THE
VALCOURT
HEIRESS

MEDIEVAL NOVELS BY CATHERINE COULTER

Warrior's Song
Fire Song
Earth Song
Secret Song
Rosehaven
The Penwyth Curse

For a complete listing of all Catherine Coulter
novels, visit www.catherinecoulter.com.

THE VALCOURT HEIRESS

CATHERINE COULTER

DOUBLEDAY LARGE PRINT HOME LIBRARY EDITION

G. P. PUTNAM'S SONS
New York

This Large Print Edition, prepared especially for
Doubleday Large Print Home Library, contains
the complete, unabridged text of the original
Publisher's Edition.

PUTNAM

G. P. Putnam's Sons
Publishers Since 1838
Published by the Penguin Group

ISBN 978-1-61664-777-3

Printed in the United States of America

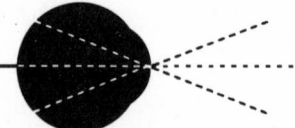

This Large Print Book carries the
Seal of Approval of N.A.V.H.

TO TOM POTWIN,

*who has been my Webmaster since almost
before the Web was born.
Many thanks to you and Diane.*

C.C.

THE
VALCOURT
HEIRESS

1

VALCOURT CASTLE
MAY 1278

She knew she had to do something. If she did nothing, her mother would force her to wed Jason of Brennan.

Her mother, Abbess Helen of Meizerling Abbey, had swooped in before nightfall, surrounded by her own contingent of soldiers, imperious and arrogant, recent widow of the Earl of Valcourt, and taken charge. Men stared at her beautiful face, at her white skin and golden hair untouched by gray, heard her velvety voice carry to every corner in the great hall, and quickly obeyed every command that flowed from her lovely mouth. As for her grief-stricken daughter, Helen informed her that she would wed in two days.

She'd stared at the woman who was her mother, a woman she didn't know, but knew what she was—a witch with unimagined powers, people said. They spoke of her behind their hands, their voices low, their fear pulsing in the air.

She'd never seen her mother do anything magick the three times she'd been in her presence. Ah, but the stories—the neighbor's wife choking to death because Lady Helen had wanted to buy her mare and had been refused; the plague striking down a village where Lady Helen had been insulted by the local monk; and now her own father, lying dead, no reason for it that their healer could see, hale and hearty but two days before. Now he lay stretched out on his bed, his hands folded over his chest, dressed in his finest tunic and hose, his beautiful sword strapped to his waist, his men below in the great hall drinking themselves insensible. What would happen now? There was no heir, only a daughter who had no power, and her newly arrived mother, a witch who could smite them all with but a wave of her hand, and the soldiers who surrounded her.

She had to do something or she would be sold to Jason of Brennan, a man she'd seen only once, just an hour before, well-made and young, but something deep inside her had recoiled when he'd turned his dark eyes on her. There were black secrets in those eyes of his. Her mother's eyes were the light gray of storm clouds, and she feared her more than the Devil.

She slipped out of Valcourt's great hall, pulling her cloak about her, for rain-bloated clouds hung low in the sky, obscuring the few stars, and the chill night wind howled. It occurred to her only after she'd crept across the inner bailey to the stables that she had no idea where she'd go. It didn't matter, she would think of something. She usually did. When she heard a man's voice, she nearly screamed. It was coming closer. What to do?

2

EAST ANGLIA, ENGLAND
MAY 1278

They rode single file on the narrow rutted
path through the Clandor Forest, a place
of ancient magick, it was said, and wicked
magick. Thick pines, oaks, and maples
crowded in on them, canopying overhead.
The leaves would tangle together in another month. Warm afternoon sunlight
speared through the rustling leaves.

Garron lifted his face to the sunlight,
felt the soft breeze against his skin. It was
a day a man was pleased to be alive, a

day that gave optimism to the days to come. And God had also wrought a miracle—no rain for three straight days. Aye, a holy miracle, Aleric said to all the men, and told them how his grandsire had once bragged about a two-day trek with no rain. But three days without the heavens pouring buckets of rain down your neck? It was unheard of. They were blessed, surely it was a good omen. Everyone was quiet, thinking his own thoughts. Garron thought of his brother Arthur, and wondered how he'd died; he'd been a young man, only thirty years of age. The king hadn't known. As for his men, Garron imagined most were probably wondering what their lives would become now that he was Lord Garron, Earl of Wareham, a nobleman with land and a castle, and income from farms, two small towns, and two keeps. And mayhap they were thinking of their visit to Lord Severin and Lady Hastings, wondering if Wareham would be as impressive as Oxborough.

"It will not delay you overmuch, Garron," King Edward had told him. Then those famous Plantagenet blue eyes had sparkled cajolery and a bit of humor to leaven the effect. "Before you travel to Wareham, you can deliver this request to Severin from his king." He nodded toward his secretary and the Chancellor of England, Robert Burnell, who handed Garron a tightly rolled parchment tied with a thin black cord. Even at the most inconvenient of times, which this most assuredly was, a man never turned down his king's request, and so the king's parchment, carefully wrapped in oilskin, rested safe against Garron's chest all the way from London to East Anglia, to Oxborough, the seat of the Earl of Oxborough, Lord Severin of Langthorne-Trent.

He didn't have the slightest wish to read the king's missive, and only sighed, thinking of the three days added to his journey to his new home. On the other hand, Garron hadn't seen Severin since the king had sent him to Oxborough nearly a year and a half before, to become the dying Fawke of Trent's heir and son-in-law. He'd become a husband and the Earl of Oxborough in a span of three hours. And now Severin had an infant son.

Garron smiled to himself as he remembered the look of utter contentment on his friend's hard face when he'd held his babe, Fawke, named after the former earl, and remarked in the most foolish way that he was surely the handsomest babe in all Christendom. And Lady Hastings watched, smiling, sitting in her countess's chair, humming as she sewed clothes for the future earl.

Near midnight, when all had retired, Garron and Severin sat alone in Oxborough's great hall, in front of the massive fireplace, a chess board between them. Severin moved his king's knight, sat back in his chair, laced his fingers over his hard belly, and sighed. "Do you know I find myself missing de Lucy, the madman who poisoned his own wife so he could have Hastings?" He studied Garron's pawn move, quickly slid his queen's bishop to a safe square, and again sat back in his chair. "There are no more unruly neighbors, no French mercenaries to harass my fishing boats, no smugglers of any account at all. Well, there are always malcontents, an occasional villain, but they are nothing, really."

Garron laughed. "You have your heir,

Severin, the handsomest babe in the world, so you yourself told me. You have a comely wife who sees well to your needs, Oxborough prospers. Be content." Garron paused a moment, his fingers hovering over a pawn. "Did you read the king's missive? Surely what he wants would relieve your boredom. Does he not want you to execute some daring commission for him?"

Severin moved his queen, and announced, "Checkmate, Garron."

"Hmmm." He studied the board, gave Severin a twisted smile, and gently laid his king on his side. "The game is yours. Come, tell me, what does the king wish of you?"

"He wishes to breed one of his favorite stallions, a gift from Philip of France, to Lady Hastings's mare, Marella. He wishes me to send Marella to London when she is next in season."

The king had sent him here for *this?*

"Ah, Trist, come and bid welcome to Lord Garron. You spent all your time watching over Fawke this evening, ignoring me, the one who has fed you and saved your furry head more times than you can count, and I know you can count, since I've seen you equally divide acorns among your own babes."

The marten climbed up Severin's arm, settled himself on his shoulder, bathed while he watched Garron.

"Hello, Trist. I am not a bad fellow. If I had a bit of pork, I would give it to you. I did not know you ate acorns."

"He doesn't. He is, I believe, teaching his own babes how to count, though they're very nearly grown now and ready to leave us for the forest. Why would they count anything, I wonder?"

Garron laughed.

Trist appeared to consider the laughter and the acorns. After a moment, he extended a paw. Garron lightly ran his fingertips over the marten's paw, then up his back.

"He spends most of his time guarding Fawke. I have told him it is not necessary, but he doesn't heed me."

Trist mewled and wrapped himself around Severin's neck.

"Ah, Garron, the king made other requests. He does not write it in so many words, but he sent you here to ensure we will support each other against mutual enemies since Oxborough and Wareham are not too far distant from each other. 'Tis true that he encourages some strife between his barons and earls, not wanting to have too much complicity brew up between his vassals, but since we are both known by Lord Graelam de Moreton and approved by him, the king wants us strong, should he need us."

"Need our soldiers at his back and our money in his coffers, you mean."

Severin's mouth twisted in a grin. "Aye, that's it." Trist mewled.

Garron raised his goblet, fashioned of a beautiful dark green glass from the Rhineland, and saluted Severin. "I am ready for your friendship and I willingly offer you my assistance should you ever need it."

"I, too," said Severin, and raised his own goblet.

The men drank. Garron said, "But you know, I am tired of fighting. I am also tired of men's duplicity, something that abounds at court. I believe I should enjoy boredom, Severin, mayhap a good six months of it."

The men drank more of Severin's precious wine, and Garron lost another game of chess.

Garron was jerked back at the loud yell just ahead. He held up his hand to keep his four men in place. He patted his destrier's neck, calming him, and Damocles immediately quieted. They heard another yell, men cursing, arguing, horses whinnying and thrashing about.

Garron said low to his man Aleric, "Stay. I will see what's happening ahead."

He dismounted and drew his sword as he walked quietly through the thick trees and the tangled undergrowth toward the men's voices, louder now, curses filling the air. Through the branches of an ancient oak tree, he stared into a small clearing. A huge man, surely the size of a sixteen-hand stallion, his face covered with a filthy black beard, was trying to hold a struggling boy who was slamming his fist into the man's face, his neck, his chest, whatever part he could reach. The man tried to avoid the blows, not retaliating. So, he didn't want to break the boy's neck. He tried to grab his hands, but the boy lurched back and slammed him in the belly. Garron was impressed. The boy wasn't about to go down without a fight. The boy yelled, his voice shrill with fear, "Let me go, or I will kill the lot of you! You fools, this man, your leader, he lies to you! I will bring you no gold, I will bring you nothing but misfortune. Let me go!"

The boy had bravado, Garron would give him that. As for this villainous lot setting the boy free, that didn't seem likely. There were two other men, both hard looking as the man mountain, ready to jump into the fray, their clenched fists holding thick-bladed knives.

"Don't kill him! No, the rest of you stay back."

This was from their leader, who looked like a king surrounded by beggars. He was richly dressed in a red wool tunic, a fine sword strapped at his lean waist, his armor well made. One of the men stepped toward the struggling boy, and their leader raised a gauntleted hand and called for him to stop.

Garron watched the boy suddenly free himself, rear up, and clout the big man in his nose. He heard the bone crack from where he was standing. Blood gushed everywhere. The man bellowed, jerked the boy up by his collar, and flung him three feet away from him, against a pile of rocks. "Ye little cockshead! Damn ye to hell and back for busting me nose, you puling little sprat!" He charged the boy, flinging out ribbons of blood in all directions.

3

Their leader yelled, "Stop, Berm! You idiot, I told you not to harm the boy! Look what you've done. My lord will kill all of us if his head's broken open. You'll be without your liver before the night falls if you've killed him."

Berm swiped his hand over his nose, and looked with loathing at the boy, now lying unconscious on his back. "He bain't be dead, the little bastid." But his fists smoothed out as he bent down to pull him upright. Fast as a snake, the boy struck up with his legs into Berm's groin and sent him pedaling backward, yelling as he grabbed himself. "My manhood is dead! The little spittlecock kilt it!"

Good blow, Garron thought, and now was the time to intervene before the others fell on him like a pack of wolves. He shouted, "Aleric, *á moi*." He leapt out from the trees into a small clearing, his sword held high.

He yelled, "That will be quite enough, lads!"

Garron felt their surprise, their terrifying joy when they saw him, prey more meaty than this scrawny boy.

Their leader shouted at Garron, "This is none of your affair, sirrah! Get you gone now and we will not kill you!"

Garron glanced at the three villains, then over at the boy, who was scooting away from them as fast as he could move. He came up and pressed against a tree, drew his knees to his chest. Garron saw the wild hope in his eyes. Garron smiled at him.

Berm was bent over, still holding himself and moaning while blood gushed from his nose. Garron couldn't make out his features what with the filthy woolen cap pulled over his forehead and the huge tangled black beard that covered his face and neck. He looked back at the man in the rich red tunic, and said easily, "I've a fancy to save the boy. Would you like to tell me what you're doing with him?"

Red Tunic said, "He is my nephew, a spoiled and heedless boy, and disobedient. I was merely taking him back to his father."

The boy yelled, "You're a mangy liar! I never saw you before in my life until you and these nasty louts kidnapped me!"

Red Tunic took two steps toward the boy. Garron stopped him with a raised hand. He said, his voice cold as the winter solstice, "I suggest you and your men leave at once. If you do not, then Saint Peter may find himself judging you this day. Given what you've done, I doubt you would like the outcome."

One of the men growled as he slashed out with his knife, "'Tis nay likely, ye cockhead. I can send ye to hell meself. Saint Peter will never have a whiff of ye."

"Look behind you," Garron said, as he leapt backward.

Aleric called out, "Aye, fill your eyes, you fool! We are here, my lord."

Garron said easily as he slashed his sword before him, "Either you leave now or you will die. It is your choice."

Red Tunic shouted as he pulled his sword from its scabbard, "Kill them!" He ran straight at Garron. Garron saw furious concentration and intelligence in the man's dark eyes, unlike his men, who were all violence and no brains. This man was a formidable opponent, single-minded in purpose, and filled with pride. Was there desperation as well? No, he didn't think so. He was a good fighter and he knew it. Garron saw one of the men run toward the boy. He jumped back from Red Tunic's sword, pulled his own knife from his belt, and released it all in one smooth motion, so fast it was a blur. The man grabbed at the knife that stuck out the back of his neck. He whirled around, stared at Garron, and crumbled to the ground. There was an instant of frozen silence, then Red Tunic yelled, fury lacing his voice, "Bastard! I'm going to kill you now!"

You're still not afraid of me. Garron smiled, then yelled like a berserker as he ran toward Red Tunic, his sword directly in front of him like a lance. He heard the horses scatter into the forest.

"Aleric, dispatch the others," he shouted over his shoulder. "Protect the boy!" He saw the man wasn't so cocky now. He paused, stroking his chin a moment, goading his opponent. "If you weren't so meager, I would take your rich red tunic after I slit your throat. Mayhap I'll spare you if you offer it to me on your knees. I'll give it to the boy."

"I am not meager, you whoreson!"

"If you are not meager, then just who and what are you?"

"I am—it is none of your affair. There is no reason for you to interfere. You have killed one of my men. You will pay for that." He slashed his sword in front of him. "You'll not have my tunic, damn you."

"I'm thinking if the boy doesn't want it, I will use it to wipe down my horse after I have sent my sword through your belly. Why are you afraid to tell me who you are? Who is your master? If I don't kill you, mayhap he'll relieve you of your tunic when you return to him empty-handed. You are so scrawny, mayhap he'll use your tunic to rub down his horse."

The man squared his shoulders and cursed, loud and fluent.

Garron said over him, "Four men with a struggling boy. You stole him, didn't you?" His smile was ferocious. "What are you, a pederast? Or is your master a pederast?"

Red Tunic growled deep in his throat and lunged. He was well trained and agile, Garron thought dispassionately as he sidestepped, watching how the man moved, watching for a weakness. Then he saw it. The man was furious, not thinking hard and cold, as a warrior should. Garron knew the man didn't have his strength, but he didn't want to kill him just yet. He wanted to know who he was first, and who the boy was, and so he contented himself with hacking a wide circle in front of him, keeping him back, wearing him down. He knew the moment the man realized he wouldn't survive this fight. He chose to run, shouting over his shoulder as he jumped a tree root, "You'll die for this!"

Garron was after him in an instant, but Red Tunic had a stout warhorse nearby, and Damocles was back in the forest, tethered with his men's horses. He was mounted and away before Garron could catch up to him. He stood there panting, watching the bright red disappear into the thick of the trees. He wondered again who the man was as he slid his sword back into its scabbard. He knew if he chanced upon the man again, he would certainly recognize his thin face, his dark, hot eyes beneath heavy black brows. He'd also recognize his warhorse, a bay with four white fetlocks, a horse he would take after he'd dispatched the man to hell.

Garron flexed his hand as he walked back to the clearing only to see Pali, his eyes red and watery, stick his sword in a man's chest, then kick him onto his back.

It was dead silent now in the clearing.

Garron said, "Where is the boy?"

Aleric looked around. "He was—well, the ungrateful little bittle's gone. He must have been frightened and run to hide in the forest."

"No wonder," Garron said. "What were they going to do with him? Ransom, I suppose, and that would mean he's of some importance to someone."

Aleric asked, "Shall I send Pali to search for the boy? With those long legs of his, he can cover more ground than the four of us put together. Or Hobbs, he can see better than an eagle."

Gilpin, Garron's squire of nearly two years, laughed. "Aye, Hobbs can see a worm hiding under a leaf."

Garron looked at the dying afternoon sun overhead through the thick trees. It was growing late. Still, he couldn't simply leave the boy alone. He and his men searched, kept assuring him they wouldn't hurt him, that they would protect him.

They didn't find the boy, even though Garron called again and again to him.

Finally, Garron said, "We have only another hour or two of daylight. I wish to be at Wareham before night falls. I wish to sleep in my own bed this night." How odd that sounded—his own bed, the lord's bed, not the small narrow cot he'd shared with his younger brother, Kalen, years before, a younger brother long dead.

He kicked the boot of one of the dead men as he said, "We have no tools to dig graves, so we will leave them." He looked again at the sun, wondering if he should search more for the boy. How far from home was he? And that damned man in his red tunic who'd kidnapped him, who was he? Garron shouted yet again, "Boy! We mean you no harm. We have killed your captors. I promise you safety. Come out now!"

After a few minutes of silence, Garron realized there was no hope for it. "We've done our best—either he'll survive or he won't. Let's go home."

As they walked back to their horses, Garron asked, "Did any of you recognize their leader, the man in the red tunic? He would not tell me his name or that of his master."

"Nay, but he's an old hound," Gilpin said, and spat on the ground.

"You are but fifteen years old," Garron said, and buffeted his squire's shoulder, nearly sending him to the ground to land on his own spit. "I am an old hound to you, and Aleric yon is a veritable gray-beard."

"No graybeard there," said Gilpin, his voice cocky, his hands on his narrow hips, "since Aleric is bald as a river rock and his chin as smooth as a pebble."

Aleric waved a fist at the boy. "Well, puppy? Think you I'm an old hound? With my bald river rock head?"

Gilpin gave Aleric a singularly sweet smile. "Oh, nay. My lord is nearly my own age and you, Aleric, you are a wise and generous protector, of no particular age at all. Your head is a beacon to all those who seek justice and hope."

Aleric shouted with laughter.

Garron shook his head at the two of them. "I shall surely puke."

Gilpin said, "Nay, my lord, do not since I should have to clean your boots. Methinks the boy is afraid to come out because he saw Pali's red leaky eyes and believed him the Devil."

Pali, those long legs of his making him even taller than Garron, gave Gilpin a terrifying smile. "If the boy saw me, Little Nothing, he'd fall on his knees before me."

"What?" Gilpin said. "You are God, not the Devil?"

Garron said, "Were I you, Gilpin, I'd shut my mouth. It might save you a hiding."

"Or Pali would wrap one leg around me and squeeze the life right out of my heart."

"Half a leg," said Pali, and scrubbed

his fists over his eyes. "I can do nothing about my eyes, they turn red with the coming of spring."

Garron said, "Stop rubbing them, Pali, it just makes it worse. Pour water on your eyes. Now, enough. Let's leave this place." His voice deepened. "Let's go home."

Gilpin looked around, and said, "I hope the boy will be all right. He had guts. Did you see him kick that hulking brute and bloody his nose?" And he threw back his head and shouted, "Boy! Come here, we'll take care of you! I'm a boy too, like you, come out."

A horse whinnied, making Garron smile. "Hobbs, get the villains' horses. We've just increased our stables." Horses loved Hobbs; he had only to speak in his low musical voice and they came trotting eagerly to him, legs high, heads tossing. In just minutes, three horses were blowing into Hobbs's big hands.

An hour later, Garron pulled Damocles to a halt. He raised his hand to stop his men behind him and looked toward his home. Wareham Castle, just shy of two hundred years of age, sat like a great fist of gray granite in front of them, a massive sentinel atop the end of a desolate promontory that stuck out into the North Sea. From the sea, Wareham was impregnable; black basalt rocks surrounded the promontory, spearing up twenty feet into the air, and the tide would do the rest, ripping boats apart.

Garron felt an odd surge of satisfaction as he looked at the stark fortress that now belonged to him. It would be his line to call Wareham home, not his brother's. This was the first time he'd been back in eight long, gritty years.

It was a beautiful spring evening, not yet dark, an early, nearly full moon beginning to climb into the sky beyond the castle walls. Stars would stud the sky tonight, another hour, no more. An evening breeze was warm and soft against his flesh. It was completely unlike that night eight years before when a storm from the sea had raged hard, hurling heavy rain, frigid winds, and a thick curtain of cold fog on anyone unlucky enough to be outside. He'd been sixteen the night he and his best friend, Bari, the armorer's son, had ridden into the storm, not waiting for morning, only two days after they'd buried Garron's father, his brother's words sounding stark in his ears, "There is nothing for you here, Garron. You are strong and you have a brain. 'Tis time you made your own way." He'd never forget the moment he'd turned in his saddle for a final look at Wareham. The black clouds had suddenly parted, the swirling fog had lifted, and he'd seen the castle outlined by a hit of lightning, stark against the black sky, an eternal beacon, and he'd wondered bleakly if he'd ever see his home again in his life.

Well, he was here now, but Bari wasn't with him, hadn't been since he'd choked to death, coughing up wads of blood so many years before. Wareham Castle and all its surrounding towns and farms were his, his legacy, his future, his responsibility.

4

I have surely vomited up my guts on the ground." Merry moaned the words into the soft, soundless air, so weak and shaky she didn't yet try to move. At least the fighting was over, her captors dead, except for their leader, Sir Halric, Jason of Brennan's man. She lay not twenty feet away from her saviors, tucked beneath leaves in the hollow opening of an oak tree, listening to them talk, praying they wouldn't come after her. In truth, she might have answered when their leader had called out to her, but she was vomiting from the clout on the head that huge man with his smelly beard had dealt her. It hadn't killed her, praise St. Cuthbert's padded belly.

She managed to crawl away from her own sickness to lie on the floor of the forest, breathing lightly, waiting for her innards to settle and her head to stop pounding. She remembered their laughter. Surely they couldn't be bad if they laughed so much. But how could she know? To jump from a boiling pot into the flames, it would be just her luck. And so she'd kept her mouth shut, too afraid to do anything.

The large man dressed all in black—he was a young man, strong and hard, and he had saved her. She'd watched his knife plunge through the man's neck, and she wished in that moment she'd had the knife and done the throwing. She didn't know if she'd be as accurate as he'd been, but she'd have liked to give it a try. Aye, he'd been very sure of himself, and he'd not doubted his own skill. She liked the looks of him but she knew all too well he could be as rotten as Sir Halric. With men, she'd learned in her young life, one simply couldn't be sure. As for women, she shuddered, her mother's beautiful witch face, surely too young, clear in her mind.

It was a pity Sir Halric had escaped, but she'd learned too that evil usually managed to slither safely away, never to die, always to return and wreak havoc.

Such rotten luck. She'd crept out of the great hall, stolen a stable lad's clothes, pausing beside an outbuilding when she'd heard the soft breathing so close by.

And then the shock of pain in her head and she'd heard nothing else. She'd awoken soon thereafter to find herself a prisoner, thrown over the legs of a huge, smelly lout whose hand lay on the small of her back, holding her steady.

When he'd seen she was awake, Sir Halric called a halt. He told her who he was and said he was going to give her a rare surprise, and then he laughed. "A different destination for you, lass, and a surprise for all. What luck, and all because of me and my quick brain."

"Your quick brain had nothing to do with aught," she'd whispered, and thought he'd clout her, but he didn't. Surely he was going to give her over to Jason of Brennan. What did he mean about a different destination? With her spate of bad luck, whatever his plan for her, she knew it wouldn't be good.

Life was not fair.

But now everything had changed.

Three men were dead, but Sir Halric had escaped, curse the fates. What would he do? He was running for his life away from the young warrior, this Garron, she'd heard his men call him, so Sir Halric probably believed she was with him, believed she was now safe. He'd lost, he'd lost. She fancied she would turn those lines into a fine song.

She came up on her hands and knees, her head down, breathing slowly, waiting for her belly to settle. She slowly raised her head, waited for the dizziness to pass, and looked around. She could ignore the headache pounding over her left ear. It would be dark soon. She wasn't more than ten miles from Valcourt—not that it mattered, because that was the last place she could go.

Valcourt was no longer her home, not since her mother had come back, not since she'd brought Jason of Brennan. She wondered what the king would do now that there was no male heir, that there would be no male heir after what had happened. He'd find her a husband, that's what he'd do, mayhap a man as rotten as Jason of Brennan.

Once the king's man arrived at Valcourt, what would her mother say about her daughter's disappearance? She'd lie, of course.

Merry felt tears burn her eyes and blinked them away. After all, she was not at this moment being forced to wed Jason of Brennan. She was alive and free, all but one of her captors dead. Surely that bespoke a benign God. Surely that meant her luck had changed.

Now all she had to do was survive. And she would. She wasn't a helpless girl, she was a boy. What's more, she could read and write and make lists, and she would survive.

Her father was dead. She felt again how his hand, squeezing hers so tightly, had suddenly become limp. She'd known the exact moment he'd died. She swallowed tears. She would grieve later.

She'd never forget the young warrior's name—Garron—he'd saved her life. All right, he'd saved a boy's life, but he need never know the difference. She'd heard of Wareham Castle, who hadn't? It wasn't as large as Valcourt, but still, it was of great strategic importance, she'd heard her father say once. Why not go there? She could hide herself easily within those massive walls, mayhap she could assist the steward. Maybe she could become the steward. She dragged herself to her feet, gritted her teeth against the pain in her head, and trotted after the five men.

5

WAREHAM CASTLE
ON THE NORTH SEA

Garron couldn't believe the pleasure it gave him to ride across the drawbridge, horses' hooves loud on the wood and iron. He looked up at the four large square corner towers, the high stone walls. Wareham Castle, now his.

But wait, where was everyone? Why were there no soldiers lining the ramparts calling down at him? And why was the drawbridge down? With night coming quickly, that wasn't wise. He threw back his head and yelled, "I am Lord Garron, Earl of Wareham! Raise the portcullis!"

There was only silence.

Aleric yelled, "Raise the portcullis! Your master is here!"

Still silence.

He felt sudden fear, cold and heavy. Something was wrong, very wrong. Then he heard a shaky old voice call out, "Are you really the new Earl of Wareham? Are you really young Garron?"

"Aye, I am Garron of Kersey. Who are you?"

"I am Tupper, my lord."

By all the saints' hoary elbows, old Tupper, Wareham's porter since long before Garron was born, he was still alive? "Have men winch up the portcullis, Tupper."

"There's no one save me here, my lord, but I can do it!" Garron heard the sudden grit in that old voice.

Hobbs said, "Is that old varmint as ancient as he sounds, Garron?"

"Older." Tupper had been stooped with years and worry and very few teeth in his mouth when Garron had seen him last eight years before.

No one was by the portcullis, save Tupper? But that made no sense. What was going on here? His fear grew. He and his men watched, amazed, as the old iron portcullis slowly rose, the sound of the chain loud in the still air. Somehow, Tupper had found the strength to turn that huge winch. Tupper managed to winch the portcullis high enough for Gilpin to crawl under. After a moment, the portcullis winched up smoothly, the huge chain flying upward. When Garron rode into the outer bailey, he saw Tupper, scrawny as a dead chicken, staring hard at him. Then he shouted, a lovely full-bodied yell that reached the North Sea. "Young Lord Garron! Aye, 'tis you, my boy, ye're home at last! Oh aye, 'tis a wonder! Bless all the saints' burned bones!"

"Aye, 'tis I, Tupper." As he spoke, Garron was searching the outer bailey for danger, but he saw only what should be there—the barren strip of land twenty feet wide with rusted sharp spikes stuck up three feet into the air, ready to shred an enemy if he managed to get over the outer castle walls. If the enemy managed to get across those twenty feet, he was faced with another high stone wall and another iron portcullis.

Tupper cupped his mouth and yelled at the top of his aged lungs, "Eller, winch up the portcullis! 'Tis Lord Garron home again! Aye, I know it's him! We're saved!"

Saved? It was nearly full dark now, dark clouds thick overhead, hiding the stars. Garron saw nothing but shadows. His fear fair to choked him now.

Damocles felt his tension, snorted and reared. Garron leaned forward to pat his neck. "We're home, lad. Go easy, we'll find out what's happened quickly now." They waited for Eller, the armorer, Garron remembered, to winch up the smaller portcullis, then rode single file into the vast inner bailey, ringed with soldiers barracks set into the walls, an apple and pear orchard fenced in to the side, a large space for the kitchen garden, pens and byres for the animals, stables for the horses, all dominated by the huge stone keep that rose forty feet into the evening air. His keep.

But there were no people in the inner bailey, an area that should be mad with activity any time of day. There were no lights pouring from the keep, no voices, no screaming children, no flocks of chickens squawking and flying about, no dogs barking their heads off, no cattle lowing in their sheds, no pigs rutting and snorting about in their byre.

He didn't see a single soldier. He didn't see any sign of life at all.

Garron dismounted slowly, handing Damocles' reins to Gilpin. There wasn't a single lit rush torch anywhere he could see, only dark shadows, grim and thick. It was utterly quiet, as if everyone within this vast keep was dead, and he and his men and Tupper and Eller were the only ones alive, and their hours were numbered. He heard Gilpin draw in his breath, knew his men were becoming more alarmed.

Suddenly he saw several shadows move in the darkness.

He called out, "I am Lord Garron. I am home now. I mean none of you any harm. Whoever is here, come out now. Tupper! Eller, come to me!"

Gilpin whispered, "There is no one, my lord. There's naught but ghosts here."

Aleric drew his sword, Hobbs and Pali drew theirs as well. They formed a circle, their backs to Garron. Garron heard Pali sniff, then whisper, "Something is very wrong, Garron. Did a plague strike? Why don't your people come out?"

"For some reason, they're afraid." Garron shouted again, "Tupper! Eller! Come to me!"

The old man finally came out of the shadows, shuffling as fast as he could, panting, his back more bowed than when Garron had left so long ago, his clothes filthy and ragged, but he was smiling, showing two remaining teeth. Garron took the old man's arms in his big hands and pulled him close. He looked down into that old, weathered face and saw tears in his eyes. He said, "It is good to see you, Tupper. I am very glad you are alive."

"And I, ye, Lord Garron. Ah, bain't life odd, my lord? You become stronger and larger and I shrink down into nearly nothing. It's a fine man ye've become, strong and straight. Jes' look, I don't come to yer shoulder."

So small he was, Garron thought, so very slight, a fist to his shoulder, and he'd be dead. Sometimes, Garron thought, life was more than one could bear. He said, "You're not nothing, Tupper—you managed to winch up the portcullis, no mean feat. Thank you. Tell me what is wrong here. Where are all our people? All my brother's soldiers, where are they?"

Tupper shook his head violently, the tufts of gray hair so dirty they didn't move on his head. "Since it's dark, my lord, ye can't see it—'tis the Retribution, my lord," he whispered, deadening fear in his voice. "The Retribution," he repeated, softer still. "All is destroyed, naught but splinters and death. We buried so many— the little ones were the hardest—the stench of death still lingers if ye breathe deeply."

Splinters? Death? Garron wanted to explode. By all St. Hermione's teeth, what damned Retribution? What was Tupper talking about? He didn't want to yell at the old man, and so he drew a deep breath and said, his voice low and calm, "Tell me. Tell me about this Retribution. Was it a plague?"

"Aye, it were a plague, but a human sort." Before the old man could say more, a shadow detached itself from a doorway and straggled toward them. It was a woman, as old and bent as Tupper.

"My lord?" Her voice was thin and quavery. "My sweet little boy? Garron? Tupper, you're standing with him, is it really our boy? Eller, I see you hanging back. Come here to me. Tupper, tell me, is it our boy?"

"Aye, Miggins, 'tis he and he's proud and strong. Jest ye look at him, here to save us."

And Garron remembered her, of course. How could she still be alive? "Is it really you, Miggins?"

"Aye, my boy."

Eller, the armorer, so thin he could hide behind a sapling trunk, hovered over Miggins, his hand on her thin shoulder. He wasn't all that old, but he looked beaten down, gaunt, his face leached of color, as if he knew life was over and he was simply waiting for death to haul him off.

Miggins pulled out a stub of a lit candle from behind her back and she held it high to shine it on his face as she walked slowly to him. He saw that her gown was filthy and torn. She shuffled along, indeed an old woman. So thin, her cheeks sunken in, like the two men's. She stared up at him, studied his face.

"Aye, jest look at ye, yer so big now. Ye were gone so many years, and they weren't all bad, those years, and they passed quickly, as years are wont to do as the years press down on ye. At least Tupper and Eller and I still cling to the earth rather than lie dead beneath it with all the others." Then she smiled at him and gave him a curtsey.

"Why didn't you come to me sooner?" Garron asked as he lifted her to her feet and embraced her.

The old woman said, "Ye might not have been my boy and ye'd have taken my candle and burned off my nose."

"Your nose is safe, Miggins. I am here now. You and Eller and Tupper must tell me what has happened. Where are all the soldiers? Where are all my people?"

Miggins craned her neck back so she could look up at him again, holding her candle high. "Ye have yer sweet mother's face, but not her eyes, no, you have his eyes, but I see no madness there, thank Saint Rupert's clean heart. Ah, now I can see him in you, that jaw, stubborn as a stoat's, that jaw, and yer strong neck, but pray God what's him is only on the outside—no rot in yer soul. Poor Lord Arthur, his insides were very like yer father. Ye aren't like yer father or yer brother, are ye, Lord Garron?"

"No, I am not like them." Garron rarely thought about his father anymore, a hard man who was wont to strike out with his fists when suddenly rages would come upon him. Garron remembered now that he'd once struck Miggins when he disliked a gown she'd sewn for Garron's mother. His fist had jerked her off her feet and slammed her into a stone wall. It was one of the few times Garron could remember his mother crying.

But surely Arthur hadn't been a bad man or a wastrel master, had he? *But his rages*, Garron thought, he'd forgotten about Arthur's rages, unleashed when one didn't expect them, then gone in a flash, but only after spilled blood, broken bones, and curses. Arthur was taller than Garron had been at sixteen, bigger, and hard with muscle, his voice loud enough to reach fishing boats at sea.

Miggins whispered, "I prayed the good Lord would save us and He did, though He waited until there nearly wasn't anything left to save." She crossed herself and looked around at the heavy, silent darkness.

Tupper whispered, as if afraid someone would leap out and shove a knife in his throat, "There are a few others here, my lord. Most are gone or dead. Will everyone return? Mayhap now that ye are here they will. Those who still live, that is."

Garron couldn't take it in. He asked again, "This Retribution, Tupper, you said it was a plague of a human sort."

"Worse than a sickness plague," Miggins whispered, "much worse."

He wanted to yell at them to spit it out, but held to his patience. They were old, they were starving, and why was that? "If it wasn't a sickness plague, then tell me why everyone is dead or gone. Where are Wareham's soldiers? What was this Retribution?"

6

Tupper's voice was so thin with fear it nearly disappeared in the chill night air. "What happened here, ye ask, my lord? I'll tell ye and pray my liver doesn't fall out of my belly for saying his cursed name. The Black Demon came, my lord, and he shouted to all of us that he would unleash the Retribution on Wareham if we didn't turn over Lord Arthur to him. But how could we? Lord Arthur was already dead and buried, along with the prized sword he'd won off that Flemish knight. We shouted the truth down to him. But he didn't believe us. Then he claimed he would spare us if we told him where yer brother's silver coins were hidden, but none knew what he was talking about. None of us ever heard that Lord Arthur had a stash of silver coins. We told him Lord Arthur was dead, and he laughed, jest laughed and laughed. It fair to shriveled yer soul to hear that black laugh."

Miggins whispered, "Mayhap the Black Demon believed Lord Arthur a coward, my lord, that he was hiding behind us. Can ye imagine such a thing? Lord Arthur would have fought until he was hacked to death, and his spirit would have continued to fight until he was naught but dirt and air."

Aleric said, "But how did this Black Demon and his men get into Wareham? It's a mighty fortress, not a puling little cottage."

Tupper said, "We believe that foulbreathed steward Eisen was a traitor and let the Black Demon's men in through the hidden postern gate that leads down to the beach. He let in a string of soldiers dressed just as ours are, and they lowered the drawbridge and raised the portcullis before any knew what they were about."

Miggins said, her old voice breaking, "The Black Demon unleashed devastation and misery, and he gloried in it, I swear that to ye, jest as he swore it was his right, his pleasure, what was due him. When he destroyed everything, when he could find no one else to kill and torture, he fell into a rage and killed one of his own men who dared to question him. Then he and his men left. When the dawn comes, ye'll see, my lord, ye'll see the desolation that demon wrought."

Tupper wove where he stood and Garron grabbed him and held him upright. "It's all right, Tupper. Tell me the rest of it."

"Yer brother's few remaining soldiers melted away, for they had no master to direct them or to pay their wages, and why would they remain in a place of death?

"We pray that some escaped to the Forest of Glen. But we do not know, since no one could come back. Even if they could, why should they? There was naught left here, naught but the smell of rot and death."

"Do you know who this Black Demon is?"

Both Miggins and Tupper shook their heads.

"Do you know, Eller?"

The man shook his head.

Miggins stepped away from Garron, took Eller's thin arm, and squeezed. "Poor Eller, one of the Black Demon's men cut out his tongue because he cursed him for killing his boy and thass why he can't speak to ye."

"Eller?"

The man nodded.

"Show me."

Eller opened his mouth. What was left of his tongue was no longer raw, thank the good Lord, and it was healing. But now he was mute.

Garron lightly laid his hand on the old woman's shoulder. "How many days after Arthur's death did this happen? How long ago?"

Miggins scratched her scalp. "Four days after we buried him, the Black Demon came. Now there are naught but spirits here, and barely a score of us left, all of us starving."

"I am sorry. I am sorry for all of this. But I will do the best I can to restore Wareham."

Tupper nodded, squeezed Garron's big hand.

Garron said, "It will be all right. Now, you said there are only a score of our people here besides you, Miggins, and Eller?"

Tupper nodded.

"You said no one could come back after the Black Demon left. Why is this? And why did no one go hunting in the Forest of Glen for food?"

"After the Black Demon left, those who were able went to hunt game, but the Demon's men were lying in wait and killed them. We thought we could fish, but he'd left men on the beach as well, hiding in those fang-toothed rocks. A few have managed to sneak back in during the night, though I thought they are mad to do so since there is naught here but misery."

Miggins said, "Three more men went out again three days later. The soldiers were hiding, jest waiting for us to come out. They killed our three men. No one else went outside the walls."

Tupper said, "Turp, the blacksmith, was hiding in the Forest of Glen. He came back today jest when dusk was falling, said the soldiers were gone, and begged Tupper to lower the drawbridge and raise the portcullis and let him enter because he'd brought game, and he had, but only two small pheasants, barely more than a single bite for each of us. Have ye food? He and Eller were going to go back to the forest at first light to hunt. Everyone else is too weak."

So that was why they were starving. Garron wondered how many had died, but he didn't want to know at the moment. He heard his men whispering behind their hands. Since he was the only one who had lived at Wareham, only he knew that dozens upon dozens of people had once lived within the walls, that the inner bailey usually rang with noise and activity, shouts, curses, laughter. The pervasive silence was like a heavy weight on his shoulders.

He shouted, hoping to reach every corner of the inner bailey, "I will set everything aright. Come out now." He looked again at Tupper. "Did Lord Arthur ever mention another man he considered a particular enemy?"

Tupper whispered, "There were always enemies, my lord, but none like this one, this one who loved the smell of death, the screams of those he tortured. He took pleasure in destroying us when he didn't find Lord Arthur's silver coins. He yelled over and over, 'Tis a just Retribution, but if ye give me the silver coins I'll stop.'"

Miggins said, "First, he tortured the soldiers who'd survived the fighting, but they couldn't tell him anything because they didn't know, and so those few who didn't escape died. And then he turned to us. He didn't stop. Ye'll see the blood dried on the stones, my lord, black now, so much."

Tupper whispered, "When I saw ye, young Garron, I thought he was returning, and my heart withered in my breast, and I could not answer ye." Tupper's voice hitched. "But it was ye, thank the good Lord. We've buried all in the cemetery behind the castle. There were so many, my lord." Then Tupper began to cry, deep wracking sobs. Before Garron could move, Miggins put her thin arms around Tupper's bony shoulders. Her broken old voice suddenly sounded strong. "The new master is here, Tupper. All will be well again. He will set everything to rights now."

Garron certainly intended to. Who was the Black Demon? He would find out soon enough, but first things first. Garron mounted the deep stone steps and entered the great hall, Aleric and his men behind him, standing alert, hands on their swords and knives, ready for anything. Where were the people who remained? *Hiding still*, he thought.

The great hall of Wareham was as black as a cave. Light was the first order of business. Gilpin and Pali followed Miggins and her single candle into the granary, where she showed them rush torches piled up against a wall, ready for use. Once they were lighted and fastened into wall sconces, people began to make their way into the great hall. Miggins stood on the top stairs of the keep, cupped her mouth, and yelled, "'Tis safe now. Come out, the new master is here! He will feed us! Come out, Lord Garron is here! We have light."

As people crept into the great hall, all

of them frightened, ragged, starving, Garron said over and over, "All will be well now. We have food enough so everyone will have something to eat. Do not fear me, I am Lord Garron. Come in, come in." He turned to Aleric. "None of us need to eat tonight. We can wait to fill our bellies after we hunt tomorrow." He looked at his people's faces as Hobbs and Gilpin divvied up all the food Garron and his men had with them. This ragtag lot of people were his. He counted heads. Only twenty-two, twelve women, ten old men, no children. Their gaunt faces, however, were no longer blank with despair; he saw burgeoning hope.

Everyone slowly ate the bread and beef strips, savoring every single chew. What of his farmsteads? What of his two villages? He would find out on the morrow.

Everyone was still hungry, of course, but at least now they had something in their bellies. And at least the Black Demon hadn't poisoned the castle's well.

In a castle that housed more than one hundred souls, fifty of them soldiers, he had only twenty-two people left, his own three soldiers, and his squire. As he looked out at those faces, he smiled. To-morrow he would find out what skills he had remaining in his castle other than his armorer, Eller, and Turp the blacksmith.

Aleric came to him. "I had hoped more poor souls would straggle in, and thus we did not raise the drawbridge or lower the portcullis when we came in. But it's late now. I sent Gilpin and Hobbs to close us in for the night." Aleric shook his head. "How Tupper managed to raise the port-cullis as high as he did, well, I believe it was God himself helped turn that winch. The chain is thicker than he is." He looked at the scraggly group of people, still hud-dled together, heard some conversation amongst them now, and that was heart-ening. "We also searched both the outer and inner baileys but saw no one else."

Garron nodded. "I still cannot believe this Black Demon left men outside the walls to kill anyone who came out to hunt."

"He wanted all those left to starve," Aleric said matter-of-factly. "He wanted no witnesses to what he had done. That action alone bespeaks a rancid soul, Gar-ron, a soul the Devil stole years ago."

Garron could not disagree.

It took a crackling laugh from old Miggins to cool the rage in his blood.

At least the weather was warm, Garron thought, when he wrapped himself in a blanket late that night to sleep near the great doors, the double thick wooden bars in place. He prayed the weather would hold. Two more days without rain, that's all he'd pray for, no more. He didn't want to tempt the fates. He'd briefly gone up the keep stairs to the solar and looked into the bedchambers. All the beds were broken apart, the few rugs in the master's bedchamber gone. There was naught but mayhem, willful and vicious. Arthur's enemy, this Black Demon, had been thorough.

But not the castle well, thank God, not the castle well.

Life, he thought, had changed irrevocably. Now life was about survival, not basking in a joyful homecoming. Not just his survival, but the survival of the souls who were now sleeping on the stone floor in the great hall. *His* souls. And they depended entirely on him.

The Retribution—what an odd thing to call the reign of terror that had very nearly consumed Wareham Castle. He wished now he hadn't stopped at Oxborough Castle to give the king's message to the Earl of Oxborough. If only he'd come here directly—but no, what difference would two days make? Not that much.

He waited until he knew all his people were sleeping before he let his mind stop making its endless lists and drift into sleep. His last thought was of the Black Demon, the man from whom Arthur had stolen silver coins.

7

Despite the Retribution, Wareham Castle was magnificent, Merry thought as she chewed on a small bit of bread Lord Garron's squire gave her. The coarse brown bread was stale and gritty and tasted wonderful. Of course she'd recognized him; he was the first one who'd called out to her when she'd hidden. She said, "What is your name?"

"Me? I am Gilpin, Lord Garron's squire." He showed no recognition of her at all, thank St. Coriander's white gums. Now that she thought about it, she didn't think he'd even seen her. Gilpin said, "Everyone can speak only of the Retribution. Can you tell me what happened?"

She kept her head down and chewed on the bread, one tiny bite at a time. "Nay, I'm sorry." He reached out his hand to take the last bit of bread from her, and she jerked her hand back. "Nay, I am very hungry. Truly."

"You don't look to be on the edge of starvation like the others."

He was right. She was a selfish stoat. Merry realized he was looking at her closely now. She also realized she'd not spoken as a serf. She said, "It were bad, this Retribution, thass all I know."

"No longer," Gilpin said, patted her shoulder, and strode off, a slight frown on his forehead. She watched him hand the small chunk of bread to a bent old woman.

She hung in the background, watched all the people eat their small portions, and found herself making lists in her head, something she'd done since she was a young child, something her father had taught her. She watched the new lord as he spoke to everyone, questioning them about what had happened, and reassuring them endlessly. She could feel the rage pulsing in him, hotter and harder than the rage he'd felt facing Sir Halric, that mangy devil. But he'd controlled the rage when he'd fought Sir Halric, and he controlled it now. She imagined he did what was necessary, what was needful, and then he moved to something else. He was dark, his hair black as the North Sea on a moonless night, his eyes a pale blue, unusual, she thought, and wondered if those pale blue eyes of his would see she was the boy he'd saved. He was the only one of the four men who'd seen her clearly. She heard him speak calmly, heard him jest with his man, Pali, whose legs were so long old Miggins told him they could lay planks on his legs and three men could sleep on him, all stretched out. His eyes were red and weeping, Merry saw, the spring season tears, she'd heard the healer at Valcourt call it, but she didn't know the recipe the Valcourt healer had mixed in his potion's kettle to help him.

When at last everyone was settled, she watched Lord Garron check the huge double doors himself and see the two thick wooden bars were set firmly in place. She watched him wrap himself in a blanket and settle in by his men near the great front doors. Everyone slept in the great hall, and so she huddled next to old Miggins, who belched once and snored throughout the long night, louder than Merry's pet pig.

The next morning, after Garron and his men rode out to hunt, Merry sidled up to Miggins. She recognized the scrawny old woman as the leader here. She said in a quiet voice, "Look at me."

Miggins squinted up at her.

"Who are ye, boy? I don't know ye. Did you come with Lord Garron?"

"Nay. I followed Lord Garron and his men. He saved me from kidnappers. He does not know I'm here. Who are you?"

"I am Miggins. I don't remember my first name. Mayhap 'tis Alice, but all know me now as Miggins."

"Miggins," Merry said. She drew a deep breath and spit it out. "I am not a boy."

Miggins gave her a long look and slowly nodded. "Nor are ye jest any girl, are ye?"

"Of course I am. I am a girl of no account at all."

"Then why would anyone kidnap ye?"

Good question. "All right, not just any

girl. I swear I will tell you everything, but not yet. Is there a gown about I could borrow? These boy's clothes are dirty, and they smell."

Old Miggins eyed her up and down, studied her clear eyes. "Nay," she said at last, "yer not jest any girl. There's the Lady Anne's gowns and chemises, hidden away by the master who wanted to give them to his mistress, but she died only two days after his lady wife, both of the bloody flux. Why did you follow Lord Garron here? Why didn't ye go back home? Do ye know about the Retribution?"

Merry looked out over the great hall. "I know nothing of this Retribution or this Black Demon. I can't go home because my mother wants to wed me to a man with a blacker soul than this Black Demon has."

"So, I suppose ye also have to hide from those men who kidnapped ye."

"Your master killed the men who kidnapped me, well, all but one of them, but I still have to hide from my mother. When your master saved me, he believed me a boy and so he will not recognize me. Since I hear he hasn't been here in many years, he will believe I belong here. Can you help me?"

"Hmmm, seems hardly fair, does it? To have to hide from yer own mither, 'tis a putrid thing. Why don't ye jest tell him the truth? Lord Garron is a fine lad, pure of heart, straight in his thinking. At least I pray he is."

"I cannot take the chance. He would have questions. Please, Miggins, let me keep my secrets for a while. I swear to you I am no threat to you or to Lord Garron or to Wareham."

Miggins scratched her dirty elbow as she studied the young earnest face, the cheek smudged with dirt. "Take off yer cap."

Merry pulled off her cap. A long, thick braid fell out and dangled down her back.

Miggins nodded, raised a gnarly hand, and touched the braid. "I niver before seen such a beautiful color—hair redder than my pa's sins. What is yer name?"

"Merry."

"Merry? That has a nice sound to it. Nay, ye're not jest Merry. Yer a lady."

"It truly doesn't matter. Please, just

Merry. Mayhap you can tell everyone to call me Merry and not tell Lord Garron or his men that I'm a stranger at Wareham. I must be very careful. I don't want anyone to find me. It would be very bad, especially for Lord Garron. Please, Miggins, will you help me?"

"We'll have to see about that, won't we now?" Merry could hear a sudden craftiness in that robust old voice. "What have ye to say to that? What will ye do if I give ye the mistress's clothes?"

"If you keep my secret and give me some gowns, I will set everything to rights. I was mistress of my father's keep until he died. It is bigger than Wareham."

"Hmmm, there is much to ponder here. Ye're but a little mite of a girl—"

"I'm not a little mite, I'm a big mite, and I'm not young, I am just turned eighteen."

"Yer a baby mite compared to me. Ye can fix things here? Ye really can do it, Merry?"

"I can do it."

Old Miggins thought and thought and scratched her elbow again, and finally she nodded. "If ye fail, ye fail. What difference? Come wi' me." Merry followed

Miggins and a thin, hollow-eyed woman named Lisle up the curving stone stairs to the bedchambers. Lisle said, "I was Lady Anne's personal servant. I kept her things safe. When the Black Demon came, I hid everything."

8

When they walked into the lord's large bedchamber, she couldn't believe her eyes. The huge lord's bed was smashed into kindling. The chest that had sat at its foot was in shards, the clothes pulled out and shredded. The stone floors were bare.

"There was once a beautiful tapestry on that far wall," Miggins said, pointing. "The Demon's men didn't destroy it, jest took it along with the rugs. Lord Garron's grandmother wove the tapestry."

"Greed got the better of them."

Lisle nodded at Merry. "'Tis so." She

sighed, and walked straight to the window that had once held a pane of valuable glass. Chill morning air poured into the room. "Be careful," Lisle called out as she gingerly walked over the stone floor. "There are shards everywhere."

"I wonder why the Demon didn't take the glass," Merry said. "It is very wasteful of him to break it."

Miggins said, "Probably one of the louts with him smashed it before he could be stopped. We had two large glass windows, one in here and one in the chapel. I'll wager that one's shattered too. Lisle, has anyone been to the chapel?"

"Tupper found poor Father Adal's body amid the wreckage of the altar, run through his chest with a sword. The beautiful altar, carved nearly two hundred years ago by the first lord, the Demon smashed it to splinters. No one else has gone to the chapel since, no one has any faith left. Do ye know, I dusted that altar for seventeen years. I ask you, how can a man destroy an altar?"

"The Black Demon," Miggins said. "He bain't afraid of anything or anyone, God included."

After seeing the wreckage of Wareham, Merry had to agree.

"Here," Lisle said, knelt down, swept away shards of glass with her strong hand, and gently pried up one of the stones against the wall.

Merry fell to her knees beside Lisle to lean over a hole two feet deep and two feet wide. Folded neatly within were gowns and shifts, a tangled flow of ribbons, even three pairs of slippers, all sadly out of fashion now, but who cared about that? She knew pointed slippers were now worn at Queen Eleanor's court in London, and these toes were rounded, but they were finely cut leather, covered with red velvet, a bit faded, darned here and there, but again, it didn't matter, they were beautiful.

Lisle picked the clothes out of the hole and handed them to Merry. "They're sound enough still." She stuck her hand into the slippers. "Lady Anne had big feet."

Merry sat on the floor, pulled off the filthy boots, and slipped them on, tied the ribbons around her ankles. She grinned up at Lisle and Miggins. "I have big feet too. They are perfect. Thank you, Lisle."

"Now a shift and a gown."

The shifts were well-tended, but Lady Anne had been shorter than she was and they came only to her knees. As for the gowns, there were four. Merry chose the oldest, a green wool, shiny from many brushings, that came only to her ankles. Who cared?

"I didn't see any stockings else I would have stuffed them into the hidey hole as well. I wonder what happened to them?"

"No matter," Merry said, and pulled off her cap and began to straighten her braid.

"Allow me," Lisle said, and began to twine the matching green ribbon through the thick braid.

Miggins stood back and looked her up and down. "What a fine little mistress ye are, Merry. That's right, Lisle, make her look a lady, wipe those dirt smudges off her pretty face. The finer she looks, the faster all the people will look to her and obey her."

Merry certainly hoped so. Before they left the wrecked bedchamber, Merry lifted her eyes upward and thanked Lady Anne for her bounty. As for the boy's clothes, let Lisle burn them.

"Thank you both. Please, Lisle, Miggins, there is so much to do, please do not ask for explanations just yet. Father Adal, how old was he?"

"Not a young man, but he had a head of hair left," Lisle said, "and usually a pleasing breath."

"Did he read and write?"

"Oh aye, and he spoke beautiful Latin, at least that's what Lady Anne told everyone."

Merry thought about this for a moment. "If you would consent to it, I would be Father Adal's bastard. Surely God will not mind, since our cause is just. I read and write too, you see, and thus that would explain it, since he would have taught me. What think you? Will you agree to it?"

"Hmmm, Father Adal came after Lord Garron left, mayhap some five, maybe six years ago. Why not? Lisle, we will see what the girl can do. If she fails, it doesn't much matter."

"Thank you. Thank you both."

"We will tell the others," said Lisle.

Merry hugged both of them, then rubbed

her hands together, her list already clear in her mind.

The girl, Miggins thought, fair to bristled with energy.

She laughed when Merry said, "Now it's time to begin setting things aright."

Miggins said, "I'll bet old Tupper's last tooth that Mordrid stole Lady Anne's stockings far before the Retribution came."

"Who is Mordrid?"

"She was one of Lord Arthur's lemans, fair to bursting with arrogance, she was. Ah, I shouldna said that." Miggins shook her head at herself. "She were taken in the Retribution, a bad thing, a terrible thing."

Merry wanted to know more about the Retribution, but now wasn't the time. "Miggins, Lisle, gather all the people who are strong enough and bring them here to the great hall. I want to know what each person's job was before the Black Demon came."

Twelve women and ten old men stood in front of her, all of them alive, Tupper told her, because they simply fell over and pretended to die and thus the soldiers ignored them and they survived. None of the women were young, Lisle and Miggins the oldest. The girls, Lisle said, crossing herself, grief in her voice, had been ravished and taken by the Demon's soldiers.

Miggins spoke to the group of pitiful men and women, then pointed to Merry and gave her each name.

9

Merry nodded to each person, repeated each name, and asked all what they could do. There was a lot of experience standing in front of her, thank St. Anthony's arrow-pierced liver, and faces that were simply too weary and too hungry to much care.

Merry saw some distrust, she wasn't blind, and surprise on those faces that hadn't noticed her before. What could she say?

She could but try. She smiled at them. "I know I am a stranger to you. I know you have no reason to trust that I will set everything aright. I know you don't like to keep silent, for Lord Garron is honorable and just, and he is the new Earl of Wareham, but if you will keep the truth about me to yourselves, if you will but say that I am Father Adal's byblow, just for a little while, I give you this vow. I will make this great hall clean and help Lord Garron make Wareham prosperous again, if you will give me a chance."

"Why don't ye jes' tell Lord Garron the truth?"

Merry looked at the wizened old man she didn't really think was all that old. "If I did tell him the truth, he would have to return me to my home. I would be forced to wed a monster. I must stay hidden for a while until—" Until what? She didn't see how everything could resolve itself in her favor. She drew in a deep breath. "Until the king goes to my home to take charge."

"Be ye so important the king hisself would stick in his nose?" This from a woman so thin she looked ready to cave in on herself. Ah, but there was a bit of vinegar and wonder in her voice, and Merry smiled.

"Aye, I suppose I am, but no matter. I'm here and I need you to keep silent so I may keep my vow. Until a short time ago, Wareham was a great castle. I believe that all of us can work to make it great again."

If she managed to succeed, then what would she do? What if the king did indeed stick in his royal nose, what would change? She would still be sold to a stranger, it was the way things were done. She would have no say in the matter. She saw Jason of Brennan in her mind's eye and felt bile rise in her throat. But her mother wasn't here. Jason of Brennan wasn't here. Merry realized in that moment that she felt as much hope as she hoped this pathetic group of people would soon feel.

They were speaking amongst themselves, grumbling, clearly not certain what to do. She said over them, "Listen, all of you are skilled, but you are weak and hungry and everything has looked hopeless for so long, you cannot see anything good happening, but I swear to you, the worst is over. Know that Lord Garron will bring food in a matter of hours, more than enough food for all of us, do not doubt it. I know you cannot imagine that your bellies will ever be filled again, but I swear you'll be full to bursting by the end of this day. I swear all of you will have some laughter too by the end of this day." *And maybe even some hope*, she added silently.

And Merry was certain of that, for when Garron set out to accomplish something, she knew to the soles of Lady Anne's big slippers that he did it. "Bullic, you assisted old Clerc, the cook who was killed. You will now direct the cooking. Since feeding all of us is the most important task before us, let's look at the cooking shed first. We want to be able to prepare the game the moment Lord Garron brings it into the keep.

"Keep faith with me, that's all I ask. Now, I also know you are all weak from hunger, so we will do everything very slowly, and rest often. At the very least, we have water."

She studied their faces as she stepped back. There was more discussion, some rumblings, but soon even the creaky old men began to nod. She even saw a smile on two faces, and an old man shouted,

"Let us do it! Let us make Wareham great again!" There was a weak cheer, but it sounded wonderful to Merry's ears. Merry felt like shouting to the blackened beams with relief. She looked out over all the people, and saw straighter backs, higher heads, not a surprise really. Now everyone had purpose, they knew they would survive.

As soon as everyone was busy collecting cleaning rags and hobbling brooms together, Merry accompanied Bullic to the cooking shed. The Black Demon had searched for Arthur's silver coins even here. Crockery was smashed, cooking tables overturned and cleaved with axes. Filth was everywhere. It smelled terrible. Merry assigned Bullic and five other men to find wooden fragments large enough to make spits to cook the game in the huge great hall fireplace. The huge beams overhead were black, she saw, but the flames would kill the smell of rot and grime. She set the women to work inside the cooking shed, mending plates and platters, and cleaning the few cookpots that survived.

The keep itself was outrageously dirty—

the stinking reeds were filled with spoiled food, bones, and dead rats. There were no fresh reeds to cover the floors, so Merry had the stone floor swept out, and all the refuse tossed onto the midden.

It was a dreadful job, and done very slowly, since everyone was so weak. Exhaustion was the enemy. Merry called a halt to the work many times and sent people to rest in the inner bailey. And she encouraged them endlessly. Finally, the great hall began to look less wretched, and the smell was no longer quite so bad.

Since the dozen trestle tables had all been smashed, leaving nothing but sharp stakes of wood, she sent the men out to find large boards to set upon stones gathered from the destroyed soldier's barracks. They managed to cobble together ten low tables.

"'Twas a good idea, mistress," Tupper said, and patted her arm.

Merry grinned at him.

When Garron returned three hours later with a huge boar tied to a pole, loud cheering filled the inner bailey. Garron was their hero.

"The cook, Old Clerc, died in the Retribution," Miggins told him, "but yer not to worry, my lord."

"Why not?"

"We have Bullic. And our little Merry can direct him, she knows what to do."

"Who is our little Merry?"

"She, poor little mite, is the daughter of Wareham's priest, Father Adal, who died in the Retribution from a knife in his chest. He was learned, he was, and thus he taught her to read and write. Lady Anne gave her household instruction before she died. Ye will see what Merry has accomplished whilst ye were gone." And Miggins gave him a big toothy smile and hoped she had not overpraised.

Garron didn't change expression, and he knew a lie when it hit him in the nose, but what part of what she'd said was a lie? He didn't know, and at the moment, he didn't care. Facing the enormity of what was ahead, he simply dismissed it, and smiled over at the girl, who kept her head down, as if afraid of him, or afraid he would see too much. He wanted to ask her why she hadn't done anything until this morning, but again, he let it go for now. Maybe, like the others, she hadn't bothered because she'd had no hope of survival.

"Ye go get the beast's blood off ye, my lord. Merry will see to the food."

Once Garron had stripped off his clothes in the inner bailey, rubbed himself all over with their single chunk of soap, Gilpin poured a pail of water from the castle well over his head. Garron shuddered and shook himself like a mongrel. "Tupper told me the devils missed this one bucket. He found it beneath a thick branch of a pear tree in the orchard. They'd chopped down the tree but missed the bucket." Garron and his men shared the soap, except for Pali, who said there was only a sliver left and that wouldn't even wash one leg, and he smelled sweet, did he not?

Garron strongly doubted there would be any more soap to be found in the keep. He prayed one of the women knew how to make soap. This girl, Merry—the priest's bastard daughter—he also prayed she was as competent as old Miggins had assured him she was. First things first. Now there was enough food for everyone.

Garron hummed as he dressed himself in the clean clothes Gilpin shook out and gave to him. He paused a moment, realizing he heard men and women speaking, then a shout, even a short laugh. The silence was over, he thought, pleased. Where was the girl Merry?

10

Bullic was in charge of roasting the boar steaks. Merry watched him show six men and four women how to cut the meat. While he gave instruction, she saw him swell with pride. He himself spit all the steaks, grinning maniacally, and giving his cohorts orders without a pause, which no one seemed to mind. Everyone, she saw, moved more quickly, their heads higher, their voices stronger because now there was food brought to them by their new lord, and they knew their stomachs would soon stop cramping from hunger.

She grinned when she heard Miggins

tell people how Merry was a young angel sent from God to help them, and they were to treat her well, and they must not forget—her voice dropped to a whisper— her name was Merry and she was Father Adal's bastard daughter brought with him when he'd come to Wareham some six summers ago. Who was her mother? Who cared, Miggins said, and shrugged her scrappy, thin shoulders.

Flames roared in the huge fireplace. The smell of searing meat filled the great hall. Those few who'd grumbled now smiled. No one cared who exactly she was or where she came from. They might care in two days, but not now. She imagined they'd be willing to swear she was sent by Queen Eleanor herself if they had enough to eat. She smiled at that, remembering how she'd rubbed the queen's back to relieve the aches from her child-swollen belly.

Soon, the smells—divine as baking figs, according to one old man—filled every nostril, and made all the trapped blue smoke well worth the watery eyes.

At last, Miggins in the lead, followed by Merry and her workers, carried the meat, still sizzling, stacked upon various small slabs of wood, and set them upon the planks placed carefully atop the stacked stones. No one worried about sitting on the hard stone floor.

There was instant silence, then sounds of chewing, and groans of pleasure.

Garron didn't mind that the girl served him and his men last. He watched her as she brought a large plank piled high with meat to where he and his men sat cross-legged, and eased it down. This plank was wider since it was, after all, the lord's plank.

A priest's byblow? He wanted to question her more closely, ask her why she wasn't starving like the others, why she hadn't been ravished and taken by the Black Demon's soldiers, but he smelled the meat, and realized he was hungrier than he'd been just the moment before.

He breathed in deeply. "You have done well."

"Bullic found a bit of salt and sprinkled it on the meat."

"I like salt. Now tell me, your name is Merry?"

"Aye, my lord."

"'Tis an odd name. Your full name is Merriam?"

"Nay, simply Merry. I was told my father was endowed with a dour nature until I was born and smiled up at him, and thus he named me Merry."

"Your mother was a castle servant?"

A castle servant? Why not? She nodded, marveled at how a little practice made it easier to lie. "She wove beautiful cloth."

"She died?"

"Aye, when I was born."

"I am sorry your father was killed in the Retribution. His name was Father Adal?"

She bowed her head, and merely nodded. She was aware of Gilpin staring hard at her, puzzlement writ clearly on his young face. Did he recognize her as the boy he'd given bread to the night before? Thankfully, Aleric handed him a steak speared on his knife. She watched Gilpin inhale the magnificent scent, and quickly transfer the steak to his own knife.

"Where were you last night?"

"Miggins wasn't certain you weren't as bad as the Black Demon. She insisted I remain hidden until she was sure of your intentions."

"So now she is certain?"

"Aye, she is."

"You weren't here when I was."

She shook her head. "My father brought me from another keep farther to the south."

"What was the name of the keep?"

It came out of her mouth without thought. "Valcourt."

"Valcourt? That is a very rich holding. Why did your father leave?"

"Lord Timothy wished to give the post to another, and so we had to leave. We came here to Wareham. Lady Anne convinced Lord Arthur to take us in since there was no priest in residence, and so he did."

Garron made room on the floor beside him. "Sit here and eat."

She hadn't expected this. Thanks to Lady Anne's full-cut skirts, she was able to sit cross-legged beside him. Garron speared a piece of meat for her.

She pulled it off with her fingers and simply smelled it before she took a lovely big bite. She didn't realize she'd closed her eyes, but Garron did.

He grinned as he took his own bite. He chewed. "This is very good. It appears you got all the people together and assigned them tasks. The great hall looks much cleaner, and the sour smell is mostly gone. Why did you not do anything before I arrived?"

A very good question. She chewed another bite, swallowed, said simply, truth in her voice because she knew it was true, "There was no hope. Every man who left to hunt food was murdered by the Black Demon's soldiers. We were helpless and trapped within the castle walls. Why sweep the floor when death is coming? When you went out this morning, did you see any signs of the Demon's soldiers?"

"Nay, we saw no one. We went directly into the Forest of Glen and hunted. Perhaps you will tell me about the Retribution? And this fellow who titles himself the Black Demon, which sounds like a name meant to scare small children."

Thank St. Hermione's scarred knees the people of Wareham had spoken of the

Black Demon within her hearing during the day. "He did more than scare children. He and his men butchered them." Her voice caught on that, for the actual saying of those words was terrible indeed. She wondered if she'd even be able to speak about it if she'd actually been here, to witness the death, hear the screams, see the horror, and see to burying all the dead.

"I was told the young women were raped and taken away. Why were you spared?"

"Miggins hid me in the jakes. The soldiers did not go there since there was nothing for them to destroy, and I suppose the Black Demon didn't believe the silver coins to be hidden there."

He cocked a black eyebrow at her. "You were lucky none of them wanted to relieve himself."

"Aye, I know it well," and she shuddered at the thought.

"You're also lucky they didn't poison the well so you could clean yourself up after your stay in the jakes."

She smiled just a bit, and finished what was on her plank. Garron speared another steak for her. "It is odd not to hear children's voices. None survived?"

"Some managed to escape and hide in the forest." What was the forest's name? She couldn't remember. "The Black Demon's men were merciless. When they couldn't find the silver, the Black Demon was enraged and encouraged his soldiers to kill, and so they did. The young girls they didn't kill, they took with them, as you know.

"I never realized how the laughter of children filled the air, but now, there's only silence. It's a fearful thing. Mayhap by killing or taking the children, the Black Demon wanted to erase the future of Wareham."

"Aye," he said thoughtfully, and wondered for perhaps the dozenth time why Arthur had stolen the man's silver and brought it here to Wareham. Hadn't he realized this Black Demon knew who he was? "I see you are not as thin and gaunt as the others."

Her brain went blank. She shrugged. "I was heavy. I had flesh to lose."

She saw clearly on his lean face that he didn't believe her. What else didn't he believe? She added quickly, "Did you come from London?"

He chewed, swallowed. "Aye. I was in the king's service. It was he who told me my brother Arthur had died and I was now the Earl of Wareham. However, the king had not yet heard of this—Retribution. Do you know the Black Demon's real name?"

She shook her head. "Mayhap another will know, but I do not."

"No one appears to know. Very well. What do you know of my brother? What sort of master was he? Did you know about the silver coins he'd stolen?"

"No one knew anything about it. I know only that the Black Demon was powerful and deadly. I am sorry, my lord, but may-hap others, once their bellies are filled, will be able to tell you more."

He chewed slowly as he looked out over the great hall, watching his people finally eating their fill. He wouldn't be sur-prised to see them licking the juices off the planks. A fine idea, these makeshift tables, and probably hers. "Everything looks better. The filthy rushes are gone from the floor, and it seems some of the stone floor was washed as well." He paused a moment, then added, "There is something else as well. The very air feels different. It no longer seems to weigh down on my head."

"That is because it no longer smells bleak."

She'd put his thoughts into excellent words. "Aye, that's it."

"There is still so much to be done. Everyone was so very weak, I didn't want to risk anyone collapsing. Tomorrow, everyone will be stronger, and we will accomplish more."

He watched her lick the steak juice from her fingers. "How did my brother treat you, the priest's bastard?"

He watched her lick her fingers frantically.

11

Her father had always told her she had quick wits. *Prove it, prove it.* "He ignored me for the most part. It was his wife, Lady Anne, who was kind to both my father and me, who taught me housekeeping."

Arthur ignored her? He looked at her beautiful red hair, at the thick plaits wrapped around her head and threaded with a green ribbon. He looked at her dark blue eyes, and her white skin, her white teeth. The older brother he remembered wouldn't have ignored her; mayhap when she was a child, but not now, not in the past several years. Come to think of it,

no breathing man would ignore her. Garron looked over at the four remaining
boar steaks on the plank of wood in front
of him. He was full, he realized, but he
knew Pali was always hungry, his long
legs empty until he'd stuffed himself with
enough food for three fat women, Gilpin
would say, then run before Pali could
clout him.

He pointed his knife at Pali and the
meat. "I can hear your knees knocking
together, Pali. They still sound hollow.
Feed them."

He turned back to the girl seated cross-
legged beside him. "How old are you?"

"I am eighteen."

"How old were you when you arrived at
Wareham?"

"Twelve."

So Arthur had watched her grow into a
woman. He'd ignored her? Not likely.

"How old are you, my lord?"

"I am just turned twenty-four in April.
Do you know how to make soap?"

She grinned. "Aye, I can make soap. I
will put it at the beginning of my list."

He could but stare at her. He was the
only living being he knew who made

lists. A dark eyebrow shot up. "You make lists?"

She sounded proud as a peahen as she said, "I am the grandest listmaker in Christendom, so my father told me. Unfortunately, lists are much better when they are written down, and thus cannot be easily forgotten. We have no parchment and no ink."

"Put them on your list, with the soap."

She smiled. "And candles," she added, then sighed, "and so much more. Everything is destroyed. Everything."

"Your gown isn't."

"There is a hidey hole in your bedchamber, my lord. Lisle had hidden some of Lady Anne's clothing there."

"Is your belly full?"

"Oh aye. It's a fine thing."

He turned to Aleric. "The king needs to know of our plight. Have Hobbs ride back to London tomorrow and speak to Robert Burnell. He recites accounts accurately, he is fluent, even when he has drunk enough to piss full a lake. We must have soldiers to guard Wareham against this Black Demon should he decide to come again to search for the silver. I am hopeful the king will agree and send us some men."

How she had heard him from at least twenty feet away, Garron had no idea, but not an instant later, Miggins shouted, "Tupper believes we can call upon Lord Severin of Oxborough for aid. 'Tis wealthy he is, with land and men and goods. He's closer than London. He did not like Lord Arthur, but he doesn't know you, my lord."

"Aye, he does," Garron called back.

"Does he hate ye?"

"No, he does not. I will consider this, thank you, Miggins." But he knew he needed the king, his backing and protection.

He wiped his knife on his tunic as he said to Merry, "How long was Lord Arthur dead before the Black Demon came?"

Garron didn't miss her quick look toward Miggins, who promptly shouted, "Four days, my lord."

Tupper called out, "Aye, barely four days. We buried him with all honor, my lord, all his men surrounding his grave."

"Few wept," Miggins said with no

hesitation at all since she knew she had an old retainer's privilege. "Lord Arthur abused Lady Anne, and all liked her."

His brother abused his wife? He'd known about his brother's rages, but he hadn't known his brother was the kind of man who hurt women, though many thought nothing of striking those weaker than them. So, he'd been dead four days before the Retribution. Garron wondered if the Black Demon would have killed and destroyed even if he'd managed to find the silver. Probably so.

What his brother had or hadn't done, none of it mattered at this moment. What mattered was Wareham. Garron looked out again over his great hall, and felt suddenly blessed. Since people's bellies were full, it meant once again there'd be life to live and friends to argue with. There was noise. But no children.

Garron would speak to his men later. He wanted them to go among the people and find out which children were taken by this Black Demon. They would try to find them. He also wanted to visit all the graves, make certain all were properly marked. And Arthur's grave, he thought, he wanted to visit his brother's grave.

He asked Merry, "Did the Black Demon disturb my brother's grave?"

There was a moment of stark silence. Merry looked perfectly blank.

"I forgot," Garron said, "you were, after all, in the jakes."

It was Tupper who called out, "The Black Demon paid no attention to the cemetery. His soldiers did not touch any of the graves."

Garron said, "The king told me Lord Arthur's men said that my brother died suddenly, with no lingering illness, with no warning at all."

Miggins said, "'Tis so. There was naught anyone could do. He was eating a lovely stew of hare, fava beans, and cauliflower when suddenly he stiffened in his chair and his face fell into his trencher. All saw he was dead. There was naught anyone could do."

Garron fell silent, wondering at the vagaries of fate and man. *How did you know of this man's silver, Arthur? How did you manage to steal it? How did you keep it a secret?* Arthur's master-at-arms, Elkins, was dead, killed in the fighting, he'd been told, before he could be tortured. Surely he'd known of the silver, surely he'd helped Arthur steal it. A cache of silver coins would be impossible for one man to handle.

Miggins, boar grease slicking her face, sidled up to him, and grinned hugely, showing the few remaining teeth in her mouth. "Is your belly happy, my lord?"

"It is."

"Iffen ye have money, my lord, Merry can buy all the provisions we'll need at Winthorpe. Ye surely remember, Winthorpe is a goodly sized town right on the coast, so the trading is brisk. She said we must buy wheat for bread. And since our miller died, we must find a new man and rebuild the millhouse. We must plant seeds for vegetables and find young fruit trees to plant. We must have cloth, or wool to weave into cloth. Borran, our weaver, is alive, thank Saint Whisken's bonny head of hair. What say you?"

"I say if there is enough meat to last for a couple of days, then we will travel to

Winthorpe in the morning. Merry, I will even buy some parchment and ink so you may make formal lists." Garron paused a moment. "I have trained my memory to keep my lists in my head, a skill you should learn."

"Aye, a useful skill. I have always had parchment to write down my lists, but I will try." She looked out over the great hall. "There is so much to be done, mayhap too much for me to remember since I am but a female." She turned back to him and gave him a fat smile.

Whatever else she was, she wasn't afraid of him. He said, "I have always believed females have too many brains."

That was a novel thing for a man to say, especially a man who was a warrior, and she could but stare at him. Then she got to her feet and gave him a small curtsey. "I think you are wise to acknowledge it, my lord."

He waved away her words. "The hall is no longer an airless, filthy tomb. Aye, it is better now."

It was indeed, she thought, it was indeed.

"Is there enough meat to feed everyone until we return from Winthorpe with provisions?"

"Aye, there is."

"I am not surprised Father Adal succumbed to matters of the flesh. Even the pope has bastards, herds of them, I've heard."

She allowed a small smile. "That is what my father told me when he at last confessed to me I was his bastard. *'A priest is naught but a weak man withal, despite his Latin.'* That was what he said." Merry knew that to be true. The Valcourt priest, Father Minsk, was a learned man who loved God and women, in equal measure, and mayhap not in that order since he was particularly pleased when the young maids of Valcourt confessed to him in private.

"What happened to your mother?"

Merry's brain blanked for an instant. "Did I not tell you? She died birthing me."

"I see." He was testing her, she realized, and that meant he suspected she wasn't what she'd said. Oh dear. She needed better lies, ones she could call up with no hesitation. She needed to have

Miggins ask her questions so she could fashion believable answers before she left with Lord Garron on the morrow for their trip to Winthorpe.

Garron turned away from her to speak to his master-at-arms, Aleric, his bald head a beacon in bright sunlight, so shiny it was. She wondered if he polished it.

Merry looked toward Miggins, who was wiping meat juice from her chin with the back of her veiny hand. She was laughing, punching an old man on his shoulder.

She hated lies.

But they didn't journey to Winthorpe the following morning.

12

After breaking his fast the next morning with a boar steak and the last of his ale, Garron looked up to see Merry pacing, obviously anxious to leave. She looked, he thought, young and fresh and eager.

Where had she come from?

When he rose, she nearly danced to him, so excited she couldn't hold still. He laughed. "You are ready, I see."

She crossed her arms over her chest and began tapping the toe of her slipper. She fell into step beside him as he walked into the inner bailey.

"Do you ride?"

"Oh yes, I love to ride, my lord." Her voice fell off the cliff. "Ah, Lady Anne—"

"Aye, the gracious Lady Anne taught you herself, is that what you were going to tell me? Did she teach you to groom a horse as well? Mayhap birth a foal?"

His sarcasm hit her broadside. Well, she knew he hadn't believed her. She'd tried. Without thought, her head came up, her chin leading the way. "She did not have the opportunity, but it would have been as nothing to her. Lady Anne could do everything."

"That is not what I heard," Garron said, although he hadn't heard anything at all about Wareham's former mistress. He'd said it just to see what she'd do.

She jumped instantly to the bait. "There are always those who are jealous, who are mean-spirited, who are—"

"Aye, that is all quite true. Let us hope she taught you to ride well. I don't wish to see you thrown into the dirt."

"I can ride anything you put me on."

He immediately turned away to help an old man carry a large plank of wood across the inner bailey to the barracks. He kept his head down so she wouldn't see the huge grin on his face at what she'd said so unwittingly.

He met her at the portcullis, not smiling now. "I was also told my brother abused Lady Anne."

Her jaw dropped. "Surely not! No man would, that is, well—"

Garron eyed her a moment, wondering yet again who she was, what she was, and why Miggins, and all the Wareham people for that matter, was protecting her. He turned at a shout from Tupper. He looked up at the ramparts to see the old man's face so filled with fear he looked ready to fall over. "My lord! 'Tis a band of men, nay, an army of men, at least one hundred of them, mayhap more, all vicious looking and hard, waiting to sever all of us in two equal parts. 'Tis the Black Demon come back to butcher the rest of us and crow over our severed bodies. One Retribution wasn't enough for him. They're riding like the hounds of Hell toward Wareham! At least God will receive us with full bellies."

Tupper crossed himself, eased his old bones down to his knees, and started praying, loudly.

Garron shouted as he ran to the ramparts, "Keep the drawbridge up and the portcullis down and all will be well. Aleric, get our men in position. Keep our people calm."

He climbed the wooden stairs that led to the ramparts, broke into a run along the thick-planked walkway that went around the perimeter of the castle. He couldn't wait to see the man who'd tried to destroy Wareham. He couldn't wait to carve him into little pieces.

Well, damnation. He stared down not at a hundred soldiers riding at Wareham like Arabs from the Holy Land, more like thirty, all of them seated quietly on their mounts in front of his castle. Their leader wasn't wearing mail. He was wearing a dark gray cloak and, of all things, a thick woolen scarf wrapped around his head. Garron recognized that scarf.

"My lord Garron! 'Tis I, Robert Burnell. I come directly from our mighty and beneficent king. May I enter?"

Garron grinned. "Is it really you, sir? A moment—we will lower the drawbridge and raise the portcullis."

Merry stood in the shadow of the deep

steps leading up to the great hall and watched the soldiers ride into the inner bailey. She watched Garron step forward and help the man in the shawl to dismount.

"That is Robert Burnell," Gilpin whispered to her. "He's the Chancellor of England and, more importantly, the king's secretary. Lord Garron says he's the king's fist, and his ears as well. Lord Garron says there's always a candle lit in his chamber and he works harder than the lowliest serf."

She started to say that all at court knew Robert Burnell's habits, but held her tongue. "Wasn't Hobbs going to see him in London?"

"Aye. I wonder why he comes here?"

Merry started to take a step forward, then realized it was the very last thing she should do. She was nothing, no one. When the soldiers parted, her jaw dropped. She saw at least a dozen pack mules laden with corded bundles. Everyone was gathering in the inner bailey, clustering around her, talking, pointing toward those mules, so excited they were very nearly bouncing on their feet. She heard Miggins break into a cheer, and soon everyone joined her. As their cheers rang through the inner bailey, several of the soldiers' horses moved restlessly, and Merry saw the soldiers looking at each other as they quieted their mounts, then at the ragged lot of people cheering them. One soldier, ugly as a tree stump, waved a fist in victory and laughed. The cheering grew louder.

Garron waited until his people quieted, then took Robert Burnell's hand in his. "I am delighted to see you, sir. One of my men was leaving this morning to go to you in London. About this," he said, and waved around him. "As you can see, we are in a very bad way here. But what brings you here? Dare I inquire about those heavily laden mules?"

Burnell, who would rather have ridden a pack mule than the huge destrier the king deemed to be worthy of him, beamed. "Our king sends you bounty." He waved his ink-stained fingers toward the long line of mules. "Two days after you left, several soldiers from Wareham arrived to tell us what happened here. Our dear king knew you would be in sore need, and he acted quickly. Mayhap it was our beautiful queen who acted more quickly, but no matter, all the mules were packed in haste. We made excellent time."

"You said my brother's soldiers came?"

"Not your brother's soldiers since he is dead." Burnell looked about him at the devastation. "Your soldiers." He sniffed the air, studied the huddled people, then pulled the scarf from his head and wrapped it around his neck. "They did not know the name of the man who attacked Wareham, just called him the Black Demon, of all things. They said those who did not manage to escape were slain, and all was destroyed. I see they did not exaggerate. We brought the two soldiers back with us, though they are in a bad way. You may question them yourself. They also told of torture and the search for Lord Arthur's silver coins, coins this Black Demon said your brother had stolen from him."

Garron looked at the two men, who seemed exhausted to their filthy boots, then to the mules and back again to Burnell, who was rubbing his buttocks. He saw Merry standing in the middle of his people, Gilpin at her side. "Merry, come here and meet the Chancellor of England and our king's secretary, Robert Burnell."

Garron hadn't thought about it, just opened his mouth and the words had fallen out. He watched her walk gracefully to Burnell, give him a smile and sink into a deep, very graceful curtsey. She was wearing a dark blue wool gown, a blue ribbon in her braids. He did not realize the gown was two decades out of fashion. Merry said, "Sir, it is an honor."

Burnell stared at the lovely girl with her too-short gown that his brave mother could have worn, and thick fiery red hair braided up atop her head, hair his mother would have called a curse from Satan, threaded through with a blue ribbon that matched her eyes. She looked familiar. Aye, this girl reminded him of someone, and this someone, he realized, heart speeding up a bit, had something about her that alarmed him. Was it her red hair? He simply couldn't remember. Alarmed *him*, the king's secretary, the king's right and left hand and mayhap on occasion all his digits as well? No, that couldn't be right. Who was she?

Burnell arched a thin dark eyebrow. "I had not realized you had wedded, my lord. The king said nothing of it to me. Indeed, how could you have found both the lady and the time in so few days? This could be a disaster." And he crossed himself, twice.

Garron nearly jumped a foot off the ground. "Nay, she is not my wife, sir, she merely resides here at Wareham. I am told she is the daughter of Wareham's priest who was killed. She"—Garron paused a moment—"is smart."

Burnell studied the strong young face, the intense blue eyes, the dark red eyebrows. Her skin was as white as the snow he'd seen three winters ago in York before human boots had blackened it.

"But priests do not wed, Garron."

"No, they do not."

This girl was a priest's byblow? So, he was wrong, there was simply no way he could have seen her before. There was nothing in this girl to alarm him. His mind was getting rusty with the years. She was smart? What a thing for a warrior to say. Burnell never looked away from her. "Ah well, these things happen, do they not?" But it gnawed at him. Who did she remind him of?

"So I have been told, sir, many times." Merry searched his face, knowing from the way he'd looked at her, that somewhere in the depths of his brain he remembered her.

Burnell waved at the men behind him. "Our dear king, our bountiful lord, sent these soldiers to protect the mules, Garron, and mayhap his lowly secretary as well. Four of the men are yours if you decide you can use them. The king said you could pay them since his, the king's, ah, generosity, does not extend that far." Actually, it was simply a timely accident that had brought Sir Lyle of Clive and his three men to London, so, in truth, the king had done very little, but Lord Garron need not know that. Actually, he had done nothing at all, merely nodded when Burnell told him what should be done. He said now, scrupulously honest as a man could be when he served a king, "It was our gracious queen who had household goods packed for you. As I recall, our king snorted a bit when he counted the number of bundles and the number of mules required to bring you all this bounty, but he allowed it as you served him well for three years. The queen had also just presented him with another royal princess, and that softened him. He, ah, has demanded that you return the mules to him."

Garron managed to quash the insane desire to laugh. He'd fallen into despair and now King Edward himself had seen to his salvation, or rather he hadn't quibbled overly when his queen had seen to his salvation. He doubted such a thing would occur again in his lifetime.

Burnell introduced him to Sir Lyle of Clive, a younger son born without lands, just as Garron had been until three weeks ago. He was Garron's senior by at least ten years, dark as a Spanish Moor, hard and lean as the whip he carried in his wide leather belt, its leather-wrapped handle twisted around his sword hilt. His eyes were set close beneath heavy black eyebrows, eyes as black as a sinner's soul. Why had he thought that?

Sir Lyle bowed. "I was knighted eight years ago by Lord Alfred of Crecy when I saved his life in battle, but there was naught to go with the title. I was at his side until his death two years ago.

"Last month I nearly died in a battle fought over a putrid swamp near Kettlethorpe. The mangy baron who hired me then refused to pay me and my men. He had ten soldiers surrounding him so I couldn't kill him. When I met with the king to air my grievance, he had just heard of your troubles here at Wareham. My men and I are looking for a home, my lord, and the king said you needed men. There are four of us. We fight well and we can work just as well."

Garron studied Sir Lyle a moment longer. His life depended on making the right decision about a man's character. It was odd, but he simply wasn't certain about Sir Lyle, those black sinner's eyes of his. Was he honest or was he a villain? At the moment, it didn't matter. He'd brought three men, strong men by the looks of them, well fed, and that meant more hands to build and repair. He clasped Sir Lyle's sword hand.

"Welcome to my service. I have two other small keeps within a day's ride of here, Furly and Radstock. I have no idea if this man—the Black Demon—and his men also attacked and destroyed them. As you can see, there is much to be done here. Look yon, all the barracks are destroyed. If you wish Wareham to be your home, you must needs assist in rebuilding it."

Sir Lyle said calmly, "My three men are hardy, my lord, all of them eager, as am I. I believe all of us would like to build for a while rather than lay waste to other men's lands. My men are all trustworthy—well, for the most part." Lyle gave a crack of laughter. "I saw both the outer curtain wall and the inner wall are sound and that is a relief. This Black Demon, I have never heard the name. Have you any idea yet who he is?"

"Not as yet."

"Was your brother killed by this man?"

"No, he was not. He died suddenly before this man arrived with his soldiers. Once all is set to rights here, I will discover his name and then I will kill him."

Sir Lyle nodded. "Aye, he should be killed. It's easy to see the barracks were once fine indeed, and that was once a fruitful orchard. Allow me one sword slice of the fellow, my lord, when we catch him."

Those were fine words, Garron thought, but still, he simply didn't know about Sir Lyle of Clive. Well, he would see soon enough. No man could hide what he really was for long. He would challenge both him and his men—no, now they were Garron's men, and Sir Lyle was his man as well—with backbreaking work and tasks they'd likely never attempted before. He saw Aleric eyeing Lyle of Clive, his seamed face utterly expressionless, then turn to the three new men, asking names, getting a feel for what each man could do, and if they could indeed be trusted.

Garron spoke to the two soldiers who'd gone to the king, saw they were both wounded, and called to Merry.

When she was at his side, he said only, "They were my brothers' soldiers. Now they are mine. They are brave men and both are hurt. Please see to them."

Even before Robert Burnell was settled into a makeshift chair, its rough-planked seat hurriedly covered with blankets, Garron heard the sound of a single hammer in the inner bailey. It was the most beautiful sound he'd ever heard in his life.

13

Clouds hung low, the air was chill, but it didn't rain.

Garron rubbed his hands together, told Tupper he was the porter and he trusted him to keep sharp, which made the old man square his meager shoulders. He stationed the king's soldiers on the ramparts, then ordered the portcullis left winched up, the drawbridge down. During the day, two dozen more Wareham people straggled into the keep, all starving and in rags, but now, at the sight of all the activity, at the sight of all the sheathed swords, at the smells of cooking food, there were wondering voices, even one rumbling laugh, but most of all, there was hope. Garron had never thought much about the quality of hope before, but he realized now it was a tangible thing, something he could feel, even smell in the very air.

A dozen soldiers, most wounded, returned as well. Merry cleaned and bound their wounds while Garron questioned them closely, but they knew nothing he didn't already know.

Aleric managed to mix the groups together, with no arguments or broken heads, and set all the men to work, each to his skill.

What pleased Garron the most, he realized, was the young woman who came straggling into the inner bailey with two small boys, their dirty hands clasped in hers, along with three dispirited dogs, their tails down. Her name was Elaine. Her husband had managed to spirit his family out of Wareham and hide them in the Forest of Glen. Then he'd returned to fight.

Elaine bowed her head. "My husband never returned to us."

Garron hoped Tupper or Miggins would know where the man was buried. While he spoke to the mother, he saw Merry give the two little boys and the three dogs milk from the goat Queen Eleanor had sent.

He heard her say, "Ivo, Errol, what shall we name our new goat with her delicious milk?"

"Eric," Ivo said. "It was my father's name. The bad men kilt him after he hid us and came back to fight. 'Tis a good name. Ma cried and cried when he didn't come back. I didn't, but Errol did. He's just a little boy." It didn't matter the goat was female. From that day on, her name was Eric.

Their mother, Elaine, a woman whose pale bruised eyes were no longer blank with fear and grief, heard what Ivo said. She turned to Merry and curtsied. "Thank you, my lady. I believed we would die, but no longer. Thank God, no longer. We saw Lord Garron and his men hunting but I didn't know who they were, so we were afraid to come out. Then, I supposed it didn't matter. We were so hungry and cold. Then we saw all those mules with the packets." She sighed, hugged her boys against her. "The little dogs followed us. Now even they are happy again, with milk in their bellies. We are so glad to be home. I was in charge of all the sewing once the weaving was done. I see everyone is in rags. If you can give me cloth, I will make new clothes. I see Talia has survived, thank the good Lord. She is an excellent seamstress as well. My husband, Eric—" She swallowed. "He was a good man."

Merry lightly touched her hand to Elaine's shoulder. My lady? She had to correct her, she had to— "I will see that you have the cloth and needles, but first you must eat and rest, your boys too." She leaned down to pat one of the dogs.

Merry went through every single bundle. Three mules carried food, another carried seeds for the vegetable garden, even some cuttings for rosebushes, and packets filled with spices. Two mules carried bolts of sturdy wool and a dozen needles, and praise be to St. Catherine's bonny face, there were three small pear and apple trees, their roots bound up in damp cloth. There was so much, Merry felt tears start to her eyes.

When she found candles, she started singing. But she didn't find any soap. She was in sore need of a bath. Well, she knew how to make soap, and given the odors coming from all the people, herself included, she should do it this very minute, though she wondered if she could talk them into bathing, something few of them did in the best of years.

Everything moved quickly. Sir Lyle and his men went hunting, led by three of Arthur's former soldiers who surely knew the lay of the land and where the best game could be found. Every other able-bodied man was out chopping down trees in the nearby Forest of Glen to make trestle tables, benches, and beds.

Merry served Robert Burnell some of the sweet red wine he had brought from the king. She smiled when she filled Garron's wooden cup, one of the dozen sent by the queen. He handed her the soap. "I heard you muttering about not having any soap. I have only this one sliver left."

She gave him a lovely white-toothed

smile that charmed and warmed him to his belly, had she but known it. She'd seen him washing at the well that day and envied that soap. He shrugged. "I learned in Moorish Spain that I preferred being clean to having fleas crawling in my hair."

She took the precious sliver from him and stared upon it as if it were a royal jewel. He laughed. "Perhaps you can use a recipe that smells like this does. I bought this soap in Marseilles. I was told they blend in lavender with the olive oil and ash."

"My father once gave me soap from Marseilles—" Her voice fell off the cliff. "Oh dear." She quickly sniffed the sliver of soap. "I can smell the lavender. I will try, but I don't know where I can find lavender. Mayhap there is some rosemary, hmmm, I must think on this, my lord."

Please don't ask, please don't ask— Of course he was brimming with questions, but in the end, thank all God's angels, he only nodded.

"I will adjust my list for what we still must purchase when we travel to Winthorpe—

it will be much shorter now, thanks to the king."

"It is good your father taught you to write."

She nodded, for indeed, her father had had her educated. She remembered the hours spent with Father Kustus, who begrudged her every moment, believing his task to be a waste of his time. A memory came back: her father speaking to their priest, telling him Merry's mother would be furious when she heard, and he'd laughed. Why, she wondered now as she had many many times in her eighteen years, had her beautiful mother hated both her and her father? She shook it off. "You can trust me, my lord. Do not worry."

Trust her about what, specifically? She was an obvious liar. He opened his mouth, only to shut it again when one of his men approached him with a question, and he was distracted.

Merry continued to serve food throughout the day in the great hall for anyone who was hungry, which everyone was. Sir Lyle's men brought in more deer, pheasant, and grouse to go with the piles of baked fish.

When everyone was called in for dinner, the planks were once again filled with roasted meat and fish, and from the queen, stewed carrots and onions, and piles of dried fruit.

Everyone looked up when Gilpin called out from the huge open doorway, "Behold what our men have wrought!"

Four men carried in a new trestle table and two benches. A loud cheer went up, even though those cheering wouldn't have the privilege of sitting at the trestle table.

It was a feast.

Once again, most everyone ate on planks set upon the piled stones, and everyone rejoiced. Merry saw Sir Lyle looking around the great hall, his expression bemused. Then he met her eyes and stilled. Merry saw something change in his eyes. What? She didn't know. He seated himself at one end of the trestle table, and he looked at her again. A brow went up when she didn't join Garron, but sat beside Miggins, cross-legged on the stone floor. Had he believed her Garron's wife? Now did he believe her Garron's leman, low-born and thus not worthy to sit beside him? And obviously, not worthy of Sir Lyle's notice or respect.

Merry looked at all the wonderful food and realized she wasn't hungry. She was simply too tired, too excited, too pleased with everyone and everything. She didn't remember ever feeling like this before in her life. Naturally she'd overseen the women's work at Valcourt, but everyone knew what to do and did it willingly. They'd all trained her and loved her and protected her since she was the little mistress.

But not here, not at Wareham. This was a revelation. For the first time in her life she was truly needed. When she looked at Garron sitting at the new trestle table, chewing on a thick slab of venison, nodding at something Robert Burnell said, she knew she'd never felt anything like this either. Here was a man to trust, a man to admire. And so very young. She had never questioned her father's exquisite control, and she now realized that Garron of Kersey, Earl of Wareham, had control as well. Like her father, she knew violence ran deep in him as it did in most men, but she knew he would never unleash it until it was necessary, as it had been when he'd saved her in the forest.

Garron swallowed some stewed vegetables and glanced up to see Merry leaning against Miggins's scrawny shoulder, sound asleep. He frowned. He should have insisted she sit with him after all she'd accomplished, but Burnell hadn't stopped talking, all of it advice, supposedly from the king, though Garron knew it was from Burnell himself. He drank the sweet wine and let the overwhelming responsibility of what he now faced fall quiet in his mind, at least for a while.

Burnell found himself wondering yet again how a priest's bastard had managed to gain such loyalty. He chewed on some carrots. "I see the girl sits with the servants. I suppose it is fitting."

It wasn't fitting, Garron thought, but exactly why it wasn't, he couldn't say. "Mayhap she sits with the servants because she fears we will belch at all her good food."

Burnell didn't laugh, for he was not a man of humorous parts. He ate a mouthful of soft black bread. "A priest's by-blow. It is amazing how well your people accept her, even do as she bids them, and none of them appears to want to shun her or kill her."

Garron nodded.

Burnell then wondered where he would sleep this night. It did not look promising. Perhaps Garron expected him to wrap himself in a blanket and sleep atop this table, here in the great hall, with dozens of people snoring all night around him. Not a soothing thought.

Garron stood and raised his cup high. Soon all conversation fell away and there was silence in the vast hall. He shouted, "Our thanks to the King of England. Long may Edward the First rule our great proud land!"

Cheering filled the great hall. Since there weren't wooden cups for everyone, those without pretended to salute the king and themselves, and passed around a wooden dipper filled with ale.

Merry, awakened by all the cheering, re-alized she had to add more wooden cups to her list. *And ale*, she thought, she knew how to make ale. She took her sip when the wooden dipper passed to her. She'd make better ale than this.

Garron raised his cup again. "We will survive. We will rebuild. We will become strong once again and then we will find and kill our enemy, this Black Demon. I also plan to travel to Winthorpe and buy every cup in the town!"

More cheering, and laughter now, and Merry, pleased with him, smiled and drank deep when the wooden dipper was passed to her again.

Burnell said to Garron, "I have decided it is my duty to visit your two holdings with you, my lord, Furly and Radstock."

Garron nodded.

"Actually, the king commanded me to. He is concerned that this Black Demon has taken control of your keeps, or else he's destroyed them." Burnell chewed on a bone before tossing it to one of the castle's three dogs. "The king will miss me but I must see that you are well received. Aye, it is his instruction. He told me if these two keeps were destroyed, then he would see."

Whatever that meant, Garron thought. "Mayhap the Black Demon is a Scot. Since the king wishes to hammer the Scots into the dirt, that would enrage him enough to send me an army. Aye, he would probably lead it himself, banners flying."

Burnell raised a brow. "I hope I did not detect a touch of irony in your voice, my lord."

14

Irony? Lord Garron shook his head, smiled. He saw Merry's head was now lying in Miggins's skinny lap. She was once again asleep.

He said, "I do not have a bed for you, sir, none were left whole and I deemed the trestle table and the benches more important to your comfort."

Even though Burnell expected this, it was still foul news. But he well understood fortitude. "I feared as much. I brought many blankets. Our gracious queen much enjoyed herself, I believe, making lists, all her ladies adding suggestions until she was satisfied you would have everything you needed. She knows how to organize, does our benevolent queen." He paused, frowned a bit. "She uses a great deal of ink with her interminable lists."

"It seems lists abound," Garron said. "I remember I heard the queen insisted all her ladies make lists as well, for greater control, she told them. Since most of her ladies could not write, she had them dictate their lists to a scribe. However, since they also could not read what was written on their lists, I wondered at the usefulness."

Burnell harrumphed. "A ridiculous thing, a lady learning to read and write, though, naturally, I would never say such a thing to our lovely queen."

"Indeed not. I hope you do not mind sleeping on blankets, sir, in the lord's chamber. At least it will be quiet. Merry said there wasn't any soap. She plans to make some on the morrow."

"Merry," Burnell repeated her name slowly. "An interesting name for the priest's bastard. She acts like a lady, my lord. She speaks like a lady. I find this all very strange."

"She is, I admit, something of a mystery."

One of Burnell's thick brows shot up. "A bastard is a bastard. On the other hand, she does appear to be more winsome than any I have met. I see kindness in her, enthusiasm, and she shows competency. You say she is a mystery. Why do you use that particular word, my lord?"

"Can you imagine her fat?"

"I cannot see her."

Garron called out, "Merry! Wake up! Attend me, the king's secretary wishes to thank you for the delicious dinner."

He watched Miggins shake her shoulder. She jerked, and even from a distance, he saw the brief confusion and a spark of fear in her eyes before she realized she was here and safe.

"Merry!"

Slowly, she got to her feet, straightened her gown, patted her hair, and walked to him.

"What do you think of our new trestle table?" Garron asked her.

"It is a marvel, my lord. However, we have no bed for the king's generous and kind ambassador. Gilpin said Aleric plans to make two beds on the morrow, one of them for you, sir."

Burnell's ears turned red with pleasure. *An ambassador*. He'd always believed it his calling, wiliness of tongue was but one of his many talents, but to be an ambassador—it was the destiny of his heart. He beamed upon the girl. "Thank you for the excellent meal. Your father, what happened to him?"

"He died in the Retribution."

"I thought I heard you call it the Devastation before," Burnell said.

Her face went perfectly blank, and Burnell thought, *She was never fat.*

"Retribution, devastation—one or the other, what matter?" Garron said, never taking his eyes off her. Burnell, sharp as an arrow tip, that old bastard, was testing her.

Burnell studied her a moment, particularly her hair. "I am sorry for your father's death, since it leaves you alone. What will you do now, child?"

Garron realized she had no ready answer to this question. "As I told you, sir, she is at present seeing to Wareham. She is good at it. What will happen later? We will see."

Burnell said, "Do you know who first called it the Retribution? Was it this Black Demon?"

Merry turned and called out, "Tupper, who first called it the Retribution?"

"The Black Demon," Tupper shouted. "When he sat atop that great destrier at the fore of his men, he announced he was here to carry out the Retribution unless we gave him his silver coins. Then he said he would spare us if Lord Arthur would come forward and give himself up for his crimes, but Lord Arthur was dead, now wasn't he? But it seemed the Black Demon didn't believe Elkins, Lord Arthur's master-at-arms. Then Murlo laughed at him, all our soldiers joined in with him because they believed themselves safe and they believed him a puffed-up popinjay. All knew that even with Lord Arthur dead, we would hold against an enemy."

"Rightfully so," said Burnell. "Wareham is a stout keep. How did the Black Demon manage to get within the walls?"

The hall quieted. Everyone was listening.

Tupper said, "A traitor let in some of his soldiers through the hidden postern gate at the beach. While the Black Demon was threatening Murlo and our soldiers, all their attention focused on him and his men, the traitor led them in single file. When the Black Demon finished talking, there were enough of his soldiers already within to take Wareham." Tupper bowed his head. "No one realized the Black Demon had divided up his men. 'Twas a black day, sir."

Burnell called out, "Who knew to call this man the Black Demon?"

Tupper said, "He called himself the Black Demon, sir, said it was his name, said, he did, we would never forget him, if we lived to tell about it."

Burnell sat silent a moment, stroking his chin. "Does anyone know who this man is?"

There was discussion. Finally, Bullic the cook shouted, "Nay, sir, no one knows. He never removed his helmet. He was garbed all in black and his destrier, a huge brute, was black as well."

"What of his standard?"

There was the buzz of conversation throughout the great hall, but none could remember a standard.

Garron said, "I know nothing of the silver coins the Black Demon claimed Arthur stole from him."

"I wonder how many coins there are?"

And Garron knew Burnell was thinking about the king's share.

15

Garron escorted Burnell to the lord's bed-chamber, followed by his servant Dilkin, a thin old man with stooped shoulders and an air of great patience. Dilkin carried a pile of blankets in his frail arms. To Garron's relief, but not surprise, he saw that Merry had cleaned the large room, which was now perfectly empty, causing their boots to echo on the stone. Sleeping on the floor would be nothing new for Dilkin, he always slept beside his master's bed. Come to think of it, it appeared to Garron that both master and servant wore the same expression as they looked around the chamber.

When he returned to the great hall, Miggins sidled up to him, Tupper standing at her elbow. "Ye're looking happy, my lord."

"Aye, I suppose that I am." Truth be told, he was seeing the great hall as it would look by Michaelmas. It would again be a nobleman's hall—sweet-smelling rushes on the stone floor, a full complement of trestle tables and benches, even a carved chair for him. He heard grunts and snoring from those already asleep, and smiled.

He noticed that the old woman was fidgeting. "What is it, Miggins? Tupper? Why aren't both of you sleeping? Is there a problem?"

Tupper gave Miggins a look. She nodded, drew in a deep breath. "Not long before his death, I overheard yer brother tell a visiting knight about ye, and how ye'd grabbed an assassin by his throat, clean lifted him off the ground, and snapped his neck before he could get within six feet of the king. Proud he was of ye, my lord, very proud indeed."

How had Arthur heard of that? In that instant, Garron saw his brother at no more than twelve years old, and he was showing Garron, only six years old, how to wield a sword. "I did not know, Miggins. Thank you for telling me."

She paused a moment. "Ye believe yer brother's death was a tragedy, that he was struck down for no good reason. But Tupper and I don't believe his heart jest stopped beating. It was so strange, Lord Arthur was laughing one minute, stroking Mordrid, his leman, and the next instant, he simply fell over his trencher my lord, dead." Miggins sucked in a deep breath and spit it out. "We believe Lord Arthur was poisoned."

Tupper said, "But the problem is, no one can prove he was poisoned."

Garron's world tilted. Poison? His brother was dead because someone poisoned him? He remembered tales of how the sheiks in the Holy Land feared poison more than being cleaved in two by their enemies. He felt his own heart, beating painfully slow, thudding inside his chest.

"But why?"

Tupper said, "Iffen he was poisoned,

my lord, mayhap the one who kilt him knew of his silver coins and wanted them for hisself."

Miggins laid her hand lightly on Garron's shoulder. "There are others besides Tupper and me who believe he was poisoned, my lord. We jest wanted ye to know, mayhap keep more alert even here at Wareham, take more care of yer food and ale."

Garron stared blindly down into his empty mug. Would someone try to poison him as well? But there could be no reason. He hadn't even known about the silver coins.

Those damnable silver coins. Garron's head ached. He looked up to see Merry watching him. Oh yes, they'd told her about this before they'd told him. Had she counseled them to tell him what they believed? In order to make him more careful, to protect him?

Garron rose from the bench. "Thank you for telling me. I will be careful."

He supposed he should inform Burnell, but at the moment, he could not get his brain to take it all in. He needed time to think. He flicked his fingers toward Merry and together they walked to the great hall doors, open to the cool evening air. For the first time, Garron realized that this girl beside him wasn't a small, mincing maid. Nay, she was tall, the top of her head coming nearly to his nose. She was long legged, capable of covering a lot of ground. And she stood straight, her chin up, as if she had worth and value, and she no longer sought to hide it from him.

She followed Garron to the ladder that led to the narrow walkway atop the inner bailey ramparts. The outer curtain walls at Valcourt were eight feet thick. These walls were perhaps two feet less. When she reached the top of the ladder, he took her hand and pulled her up.

She straightened Lady Anne's skirts and turned with Garron to look at the half moon hanging over the Forest of Glen, at the stars studding the black sky. Merry drew in a deep breath, felt the cool night air stir around her. Rain was coming. It felt heavy, like a cloak weighing on her shoulders. She breathed in the smell of the sea and tasted salt on her tongue.

"I am surprised they didn't destroy the ladders. Look yon, the ladders to the ramparts on the outer walls are also intact."

"I wondered about that as well." He paused a moment, then turned to lean his back against the rampart wall. He crossed his arms over his chest, eyeing her thoughtfully. "I could threaten to toss you to the ground if you don't spit out the truth now. It is a long way down. Or I could give you over to Aleric. He has a gift for convincing men—and women too, I suppose—to tell him what he wishes to know. What do you think?"

"I think—I think that would be wasteful of you, my lord."

Wasteful? Garron nearly laughed at that. Yet he thought he heard a tremor in her voice. Was she afraid of him? Well, she didn't know him. He could be one of those men who spoke calmly, even kindly, before they struck. Or maybe she wasn't afraid of him at all, he simply didn't know.

He held out his hand to her. She eyed it a moment, then took it. As they walked the rampart walkway to the seaward side of the castle, Merry realized she didn't want to tell him she was the Valcourt heiress. He was the king's man, first and foremost, and that meant his loyalty was to Edward. The king might not force her to wed Jason of Brennan, but she had no doubt he would select a man who would bring him great gain, be it silver or loyalty and men. He would sell her just as her mother planned to do. Well, it was the way of things, now wasn't it? Marriage was about building wealth, gaining land and power, establishing or strengthening alliances, nothing more, nothing less. But it terrified her to be the one bandied around. She didn't want to return to Valcourt, not yet; she wasn't ready to lower her head, accept a yoke on her neck, and accept her fate.

What she had here at Wareham, it made her swell with pleasure and pride. She was important here. She was making a difference, people looked to her, counted on her. *Please, God, let me remain here for just a little longer, mayhap a fortnight longer, then when it ends, I will not complain.* Well, she knew herself, now, didn't she? She would complain, but not in a prayer to God.

She found herself wondering if a Wareham carpenter still lived, and perhaps a stonemason, and a smith as well? Well, that was Garron's problem, not hers, blessed be St. Leonard's crooked teeth.

"Wasteful, you say?"

She looked up at him, his profile silhouetted in the dim light, and she saw him fighting Sir Halric and remembered she'd known he would win, known it to her soul, and he would have if Sir Halric hadn't run. And he'd also seen through her quickly enough, known she was lying, and now he wanted the truth. He turned to give her a lazy look, no threat in it at all, and it was hard to look away from him, from his dark hair blowing off his forehead in the night breeze, to his eyes, so much lighter than hers, such a light blue to rival a summer sky.

"Aye, wasteful, my lord. Aleric believes me useful as well. On the morrow, I will help Pali stuff mattresses. Mayhap one will be for you." She frowned up at him. "You are very young."

"Not so young. You already know I am just turned twenty-four."

"How old was your brother?"

"Arthur was my senior by six years, far

too young to die. Do you agree with Tupper and Miggins? Do you believe someone poisoned him?"

"How can I know?" Her face froze. *Lie, but make it smooth and easy.* "Actually, I wasn't in the great hall when it happened. I was in the cooking shed, so I know only what they have told me, still—"

"You are a very bad liar. You need lessons. No, no, don't lie more. You told Miggins and Tupper to tell me, did you not?"

"Well, of course. If it was poison, I did not want you to be ignorant of the danger to you. Do you have other brothers and sisters?"

A dark eyebrow shot up, but he merely shook his head at her. "Thank you, I will be careful. There were three other sons and two daughters besides Arthur and me, but they died."

"Life is many times difficult," she said, "particularly for babes." *And for everyone else as well*, she thought.

He stopped and they both looked toward the North Sea, the calm flat water glistening. Below them was the hidden postern gate leading down to the beach.

She said, without thinking, "You are quite well made, my lord."

The dark eyebrow shot up again. "Young and well made?"

"It's the truth, as well you know."

"Do I? Are you trying to distract me?"

"The truth is never a distraction. It wasn't a compliment, merely an observation."

"Give me more of your observations."

"You smell good."

She saw a tug of a grin on his mouth, but then he only shrugged. "I have always disliked filth, particularly on myself. That is all you've got to offer up—I don't stink?"

"There is more, but if I tell you, your head will not fit through the doors into the great hall. Now, attend me. I have made a list of all that must be done within the keep. In my head. If Robert Burnell will give me a bit of parchment, I will write everything down and show it to you."

Garron looked at the low-hanging dark clouds rolling toward them over the sea, obscuring the moon. He turned back, studied her for a moment. "Even though your gown is too short, you are also young and well made."

She shook her head. *She was well made?*

"You always wear your hair braided, yet you are a maid. I like the little braids you've stuck in the big ones. I have counted three of them."

She touched her fingers to her hair. "My father liked the little braids as well."

"Where did you sleep before the Black Demon came

"In the small room assigned to my father."

He slashed his hand through the air. "By Saint Andrew's rotted teeth, you are too smart. When will you tell me the truth? When will you tell me who you are? When you came here? How you came here and why you were not killed? What does it matter now?"

16

She wondered if he could hear her heart, it pounded so loudly. She had to say something. Her chin went up. She lightly laid her hand on his arm. "I swear to you, my lord, that I will bring you no trouble." *Please, God, please, God, make that the truth, make my promise hold.* "I am of no importance at all, well, mayhap there are people who want me, mayhap they want me badly, but I do not want them. I never want to see them again." But what if her mother found her? Or Sir Halric? Or Jason of Brennan? No, not here at Wareham, it would be all right. No one knew she was here, there was no reason for anyone to ever find out. But there was Sir Halric. Would he figure out where she was and tell his master, Jason of Brennan? Would he tell her mother? Could her mother then simply come here and demand to have her back?

No, it couldn't happen, wouldn't happen. She was safe as long as she was useful to him. She planned to be very useful to him.

"If you are of no importance, then why keep your identity from me?"

She was silent as a rock.

"But you admit there are those who want you. Tell me who they are. Do you not believe I will protect you?"

She looked up at him. She had no more words.

Garron said, "It is your father who searches for you, isn't it? You ran away, didn't you? Why?"

"No, no, not my father."

"Ah, so it is someone else who wants you. Your mother, perhaps? A woman has no power, there is no reason to fear your mother."

If you only knew.

"Don't you believe I can protect you?"

"Maybe."

Well, that was something. "Yet you want me to trust you? Trust you when you will not trust me with the truth? And for no logical reason I can think of?" He paused a moment, stroking his chin. "Mayhap you do know of the silver. You are a thief, here to steal it. Mayhap you are the one who poisoned my brother."

"Don't be ridiculous. I wasn't even here at Wareham! Listen, Garron, my lies are of no importance either. I am simply trying to protect myself. In truth I am a simple girl, young, and as you say, well made."

He did not smile. He leaned back against the rampart wall and crossed his arms over his chest, an intimidating pose, one she suspected he used quite often.

"The fact is, I am here and I am able to help you return Wareham to its former glory. You are fortunate the keep wasn't razed to the ground. We can rebuild all that needs to be rebuilt. Surely you can trust me in that, can you not? Were the roasted meats not delicious? Were not the stones in the great hall cleaned and swept? I can do more, I will do more. Your people will help me. They approve of me."

He stared down at her a moment. The black clouds had moved in, bringing instant darkness. He couldn't see her expression clearly. "You could be an enemy," he said slowly, "you could be here to murder me as my brother was murdered."

She didn't move; he saw her hands clench into fists, but she didn't rise to the bait. "I am not your enemy. Indeed, I am very happy to be here. Please, let me earn my keep. Let me help you and your people."

"Who taught you what to do?"

"Mayhap you could think of me as a witch. A witch can do anything." A door suddenly opened in her mind. She was perhaps six years old, the first time she could remember seeing her mother. She had come to Valcourt to see Merry's father, why, she didn't know. She remembered soldiers followed her, even into the great hall. Merry crept after her to her chamber that night, the child wanting to be close to her mother. Instead, she'd watched her mother fall gracefully to her knees before a small pile of what looked to Merry like dried weeds. She listened to her mother's beautiful voice chant strange words even as she crushed more weeds in her hands and threw them on the pile. Then she made a strange circular sign with her fingers. Merry watched her sprinkle what appeared to be sand over the weeds. They burst into flames. She'd never been so afraid in her life.

She'd said nothing to anyone. She was too afraid. And she'd begun to hear the whispers then, everyone at Valcourt spoke behind their hands of her mother, and witchcraft. Was her mother really a witch? If so, why had she sought out a religious life? Why had she left her and her father and entered Meizerling Abbey?

Garron gave a sharp laugh. "You, a witch? You are too guileless to be a witch. Besides, there is no such thing." He looked away from her, back out over the sea, searched to see the horizon. "Just a moment ago, the water was flat, running smooth and black. Now you can practically feel the water pulse deep beneath the surface. Listen to the waves boiling up, soon they'll strike the rocks. The storm is coming.

"Tupper tells me he has a fine nose, something I don't remember. Mayhap he has grown this fine nose in the past eight years. He tells me we will have howling winds and rain throughout the night, but the morrow will bring warmth and a sun high in the sky. If this comes to pass as he says it will, then we will go to Winthorpe." He turned to stare down at her with a good deal of dislike. "Very well, I will let you keep your secrets if you continue to be useful to me."

He was going to leave it, thank St. Cladawr's bulging eyeballs. She bowed her head, feeling light-headed with relief. "Thank you, my lord. I swear you will not regret it."

He had the distinct feeling, however, that he would come to regret it greatly.

She said, "The queen was very generous, but there are still many items we must purchase. We need wool. Elaine, the woman with the two small boys, she is a seamstress, as is Talia. Borran is Wareham's weaver. I too know how to spin and weave thread into cloth. I can help him since there is so much to be done. I can teach other women since there is so much need. I know Borran has already begun repairing the looms smashed by the Black Demon. We must make palliasses and stuff them with straw so our old people can sleep better."

He let her run on. Finally, he raised his fingertips and laid them against her mouth. "I'm certain you can do all these things. If you cannot, then we will see." His fingers touched her bottom lip. *Madness*, he thought, it was madness to feel lust for this unknown girl. She had drawn his people in, so easily, it seemed, beginning with old Miggins. He dropped his hand to his side. "I have coin, but I will have to spend most of it on skilled laborers. Wareham's carpenter wasn't killed, but Inar is an old man. I am hopeful to find a new carpenter in Winthorpe he can teach. The steward was killed. At least Eller the armorer survived. The Black Demon did not destroy my farms, but the farmers need more seeds, something my brother had not provided them before he died." He gave a short laugh. "I had believed myself rich, but I do not have enough to rebuild Wareham."

"Mayhap you could ask the king to find you an heiress." She hadn't meant to say the words, but they'd popped right out of her mouth. And just why was that?

He laughed. "It is not a bad idea, except that heiresses do not fall like snow upon the ground. There are very few of them. Heiresses are also, I've heard, a very bad business."

"Surely that cannot be true."

"Of course it can. Indeed, it is common knowledge."

"A bad business? What do you mean, bad business?"

"An heiress knows her own worth and thus she is too proud. She complains endlessly, she whines, she casts out orders, and all dislike her heartily and hate to look at her because she very likely has rabbit teeth and foul breath. To be a husband to an heiress curdles my guts."

"That is nonsense. Only a blockhead would believe that."

"You, a simple girl of no importance at all, dare to call me a blockhead? Do you know, if you were a man I would likely throw you off this wall for calling me that? As for you, if I wished, I could throw you off this wall with one hand."

She appeared to think about that. "Very well, in that case, I will mind my tongue even though it is sometimes difficult."

He could but stare at her. She'd sounded wicked, and she'd done it on purpose. He found he was charmed to his boot heels. He said suddenly, "I remember my father believed a woman should be chastised whenever she misspoke to her lord."

"I should chastise a man if he misspoke to me. What is your point?"

"I mean he struck her when it pleased him to do so."

"I should kill my husband whilst he slept if he struck me."

"You sound much too fierce to be a girl of no importance at all. No, now don't make up a new lie. Actually, I do not remember his ever striking her. But enough of that. Last night I could hear Miggins snoring from thirty feet away, over all the snoring of my men. And you slept beside her." He eyed her. "Ah, why do you not sleep in the small chamber where your father slept?" He immediately raised his hand. "I know, I know, it pains you too much to sleep there."

"Very well, I will not tell you that."

"Then tell me how you slept with Miggins snoring in your ear?"

She gave him a big grin that made him stare at her mouth and at the deep dimple in her cheek.

"I sang to myself," she said, "sang every song I knew until I was so bored I fell asleep. When I opened my eyes, it was morning."

"Sing me one of your songs."

She cocked her head and sang in a pure, sweet voice,

"I was a simple angel,
Sitting on a cloud,
A fair knight smiled up at me
And beckoned, voice loud
to come to him.

"I left my cloud and flew to earth
But it was not my fate.
I died since I'm an angel,
Not meant to pass through earthly gates."

"I have never heard that song before. Your voice is acceptable, but your song is too sad. It is the saddest song I've ever heard."

"Sad? Aye, I suppose that it is, but surely not the saddest. I wrote it myself and I will tell you, it is not easy to make rhymes." And then she puffed right up. "I sang it to our jongleur and he praised it."

"I did not know there was a jongleur at Wareham."

That chin of hers shot up. "There was a jongleur where I once lived."

"Mayhap I'll change my mind and demand the truth from you once I have seen your list."

"Mayhap, if you do not leave me be, I will not show you my list."

"You may go back to Miggins now and sing your songs. I will see you and your list on the morrow." He nodded, turning away from her to stare out over the North Sea. "Do you know, during dinner, I heard laughter and arguments and belches. It was a fine sound."

She turned, climbed carefully down the ladder, raised her skirts, and ran back across the inner bailey to the great keep.

He called out, "An angel? Did your father believe you an angel?"

She paused a moment, shouted back at him, "My father believed the sun rose only to shine upon my head."

17

Robert Burnell chewed the last bit of sweet brown bread, patted his belly, and said to Garron, a bit of a frown on his aesthete's face, "The king finds you useful. He believes you still innocent of guile and slyness."

Innocent of guile? Garron didn't think he liked the sound of that. Was he as useful to the king as Merry was to Wareham?

"The king also told me once you had remarked that violent intent had a distinctive smell to it, that you had smelled it on every man who had tried to attack him. I told him that sounded too mad not to be true."

Garron merely nodded.

"I am sending two of the king's men to Furly and Radstock to see if this Black Demon attacked them. When they return, we will know if your keeps are safe and what are the inclinations of your castellans before we ourselves visit them upon your return from Winthrope. If Sir Wills and Sir Gregory know what is good for them, they will readily accept you as their new lord. Now, do not argue with me, the king wishes me to ensure that you will be safe. I will guard Wareham in your absence. The king also said you have a rich and cunning brain."

Garron liked that better than smelling violence.

"I wonder what will next year bring?" Since Burnell was vigorously rubbing his buttocks as he spoke, Garron grinned. No matter the number of blankets atop the straw-filled mattress, a cold stone floor wasn't what Burnell was used to.

"I will use all of my rich and cunning brain as well as prayer that next year brings renewal to Wareham," Garron said. "Walk with me, sir."

"A thorough prayer, I have found, requires a good deal of exertion to be done correctly. Sometimes a thorough prayer, one of great length and complex composition, makes one chafe."

When they stepped into the inner bailey, Garron said, "But look, sir, every able-bodied person is working—yon, a man is drilling holes in a plank of wood with an auger, another is wielding a pitchfork, digging into sheaves of hay to make new mattresses, another carefully makes pegs to be driven by hammers into wood for benches and tables."

"Aye," Burnell said, "and I know men are bringing in trees cut from the Forest of Glen, supervised by that that old gizzard Inar, a man of great talent, so his equally old sister told me when she served me ale."

Garron said, "Tupper told me it was good to see Inar smiling again. He is calling out orders, there is a bit of a strut in his walk."

But he needed more skilled men. Garron felt himself worrying again until he heard the loud braying of Eleanor's goat, Eric, who was trying to tug an ancient boot from the little boy Ivo. His brother Errol was stuffing a piece of bread into his mouth, as if he feared there would be no more. He saw the boys' mother, Elaine, speak to each of her sons, then walk briskly across the inner bailey toward the weaving shed, her arms filled with bolts of woolen cloth. Her shoulders were back, her head held high. He was pleased. Her husband had been one of Arthur's best archers, Tupper had told him, a fine man, and they'd buried him with great care. Now it was time to have new looms made. Old Borran told him two of the looms could not be repaired.

He watched Merry skip down the stone steps, watched her speak first to Miggins, then to every single woman she passed. They all nodded and smiled. She was the mistress, he thought, and they accepted her as such. She'd taken over so effortlessly. He wondered for an instant what it would be like if Merry weren't here, if it was only Miggins. It was a thought to make him shudder. Ah, but he had a brain, a rich and cunning brain according to the king, and he would have managed. Garron saw that Burnell was watching her as well.

She called out to him, waving a small rolled parchment. "Here is my list, my lord. I have consulted all the women and compared my list to the goods the queen sent us. I have heard Winthorpe is an excellent marketplace, much larger than your closer towns, although I think it wise to purchase as much as possible from your towns since you will want them to flourish. You will be able to hire men to come back with you and I—"

He held out his hand to silence her and she immediately shut her mouth. She proudly handed him the scrap of parchment he'd given to her the previous evening. He unrolled the parchment and looked at the beautiful script. There were no ink splatters. Couldn't she have made at least one mistake? His writing looked like a savage's in comparison.

He scanned the list, then pulled out his own very different one.

He broke out with a laugh when he realized they had both written soap near the top of their lists.

"It is probably the least useful item on our lists," he said. He sniffed her. "Ah, you smell like the soap I gave you. Is there any left?"

"Nary a bit. I did offer the soap to Miggins before I used it. I thought she would faint she was so revolted. She told me her mother bathed once a year and had to spend a week in bed afterward to recover."

"So the gracious Lady Anne taught you the glories of bathing?"

She grinned at him shamelessly. Bless St. Cuthbert's boiled bones, there was humor in his voice now. She remembered there'd been no humor in her father's voice the sicker he became.

"Just so," she said.

"Ah, you have written down a score of herbs I have never heard of."

"There is no healer here. The queen sent some herbs—rosemary, bramble, betony, chamomile, and horehound—but I will need—"

"How do you use horehound?"

Burnell cleared his throat. "Horehound is used for stomach pains, for colds in the head, and to counteract various poisons."

Garron wasn't surprised Burnell knew about horehound. In his experience, the man knew a bit about everything. He raised an eyebrow at Merry. "So you feel I must find us a healer?"

"Perhaps not. I had begun lessons with our healer, even though he didn't wish to teach anyone what he knew, but he knew he would die soon, so even though he hated it, he began my lessons. I learned enough to make a difference." Merry thought of her father's devastating stomach pains, the constant vomiting at the end, the wasting of both his mind and his body, and how the little she'd known about herbs hadn't helped. She'd sent a message to her mother since she'd been told her mother was vastly learned in the ways of herbs and their powers, and the power of other things as well. But her mother had not even acknowledged her message.

"The cloak you are wearing, it belonged to Lady Anne?"

She nodded and gave it a tug since it, like the gown, was too short, and its overlong sleeves made every task difficult. Merry didn't care. It was beautiful.

Ten men and one woman rode from Wareham an hour later, Burnell looking down at them from the ramparts. Merry rode on Garron's right, Sir Lyle of Clive on his left. He wanted to get to know the man. However, he knew he wanted to know about Merry more. Exactly who she was didn't seem so important at this moment.

He hadn't been around women all that much, the ladies at Edward's court, certainly, and he'd enjoyed several of them when they'd cast him their sloe-eyed looks, but he'd never understood them, these soft-skinned creatures with their beautiful bodies who seemed to enjoy stroking him. He remembered his first girl, Constance. He'd been twelve, she an ancient fifteen, married to the fat draper, twenty-five years her senior. She'd died the following year in childbed. He remembered the draper had remarried three months later. *So very young*, he thought, and he heard her laughter in that instant, remembering how she had shown him what pleased her. He gave a sideways look at Merry. Her face was raised to the sun, her eyes closed. Did she yet know anything of a man's mouth caressing her?

He didn't think so. When she'd told him the night before that he was well made, there had been no knowledge in her voice or her eyes.

She was riding one of the horses they'd taken from the dead robbers. He worried the coal-black brute was too big for her, too vicious, but she was handling him well.

Garron wasn't wearing armor today. His tunic was dark gray as were his trousers, his sword fastened to the belt at his waist, his stiletto snug in its sheath inside the right sleeve of his tunic, strapped to his forearm. He wore dark hose and boots. He was bareheaded. He felt good. The morning breeze cooled his face, ruffled his hair. Tupper had been right—the storm that had raged throughout the night was gone, and in its place was a beautiful day. He heard a quiet laugh and looked at Merry.

He said, "The horse you are riding belonged to a robber. I don't know the horse's name. If you like him, you can name him."

Of course she knew the horse; she'd ridden on it, seated in front of that huge villain with his foul breath and heavy fist, now dead, thanks to Garron. She remembered his name was Bollon. She cocked her head at Garron, and the hood she wore fell away. She wore her red hair in her typically neat braids twined atop her head, blue ribbon plaited through it. He remembered the ladies at court tended to wear their hair in coils over their ears, or if they were maids, their hair was loose, with silk bands around their heads.

He frowned. He was becoming an idiot.

He gave a start when she said, "To honor his former owner, I will name him Satan."

For an instant he didn't realize she was talking about the damned kidnapper's horse.

A horse whinnied and he turned in his saddle to see Gilpin's horse bite the neck of the horse next to him. For a moment, there was pandemonium, horses rearing, shouting, and ripe curses, until a ferocious-looking man with a pocked face separated them.

Garron turned to Sir Lyle. "Your man, his name is Garn? He handled the horses well."

"Garn is a magician with horses," Sir Lyle said. "I would say he is better with horses than he is fighting, and thus his worth to me. He can break them, train them, determine their abilities. He told me your man Hobbs is also excellent with horses."

"Aye, he is." Wareham's head stable lad had been killed, and there was no one to take his place. Hobbs was in charge of the stables at the moment, but Garron needed to hire a new head stable lad. He'd forgotten to write it on his list. He saw that Merry was looking at the trees surrounding them, so at ease he feared she might fall off her horse.

Garron felt a punch of lust as he looked at her damned hair. One of those ridiculous ribbons had come unthreaded and was dangling in front of her ear. Hair was hair, who cared? Was that a small braid he saw twined in that ribbon?

He said, "You don't have freckles."

She jerked in her saddle and he reached out his hand to steady her. "What? No, I do not. Neither does my mother—I mean, my mother didn't either, so my father once told me."

So now I am a party to your lies and you expect me to swallow them. He realized he would. He said to her with a good deal of dislike, "I will leave you be, so long as you are useful to me."

18

They stopped briefly at the two small towns now under Garron's protection. Thanks be to St. Allard's beautiful voice, neither Abbenback nor Stour had been visited by the Black Demon, but both towns had heard what had happened at Wareham. They welcomed the new earl enthusiastically, particularly when they realized he was buying goods. Everyone treated Merry like his wife.

They spent the night near Stour after Garron sent back three men with goods purchased at both towns bound for Wareham.

Late the next morning they arrived at Winthorpe, a much larger trading town set at the mouth of the Porth, a short snaking river that fed into the North Sea. Winthorpe's protector was Baron Norreys, a foul man Garron had met when he was but a young boy, a man no one considered friend, including, Garron remembered, his own father.

The road that bisected the town was hard and dry. Clouds sat high in the sky, the air was warm and ripe with the smells of bodies, manure, fish, and, oddly, jasmine. There was activity and noise everywhere. Stalls filled both sides of the main roadway. Haggling was loud and fierce, the very air pungent with arguments and insults.

He learned quickly enough that Merry could bargain with the craftiest of merchants. When he was satisfied she would spend his money wisely, he left her with the four mules and the three men he'd assigned to assist and protect her. He found skilled laborers, including a master carpenter to join Inar, a smith, and an assistant mason. He offered them all steady work until Michaelmas, with the possibility of remaining at Wareham. Twenty of them accepted.

He was rubbing his hands together, praying Merry hadn't spent all the coins he'd given her, when he spotted her near a stall at the very end of the vast trading center. She was surrounded by his men, the pack mules now piled high with roped bundles.

As if sensing his presence, Merry looked up and gave him an excited smile.

"What have you got?"

"It is Book One of *Leech Book of Bald*, written two hundred years ago. Our healer told me about it, told me how amazing it is, how he'd studied from it, but did not have a copy. I was told my mother also has—had—a copy. And now here it is in Rabel's stall. This is Rabel, my lord. He told me it once belonged to a monk who stole it from his monastery many years ago. He says its infusions and decoctions are still as effective in this modern day as they were in William the Conqueror's time. Look, in Chapter Sixty-three, it says to cure lunacy one must add a goodly number of different herbs to ale and drink it for nine mornings. Hmmm, it also says to let the lunatic give alms and earnestly pray to God for his mercies."

She raised her face to his, holding the book tightly to her chest. "Rabel sells all the herbs I will need as well." She drew a deep breath. "I think it would be wise to have this book and the herbs."

"Would it also be wise to see if Rabel wishes to live at Wareham?"

"Why did I not think of that?"

But it was not to be. Rabel, nearing his fiftieth year, his stiff white hair haloing his head and his seamed face, could not leave Winthorpe. He lived with his daughter and her husband and three boys, and helped support the household.

"With this amazing book, my lord," Rabel said, "the lady will be able to become a fine healer."

"There are not many pages in it," Garron said as he paid out surely too many of his few remaining coins. "How many illnesses can you cure with so few pages?"

"Look here, Garron, fennel is used for insomnia, indigestion, and vomiting. And just look at the beautiful illustrations,"

Merry said, pointing. "One can see exactly what to do. Rabel is right. I can learn, my lord. I will learn."

"I now have barely enough coin to buy the additional tools to repair the barracks at Wareham."

"To make a man well again is surely more important than giving a sick or dead man tools, my lord."

He eyed her with dislike, as Rabel, trying not to look too pleased with himself, carefully wrapped white linen around the book and reverently handed it to Garron. "You will guard it, my lord. I am glad it is now yours, in your protection. I feared someone would steal it. It was my own grandmother who bought it from the monk. She was a witch, a very good one."

Garron looked down at Merry. "It appears to form a circle since it comes to a witch."

"A witch's daughter." She came up on her tiptoes to say close to his ear, "I read that if a poisoned man drinks old wine with the ooze from the white horehound, the poison will soon pass off. Now you are safe, my lord."

"It is a pity my brother did not know this."

She frowned. "Miggins said it happened so quickly there was nothing to be done."

He told her of the twenty workers and their families he had hired to come to Wareham.

"I trust the families will bring sufficient clothing and bedding. Ah, we must build dwellings for the families. The unmarried men, how many are there, my lord?"

"Six are unwedded."

"Where will they live?"

"We will add to the soldiers barracks, a large dormitory, perhaps."

"Are any of these men older?"

"Aye, three are, and they are masters at their crafts."

"We must build them dwellings as well. They will not want to spend their time with heedless young men, cursing and spitting and butting heads."

When Garron stopped a moment to examine a handsaw, Merry, standing just behind him, saw Sir Lyle speaking to one of his men. The man nodded and slipped away. What was that about? She didn't like Sir Lyle, hadn't the moment she'd met him, hated the way he'd looked down his nose at her as if she were worth less than nothing.

But she forgot Sir Lyle when Garron began discussing each of the new workers he had hired, and where they would build their dwellings.

Night was falling, warm and clear, when Garron heard the sound of a stream and called a halt. Pali found a nearby clearing large enough for all of them, the mules and the horses. Merry watched the horses docilely follow Hobbs to drink from the stream. He returned humming to the camp, again, the horses following him. Garron smiled at Damocles, that mean irritable animal who would delicately eat a dried apple from Hobbs's hands. Gilpin removed all the bundles from the mules' backs, fed them, and led them to the stream.

Aleric brought down two rabbits for dinner and Pali roasted them over a blazing fire. Merry wanted to help, but she quickly saw this was a routine and each man knew what he was to do, and so she sat down cross-legged and sang them songs. After they ate the rabbit, she sang more songs. Pali told her a voice like hers had made the stars shine brighter. "Ha," Garron said.

She pointed upward. "Garron, but look at that star just over Gilpin's left shoulder. It is so bright I can see Pali's red eyes reflected in its light. I am good, am I not?"

He laughed and threw a rabbit bone at her.

The following day dawned warm. They stopped at a small alehouse, the Hoary Rabbit, in the tiny hamlet of Kersey-on-Dale, halfway through their remaining five-hour trek back to Wareham. Garron wanted to see if anyone here knew anything about the Retribution at Wareham and the Black Demon. He discovered quickly enough that everyone knew. However, no one knew the Black Demon's identity, or admitted to knowing.

Garron bought a flagon of ale for Sir Lyle and invited him to sit with him on the long bench in the alehouse.

"You are missing one of your men. Solan is his name, if I remember aright."

Sir Lyle said, "Aye, Solan had belly

cramps. I left him to take his ease beneath an elm tree. When he recovers, he will return to Wareham."

Garron took a drink of the tart ale, wiped his mouth with the back of his hand. He looked out the narrow window at a bent old woman tugging at a rope tied around a pig's neck.

A reasonable answer, but Garron wondered.

Sir Lyle stilled, no part of him moved, even his eyes. He slowly lowered the cup of ale to the scarred tabletop. He said easily, "You doubt my word? I am your man, my loyalty is to you, to none other. I came with England's chancellor, the king approved of me."

This was true. Garron nodded slowly.

"I will go keep watch over our supplies." And Sir Lyle strode out of the tavern.

When Garron emerged, he heard a small gasp. He stilled immediately. "Merry?"

"Ye tell me where yer silver coins be, my lord, and ye can have the wench back with her gullet still inside her neck."

He turned very slowly to see a man holding Merry tightly against him, a knife point against her neck.

Be calm, be calm. "Very well," Garron called out, "I will tell you where the silver coins are but you must release her."

"Ye think me a fool? I'll not trust a big'un like ye to keep yer word. Url, show our fine young lad what ye can do."

Garron felt the sharp tip of a knife press into the middle of his back, through his thick tunic, to stick into his flesh. He heard the man's breathing, ragged, and knew he was afraid.

"Aye, ye hold yerself still and Url won't shove it through yer back. Now, where did yer brother hide the silver coins?"

Merry gave a soft, terrified cry and slumped forward in a dead faint. The man automatically loosened his hold, yelled, "What are ye doing, silly wench!" and Merry slipped unconscious to the ground. When the man bent down to pull her up, she rolled onto her back, raised her feet, and struck him as hard as she could in the groin. The man dropped his knife, grabbed himself, and doubled over. Merry struck him again in his side, and this time he fell to the ground, moaning and crying. She grabbed up the knife.

The knife against Garron's back shook,

and he smiled even as he whirled about and cuffed Url on the side of his head with his fist. He yelled, "Aleric! *A moi!*"

"Garron, behind you!"

Garron whirled about, brought up his fist, and slammed it into the new man's jaw. His blow was so hard, the man went flying backward to land hard on his back. He didn't move. Merry watched Garron calmly bend down over the man and pull the knife out of his hand. He slapped him once, twice.

But he didn't move.

Garron stood when he saw Aleric, Sir Lyle at his side, both their swords drawn, running toward him. In that moment, the man jerked up, rolled up onto his feet, and ran into the woods behind the inn. "Let him go," Garron called out when Aleric would have gone after him. "We still have two of them. They will tell us what we need to know."

Aleric sheathed his sword. "Well done, my lord. You kicked that one cockshead in his parts?"

"Nay, Merry did that." He saw in his mind's eye the dirty lad he'd rescued kick Berm in his groin right before Garron had hurled his knife into his throat. He frowned, then dismissed it.

"This one here, I clouted in the head. And for the one who ran, I hit him in the jaw, but evidently not hard enough. Have you seen either of these two before?"

Both Aleric and Sir Lyle studied the men, then shook their heads. Sir Lyle called out to his men, but neither knew the two scoundrels.

Garron went down on his haunches beside the man who'd held the knife to his back. No, not a man, more a boy, and he was filthy. His eyes were open and he was sniffling. He moaned and raised his hand to press against his head. Garron leaned close. "Tell me, Url, who hired you?"

The boy was so afraid he was shaking. "I dinna know, I swear it, my lord."

Garron drew his knife and began to slide his fingers up and down the blade. "I won't kill you if you tell me. Who hired you? How much did he pay you?"

The boy shook his head again, his eyes on that knife, and moaned at the pain in his head. He whispered, "After we found out where yer brother hid the silver coins, after I kilt ye, then he said he'd pay us. I don't know who he was, niver saw him afore."

"What did he look like?"

"His head were down, I couldna see him."

"You agreed to kill a man without seeing a single coin?"

"Aye, why not? But the man, he gave us each a bit to make us want to gain the rest after we kilt ye."

Aleric knelt down beside Garron and shoved his hands into the boy's pockets. He pulled out three half pennies. "Evidently he did not believe these young louts needed much to urge them to murder."

Garron walked to the other man, still lying on his side, moaning and holding himself. "Who hired you?"

This man was older, as dirty as the boy, only there were years of meanness in his eyes. He looked beyond Garron to Merry, and there was bone-deep rage in his eyes. He spat in the dirt. "I'll kill ye, wench, I'll kill ye with me bare hands! Yer a female, yer not supposed to hit a man like that, it's vile and unnatural!"

Merry growled deep in her throat, took

a step toward him, and raised her foot. The man yelped and tried to roll away.

Garron leaned down and struck him in the jaw. The man fell back, unconscious. He looked up at Merry, her foot still raised. "Well, that was a mistake. I should have left him conscious to enjoy some more pain and answer my questions. We'll take them back to Wareham, question them there. We'll find out who hired them. I believe this fellow knows."

"Oh aye," Aleric said, and rubbed his hands together. "Remember that French assassin who wouldn't tell you who had hired him to kill the king? Ah, that was fine sport, wasn't it, Garron?"

Garron realized Url was listening. He laughed. "The man was a coward, he yelled so loudly when you pulled out his fingernails and toenails, the king remarked that it curdled his cow's milk." Garron paused, saw the young man's face was perfectly white, a feat since he was so dirty. He rose, dusted his hands on his breeches. "They can think about their fingernails whilst we ride home."

Garron felt his blood begin to slow. He

turned to Merry, the anger still burning hot in her eyes. "You should have stayed with Aleric. Now, breathe deeply, and calm yourself. Do you know, not long ago I saw a boy kick a scoundrel in the groin just as you did. And you did it well, Merry, although you were an idiot, since that lout could have shoved that knife into your neck in an instant."

He was right, she knew, she hadn't thought, hadn't considered. She'd found a recipe for curing hiccups and wanted to tell him. She began frantically rubbing her throat. "Oh dear," she said, staring up at him, saw that knife slice right through her neck. "Oh dear," she repeated, and she fell over in a dead faint.

As Garron lifted Merry into his arms and carried her to Damocles, Aleric spoke calmly, "Pali, Gilpin, bind the two scoundrels, Garron wants to question them when we reach home." He said louder, knowing both men were listening, "And I will leave my knife dull and dirty, 'twill be more fun shoving it beneath fingernails." He slanted a look at Garron, said quietly, "It was a fine tale of torture you spun to the boy. I doubt not that he, at least, will be more than willing to spill everything he knows. As for the other one, he's hard, that one. Gilpin, bring Merry's horse. Sir Lyle, will you keep watch on the two prisoners?"

Sir Lyle nodded. He looked angry. And Garron wondered if his anger was because these men had tried to kill him or because they'd failed.

Garron mounted his horse, still holding Merry against him. He let her be for several minutes, then slapped her face. "Come on, wake up. One moment you are a hero and then you collapse like an empty goat bladder."

"I am not a goat bladder."

He grinned over her head as he clicked Damocles forward.

"Oh dear, I did not really faint, did I?"

"You fell to the ground like a rock." And he began whistling.

"It is not fair. I am a hero."

19

It could all have ended so differently, she kept thinking, and found herself again rubbing where the man's knife had pressed against her throat. To distract herself, she began chanting a recipe for curing loose bowels from *Leech Book of Bald*. Everything had turned out all right. She and Garron were both fine, and they were now nearing home.

Only days, she thought, since she'd been kidnapped by Sir Halric and his three villains. Yet it was beginning to feel distant, just as Valcourt and her life there was receding with each passing hour.

She looked up to see the sun had disappeared, locked behind darkening clouds. The afternoon was growing colder, and she shivered.

She pulled her cloak tightly around her and drew Satan closer to Damocles. "How did those three men know?"

Garron said matter-of-factly, "In all the towns we've visited, everyone knew about the Black Demon's attack on Wareham and why. Someone realized he could make a lot of silver and so he hired the three men, though his selection did not show particular intelligence on his part. But he did have to act quickly."

"Or it could have been someone in Wareham who knew where we were going."

"Aye, so it could. I dislike traitors. I really do."

Merry said without thought, "I saw Sir Lyle speaking to his man Solan, and then Solan disappeared."

A black brow shot up as Garron turned to look at her. "What is this? You doubt Sir Lyle, believe he is the traitor?"

"There is something about him I do not trust."

"What is that?"

"I am not sure how to say it. I suppose it is the way he looks at you."

"I am a stranger to him. He doubtless looks at me because he wants to gain my measure. The king himself sent Sir Lyle to me." His voice sharpened. "Has he bothered you?"

"Nay, but he does not like me either."

"How do you know this?"

"Come, you can always tell when another doesn't like you. He looks at me like he doesn't trust me and his eyes are always so cold."

"Mayhap he does not trust you, Merry. Mayhap he realizes, just as I did, that you are no priest's byblow, and he fears you will try to harm me."

"For anyone to think I could hurt you— that is idiocy."

"Aye, it is. I could wring your neck as easily as a chicken's."

She wanted to strangle him. "That is not what I meant and you know it. This is not a jest, Garron."

"Aye, I know it."

"This is very serious."

He gave her a small smile. "After what you did to that lout who stuck his knife to your neck, I suppose I must now take care around you."

Her shoulders went back, her chin up, and his smile grew just a bit. "Aye, I did well, did I not?" She said very deliberately, "My father taught me. He told me kicking a man just there would stop even a giant in his tracks. And he laughed at that. I had never tried it before." *Lie, lie.* "It worked. I have proven myself to you, to your men." She flung out her arms. "I have proven myself to the world."

He laughed now, though his fear for her was still a knot in his belly. The fear was gone from her eyes. As a matter of fact, she looked proud as Gilpin had the time he'd managed to trip a man who'd tried to slit Garron's throat in Marseilles.

Ah, but that villain could have so easily slid that knife into her neck and she'd be dead, and— No, he wasn't going to say any more about it. "Aye, you've proved yourself to the world. You were a warrior. Tell me, Merry, have you ever seen Sir Lyle before?"

She frowned, shook her head.

Did he himself trust Sir Lyle? Down in his gut where it counted?

An hour later they were back at Wareham and greeted with loud cheering and great excitement when all the laden pack mules were in the inner bailey. Garron turned the twenty men he'd brought back with him from Winthorpe over to Aleric. Their families would be arriving within a sennight. Until dwellings were constructed, the great hall would be full to bursting.

He did not go to the granary to visit his two prisoners until it was nearly time for the afternoon meal. Merry was on his heels the instant she realized what he was going to do. "Leave me alone with them, I will make those worms tell you the truth," she said, chin up.

Ah, the arrogance, he thought, and found himself smiling at her. "No, Aleric and I will question them first. If we fail, you may be certain I will call upon you. They have enjoyed several hours by themselves to consider their sins and their fingernails. It's very dark down there, the walls oozing damp and cold. It should make their tongues loosen."

"But—"

He patted her hand, and left her. He and Aleric walked down the stairs, and Aleric unlocked the granary door and shined a rush torch inside. The two men lay on filthy straw, their backs against the cold stone walls. Both appeared to be asleep.

"Do you think they're ready for your fine care, Aleric?" Garron called out, his voice echoing back to him.

There was no movement from either man.

Garron frowned, then he cursed and ran to where they lay. They were dead. Both had been garroted, the ropes still around their throats.

He cursed until he was repeating animal body parts. "They're cold to the touch, Aleric. They were murdered not long after we arrived home." Garron rose slowly to his feet. "We have a traitor right here in Wareham. By all the disciples' martyred sisters, I do hate traitors."

Garron wondered what Robert Burnell would have to say to this.

Burnell had plenty to say when Garron told him during dinner. He carefully laid down the pheasant bone on his trencher.

"I cannot accept this, I cannot. Yet another traitor here at Wareham?"

"Evidently so, sir. Since both the prisoners are dead, there is no way I can determine who hired them. Tell me about Sir Lyle."

"Sir Lyle? Come, Garron, that is not possible, surely it is not. I cannot credit it, I cannot, for it would mean I was duped, and surely that cannot happen."

"Then mayhap it was one of the king's men you brought with you, sir. My own men and I have been together since I was a green lad. There is no one else. Miggins or Tupper would have told me if there was a stranger lurking around."

Burnell ruminated. "It cannot be Sir Lyle. He asked to see me when I was preparing to journey here to Wareham. He said he owed allegiance to no man and when he'd heard you were the king's man, a fair man withal, he said he wished to swear fealty to you. The king himself said he'd heard Sir Lyle was stout and loyal. Others agreed with him. I had not met Sir Lyle so I did not know, but I liked how he looked me straight in the eye and kept himself sharp and straight in his manners and speech. Ah, mayhap it was one of his men, ah, that is it. But Sir Lyle? Ah, if he is false, it means I failed my precious king."

And you surely failed me as well.

Burnell was tapping his fingertips on the table. "I saw that Sir Lyle was distraught when he heard you telling me of the attack on you and Merry. I saw his anger, his confusion."

"Aye, I saw it too when he first came with Aleric right after the attack." Garron looked over at Sir Lyle. He was sitting at a newly made trestle table, hunkered down next to his three men, a roasted pheasant leg in his hand. He said, "I saw Sir Lyle speak to his man Solan, and the man disappeared. When I asked Sir Lyle about Solan, he told me Solan suffered from belly cramps. He looks fit enough now." He paused a moment, chewed on a hunk of brown bread, tasty it was, slathered with rich butter. "Merry distrusts him."

Burnell said, "The priest's bastard? She distrusts a knight?"

"Aye, she does."

"She is making up tales, exaggerating. I mean, just look at all that red hair."

Garron called out, "Sir Lyle, attend me!"

When Sir Lyle stood quietly beside him, Garron asked him, "Where did your man Solan go today?"

"Solan? Do you not remember asking me that before, my lord? Do you not remember I told you that his belly pained him? I had warned him, but he wouldn't stop eating the winterberries. I sent him to lie down under a tree. He is himself again. He, like I, like all my men, is much disturbed by the murder of the two prisoners. He does not know who it could be." Garron watched Lyle look briefly toward Merry, who sat silently next to Elaine and her sons. There was no expression on his face, but his eyes—they were filled with suspicion and something else. What was it? He didn't know. What was he thinking? Merry was nothing to him, nothing at all.

Sir Lyle turned back to him. He was smacking his fist against his open palm, once, twice, three times. "And now the two assassins were garroted right here at Wareham—by all black hearts that roam the land, my lord, it is difficult to accept that there is a traitor here, within Wareham's very walls, someone disloyal to you. If you wish, I will join Aleric and Pali and question all the new workers who came from Winthorpe back to Wareham with us. I am hopeful one of them is the traitor."

Garron nodded. He had to face the fact that there were a great many people now within Wareham's walls he did not know. And the twenty men who'd come back with them? It made the most sense. "Question them, Sir Lyle."

"Aye, my lord. But I do not understand how the murderer got himself into the granary to kill the two men."

Garron said, "There are two keys. Aleric had one, I had the other. When we went to the granary, he could not find his key. He believes it was taken from his jerkin."

"He has no idea who would have taken it from him?"

Garron shook his head. "He is speaking to Pali, Hobbs, and Gilpin. I am hoping that one of them saw something. He is furious, both with himself and with the traitor. I have also asked Tupper and Miggins to canvass all our people while you and Aleric are questioning all the new men."

"Aleric's carelessness could lead to your death, my lord."

"Aye, that is so," Burnell said. "We must find out the man's identity, else I will return to my blessed king with a black wart on my conscience."

Garron said to Sir Lyle, "I wish you to speak to your men as well, see if they witnessed anyone going to the granary, if they have heard anything suspicious."

Sir Lyle gave him a short bow, turned on his booted heel, and strode back to his table. Garron saw that Merry was watching every step he took.

Garron and Burnell drank in silence from the new mugs Merry had purchased in Winthorpe from a miserly old woman who, truth be told, had outmaneuvered her. The ale was rich and ripe, and Burnell continued to drink, staring down into his mug, that magnificent brain of his sifting facts, considering possibilities. He said to Garron, "I don't like this at all. No man's face comes to my mind."

He emptied his mug. Garron was surprised, for he knew Burnell rarely drank.

Burnell saw his surprise. "My head is harder than the writing calluses on my fingers, but you are right, my lord, I am succumbing to a weak man's crutch. It is not assisting my thoughts to reveal themselves in a logical manner. I do hope Sir Lyle is not the villain. If he is, it is possible my dear king will have me beheaded for my blindness. I deserve any punishment he wishes to mete out." He paused a moment. "Our executioner, Dalfo, can see great distances, his eyes sharp as a hawk on the wing, but up close, looking down at a man's neck, he told me all is a blur, a good thing, withal, since a man's neck has buckets of blood and gore in it. Still, he admitted there are drawbacks, since often it requires him to swing his axe several times to detach a man's head from his neck. If it is to be my own neck on the block, I might grab the axe from him and cut off my own head."

Burnell shuddered. "I need more ale, to quiet my mind from these awful visions." He poured from the ale flagon into his mug. He immediately set the mug away from him. "Nay, I must determine who is the traitor within Wareham's walls. Hmmm. I believe my brain is too sodden to wring itself out. Tell me again what happened."

20

Garron picked up his knife, tested the sharpness of its tip. He said, as he looked at the small drop of blood that appeared on his fingertip, "The attack came quickly. There was not that much time to plan it. The three men who attacked me and Merry weren't efficient. Merry saved herself, as I told you."

"A fortunate accident for the girl, nothing more," Burnell said. "Ah, Arthur's silver coins, it teases my brain, it always comes back to the silver coins, and this Black Demon."

Burnell set down his mug, sighed, and

sniffed at the newly cut wood that made up three more trestle tables and benches, raw and fresh in the air. It was a smell he remembered from childhood, a smell that brought to mind his mother, and her broom, and why was that? He drank again.

Merry marched up to the trestle table where the two men sat. "Sir," she said to Burnell, "you will have a real bed to sleep in tonight."

"That is good," Burnell said, and gave her a brooding look.

She looked down at the chancellor's empty mug, at the near empty flagon beside that mug. "I will find you an infusion to chase the Devil from your head when you awaken tomorrow morning."

Burnell thought about that a moment, and nodded. "Mayhap it is not a bad thing you can read. Garron told me about his purchase of the *Leech Book of Bald*. I would like to see it," and he poured the remainder of the ale from the flagon into his mug and drank deep. He looked up again at the young girl, standing not a foot from him, her hands on her hips, disapproval coming off her in waves. He said to Garron, never taking his eyes off her,

"She offers me a healer's potion, all kindness she is, but I wager she really believes we are both lackwits since we cannot determine who murdered your prisoners, and betrayed you to the Black Demon. Aye, she believes we are pitiful drunkards. This is not right, Garron. She is only a priest's get, a holy brother who suffered a momentary loss of virtue and look what happened. No, this is not right. You will do something."

Garron wanted to laugh, but instead he looked at her over the rim of his mug. Burnell was right. She looked disapproving as an abbess, a look that didn't suit her at all, and so he poured oil on the coals. He cocked an eyebrow, waving her away. "She is just a woman, sir, ignore her."

Just a woman? "The wine has drowned your memory, my lord. I brought down a man all by myself, not a bit of assistance from you. You said I was a warrior. You said I was a hero. Listen to me, the two of you should be planning how to discover the traitor who sits here in the great hall, eating our food and laughing at us behind his hand."

Garron knew she wanted to shout her

distrust of Sir Lyle to Burnell, her thoughts were so clear on her face. He took another drink of his ale, watched her expressions change and shift. She obviously believed they had done nothing but drink. Beside him, Burnell belched behind his hand and weaved a bit.

She wasn't far wrong.

Garron poured some more oil. "You make lists, you bargain—except for the ale—and you buy mugs, more than enough mugs for two towns because you fell for the wiles of the old woman who sold them to you." He wished he had a lord's chair so he could lounge back, and sneer, all arrogant, maybe swinging his leg, and goad her until she spit. He said, "Hold your tongue, wench, and fetch us another flagon of ale."

He watched her face turn nearly as red as those clever little hidden braids, from the neck of her pale gray gown to her hairline. It was an amazing sight. She was thumping with fury. She opened her mouth to spew forth insults, saw Burnell was frowning at her, and swallowed her words. She wasn't a dolt. He watched her turn on her heel and stomp away. He was pleased at her restraint, and smiled after her.

Then she whirled back and shouted, "Do you know, the jakes are newly limed? My father demanded I find him a recipe that would render the jakes sweet-smelling. Once I discovered the secret, my father was very pleased because he enjoyed sitting in the jakes when they didn't knock him unconscious with the smell, stewing over some problem. He told me the knottiest problem unraveled when contemplating all its various aspects whilst he was hunkered down in the jakes. Mayhap the two of you could sit side by side and ponder together, for I have used the same recipe. Or mayhap not—you might fall over since you have drunk so much." Merry strode away, like a young man, stiff in the shoulders.

Sitting in the jakes pondering problems? He couldn't imagine doing such a thing. Garron smiled. She had a fluent tongue. He saw his people leaving the great hall to go back to work, jostling each other, laughing, arguing, a wonderful sight. He wondered idly if it would rain.

Burnell picked up a bit of bread and

chewed it. "It is amazing. She is a priest's byblow, she should be modest and grateful, yet she acts as if we were here at her behest. She is arrogant. She spoke of the jakes in the most insolent voice. I do believe she was attempting to insult me, although it doesn't seem likely since I am the Chancellor of England. The 'Chancellor of England'—the words themselves sound like music, like the majestic ringing of bells, do they not?"

Garron nodded, grave as a bishop.

"Only an idiot or a halfwit would speak to us as she just did. Sitting in the jakes! The priest pondered in the jakes? You want to smile, I can see it in your eyes, though they are a bit blurred to me just now. Why are you not furious with her? I marvel at her boldness and wonder how such a thing could happen since she is a bastard. Also, her gown is too short and her hair is too red, a willful red, and those little braids tucked inside—well. She needs discipline, Garron, she needs it badly. You will see to it."

Burnell wanted him to discipline her? How was he to do that?

Burnell continued, "Aye, I am important.

You are important, though less important than I am. I am the king's representative, so close to the king I am nearly as fitted to him as his own clothes, nay, even closer, for I share his deepest secrets, stitch and form his many ideas. Ah, this is not right, Garron."

Garron nodded. "Aye, she needs discipline, she needs a lesson in humility. I wonder what I will do to her?" He stared a moment at his mug. Here he was drinking simply because Burnell was drinking. He was an ass. He had a traitor to discover. He looked toward Sir Lyle, who was in close conversation with Solan, the man with the belly pains. What were they talking about?

Garron left Robert Burnell to brood over his ale, and strode out of the great hall. He poured several buckets of well water over his head to clear all that excellent ale out of his brain before he went to look for her. Tupper told him the mistress was in the weaving hut. Mistress? It was amazing. He was beginning to believe she was a witch.

Miggins stood in the doorway of the weaving hut, her arms crossed over her scrawny chest. "Ye wish to see Merry, my lord?"

He nodded. "You came out here quickly. To protect her from me, I wonder?"

Miggins scratched her head. Garron wondered what lived amongst those scrawny braids. "There is no need, for Merry is a warrior."

Garron was beginning to think those words would haunt him to the grave. "Tupper said she was within."

"Aye, she is, trying to fix the spindle on one of the looms." Miggins crossed her arms over her sunken bosom. "Ye'll not hurt her, my lord."

"You believe me angry at your little pigeon, Miggins?"

The old woman didn't move. She tried to stare him down. She scratched her armpit, then yanked on her old gown. He looked past her to see Merry sitting on the straw floor, her face shiny with sweat because it was so hot in this small, airless room, trying to fix the spindle that looked ancient and far beyond repair to him.

"My little Merry is near to screaming blasphemy to the heavens, or mayhap drinking more ale than she should"—she gave him the eye—"but then how could she when you and the chancellor swilled it all down your gullets, sots, the both of you, and here there is a traitor to find. Oh aye, I have eyes in my head, I see everything." She pressed her fingers to her temples and stared at him. "I see a man whose loins are heavy with lust, a man who better not relieve his lust on the priest's sweet bastard."

He lifted Miggins under her armpits and set her away from him. She weighed nothing at all. He hated it. "Go eat some more dinner," he told her, "and stop looking at my loins," and he walked into the room, past three women sewing, none of them looking at him.

Merry was on her hands and knees fiddling with a wooden bar that obviously should attach to something, what that was, he had no idea. He laid his hand lightly on her shoulder.

"Come," he said.

She jerked up, hit her head on the wooden bar, and yelped. She sat on her bottom and frowned up at him. "What, you have come to tell me the earth will end in two hours and you wish me to fetch you more ale so you may be unconscious when the final hour strikes?"

He eyed her. "You said quite a lot there, most of it insulting. If doomsday arrives, you may be certain my sword and I will attack it and drive it into the sea. Now, keep your mouth shut and come with me."

"You are so sodden with ale you fell on your face in the mud, didn't you? Just look at you—what have you done?"

"There isn't any mud yet, but by the looks of the clouds, it might begin at any moment. I poured water over my head."

"Good. You need sharp wits to deal with me," and the witch gave him a full-bodied sneer.

"Have Miggins fetch Borran, he should be the one to fix the loom."

"Borran asked me to look at it. He claims he is flummoxed." She got slowly to her feet, dusted her hands on her skirts, placed her hands on her hips, and gave him another sneer. "Are you really so insulted, my lord?"

"Nay, but the chancellor is. He believes you need discipline and I am to see to it."

"Discipline? What does that mean? I

did not insult the chancellor—" She frowned. "Mayhap I could have selected more mealymouthed words. Shall I apologize to him? Mayhap he won't remember since he is so drunk. It is disgraceful."

"The chancellor was right. He many times is. You are sorely in need of discipline," and he nodded to the other women, all of them busily sewing, weaving, and listening. "Come," he said, and held out his hand to her.

21

Discipline," he repeated, savoring the word, not looking down at her as he strode through the inner bailey, pulling her behind him. "It has an interesting sound to it, does it not?"

"It is a man's word that holds only threat." She took a double step to keep up with him. "At least you do not sound like a drunkard any longer. What is so important that you must speak to me this very moment?"

He stopped suddenly as one of the three dogs dashed into his path. She nearly ran into him. "Do you know, I was thinking about all the noise in the inner bailey. Everyone will work until it is too dark to see, or it rains. Listen to the hammering, the sawing, all the cursing, the arguing, all the insults that turn the air blue."

"There is also laughter and two men are singing at the tops of their lungs. I must give them better rhymes to go with their tunes. Mayhap I can sing a duet with them. It is going to rain, very soon now."

"Do not forget the families to arrive within the sennight, with children. All must be put in the great hall, I suppose. Speak to Bullic, tell him we will have at least two score more mouths to feed."

"I did. He said he will be ready. Aleric assigned a detail of men to hunt each morning. When do you think the king's men will return from Radstock and Furly?"

"In three days, if all goes well. I pray the keeps were not attacked. They would not have stood a chance, for their defenses are meager in comparison to Wareham's, and just look at what happened here." The three dogs were barking madly and he turned to see Ivo throwing them each a bone. "The great hall smells good."

She nodded. "I had rosemary and lavender strewn on the fresh rushes. A great deal of lavender, actually, to soak up all the foul smells that have seeped into the stone floor over the years. As for the sweet-smelling jakes, since you drank so much ale, you will probably visit them soon, you and the Chancellor of England. Mayhap between your two brains, you can determine that Sir Lyle is the traitor. I cannot believe you actually assigned him and his mangy men to question the men we brought from Winthorpe."

He smiled at the meaty sneer in her voice.

She grabbed his sleeve. "Listen to me, Garron—the man who attacked you didn't have a chance against you. You are a warrior, you are brave and strong. You do not hesitate. But Sir Lyle of Clive, I simply know it to my bones, he is a very bad man."

He studied her, his eyebrow arched. "You do not know that. I pray he is not bad because I need him and his strong arm. I find it odd that our very astute chancellor still believes you the priest's bastard. It is so very obvious that you are nothing of the sort, that you are obviously a lady born."

"He sees what he's meant to see. Most do."

"Discipline," he said, "our chancellor wants me to see to your discipline. Come with me." He took her hand and pulled her behind a newly rebuilt shed that held building tools. He pulled her close and placed his finger on her mouth. "Listen to me, Merry. As I said, the chancellor believes you should be disciplined. He has instructed me to see to it. I believe he wants me to thrash you."

"You would not!"

He smiled. "No, I would not, but let me tell you this. If the chancellor continues to believe you a nagging fishwife, he could easily insist you return to London with him, to accept punishment from the king himself." This wasn't at all in the realm of possibility, but Garron saw she looked uncertain now, not quite so sure of herself. Good. "The chancellor is also a very intelligent man, a man I trust above all others. Let him drink away his woes, even only for a single night. His duties for the king always weigh heavily on him."

"You would not let him take me back to London, would you?"

He hated that she was afraid, but he needed her agreement. He shrugged. "I would not have a choice. What would the king do to you? I do not know. So here is what we must do. When we emerge from behind this shed, I want you to rub your bottom, as if I'd walloped you but good, all right? You will tell anyone who asks you that this walloping was deserved discipline. And rub your bottom again. The chancellor will find out, and he will be pleased. He will leave you here with me. Can you do this?"

He watched her chew this over, and wanted to smile. Finally, she nodded. "Oh aye, I will not accuse him of idiocy anymore. I do not wish to be forced away from you, Garron."

"You will mind your tongue?"

She nodded.

"Good. All right?"

When they walked back into the inner bailey, he smiled to see her vigorously rubbing her bottom.

"Ah, one other thing, Merry. Try your

best not to sneer again in the chancellor's presence or even behind his back, for I have learned the man sees everything."

Both were aware of the silence around them, no hammering, no yelling, no little boys' voices, not one of the dogs barking. One of Garron's newly purchased cows mooed. He looked up to see nearly every one of his people staring at him, and Eric the goat stood not six feet away, chewing on an old leather strap dangling out of her mouth. And here came Miggins striding toward him, her ancient face seamed and set, her meager shoulders pulled back, mumbling to herself. This was all he needed. At least she wasn't carrying a weapon.

Merry quickly rubbed her bottom again and tried to look pitiful.

Miggins waved her fist at him, "Ye whipped her, didn't ye, my lord, ye, a big man, strong, used to violence, but this one here, she is only a dainty little mite, soft and yielding. Aye, ever so yielding. Be ye like yer brother, Lord Arthur? Be ye as rotten as he was?"

"Yielding? Where is such a girl, Miggins?" He made a show of searching the inner bailey.

"She's wrong about that, Garron, I'm not this fragile useless creature. I am a warrior. I am a hero."

"Aye, and now you're a better disciplined warrior."

Miggins shouted, "Mayhap not sweet and gentle, but she is innocent of men. Did ye jerk up her skirts? Don't deny it, young randy lord that ye are. When I was young, my handsome Ulric always did the same to me. And then he licked me behind my knees."

Garron stared at her, blanching at the picture forming in his mind. "It is difficult for me to see you as a young girl, Miggins."

"That is because ye are a man with little enough brain. It is very sad. Ye must stop abusing her. Now ye've frightened her with yer lust."

"He does not frighten me, Miggins. Look at him, he is getting scared because he knows I will make him pay for walloping me."

She was enjoying herself, the little witch. She rubbed her bottom harder.

Garron heard a laugh, then another. Soon laughter filled the inner bailey.

"Gentle sweet girl," he whispered in her ear, "by all the saints' hairy knees, *yielding?* That is nearly enough to make me burst my guts laughing." He patted her face. "Ah, what wonderful laughter. Just listen, everyone knows how yielding you are. Come now, Merry, 'tis time for you to show respect to the Chancellor of England even if he is in the sweet-smelling jakes puking up his guts with all the ale."

She stared up at him. "Will you lick me like Miggins's Ulric did to her?" Whilst he gaped at her, she turned to Miggins. "This licking behind the knees, do all men want to do it?"

Garron didn't think the laughter could be any louder, but he was wrong.

"Aye, and a fine thing it be," Miggins said, her scratchy old voice suddenly sounding girlish with memories.

That terrifying image undoubtedly flashed in every man's mind in the inner bailey.

He grabbed her arms and pulled her up close against him, to every eye, a sign he was not through chastising her. "Do you know, if you like, I will allow you to visit my bed and we can see what this licking is all about."

Merry sighed. "There is only one bed and it is for Robert Burnell."

Garron realized he had no problem with kicking Burnell out of the master's bed. "If I set the men to work, there will be another by nightfall. What say you?"

"There isn't enough time."

His eyes nearly crossed. Everyone was still laughing, listening for all they were worth. Everyone had misunderstood, which was the point, only not really. The point had changed remarkably in the past few minutes. He had to change that—and so he hammered in one more nail. He said, his voice hard and loud, "You are a nag. Even at your tender years, you have the rudiments of nagging down quite well." He saw her purse her lips, but she understood. He then tapped his finger to her nose, and said, his voice perfectly serious now, "Did you learn it from your precious Lady Anne?"

"No, my mother left and went to an abbey."

A small piece of the truth, and that was something. Her mother had become a nun? He waited, but she shook her head.

"You are stubborn as one of those mules," and he turned on his heel and walked to the soldiers barracks, where ten men were alternately looking at the dark sky and sawing wood. No more laughter now, only fierce concentration on completing tasks before the rain came.

Miggins, thankfully deceived, petted Merry, straightened her hair, tucked in two small braids that had come out of the crown of braids on her head, smoothed down her skirts. "Do ye want to tell me who ye really are? Ye can practice on me, smooth out all the hillocks in yer story before ye tell the young lord."

"The young lord is content to wait," Merry said. She noticed the women standing behind Miggins, all of them leaning toward her, worry on their faces. Worry for her? Because they believed Garron had whipped her?

Miggins said, "Heed me, Merry, he is a man, a warrior, strong and fearless, just like ye said. Oh aye, ye are a warrior too, little mite."

The women all nodded.

"Surely I did not say he was fearless. Did I?"

"Something close to that. Listen to me. Sometimes men need to drink ale so their brains will loosen their tongues so they may air their worries, their fears, their doubts. Aye, ale smoothes out all the boulders in their brains so they may begin to think again, to plan, and take action, once they are sober."

"Evidently the chancellor had a great many boulders in his brain."

Miggins nodded. "Aye. Now women fret in a different way."

Elaine said, "My Eric never drank himself into a stupor, he ate." She sighed. "Not that it mattered. He was thin as a nail, thinner than the arrows he shot."

"Like Elaine's Eric, I eat," said Tulia, who carried a bowl of almonds in her large, rough hands. She handed them around. All the women laughed.

Merry kicked a pebble at her foot. "Other than eating, what is our different way?"

Lisle, whose hands were busily smoothing a huge ball of gray wool, said, "Mayhap our ways are different because men have always drunk all the ale and left none for us."

More laughter, some of it from a few men who had drifted close.

Miggins said, "All ye little peahens, listen to me. We wring our hands, we weep hot loud tears, we shriek our woes to the heavens when something bad befalls us. I ask ye, can ye see Lord Garron wringing his hands? Mayhap crying on Aleric's shoulder, bemoaning what the fates have dumped on his head?"

Merry sighed, rubbed her bottom again. "Nay, I cannot imagine that."

Miggins said, "Lord Garron is a good man, not crooked like his brother, but straight in his body and in his thoughts. He is very young, mayhap not quite ripe enough, yet he is a dandy lad. He cares about all of us, Merry. He cares. Look around you. There is life again at Wareham, life and a future for all of us. What is a mug of ale when compared to what he has wrought?"

"Next you will call him a god." Merry walked back into the weaving shed. She turned and asked, "Was Ulric your husband, Miggins?"

Miggins gave her a huge toothless grin.

An hour later, Sir Lyle and Aleric told Garron and Burnell that the new smith Garron had hired in Winthorpe, Ronsard his name, was gone, all his belongings with him and he'd stolen a horse.

"I wonder," Burnell said, "if the Black Demon will slit Ronsard's throat when he finds out he failed."

22

Garron's men returned with good news. Neither Furly nor Radstock had been attacked. Garron wasn't surprised that neither Sir Wills nor Sir Gregory had heard about the Retribution at Wareham, for who was there to tell them? They had, appropriately, sent back a dozen men to help make repairs on their lord's castle, surely a good sign as to their intentions. The men were immediately put to work building beds.

Garron stood on the ramparts and contemplated his good fortune in the face of what could have crushed him. Not even a fortnight had passed since Tupper had managed to winch up the portcullis, and now, instead of twenty-two starving rag-tag people, there were, in addition to Robert Burnell's men, close to sixty-five people in Garron's great hall, all of them drinking from the dozens of wooden mugs Merry had bought in Winthorpe. Merry had told him at dinner, "The old woman informed me proudly that she had all the mugs I could need, as few could afford to buy them since they lasted forever." She handed him a hunk of bread and goat cheese. "When I told her I would take the lot, she broke into song with her scrawny old husband, and the two of them danced a jig. So maybe I really wasn't outbargained, since I will never forget their fine performance."

Garron laughed. He realized as he scanned all the open land between Wareham and the Forest of Glen that he couldn't recall having laughed so much in a very long time.

By the following evening there were four new trestle tables and eight new benches, all stout and sturdy, ready for a good hundred years of men's arses. Garron realized there were no more dark corners in his great hall. It wasn't the burning rush torches in the wall sconces that cleared the shadows, nay, it was the pulse of so many breaths and the pounding heartbeats of so many people.

As for the jakes, he wondered if maybe thinking about problems whilst he sat there wasn't such a bad idea.

He and Burnell were leaving the following morning for Furly, then onward to Radstock, another half day to the north. He did not want to leave Wareham and so he tried again to convince Burnell that since Sir Wills and Sir Gregory had sent men to help, it surely meant they were eager to swear their fealty to him. Surely, a visit from him could wait.

Burnell speared a piece of baked hare on his knifepoint. "I am relieved your two keeps were left unharmed. I am pleased they sent men. It means, of course, that this Black Demon believes Arthur's silver to be here, nowhere else. Still, the king believes that since neither Sir Wills nor Sir Gregory knows you, you are best served looking each man in the eyes as you accept his homage."

There was no hope for it. Garron said, "We will quickly discover if either of them is stupid since with you at my side, they know the king's shadow sits close by. If ever they considered falling out of line, they will quickly fall back in." He began tossing his knife from one hand to the other, a fine exercise he'd always found. "If there were not so much to be done here at Wareham, it might be interesting to have Sir Gregory balk a bit. I've heard he's a stubborn stoat, full of conceit and aggression. I wonder what he will do in the future? Truth be told, sir, I'm itching for a good fight. I think the king enjoyed fighting with me because I learned quickly enough to duck under those long arms of his. I tried to teach him to kick out with his big feet, but he never got the knack."

"I watched the two of you once. My brave, agile king clouted your head and sent you flying into some yew bushes."

Garron remembered his head had pounded for two days. "Aye, that was before I learned to leap backward, fast as a goat."

"Did you not get your fill of fighting when you saved that kidnapped boy in the Clandor Forest?"

"There really wasn't much to it. Because his destrier was near, their leader escaped me. You told me you couldn't think of any lad in the vicinity who might be worth taking for ransom."

"When I return to London, I will inquire." Burnell drank some more ale, then softly belched.

Garron continued after a moment. "I wonder if the boy is still alive. I must doubt it, given he was alone and black-hearted men abound on God's earth. It's a pity, the lad had grit."

Burnell pointed toward Merry, who was laughing at something young Ivo said to her. Her head was tilted and one of the small braids had worked itself loose and was lying against her cheek. "You told me you disciplined her—a good lesson, I say, to all the women, although I doubt your punishment will lead any of them to mind their tongues in the future." Burnell sighed.

"Women will not change, so our glorious queen assures me. She says it is simply not in their natures. The king agreed—I well remember the placid look he gave her when she spoke—but who knows? Stranger things have occurred, like the story of God raining locusts upon Egypt."

Garron laughed, bit off a chunk of bread with his strong teeth, looked over to where their new miller, Arno, sat stuffing down his own bread dripping with gravy. The fellow certainly knew what he was doing; there was not a single piece of grit in the bread to break teeth.

"What think you, Garron?"

He shrugged. "As long as our women do what I tell them to do, why should I care about their natures?"

"Do they always obey you?"

"They do whenever I've sought one of them out for enjoyment." Garron thought of Lady Blanche, one of the queen's ladies, who'd enjoyed coming to his small bedchamber in the middle of the night and awakening him with kisses on his belly. He shuddered with the memory.

Burnell's lips pursed. "You speak of carnal matters, my lord."

"Like every breathing man I know, I find it a satisfying subject, sir."

"You are young," Burnell said, his voice sour. "Curses upon all young men, I say. But there is more than lust, my lord, at least there is later in life when all good things have waned."

Aye, he thought, there was more than lust, even for young men. Garron saw Merry in his mind's eye, bargaining with a leather merchant, and said without thought, "Sometimes women are competent and cocky and stubborn as any man." He laughed. "Aye, sometimes they are warrior brave."

"I find it interesting your bastard makes lists like our queen."

His bastard? Was that her laugh he heard? "Mayhap it is common amongst women who know how to read and write."

"Most churchmen believe women are simple creatures, here only to birth men's children and see to their needs. You look at me like I've lost my wits. Are churchmen right, I wonder?"

"Simple creatures? A man would have to be a hermit to believe such nonsense. Have you seen Merry's writing? Have you noticed how she has gathered all the women together here at Wareham and set each to specific tasks, the men as well? The men respect her and defer to her. Aleric searches her out to ask her opinions. Now that she has Book One of *Leech Book of Bald*, I know she will become an excellent healer. She is many things, but she is not simple."

Burnell chewed on another chunk of hare, dripping rich, thick gravy on his chin. He remembered in the last century, Eleanor of Aquitaine—that contentious witch with her hellhound sons—had written beautiful script. King Henry had kept her a prisoner for more years than some men lived, and look what she'd wrought. Endless plots against her husband, murdering his mistresses, setting one rapacious son against the other. Ah, but he'd heard she'd written and recited poetry to make a man's heart bleed.

And his own precious Queen Eleanor. She read and wrote. She made lists, volumes of lists, each one to the point, each one useful. She advised the king. She kissed his bruises and bit his ear once,

then kissed it, when she didn't know anyone was about. Burnell said, "Take care,
Garron, mayhap this redheaded wench
will oust you from Wareham and set herself up as lord."

Garron smiled, his eyes drawn yet
again to Merry, now sitting next to Borran, doubtless discussing the repairs for
the looms. Her braids were clean and
shining in the rush lighting, from her own
soap. She'd told him the soap she'd found
at Winthorpe was too dear, and so she'd
bought ingredients to make Wareham
soap herself. Jasmine, she'd told him.

Garron knew, as he suspected every
single man alive knew, that women were
not simple. He also knew the queen was
right—women would not change. They
were eager when it came to passion, if a
man wasn't a lout; but during the long
days, they'd criticize and nag a man until
he went off to fight a war or he keeled
over dead to escape.

On the other hand, he didn't believe
men ever changed, either. They coveted
what wasn't theirs, they always found reasons why what they wanted should be-

long to them, and they stole and hacked and maimed. Mayhap like the castellans of his Radstock and Furly keeps, Sir Gregory in particular—a man's loyalties had to be reinforced, constantly, else he might slide off the path. Women as well?

23

That night, after he had lost two games of chess to Burnell, Garron couldn't sleep with all the snores surrounding him in the great hall, and so he woke Gilpin, who could sleep through a raging storm, and they moved their goose-feather mattresses to the lord's bedchamber. Garron spent a long time listening to Robert Burnell snore like a stoat, his man Dilkin sprawled on his back on the floor on a mess of blankets, snoring as loudly as Burnell, in harmony, it seemed to Garron.

He left, yawning and blurry-eyed, with Robert Burnell the next morning and ten men, all of them armed to the teeth. He left Aleric in charge.

Merry stood on the ramparts and watched them ride into the Forest of Glen, Aleric standing at her elbow. Garron had merely nodded to her and given Aleric a nice long list of instructions to give to her, which he did once the line of men had disappeared from sight.

It was a sunny morning, shining down on Aleric's bald head. "You seem worried, Aleric. Do you believe either Radstock or Furly will resist swearing fealty to Garron? The men Sir Wills and Sir Gregory sent seem content to be here and eager to work. Do you think their masters sent them here to spy out our weaknesses?"

"Nay, I do not think that, but I do believe it wise for Lord Garron to have Robert Burnell with him. No man with a brain would resist King Edward. Sir Gregory of Furly, now that little spittlecock has more ambition than brains, but Garron will see to him. The men each man sent are workers to build, not to spy, and they can fight if they must, so that is a relief. Hobbs told me both Sir Wills and Sir Gregory were relieved to hear Garron is not like his brother. To have their new lord the king's man is of value as well. Pali and Gilpin will speak to the men within the keeps. They will see the truth of things very quickly.

"Worry not, mistress. Despite his few years, Garron is a leader, he has taught me strategies over the years. He is a man to trust. He has a brain, bless the beneficent Saint Simian, who gave away his sandals to a beggar. He then cut his foot on a rock, and died screaming in pain a sennight later, so it was said. If there is something of value to learn in that tale, I have yet to find it."

Merry wondered why Simian hadn't been smart enough to consult a healer. "How do you come to be Garron's master-at-arms?"

Aleric's face split into a huge grin. "Now there is a tale to boil the blood. It was all about a thieving merchant, a milking cow, and a hapless gypsy. Another time, mistress. Garron will keep his possessions safe, and if Sir Wills and Sir Gregory have any brains at all, they will hold steadfast to him and his authority.

"Look yon at our magnificent cattle.

Garron allowed me to select them myself since my father was a master herdsman. I could help birth a calf and milk the mother when I was just a lad. Now, the cattle will continue to graze outside the keep until this afternoon. Then we will bring them in, the dairy maids will milk them, and we will winch up the drawbridge and lower the portcullis and be snug within, fifty cattle mooing in our ears, their sweet milk warm in our bellies.

"We don't have that many trained soldiers but we do have a lot of healthy workers. We will be fine." He massaged his shoulder, since his muscles pulled and cramped because he'd carried more stacks of cut wood than he ever had in his life the day before, and he wasn't a lad of twenty anymore, cursed be the passing years that simply never stopped to let a man catch up.

"Your shoulder pains you, Aleric. You have lifted too many heavy planks of wood, haven't you, pounded in too many nails? Let me consult my herbal."

Taking herbs for knotted muscles? Was she mad? Every soldier knew pain after a battle, and the rebuilding was worth at least three battles, but it had to be done, so no matter. He started to say it was nothing, but he said instead, "Thank you," and continued to rub. She'd been right about that. Still—afterward, not two hours later—Garron had been full of plans, balanced again, even smiling.

She said, "Let us go over our lists, Aleric, and determine what is to be done each day."

"Lord Garron did not leave me a separate list, just the one for you."

So Aleric did not read. She said matter-of-factly, "No matter, I will read you what he has written and we will see."

Aleric believed it even more amazing when he saw her beautiful script, all those elegant strange black lines and loops that made sense—to some people. He grunted as she read off items on the lists, and they made changes and adjustments. Each was satisfied that the other had the same goal: to have Wareham nearly back to normal by the time Garron returned. They were expecting three more families by the end of the week.

When Aleric sought out Merry an hour later, he said, "I have visited Arno the miller. He's brought his wife, his wife's mother, and his three children. His wheel broke and so I assigned men to repair it."

Merry nodded. "I have consulted my herbal. I have ground up horehound, marisilver, and vervain, and mixed them together in hot water. I have a paste to rub into your shoulder. It will leach out the soreness. Come with me to the solar, Aleric."

And so he went with her, and took off his tunic.

She hummed as she rubbed her sweet-smelling mixture deep into his knotted muscles. There were so many scars on his body, she thought, and so much hair as well, much of it white. She smiled as he groaned and sighed. And when he admitted the pain lessened very quickly and the soreness eased, she wanted to dance. That he smelled like wildflowers would make his men laugh, Aleric knew, but it didn't matter. Since many of the men were sore, he sent them to Merry. Garron, he thought, would have the sweetest-smelling workers in Christendom.

More than a dozen men sought her out

that day. Merry realized she would run out of the precious horehound. She had to consult her herbal for another infusion.

As she served Aleric his afternoon meal of gravied beef slices on hard brown bread, she said, "Keep sending me people; the more I practice, the faster I will learn all the recipes in my herbal. Ah, but I must plant herbs." She fell silent and Aleric knew she was planning it all out in her head. He also knew there would be a long list on the morrow. He mentally selected two young men to prepare an herb garden.

Just after dawn the following morning, Merry awoke abruptly to yells. She had slept in Garron's lovely new bed at Miggins's insistence. "Aye, little sweeting, ye need yer sleep after listening to me snore loud enough to keep the pope awake," which was true. She, Elaine, Ivo, and Errol spooned on the soft bed, the three dogs lined up like firewood at the foot. She pulled gently away from Errol, and quickly dressed in one of Lady Anne's gowns Lisle had cleaned for her the day before, tied on her slippers, and raced to the door, grabbing her cloak and pulling it around her. She left Elaine sitting up, rubbing her eyes, looking alarmed.

"I don't know what is happening," Merry said over her shoulder, "but mayhap the Black Demon has returned. Quickly, Elaine, dress and go into the great hall. I will send all the children to you. Take care of them."

The three dogs raced after her. The great hall was already pandemonium. There were at least thirty women there, awakened by the shouts, some of them weeping, wringing their hands, praying loudly to the blackened beams overhead. A woman yelled, "'Tis the enemy again! They will spit our guts on their swords and roast us over a fire!"

Then a chorus of voices joined in the refrain.

"The Black Demon is back!"

"They will rape all of us this time, even us old'uns!"

"Lord Garron took all the soldiers! There is no one left!"

Merry scrambled on top of a trestle table, waved her arms, and shouted, "Shut your mouths! What are you, bleating sheep? Wareham is your home! You defend your home. Listen to me, no one will come through the postern gate again, Aleric always has men guarding it.

"We are women, we are strong. We will show the enemy what we are made of. All of you—fetch weapons, anything that can break a man's head. This time we will make the Black Demon run for his miserable life!"

The grumbles fell away. There was dead silence, then, "Aye, I'll clout one of the whoresons!"

"I'll kick their slimy parts to France!"

"France is the homeland to slimy parts!"

24

The women stripped all the iron pots and knives from the cooking shed, Talia grabbed a long-handled metal scoop for meat pies and bread, and raced out after them. Soon all the women and the workers were standing in the inner bailey, armed with planks of wood, hammers, mallets, and all the precious knives and pots, ready to take on the Devil. As for the soldiers, they stood in a small knot at the base of the ramparts ladder, looking up at Aleric.

They moved aside to let Merry climb the ladder to stand beside Aleric on the ramparts walkway. She stared down at a band of thirty men, their leader tall in his saddle, his gleaming silver mail covering a black tunic, his destrier black as a moonless sky. She felt fear, rancid as bile, rise in her throat, choking her—was it the Black Demon? Persuading the women to have pride and fight was one thing, actually seeing the Black Demon was quite another. But why had he returned to Wareham? He had already searched Wareham for Arthur's silver, and that meant he'd learned where the silver was and had come back to get it.

There were no more than fifteen fighting men at Wareham, all the others workers, but she knew they would fight to the death. *The women as well*, she thought, pride filling her as she turned to look down over the inner rampart's wall, into the inner bailey at the women clustered together, holding their weapons tightly against their chests, looking determined. Merry saw the soldiers still standing below her—what did Aleric have in mind?

The drawbridge was tightly winched up, the portcullis down. Thank the merciful Virgin's stout heart it was only dawn and the cattle were still within the walls and not outside for the Black Demon's men to slaughter.

Merry stilled her fear and stood straight and tall, like Aleric. She watched him turn and speak to Hobbs, who was kneeling behind him. Hobbs went down on his haunches and spoke to the men now climbing the ladder, one by one, staying low and quiet. They fanned out to both sides and crawled along the rampart walls, keeping their heads low as they positioned the quivers on their shoulders and readied their bows. She heard Aleric tell Hobbs, "Three of the men are in mail, the rest are not. There aren't many archers, maybe a dozen, all of them standing in a straight line behind the horses. If it comes to shooting, tell our archers to aim for the necks of the soldiers on Zhorses, but don't kill any animals. We need them."

Aleric nodded at her, still not questioning her presence, and said more to himself than to her, "It is not much of an army the whoreson brings to Wareham, nothing really to test a man's mettle," and then he smiled, a ferocious smile that would have scared her to her toes had she been on the other side of the moat. Aleric shouted down, "Who are you? What do you want?"

Their leader called, "I heard of Wareham's destruction. Are you the last remaining man to stand upright in this blighted castle? Who is the girl standing beside you? Why was she not taken? I heard all comely maids and those even not so comely were taken. Are all the rest of your people dead or too weak to walk? Let me in and I will feed you and those who are still alive."

Aleric said to Merry, "By Saint Albert's pointed chin, I know that man, I recognize his voice and his horse—look at the four white fetlocks. Garron described his destrier to me, but I do not know the man's name. He is the man we came upon in the Clandor Forest on our way to Wareham. He and three men had kidnapped a boy and Garron intervened. He himself fought this man, but the bastard managed to escape him. Now he is here. Is he the Black Demon? I wonder. If not, then the Black Demon is his master."

Merry recognized his voice and his

horse as well. Only she knew his name and who his master was, for his standard, held by a squire, luffed out in the stiff wind. Two black eagles, wings folded down, bones piled between them.

Jason of Brennan's standard.

She calmed herself. Sir Halric couldn't get to her this time. She was perfectly safe behind Wareham's walls. "Will you tell him you know who he is?"

Aleric shook his head. "Garron always says that knowledge is vital and it is always wise to keep it close. We will see what the cur tries next." He gave a fearsome smile as he shouted down to Sir Halric, "Nay, I cannot allow you and your men to enter. You were here before, you killed nearly all of us, and those you didn't kill nearly starved to death, what with the bands of men you left outside the walls to prevent us from hunting."

Sir Halric yelled, "I have never before been to Wareham. I told you I heard of a deadly attack, and my lord, the Earl of Exmouth, wishes me to give you aid. He and Lord Arthur were friends. It pains him that such misery has visited Wareham, and thus I am here to help you."

Aleric said to Merry, "I doubt that sincerely. But one thing is clear—the Black Demon does not know Garron returned to Wareham. He sent his man here, expecting to find naught but human misery, that or an empty castle with only rotted corpses within the walls."

"Do you think he believes this time he will find Arthur's silver coins? Do you believe someone told him where to find the silver, and that is why he has returned?"

"Evidently so." Aleric looked back down at the inner bailey, at the scores of people staring up at the ramparts, all of them armed—hammers and handsaws and wooden boards and the women stood there as well, silent, ready. He saw old Miggins holding an iron pan in her gnarled hand, her look ferocious. He saw no fear on those raised faces, men or women, and was pleased. It was Merry, he thought, and wondered what she'd said to the women.

Aleric said to her, "Whoever he is, he is a bad liar," and he yelled down, "The Earl of Exmouth? He was Lord Arthur's friend? I did not know. This is an excellent, selfless offer. But where are the scores of pack mules with all this aid you are offering us?"

"I have left them under guard in the Forest of Glen. Who is that girl beside you? She looks familiar to me. What is her name?"

Aleric saw that Merry had turned to stone beside him. He called down, "How could she look familiar to you? She is naught but a priest's byblow."

"When I enter Wareham, I will look at her closely and tell you."

She turned away from the rampart wall and pulled her cloak over her head.

Aleric shouted, "I would be a fool to lower the drawbridge for you to enter and finish your butchery. You will take your leave. The postern gate is closed and guarded. Return to the Earl of Exmouth and tell him Wareham will survive without his assistance."

Sir Halric turned his head and gave a slight nod. In the next moment, an arrow flew within two inches of Aleric, but he was already in motion, dropping to his knees, pulling Merry with him. Merry was shaking, couldn't help it, with both the knowledge that Sir Halric would probably realize who she was and that an arrow had nearly gone through Aleric's chest. That was close, very close.

Sir Halric shouted, "Curse you for an idiot, let me and my men enter! I must do my master's bidding. You have no choice—it is certain death if you do not obey me."

Aleric yelled back, raising his head only enough so he could see Sir Halric, "I wonder, does the Earl of Exmouth even know who you are, sirrah? Why don't you tell me your name?"

A rain of arrows flew toward them. Aleric raised his shield over his and Merry's head, as did all the men crouched down on the ramparts walkway. He said softly, "Nay, don't move, not yet. Keep down." He didn't look away from the soldiers outside.

As for their people in the inner bailey, none were hurt, thank St. Flavin's crooked thumbs. Aleric heard angry, muttering curses, and grinned.

Aleric didn't raise his head above the stone wall. "What will you do when your archers have shot all their arrows? I have told you the traitor you planted before in our midst is no longer here to let you in. Will you swim the moat? Will you place ladders against the walls and climb them? There are enough of us to kill you if that is what you will try. We are safe from you. Leave!"

"I have told you, I had no part in Wareham's destruction! You will do as I tell you or I will starve you out! Do not be a fool, no one will leave Wareham, no one. You will all be dead in another week. Then my men will scale your walls and it will be over. I will not kill you if you allow me to enter now. I told you, I will give all of you food."

"What is it you want?"

"I search for what Lord Arthur stole, nothing more."

"You know Lord Arthur is dead. You searched for hidden silver coins before, but you did not find it. What makes you think you will find the silver this time?"

"I was not ever here before! I have been told—damn you, lackwit, allow me to enter! We will take the silver and be gone."

"Who told you where the silver is?"

"That is none of your affair! Let us enter!"

"What is this? You no longer wish to feed us? Come, what is your name?" Aleric thought he would burst out of his armor, his anger was so great.

"Don't you make sport with me. Let down the drawbridge!"

"So he is not going to give me his name." Aleric sighed, then turned and nodded to the kneeling archers. "Now!" They rose as one and shot their arrows. Three men on horseback fell to the ground. Sir Halric didn't fall, but an arrow grazed his neck, furrowing a deep trench. Merry saw the blood flow out even from where she was.

Sir Halric cursed furiously, waved his mailed hand toward Aleric, motioned to his own archers to fire again, but they had run away. Without the archers, the mounted soldiers were in a weak position and they knew it. They wheeled their mounts about and were out of range within moments, another ten arrows raining down to land on the shields covering their heads, the dirt swirling at the pounding of the horses' hooves.

Merry looked at the fleeing soldiers, Sir Halric at their head, his hand pressed against his neck to stanch the flow of blood. Why hadn't Jason of Brennan come, since he was the Black Demon? Who had told them where the silver coins were hidden?

Garron's soldiers rose to stand beside Aleric, screaming insults after the fleeing enemy.

Aleric slapped men on the backs, told them they'd beaten the cowards, and there was more cheering from those standing armed in the inner bailey.

She threw her arms around him. "That was an amazing plan, lining your men along the rampart walkway, never letting them be seen until it was too late. We won!" Aleric stood frozen, pleased, appalled, and a huge grin bloomed on his face. He patted her awkwardly on the back.

Miggins shouted, "Aleric, 'tis a good braw lad ye be. What say ye, would ye like to lick me?"

Everyone laughed, Merry included. Two archers were laughing so hard they nearly fell off the ramparts.

As for Merry, she knew there was now no hope for it. Sir Halric would remember who she was, she knew it. She said to Aleric, "Did you see the standard the squire was carrying?"

"Aye, I did. I have never seen it before." *Spit it out, spit it out.* "I have."

Aleric said slowly, "Their leader said you looked familiar. I wondered how that could be. Whose standard is it, Merry? Who is that man's master?"

"Jason of Brennan. It is his standard—two black eagles, their wings folded down, bones piled between them."

"Jason of Brennan. I know of him, as does Garron. How do you know it is his standard? You are saying he is the Black Demon?"

"Yes, he must be. Their leader's name is Sir Halric. He is Jason of Brennan's man."

"Tell me, Merry, everything you know of these men."

"I know Jason of Brennan is a bad man, greedy, ambitious. As for Sir Halric, he is a hard man, and single-minded, I think."

Aleric knew stalling when he saw it. He repeated, "How do you know these men, Merry?"

She was frantically pleating the skirt of her gown. "Please, Aleric, please, I must tell Garron first, it is only right."

"Surely it is not so very bad, is it?"

"Aye, it is."

Aleric eyed her. Her face was white as the beautiful clouds overhead. He watched her pull the hood off her head. He eyed her bright red hair. "The man recognized your hair, didn't he? How is this?" When she remained silent, he sighed deeply. "Will you tell Garron the truth when he returns? You swear you will tell him how you know these men?"

"Aye, I will, I must. It is past time, really. I do not want any of you hurt."

"Now that I know who they are, they cannot hurt us. I knew you could be no priest's byblow. Who are you?"

"Not yet, Aleric, please, not yet. There is more."

25

WAREHAM CASTLE
SIX DAYS LATER

Bless Aleric, he did not mention Sir Halric
or Jason of Brennan again, nor did he
again ask her who she was.

Now Garron was home. Merry watched
him, Gilpin, and Pali ride across the drawbridge, their horses' hooves pounding
loud on the thick wooden beams. Since
Robert Burnell wasn't with him, he must
have taken all the king's soldiers and returned to London after visiting Furly and

Radstock. This meant all was well, but it was still a relief.

She saw Sir Lyle of Clive and his three men riding behind Garron. She knew to her bones he'd been the one to pay those men to try to kill her and Garron, then he'd killed the two men, probably killed the new smith and claimed he'd escaped Wareham. But how to get proof of his guilt?

Garron had taken off his helmet and his black hair shone beneath the bright sun.

Voices swelled around her.

"Lord Garron is home!" yelled Lilo, a young daughter of a carpenter they'd hired from Winthorpe, who appeared to worship Hobbs, always standing near when he spoke in his beautiful musical voice to the horses.

Word spread fast. Soon, all Wareham's people poured out of the great hall, out of the outbuildings to gather in the inner bailey. Workers waved their tools, joining in the cheers.

Damocles reared on his hind legs, not at all nervous with all the noise; rather, Merry thought, he was announcing his arrival, ready to be admired. Merry came down the great hall stone steps and moved to stand a step behind Miggins. She wanted to cheer with his people, but could not.

Garron was home at last.

Her time was up.

Garron saw a flash of bright red hair. He saw Merry lurking behind Miggins on the stairs. Why wasn't she coming to greet him? He smelled the now familiar scents of home, and grinned from ear to ear at the sight of all Wareham's people, all here to welcome him home. It was the first time in his life he'd received such a welcome. It warmed him to his booted feet.

It was a beautiful day, the sun shining brilliantly down upon his land, his castle, his people, his cows, her glorious red hair with the small hidden braids. "Merry," he shouted, "bring yourself here now!"

He knew, she thought, somehow he had found out and now he was going to denounce her in front of all his people. She heard Eric the goat make small belching noises, saw Errol trying to pull a stick from the goat's mouth. She felt a shove at her back. Elaine said, "Go, Merry, the master is home. You will tell him all we've accomplished in his absence."

Merry threw her head back, smiled, and strode to where Garron was dismounting Damocles, who was still flinging his mighty head up and down. Garron stroked his long neck to calm him even as he listened to Hobbs speaking quietly to him.

Then he looked at her coming toward him, and smiled, simply couldn't help it. The fact was, days ago he realized he didn't really care who she was, where she came from, what her lineage was, he only knew she was here and she was smiling at him, and— Something was wrong.

"What is the matter with her, Aleric? Has something happened? Is she ill?"

"She will tell you, Garron."

Garron didn't think. He took three steps toward her and lifted her high, then swung her around. His people cheered and laughed and cheered some more.

He realized she was his as much as Wareham was his, and it felt very good. It felt right. He slowly lowered her, leaned his head down, and kissed her.

She was always talking, laughing, but now her lips were seamed tight. She'd turned to stone, and that was surely a blow to a man's pride.

He frowned, set his forehead against hers for a moment, and said low, "I will see to it that when I kiss you the next time, we will be alone," and he set her away from him. He turned to Aleric. "Six days, Aleric, and all looks nearly whole again."

Aleric said easily, "Come into the great hall and I will tell you about how a man named Sir Halric visited us with several dozen soldiers and archers and demanded to be let in. He obviously believed all of us to be dying or dead. He offered to give us food if we let him in." He paused a moment, looked briefly to Merry, and nodded. He stepped back to give them privacy.

Garron stilled. "Merry? What do you know of this? Who is Sir Halric?"

She said, "Evidently Sir Halric did not know you had returned to Wareham. I recognized him and Jason of Brennan's standard as well."

"How is this possible?"

"Jason of Brennan's standard is horrible—two black eagles with their wings folded down hovering over a pile of bones."

Garron looked back at Aleric. "Do you believe Jason of Brennan is the Black Demon?"

"It would seem so," Aleric said. "He sent Sir Halric because he didn't believe it would be difficult to gain entry into Wareham."

Garron asked, "Did you hide the archers behind the rampart walls?"

"Aye, I did. It is a fine ploy. When the enemy shot their arrows at us, all our people merely covered their heads. I covered Merry's head with my own shield. It was Hobbs who shot Sir Halric in the neck, not a death shot, but he bled like a pig. I will wager the bastard is cursing us for his pain."

Garron said to her, "You were on the ramparts wall with Aleric?"

She nodded.

"Tell me, Merry, how did you recognize Sir Halric?"

She stood before him, dumb as a post.

"How did you know he was Jason of Brennan's man?" He saw her swallow hard. "You are somehow tied to these men, are you not? Have you told anyone who you are?"

"I asked Aleric if I could wait to tell you first."

"Good. Aleric, leave us." He raised his voice to shout to everyone in the inner bailey, nearly full now, with people, his people, "We are home. Furly and Radstock are both loyal to us. You have all done very well, and I thank you."

No one wanted to move. Everyone knew something important was happening that involved Merry and Lord Garron, but Aleric ordered them back to their jobs, and no one would dare to disobey Aleric.

Garron studied her a moment. "I will not turn you away, Merry, not after you have done so much for Wareham. Tell me, are you Jason of Brennan's wife? Did you run away from him? Did he send Sir Halric to fetch you home? But how did he know where to find you?"

He'd reached the most awesome conclusion. "Jason of Brennan is not my husband. I am not wed."

"All right," he said, and waited. He watched her wring her hands. He'd never seen Merry do that.

Her words poured out in a flood. "My

mother sold me to Jason of Brennan. When I found out I was to be wedded to him, I ran away. Sir Halric is his man. He caught me, made me wear boy's clothes. I was the boy you saved in Clandor Forest."

Aleric hadn't stepped all that far away and Garron could hear him suck in his breath. Merry and that scruffy boy were one and the same? No, it was too outlandish, impossible—

"I really am the boy you saved, my lord," she said again, searching his face.

Garron said, "Why did you not come out when I called out to you?"

"I did not know who you were. You could have saved me merely to take me yourself. And I was puking up my innards from being hit on the head."

"But then you decided to follow me?"

"Aye, I'm not entirely stupid."

He gave a fleeting smile. "No, you are not. You slipped into Wareham?"

She nodded. "Miggins and Lisle took care of me."

"Why would they do that?"

"I told them I would fix Wareham if they

would help me. They believed me. Lisle had some of Lady Anne's gowns hidden beneath the stones in the lord's chamber. She gave them to me. They spoke to all the people, and everyone agreed to say I was the castle priest's bastard. Because you fed everyone that first night, I believe they were ready to give me a chance as well."

"You told no one who you were?"

"No."

"Who are you, Merry? What is your real name?"

"My name is Marianna."

"Marianna. Well, that is a nice name."

"You will not like the rest of it. Garron, I am very sorry."

He lifted his hands to her shoulders, shook her slightly. "I know you are not the Queen of England. What matter then? Tell me."

She looked briefly heavenward, swallowed, then said finally, "My name is Marianna de Luce de Mornay. I've heard I am called the Valcourt Heiress."

For an instant, his mind was blank. He stared down at her, his brows drawn together. Then his mind filled with the knowledge of her. Slowly, carefully, he set her away from him.

"I see," he said.

"You said heiresses complained and whined and ordered everyone around. You said they had rabbit teeth. I do not." And she gave him a big smile, showing small white teeth.

"No, you don't, do you?" And he turned away from her without another word.

Merry opened her mouth to call after him, but Aleric shook his head at her. "Leave him be, mistress. It is a blow, who you are. The heiress of Valcourt. It is something I never would have imagined, Garron either. And you were that boy in Clandor Forest. He must think this through, it is his way."

Merry watched him stride away.

"He is not brooding, Aleric, he is looking at all the repaired barracks and outbuildings, the cottages for our workers." She watched him walk to the large cleared area that stretched out from one of the inner walls, a short fence protecting it. It would be her herb garden.

Aleric said, "Even I have heard of you."

"Most have."

"This is very bad, Merry. I do not know what will happen. Are you really the Valcourt Heiress?"

She nodded, so filled with misery she couldn't find words.

"By all Saint Cuthbert's broken toes, this is an amazing thing, but no matter. Garron will decide what to do. How much fresh ale do we have?"

"Enough, I believe. Aleric, is there any reason to tell anyone else who I really am?"

"It wouldn't matter since none of the people would know of you and what you are. I am willing to wager Sir Halric now realizes exactly who you are, and that means Jason of Brennan now knows as well. This is not good at all. I must tell Garron that Sir Halric recognized you."

When Garron entered his chamber, he saw that Gilpin had filled his new bathing tub. As Garron sank down into the steaming water, he closed his eyes and tried not to think, but it was no use. "Leave me, Gilpin." He now knew the name of the Black Demon—Jason of Brennan. He knew the man to be more rapacious than most men, a man who would slip a stiletto in another man's back if he could not gain what he wished by looking him in the face. He was the man who had destroyed Wareham, all in search of Arthur's silver coins.

What would he do now? At least Garron now knew the name of his enemy.

If only that were all. *Marianna de Luce de Mornay, the Valcourt Heiress*. What in the name of all that was holy would happen now? Soon enough, he realized, he could very well be a dead man.

26

MEIZERLING ABBEY
NEAR CHEDDLEFORD ROWLEY
EAST ANGLIA

"You are an idiot."

Jason of Brennan wanted to leap over the huge table covered with foul-smelling vials and jars that held things he didn't want to know about, and throttle the magnificent golden-haired creature who stared at him with open contempt.

The sharp eye-watering smell of sulfur wafted to him, as if a trap door to Hell had opened. He was not afraid of her, he wasn't, nor was he an idiot. He would show her what he was made of, he would sound as calm and reasoned as one of the king's counselors, or his damned father. He knew he looked imposing in his black tunic, with the studded silver belt that fastened his gem-encrusted sword to his side, and drew himself up. "I am not an idiot. Sir Halric is not an idiot. I told you, madam, Halric did not realize Lord Garron had gone to Wareham. Who was there to tell him? Who was there to tell me so I could inform him of the fact? He expected all those remaining within the walls to be starving, desperate for help. There was no reason to believe his ruse would not work."

The beautiful witch sneered at him, contempt now bursting from her voice. "Ah, but you tell me he saw this very fit soldier standing atop the ramparts, yet it did not occur to Sir Halric to wonder if mayhap something had changed? He still kept to his fiction of offering aid? Given this, would you not call him an idiot? And given you are his master, does it not follow that you are an idiot as well?"

Her words slammed against him like

hard grit, abrading his flesh, irritating him to his soul. He looked down at his boots for a moment. What could he say to her accusation? What she had said was logical. The truth was the truth. He said finally, hating those words coming out of his mouth, "Aye, I suppose that is what happened. Still—"

"I am distressed that my excellent plan was so poorly executed." And she gave him a smile that promised more suffering than he could imagine. He hated her in that moment, as much as he hated this immense chamber filled with strange smells and thick brooding shadows since the window shutters were always closed against the sunlight. Jason imagined he could feel the bright sunlight beating against the shutters, trying to come in, but to no avail. The billowing shadows crowded in on the branch of candles on Abbess Helen's large worktable. He knew there was something malignant lying in the midst of those shadows, something waiting to rip out his throat, that or drive him to madness, and it lurked, and waited. He knew he would have no fear of her if he could grab her by her golden hair and drag her out of this malevolent room, out of this hideous gray stone abbey, away from her private army, and her blank-faced nuns who all treated her like a queen, and fling her to the ground. Would her body be as beautiful as her face when he ripped that ridiculous black habit off her?

She sat back in her finely carved chair and regarded him over her steepled white fingers. "Halric should have known everything there was to know about Wareham before he went there, but he did not. He should have known that Arthur's brother had arrived to succeed to Wareham Castle. He should have stopped at neighboring villages and inquired, but he did not. He should have sent a soldier to study the castle before ever he went to Wareham, but he did not. I should have slit his throat, were I you.

"And you, as his master, you should have ensured he knew what to do, instructed him if needed, but you did not. I cannot believe you have failed me yet again. I fear you are not a very good tool. Mayhap my loyal Abel will have to search elsewhere for a better one."

Abel was the man who led her private army, a hard man and vicious, not a dollop of mercy in him. On the other hand, Jason rarely showed mercy himself. He said, "The failures you speak about—they are about two different matters, so there is only one failure for each endeavor."

Contempt blossomed again on her white face, a face too white, too unlined, and her brilliant eyes narrowed on his face, and he wished he'd kept his mouth shut. How could she be so beautiful and yet have a daughter full-grown? But he knew, oh aye, he knew. Abbess Helen de Mornay was a witch. If she hadn't left her lord years before, he probably would have killed her, before she killed him. He eyed a line of vials on shelves behind her filled with potions to make a man's guts twist and shrivel as he said, hating the whine in his voice, "I am no man's tool."

She laughed, a melodious sound, soft and lovely. She gave him a look of amusement. "Nay, of course you are not. You, Jason of Brennan, are a woman's tool. You are my tool, defective though you be, you are still mine, until I decide otherwise." She paused a moment, looking toward the shadows, into them, he believed, and he knew he saw those shadows roil and twist. He forced himself to stand perfectly still, to show no fear, for he knew to his guts that would be fatal. He stared at the powerful abbess who had ruled Meizerling for more than fifteen years now, mayhap the wealthiest abbey in all of England, filled with learned parchments and beautifully illuminated manuscripts. She even had several women scribes, something that he'd never heard of before. Her damning words flowed into him, reduced him to nothing at all. He drew himself up again, taller this time. He was a man, he was strong, he wasn't anyone's tool, man or woman. Abbess or no, she was still a woman withal, yet in odd moments of honesty, in this terrifying chamber with its deep shadows that held evil, he knew he was afraid of her, and he hated himself more for that than for his excuses. At odd moments, he wondered if she even needed the six ever-vigilant soldiers who stood alert and at the ready outside her door, ready to pour into the room and kill anyone she pointed to. Could she point a long white finger at him, the one with the massive emerald set in finely worked silver, chant a few words, make that stinking sulfur smell fill his nostrils and choke him?

But he'd had no choice but to ally himself to her, no choice at all. He'd been desperate.

"I am no tool," he said again.

She laughed once more, and he swelled with rage. *Be calm, be calm, all is not lost. She can find no one else in time.* He dredged deep and found a smile. "There is good news, my lady."

An arched eyebrow shot upward even as she said with utter indifference, "I hope your good news is sufficient to convince me not to let Abel kill you."

"It is," he said shortly, hoping his voice sounded firm, hoping he sounded like a solid man, one who knew what needed to be done, and could do it. "Halric said there was a girl standing beside the warrior on the ramparts at Wareham."

"A girl? I don't suppose she was ill-kempt and starving either, was she? No, of course not. And how exactly is this good news to me?"

"Halric recognized her."

Abbess Helen stilled.

"Aye, it was your daughter, madam. Halric has no idea how she came to be at Wareham."

Lady Helen looked away from him, into the shadows that were warm and comforting, and wished this vain young cock would leave so the shadows could seep into her and ward off the cold. She forced herself to look at his handsome face. "So after Halric lost Marianna in Clandor Forest to a fierce warrior he did not know— and his vast army of men—she somehow made her way to Wareham, not all that distant from Clandor Forest. I do not suppose it was difficult for my daughter to sneak into Wareham, what with all the people either dead or nearly starved."

She closed her eyes and looked beyond her abbey walls, beyond the acres of trees, past the small villages, until the savage North Sea finally came into her mind's eye, and atop a promontory sat Wareham Castle. It was not difficult to see her daughter slipping in amongst those starved mongrels, blending in, helping them.

In that instant, she realized this was not what had happened at all. Everything was clear now.

Abbess Helen contemplated Jason of Brennan as he now paced in front of her worktable, turning to stride to the far shuttered windows, then back again. Did he want her to admire his excellent form? The strength and sturdiness of his back? Indeed, he was a handsome man, a man Marianna should have admired, but she hadn't. She'd detested him so much, she'd run away. How had she realized so quickly that he was a callow creature, no honor in him that she'd ever seen, only self-interest and greed and a marked need to cause pain whenever he could, failings of most men Helen had observed? Evidently she had.

Still, Helen was amazed that this particular man, whose father, Lord Ranulf, the Earl of Carronwick, a man she'd always avoided because he was far-seeing, was so blind, so stupid, so unlike the man who had sired him. "You honestly don't know what happened, do you?"

Jason stopped in front of her table. He hated it, but slowly, he shook his head.

Lady Helen said very softly, "Garron of Kersey naturally traveled to Wareham to assume his brother's title and lands. The man in your pay at Wareham, the steward, was it not? You instructed him to tip the potion into Arthur's ale, and so he did. You should have known Arthur's brother would arrive quickly. Is it not obvious to you that Lord Garron was the ferocious warrior who rescued Marianna from Halric and his men? Is it not obvious to you that he must have taken her to Wareham with him?" She examined her fingernails, noticed that one was blackening, doubtless from her recent experiment with noreweed and warboil. "Is it clear to you now?"

"That is impossible, madam. I told you that Halric dressed her as a boy. No one would recognize her. Why would he take a scruffy boy with him to Wareham?"

She was tempted to hurl the lovely black onyx statue of Minerva that stood on her worktable at his head. "So she revealed herself to Lord Garron. Did she confess to him who she was? Probably not, she is too afraid of me, probably too afraid of you as well. Is she now his leman?

I must doubt it because she has shown no interest in men, according to Ella, my own faithful servant who stayed behind at Valcourt to take care of her."

"She took no interest in me either," Jason said, and he sounded astonished that such a thing could happen.

Helen continued to examine the black fingernail, a frown on her smooth white brow. She said, more to that fingernail than to him, "Marianna draws people to her, it is a special gift she has. She calls forth their loyalty, their trust. She has managed to do the same thing at Wareham. Did you not tell me that you and your men destroyed Wareham, that you ensured all those who were left alive could not leave the castle?"

"That is correct."

"Marianna would kill herself to fix things. She is very good at it. She arranges, she cajoles, she makes her infernal lists. She has taken over Wareham, and Lord Garron, doubt it not. I do wonder if Lord Garron now knows who she is."

Helen looked toward a vial that held pulverized toad mixed with ox blood and a pinch of ground swamp panwort, said to bring clarity to the mind. She let herself sink into that clarity and saw a little rat of a girl with flaming red hair, yet her mother didn't have red hair, nor did her father, Lord Timothy. That hair of hers was a curse from the Devil. Not more than six years old she was. She drew away from the vision when Jason of Brennan said, "Halric, once he realized who she was, believes she recognized him as well. She knows, madam, and that must mean that Lord Garron now knows as well. Surely she would not keep him in ignorance."

"She knows only of Sir Halric. How could Marianna know he is your minion?"

He hadn't considered that. He felt relief wash through him. "Aye, that's right. She never saw us together. He told me he never said my name to her."

"Nor does she know you do my bidding, now does she? And that means Lord Garron is ignorant of that fact as well."

He felt the quiver of insult and drew himself up. "I am my own man. I only do your bidding because I have decided it is in my own best interest to do so." He

gave her a sneer, knowing it would enrage her, but not enough to smite him, he
hoped. "I promise you, madam, I will kill
Lord Garron, I will find where Arthur hid
the silver coins he stole from my father
and present them to you, and then I will
wed your daughter." *And then I will have
Valcourt and the king will have no choice
but to accept me. And why would he not?
He thinks highly of my father, trusts him,
so why would he not accept the son, particularly after he is already the master of
Valcourt?*

*And you, madam, even after I give you
the silver coins—if I decide to give all
of them to you—you will still be here
amongst these ancient evil-soaked stone
walls, these brooding shadows drown-
ing the light, and your strange chants
and black smoke, and screams, so many
screams, and mayhap one day you will
fall into them and disappear.*

Jason smiled now. "Mayhap, madam,
you will be a grandmother within the
year."

Abbess Helen wanted to laugh at his
paltry attempt to insult her. She marveled
at his overflowing male vanity and was

amused by what he was thinking, so clear his thoughts were on his face, his pleasure at the vision he created of himself as the Earl of Valcourt. Of course, he also saw himself besting her, keeping the silver for himself, but this would never happen, particularly since she held powers close to her breast, powers he couldn't begin to comprehend, powers beyond this world. And mayhap the next as well.

Her husband, Lord Timothy de Luce de Mornay, Earl of Valcourt, had male vanity in full measure until he finally closed those damned knowledge-filled eyes of his for the final time, and she'd known she'd won because he hadn't had the time to marry off Marianna to spite her. She'd never known what he was thinking, not like she did most men, not until he wanted her to know. Nearly twenty years flowed through her mind and it was weighed down with her hatred of his knowledge of her, her failure to control him. She remembered clearly the look on his face when he'd realized what she was, and she'd known it was too soon, too soon, she had not secured him yet. But she had gained what she'd wanted, what she knew she must have. And that was a victory over him.

And she'd cleverly spread the story that Lord Timothy was a monster, that she'd had to leave her young daughter to escape him, taking with her the vast wealth she'd brought to the marriage, and come to Meizerling Abbey, and who could blame her for that, even though she was but a woman, a wife, obedience supposedly the first commandment for a woman? But none would quibble with the religious life she'd chosen. And she'd taken over Meizerling within the year, changed it utterly, and now it was known as a center of learning, of science, and, as very few knew, a center of other sorts of knowledge as well.

Meizerling was her kingdom. Only hers. And she would dispose of Valcourt and Marianna as she wished. Of course there was another option as well, one that just might be delicious. She would think carefully about that.

She smiled at Jason of Brennan. "So you still hope to wed my daughter?"

"Of course. I must simply determine what is best done now."

"Will you slip your knife into Sir Halric's heart?"

Jason wasn't about to tell her that Halric made his own rules, went his own way, that he was something more than simply Jason's man, and that knowledge always stayed his hand, but he realized his acquiescence was what she wanted. He saw the arrow wound in Halric's neck, saw his own knife digging in, widening it. Slowly, he nodded.

Her eyes were narrowed on his face. Could she tell he was lying? Could she see into his brain and simply know? He felt a slap of stark fear, and said again, "Aye, I will stick my knife in deep."

"Then I will tell you what you must do and pray for your sake that you do not again fail me." When she finished, Jason gave her a long look, nodded, turned on his booted heel, and left the chamber. He heard her laugh. "No more failure or I will turn your hair white and your nose will fall off!" He looked back only once over his shoulder, and would swear the roiling dark shadows now surrounded her worktable, drawing ever closer to her to embrace her like a lover, and the stench of sulfur was stronger, now coming toward him to curl into his nostrils.

He closed the chamber door and ran. He didn't remember until he'd ridden away from the shadow of the great abbey: Sir Halric had carried his standard, one of his soldiers had told him that, and wasn't that a mistake? Jason was glad he hadn't told the witch. He believed she would have smote him dead on the spot. Was it possible that Marianna recognized his standard? Given his spate of recent bad luck, he wouldn't doubt it.

But there was still something the witch didn't know, something he would not tell her.

27

WAREHAM CASTLE

Garron found her in the small solar beside the lord's chamber. There was a single window, the deer hide pulled back to let in the sun. There'd been no glass window in this room for the Black Demon to shatter.

He watched her carefully remove a pot from atop a fire and carry it to a small table. He watched her carefully stir as she read her herbal. She didn't look up at him. "Good morning, Garron. I cannot stop stirring or the herbs will do something bad, exactly what I don't know. I feel so very ignorant. What if I make a mistake and kill someone?"

He waved that away as he came closer. "What is it?"

"It is an infusion for Miggins's cough."

"It stings my eyes."

She nodded, still stirring, studying the brew. "It is aniseed and sundew. It is the aniseed that stings your eyes. The thyme smells tart. I have never made this recipe before. I am being very careful with all my measurements, but it is difficult, Garron. I hope it will help her and not burn her throat out."

As she stirred, Merry's heart beat slow hard strokes. At his continued silence, she said finally, still not looking at him, "It has been a day and a half since you returned, a day and a half since you have spoken to me of anything other than improvements on Wareham. Have you decided what to do?"

"You said your mother sold you to Jason of Brennan. I gather your father, Lord Timothy, is dead?"

She nodded. "About the same time your own brother died."

"Why did your mother have to sell you if Valcourt is so very wealthy?"

"There is no cache of ready silver, since Valcourt's wealth lies in its lands and farms and towns. When I was a babe, she left me and my father and took her family's silver with her. She requires a great deal of silver for Meizerling Abbey. She must have determined that selling me to Jason of Brennan was the best way to get it. She acted quickly, found a man she could buy before the king could even be told of my father's death and bestow Valcourt on one of his favorites. Or perhaps she had been planning this a long time and Jason of Brennan stepped through her door."

"You said Meizerling Abbey. I have heard of it."

"My mother's name is Lady Helen, or most properly, I suppose, Abbess Helen of Meizerling."

"I have also heard talk of your mother, how she has made Meizerling a learning center where men may come and study." He'd also heard a story about a monk who had visited Meizerling and fled in the night, telling how he came upon the abbess kneeling in front of a strange statue that sat tall and skinny in the middle of a black circle, and she was chanting strange words to it. The monk claimed the Devil had appeared, framed by billowing black smoke. That story alone could scare the lice off a cow. It sounded ridiculous to Garron, a nightmare image to frighten children. "So when your father died, she moved quickly. Too quickly, I think. How did your father die, Merry? Was his death unexpected?"

She stared at him, her brain frozen. "You believe she made a bargain with Jason of Brennan, and killed my father?"

He shrugged. "Is she smart? Can she plan well? Is she that ruthless?"

"Aye, she is all of those things. But to murder my father—that is difficult to accept. My father died one day before my mother arrived at Valcourt with her own private army and Jason of Brennan at her side. I hope you're wrong. I hope she did not murder my father. That would bespeak evil beyond reason. Since I am of her blood, it scares me what could be inside me, waiting to reveal itself."

"Don't be a dolt. You are so far from

being anything bad or frightening, and that makes you vulnerable. Now, listen, whether she did or did not kill him, I see now that I have no choice. I must take you to King Edward. He is the one to make all decisions about who will assume authority over Valcourt. He is the only one to protect you."

She'd known, oh aye, she'd known what he would decide, for after all, he was the king's man. She said calmly, her stirring a bit slower now that the mixture was cooling, "So I will no longer be my mother's pawn, I will be the king's pawn. It is he who will sell me, not my mother."

"By Saint Florin's boils, don't sound so put upon, you know it is the way things are done. Marriage is about alliances and property. Had your father not died, had your mother not interfered, the king would have decided your future and Valcourt's. It is his responsibility, surely you understand that. The king would hardly wish to have a man not of his choosing take over Valcourt, it is too important a holding. I doubt not the king will want you to stay at court, under his watchful eye."

"You mean he will dangle me in front of

his toadies? I do not wish to visit the court again."

That stopped him cold. "What do you mean, 'again'?"

She touched a fingertip to the thickening liquid and tasted it. She nearly gagged it tasted so bad. She swallowed once, again. "This mixture is so vile, it is bound to cure anything."

"Merry—"

She reached for two open jars, carefully poured in the mixture, covered both jars with heavy cloth, and tied string around them. "When I reached my fifteenth year, my father sent me to be one of Queen Eleanor's ladies. I stayed for ten full months at court. I hated it. Not Queen Eleanor, for she was very kind to me, but the courtiers, both the men and the ladies, they would smile at you and tell filthy stories about you behind your back. It is an awful place. When I finally begged my father to bring me home, he did."

Garron had watched the courtiers play their interminable games until he'd simply paid no more attention. A fifteen-year-old girl would not have stood a chance. "Did any of the men try to seduce you?"

She snorted. "Certainly, it was one of their favorite pastimes. Wager they could not seduce a goat, and they would try."

"I trust the queen protected you?"

"No, I protected myself. My father had warned me, you see. He dinned into my head what the men at court would do, and he was right. He also gave me a small knife if a man tried to force himself on me."

"Your father should not have sent you to court."

"He knew it was time I was wed and he wished me to see if any of the men at the king's court pleased me since all the king's knights and barons, mayhap even an occasional earl, visit the court periodically."

"None of them pleased you?"

She shook her head. "The cruelty, Garron, the honeyed vicious words, the careless promises that meant nothing at all, I couldn't bear it."

"Did you have to use your knife?"

"Once. His name was Baron Landreau. He had just buried his second wife and he was searching for another one, preferably a rich one. One night, he was very drunk and caught me, probably if he raped me then the king would give me to him. I slipped the knife into his shoulder. While he was screaming at me, I ran."

"I know the baron. He is an excellent fighter." He frowned. Men drank, many times even forgot their own names. He said, "Burnell believed you looked familiar. He was right. He must have seen you in the queen's company at court."

She nodded. "Oh yes, but you see, my head was always covered so he never saw my hair." She began to tidy her worktable. "I never saw you, so you must have come to court after I returned to Valcourt."

He nodded. "You are an heiress."

It was an accusation. She couldn't help herself, she gave him a crooked smile. "It is not an affliction, Garron, but since it displeases you so much I will carefully read my herbal, mayhap find a decoction of coltsfoot and soapwort to cure it."

"Your jest does not amuse me."

She watched him dash his hand through his hair. Without thought, she reached out her hand, but he took a quick step back. Her arm dropped to her side.

"Your father was Lord Timothy de Luce de Mornay, the Earl of Valcourt. I visited

Valcourt once a very long time ago, when I was but a boy. My father knew Lord Timothy, but even as a young boy, I saw the stiffness in my father, and knew they were not friends, but I was too young to know the truth of things. I still do not know. Valcourt is larger than Wareham."

"Yes, it is."

"The wealth, Merry, Valcourt is an incredibly wealthy holding. Since the time of William, it has flourished." Indeed, he had heard men at the king's court speak of it and the daughter who was Lord Timothy's only child, and that she hadn't been ugly, a pleasant surprise, that.

"My father told me his father taught him how to manage his properties just as his father had taught him, and so it went back to the first earl." She recited, "Ensure tenant farmers have the proper tools and seeds and help during harvests, use rents to buy more farms, control as many surrounding towns as you can, maintain them, always protect them from outlaws, buy all goods from them, keep a stout fighting force, make excellent ale—and on it goes." She grinned suddenly. "My father said the first earl was a violent old man who wore a long beard wrapped around his neck, but he knew how to make his lands thrive and so he set down rules. They are written in a bound leather book, so very worn when I first saw it. My father set me to copying it. It is fresh now and easily read—for the man the king gives me to, if he can read or write, that is.

"It is a pity my father had no son, only me. Soon another man will become Valcourt's master." She shrugged. "Valcourt will probably lose its wealth in the next couple of generations."

"The Valcourt earls are not the only smart men in England. The king is not a fool. He will not select an incompetent wastrel."

She cocked an eyebrow at him. "Did your own father have such rules for administering Wareham?"

He saw his father in that moment, his face red with fury as he beat the miller because a grain of poorly ground flour cracked a tooth. He gave no help to any of his dependents. He wasn't much loved, his father. He remembered the farmers starving when the crops were poor. He shook his head. "But I will have them."

"That is good. Do you know, my father never shirked his responsibilities, but to be honest, his great love was tournaments. He told me he was the only man he knew to become wealthy from winning tourneys, and he was only eighteen. He was an excellent fighter, only fourteen when he won his first destrier and suit of armor off a French knight he'd bested. He was greatly saddened when King Edward outlawed them."

"Too many men died needlessly in tournaments. Listen, Merry, it must be done. I must take you to the king. You are of marriageable age, indeed past it. He will select a husband for you, a strong warrior to protect Valcourt and swear fealty to him. I will suggest to the king that he find a man who has rules and makes lists.

"I will escort you myself. I will ensure that you are not harmed or forced by any of the men at the court. The king will find a man to follow in your sire's footsteps and Valcourt will continue to prosper."

"Will you tell the king that Jason of Brennan is the Black Demon, that his man

Sir Halric kidnapped me? Will you tell him Jason made a bargain with my mother? Will you tell him your brother was probably poisoned by the Black Demon?"

"Aye, I will tell him."

28

He gave her a brooding look. "Now you said you ran away from Valcourt rather than marry Jason of Brennan. Tell me exactly what happened."

She turned away from him and began to pace. Her gown was so short, he could see her ankles. "I told you my father died unexpectedly. He was well and then he was ill and vomiting and sweat poured down his face and off his body. Then the fever came and he shivered until his teeth chattered. The fever never left him and he died." The telling of it, so bloodless, those words. She wiped tears away with the back of her hand.

"I'm sorry, Merry."

She nodded. "When my mother rode into Valcourt the next day with her men and Jason of Brennan, I believe I was the only one surprised by her sudden appearance. My nursemaid, Ella, said my mother would take care of me now and I was not to worry, and that I was to obey her. My mother was beautiful and very smart, she told me again and again, her heart full to bursting with kindness, and it no longer mattered that my father had hated her, and abused her.

"I didn't say anything, but I knew to my soul that could not be true. My father never abused me, never resented me because I was not a boy. He never spoke ill of her. Once, though, I saw him cross himself when someone mentioned her name in his presence." *Tell him, just tell him.* Her voice came out a whisper. "I also heard it said she was a powerful witch, that she knew things no one else did, that she could cast spells to shrivel a soul. I think that is why my father sent her away. He was afraid for me."

A witch was a creature a man couldn't begin to understand. He hated it. He hadn't wanted to believe that monk's tale, but now—this was real. "Are you a witch also?"

"I do not think so," Merry said, her voice as serious as his had been light, but, he saw, she did not speak with much conviction. Did Merry believe herself a witch like her mother? What nonsense was this?

"I told you she brought Jason of Brennan with her. She told me I would wed him. Jason appeared young enough, well made, smoothly spoken, but I tell you, Garron, when I looked into his eyes, I saw no light. Whenever he laughed, which was too often, I saw something shift in his eyes, something calculating, something that scared me to my toes, and I simply knew there was nothing good or wholesome in him. He left then. My mother told me he would soon return."

"How did you escape from Valcourt?"

"I bided my time and finally I was able to escape. Unfortunately, Sir Halric had arrived at Valcourt, unannounced, and he saw me running away. He caught me, and dressed me in boy's clothes to take me to his master."

Garron thought about this for a moment. "I wonder why he simply did not hand you over to your mother? Surely she would have had you locked in your bedchamber at Valcourt, kept you safe for Halric's master, Jason of Brennan."

"I thought that was what he was going to do, but instead, he rode away from Valcourt. Was he really taking me to Jason of Brennan? I remember how he laughed when he spoke to one of his men, said I would be a gift to his master, then he laughed and wondered aloud how such a dirty little beggar could have any worth at all. All in all, he was very pleased with himself because he had me."

Garron began to pace. "Then I found you and freed you and you made your way here. Now, why did Jason of Brennan send Sir Halric back to Wareham?"

"Because he found out where the silver coins were hidden. There can be no other answer."

"And Sir Halric believed all would be dead or nearly dead and welcome him right in."

"Do you think Jason has admitted his failure to my mother? If so, I hope she will blight him with a curse. She surely must realize now that Wareham is safe from more attacks. Will she guess that you will escort me to King Edward?"

Garron picked up a flower sprig and sniffed it. It was lavender. "I doubt either your mother or Jason of Brennan will even consider my giving over such a plump prize to the king. They doubtless believe I will keep you for myself, and gain Valcourt in the bargain."

She said clearly, with no hesitation, "Why not?"

She watched him pick up a lemonwort leaf and sniff it, then carefully set it back into its place. He slowly turned to look at her. "You believe I would force you to wed with me? You believe me as big a villain as Jason of Brennan? As your mother?"

"No, you are not at all like them. You would never force me to wed you. Indeed, you wouldn't have to force me." She thrust up her chin, stared him straight in the eye. "I would agree willingly. I would not mind being your wife."

"You are mad," he said, appalled,

turned on his heel, and strode out of the small solar, his back straight as the new barrack door.

Merry picked up one of the jars that held Miggins's infusion, shook it, watched bits of anise and sundew dance in the liquid, then settle to the bottom. The jar was cool to the touch. Time to give it to Miggins.

What to do?

And then she knew.

29

Merry knew Gilpin slept on a pallet outside Garron's door. Even though she'd
slipped a sleeping draught in his ale but
an hour before, she cupped her hand
around her candle and removed her slippers before she very carefully stepped
over him and slowly opened the lord's
bedchamber door. Gilpin didn't stir. Thank
St. Agnes's crooked fingers Garron hadn't
set the bar on the door. She nearly fell
over when she heard Gilpin whisper, "Let
me cleave his head, Lord Garron, let me
cleave his head." She jerked about to see

he was still asleep. He had sounded en-
thusiastic.

She closed the door, picked up the
stout wooden bar, and eased it into place.
The room wasn't as dark as the bottom of
one of Bullic's cooking kettles, since Garron had tied back the deerskin that hung
over the now-open window, and moonlight poured into the room. She paused
a moment and breathed in the still, sweet
night air. She looked toward the bed, saw
no movement, but she could clearly see
his outline.

She walked to the great bed and stood
over him, raising her candle until she
could see his face. He looked very young
in sleep, a slight smile about his mouth.
Was he dreaming of cleaving someone's
head, as was his squire?

He lay on his back, his legs spread, the
blanket pulled only to his waist, leaving
his chest bare. She knew the rest of him
was bare, too, a good thing, since that
step on her list had no instruction. But she
wasn't stupid. She knew what lurked beneath that single blanket.

She was here and he was here, and he

was naked. The bedchamber door was barred. It wasn't as if she didn't know how men and women mated, but making the mating happen was something she wasn't quite sure how to bring about. On the other hand, she'd heard Lisle say to Elaine that Lady Anne had often remarked that a man was always randy, and a woman had naught to do but spread her legs and think about a new gown or perhaps a new bauble as she bounced up and down and moaned.

She looked down at his chest, saw the scar high on his shoulder, another one, long and puckered, on his arm, yet another disappeared beneath the cover over his belly. She saw his new bathing tub in the corner. She leaned down and breathed him in. The smell of him was so familiar to her.

She reached out her hand. Mayhap if she touched him—touched him where? What would he do?

He made a sound deep in his throat, and his head twisted back and forth on the pillow. He flung his arm over his head, then stilled. What was he dreaming?

She drew her hand back and looked

again at him. He was big. Big was not bad. Big meant he could meet an enemy head-on and cleave him in two. That made her smile, but only for a moment. Big also meant he could hurt her. But who cared? Time to get it done.

Merry set the candle on the floor, steadied herself, slipped out of her robe. She then pulled her shift up to her waist, and slowly and carefully climbed on top of him. His eyes flew open. He jerked up onto his elbows. "Are you the enemy?"

"Nay, my lord, I swear I am no enemy." He sighed deep in his throat, his eyes closed, and his breathing deepened. She lightly shoved him back down. She carefully straddled him, and realized she didn't know what to do now. He had to come inside her, but how, since she was sitting on top of him and there was a blanket between them? She wished she could waken him and ask how to continue. He stretched beneath her, stilled again, and began to snore lightly. He would never compete with Miggins.

She leaned forward, kissed him, then straightened up, fast as a shot arrow.

The kiss was nice, more than nice

actually, even though it had lasted but a moment. Again, she thought, leaned down, and this time her mouth stayed on his. His mouth was warm, but it was more than simple warmth, it was something about the feel of him that sent a touch of heat straight to her belly. She wasn't expecting that, frowned when she felt her heart speed up. She knew mating was enjoyable to men, at Valcourt she'd heard them bray and brag about it all the time, and at court as well. Nothing else interested them that she could see. To be honest, it wasn't just the men. At home and at court, she'd heard the women giggle and whisper behind their hands when a comely man was near, but what exactly were they saying? About how wonderful he smelled? How they wanted to touch him and never stop? Curse her for a fool, she should have listened, but she hadn't, she'd always slithered away. It was clear she'd been shortsighted. She had not considered the future.

She kissed him again, this time pressed her mouth harder against his. To her shock he opened his mouth and his tongue touched her. Never had she thought about a man's tongue touching her mouth, roving over her bottom lip, and her legs tightened around his flanks. Suddenly, his tongue slipped into her mouth. She nearly leapt off him she was so shocked. She lurched up, and he moaned. He raised a hand, cupped her cheek, and whispered, "Blanche, have you come again to kiss me awake? You know I love the taste of you."

Who was this wretched Blanche? She came to him when he was asleep and kissed him awake? If the bitch were here, Merry would clout her head.

"Come, Blanche, come closer, I'll give you whatever you want. Aye, give me your breasts." He began humming the sad angel song she'd once sung to him as his hands moved to cup her breasts. How could he hum *her* song when he believed he was touching that bitch Blanche? He stopped, frowned. "What is this? I want nothing between your sweet flesh and my hands." He jerked up her shift. Merry helped him pull it over her head.

"Ah, that is much better. Give me your breasts, sweeting."

She was naked and sitting on top of a

man who was running his hands over her arms, her shoulders, dipping to cup her breasts again. His hands were callused, hard, and warm, and the way he was touching her made her want to sing. It was astounding, mayhap a bit frightening. "Ah, that is very nice. Bring me your mouth, Blanche. Aye, come down to me. Then you may have your way with me."

Even as she lowered her head, Merry never stopped looking at him. His eyes were still closed. How could he sleep through such a cataclysm? She wanted to kiss him until her mouth was numb. He moaned as he raised his head and nuzzled her breasts, then licked her flesh. When his mouth closed over her she wanted to leap straight to the ceiling, but only for a moment because she wanted his hands and his mouth to touch more of her, and she wanted what was beneath that single blanket.

His hands slipped beneath her, and his fingers skimmed inward until they touched her. She sat atop him, horrified and frozen, feeling his fingers probe.

"You are so soft and warm. But you are

not wet for me, Blanche. What is wrong?"
Wet? What was this? When he raised her
hips with his big hands, she splayed her
palms on his chest and closed her eyes
and waited to see what he would do.
What he did was ease a finger inside her.
It hurt, but not all that much. Now what
would happen? Whatever he would do
next, she only knew she wanted it very
much. As he pressed further, she realized
she was beginning to pant, her heart
speeding. It hurt, but not for long. She
wasn't stupid. She knew he wanted to
come inside her, not just his fingers, but
what was beneath that blanket. His fingers
left her. He eased her upright again, still
holding her with one of his big hands, and
with the other he pulled down the blanket. She wasn't about to look at him, even
though she wanted to, desperately. It was
going to happen. She raised herself more,
and felt his fingers, then felt him enter her.
He heaved out a huge groan and pushed.
He pushed and pushed, not that he got
very far. She gripped his shoulders, closed
her eyes and seamed her lips to keep
from yelling. He would tear her apart, she

knew it, but she had to let him do it, no choice. Pressure, too much pressure, and it didn't stop. How far could he push?

She couldn't bear it, simply couldn't. Just as she was about to pull off him and run from the chamber, he moaned, grabbed her waist in his hands, and pulled her down as he shoved upward.

She yelled and tried to jerk away, but it was no good.

Garron's eyes flew open. For an instant, he simply was unable to understand what was happening, but only for an instant. By all that was holy, it wasn't Blanche astride him with him deep inside her body, it was Merry, and he could feel how small she was and how he was stretching her and she yelled again, really loud this time, and he knew he was hurting her. But it didn't matter, for he was swamped with lust. He jerked and heaved, but it wasn't right, this couldn't happen or— "No," he said between gritted teeth, "no, get off me, Merry, now. I will not do this, I cannot do this."

She realized she was pitiful to cry out. Pain was one thing, surely she could deal with pain, but what she knew she couldn't deal with was a stranger for a husband.

Get it done, get it done. She pushed down with all her might, felt him burst fully into her, and knew she was going to die. Dead, at least, she wouldn't have to marry Jason of Brennan, she would never have this happen to her again. Garron didn't move.

Had he fallen back asleep? Suddenly he began cursing. His hands closed around her waist and this time he was trying to pull her off him, but she wasn't about to stop now. She knew instinctively she had to move and so she did. "Merry, no." She leaned forward, grabbed his hair in her hands, and kissed him wildly.

Garron cursed in her mouth, then moaned. He said her name over and over, then quite suddenly, he knew it was too late. It was all over for him and he couldn't stop it. He was stretched taut as a bow. He sucked in his breath and yelled her name to the beamed ceiling. Never in his life had he felt like this, pushed somehow beyond himself, beyond his earthbound limits, yet he was held deep inside her—

his world shattered, and he soared. Surely Heaven was his destination.

Gilpin shouted, "My lord! My lord, oh no, someone is hurting you! Someone climbed over me to get to you, to slay you, and it is all my fault. Oh mighty Saint Albertine, blessed saint of all limping beggars, I deserve to drink the poison the heretics forced down your gullet before they broke your legs and burned you to ashes!" Gilpin banged on the door, sent his shoulder and his foot into it, but that door was thicker than he was, the stout bar could keep out a dozen men, and there was no way he would get through it.

Merry heard the mad knocking and slamming against the door, but it wasn't important. What was important was that she was no longer a maid. It was done, it had to be since she felt wet inside, and she knew it was his man's seed. She looked down at him, still inside her. He was lying motionless as a dead man, his eyes closed, his hands palms up at his sides. In the dim candlelight, she saw he was smiling, and he was asleep.

Asleep! How could the lout fall asleep?

The pain was less than it had been, and that was a relief. She leaned over him, her hand cupping his cheek. "Garron, I know I am no longer a maid. I mean, how could I be since you are so deep inside me? Come, you must wake up, you must realize what has happened."

Gilpin yelled, "I will fetch Aleric! We will save you, my lord!"

Garron's eyes flew open. He was firmly back on the earth. He grabbed her about the waist, yelling as he rolled over on top of her, "Gilpin, do not get Aleric! Do you understand me? It was a nightmare, nothing more than a nightmare. *Do not get Aleric!* I am all right. Go back to sleep!"

"How can I sleep, my lord? I heard you yelling. Is there an enemy in there with a knife to your gullet?"

"There is no enemy, no knife. Go back to sleep or I will twist your tongue around your neck and choke you with it!"

30

After a moment of blessed silence, Garron looked down at her pale face. "So, you have brought me low," and he pushed. She hadn't realized he was still inside her. She tried to pull away from him, but she couldn't. Her body wanted him as far away from her as it could get. "It's done, Garron. There is no reason for you to do more to me. You can stop now, please."

He stilled over her. "Why should I?"

"It hurts."

He frowned, and pulled back, just a bit, but stayed inside her. He balanced himself on his elbows above her. He wanted her again, but now his brain was back in his head and he could at last reason. "So," he said again, "I cannot believe you came into my bedchamber and impaled yourself on me."

"You thought I was Blanche."

"I should have known. Even asleep I should have known it wasn't Blanche. Her breasts are more bountiful than both a man's hands together. And Blanche always knew exactly what to do."

She smacked her fist against his shoulder. "Stop thinking about that cow."

He grinned down at her, moved just a bit deeper, stilled again when she stiffened. "Hold still. You do not even know Blanche. She was clever, was Blanche, and she loved to awaken me in the middle of the night."

"How?"

"Sometimes she'd have her breasts pressed against my face."

"Didn't her bountiful breasts smother you?"

"Aye," and he once again fell silent and she knew, simply knew he was thinking about his face buried in the cow's breasts.

She smacked his shoulder again. "Well,

you cannot wed this Blanche, you cannot ever have her breasts in your face again. You must wed me, Garron."

He was inside her, just barely now, but lust was rising again. At her stark words, the enormity of the situation burst clear as a crystal into his brain. *Marry her?* He'd taken her maidenhead, he'd spilled his seed inside her. She was no longer pure.

By all St. Clementine's rosary beads, would the king have him drawn and quartered? Would he lock him in the dungeon away from the light and leave him to starve?

Bright clean fury flashed in his brain. He didn't deserve this. He was panting with rage and lust when he pulled out of her, and came up on his knees between her legs. He waved his fist in her face. "I cannot believe you planned this, that you actually came into my chamber and forced me to take you."

"Forced you? Ha!"

"Be quiet! You foolish girl, I cannot believe you actually did this."

"I told you I did not want to be forced to wed with some man I do not know."

"It is not your right to decide your future. Are you so ignorant you do not understand that? Your father would have selected your husband. But now it is only right that the king act in his stead. I cannot believe you are so willful or so stupid."

His outrage finally broke through and she burst into tears.

He was appalled, but only for an instant because his anger was riding him hard. He waved his fist in her face. "What are you doing? Crying? How dare you? Stop those infernal tears now!"

The tears dried up. She gulped. "All right, but it is difficult to stop once I get started. What is it you wish to do now, my lord?"

"You can cry whenever you wish to?"

"One of the ladies at court taught me, but I must think sad thoughts. I thought about what the Black Demon had done to Wareham and that was enough."

"What was her name?"

"Alice of Kent."

Not Alice, anyone but Alice. Was he cursed? "Did she teach you anything else?"

"No. She even believed I was so backward that gushing out tears when I wished was beyond me. It took me a while, but I finally proved her wrong."

How had she gotten him off his logical path?

"I would like to beat you, but I suppose that since you are an heiress, since you will soon be the king's ward, I am to be denied the pleasure."

"I cannot be the king's ward. He does not want a girl who is no longer a virgin. I know well that virginity is prized above all else. Well, except for silver and land."

"That was your fault entirely. I had nothing to do with it. I was scarcely here."

"Ha! You moaned so loudly I was nearly deafened. Then you yelled—it even woke up Gilpin. I don't hear him. Do you think he is asleep again?"

"He had better be. You be quiet."

"I do not believe you suffered any pain, not like the agony you forced upon me."

"Agony? You are ignorant as that dead pear tree in the orchard. I cannot believe you did this to me."

"Why? It appears I am simply one amongst many women who have awakened you in the middle of the night, their hands and mouths all over you."

"And their breasts. But that was different and you well know it. You are an idiot, Merry."

She hit his shoulder, felt the scar. "I am not an idiot. I am simply determined not to be given over to some man I do not know. What happened to you?"

"You were Blanche, a female I know well, and you kissed me until my lust overcame my reason."

"There was no reason involved. You did not hesitate a single minute to think. No, what happened to your shoulder? That scar is quite deep. It could have killed you. What happened?"

Surely this is passing strange, he thought, and looked down at her mouth he'd kissed too many times, and wanted to kiss again. He said absently, "A Scottish madman tried to kill the king. It was my job to protect him, and so I did."

"What happened to the Scot?"

"He is rotting in Hollow's Field. It is where assassins are buried."

She touched the scar again. "It must have pained you greatly."

He shrugged, though in truth, he'd thought he would die, what with the fever that had nearly consumed him to ashes.

And now this. He had taken a maid, and not just any maid, he'd taken the Valcourt heiress. Surely a remarkable experience, but he knew there was no pot of silver waiting for him. He sighed. "You did not consider the consequences of this, Merry, you did not realize that I will pay for it?"

"No, no, you will not pay anything. I will explain everything to the king. I will tell him that you are so very honorable that I had to force you. I will tell him I want you, Garron, I admire you, not some faceless lout he would give me to. He will see that we will deal well together. I will tell him that you make lists just as the queen does, just as I do, and he will realize that you will manage Valcourt as well as my father. And he does know you and admire you already, Garron. He will understand why I want to marry you, not some stranger who could be as bad as Jason of Brennan. The king will understand."

He was still between her legs, his hands on his thighs. She stretched out her hand and laid it atop his. "My father's book of rules—I will give it to you, and you can memorize each one, mayhap add some of your own. I know you can keep Valcourt prosperous. The king will be pleased. He will praise you. You will become so rich you can give him money and soldiers and you will become as close to him as the queen."

Garron grabbed both her hands, jerked them over her head, and came down to within an inch of her nose. "Listen to me. You do not know the world, nor do you know the king. He will have me beheaded."

She knew he believed utterly what he said. "You are saying he would have beheaded Jason of Brennan if he'd managed to force me to wed him?"

He was pressing against her again, and quickly pulled back. He stared down at her flesh, and wanted to touch her again with his fingers, with his mouth. He wanted to weep. His brain stalled and he guided himself inside her.

She yelped and jerked back, struck her head against the wall, and yelped again. He didn't move, remained still. "Get used to me," he said, and realized when a man was inside a woman, his brain ceased to work. "If I am to die for taking your maidenhead, then I might as well enjoy you again. A man can only die once."

She was panting, pressing her palms against his shoulders, trying to pull away from him. "It doesn't hurt as much as before, but I do not like it, Garron. I want you to go away, but not too far away so that we would have to shout at each other. No, truly, we must talk. I will not allow the king to hurt you, I swear it. I am a great talker, I will make a list of all important points so I will not forget any, and I will present them to the king and he will welcome you as my husband."

It didn't matter that he was panting, that his eyes were nearly crossed in lust. At her words, his brain took him by the throat and shook him hard. He jerked out of her and rolled off the bed. He stood panting over her.

Merry jerked the blanket to her neck. He continued to stand over her, naked, hard, his hands fists at his sides, and stare down at her.

"I would not have forced you if I believed the king would kill you, Garron."

"Don't lie—you did not even think of the king when you planned this. And you did not force me. You merely surprised me. A man can't be forced."

She said thoughtfully, never looking at him above his waist, "Do you know, it is almost worth marrying Jason of Brennan if you swear the king would behead him. I should demand to see it done immediately, before he could do to me what you did. It was bad enough with you and I like you, but the thought of Jason of Brennan—" She shuddered. "I will save you from the king. I will think of something. That part of you is still big, Garron."

He looked down at himself and saw her blood. He had never before bedded a virgin, but he knew virgins bled and sometimes it wasn't good. He grabbed the blanket and pulled it off her. Blood was smeared on her thighs. "Do not move," he said, and fetched a wet cloth.

She grabbed the blanket to cover herself again, and came up fast, swinging her legs off the bed. "What are you going to do?"

"Bathe the blood off you. I told you to hold still." He grabbed the blanket off her and pushed her down onto her back. "For once, just be quiet." And she was so shocked when the cool wet cloth pressed against her that she couldn't have spoken if the Black Demon burst into the chamber. She squeaked.

He touched her with his fingers, and nodded. "The bleeding has stopped. That will not happen again. It is your maid's blood." He wiped himself off with the cloth, threw it on the floor, and came down beside her. She tried to sit up. He pressed her down again. "No, hold yourself still. I must think about what I should do."

"You are not a bad man, Garron. Indeed, not only are you not a bad man, you are noble, you have wealth and land. You are an earl. Surely the king would see you as an excellent husband for any heiress."

He ignored her, and she simply saw him making a list in his mind. "First, I must see the king. If I tell him I slept through a female impaling herself on me, even though I believed it the lusty Blanche, he might understand, but he will laugh at me, he will call me a fool, he will clout me, and I will have to take it."

"No, seeing the king is second on the

list. First you must wed with me, then both of us will visit the king. The queen—"

He spoke over her, his brain moving straight and forward. "I must kill Jason of Brennan. That will give me great pleasure since he very likely was responsible for poisoning Arthur. Then I must deal with your mother." He cursed again, and Merry heard more animal body parts than she'd known existed.

He said, "Do you know, it makes no sense that no one would know that Arthur had stolen such a vast amount of silver coins from Jason of Brennan. Or more likely Arthur stole the coins from Jason's father, Lord Ranulf."

"Well, Jason knew."

He leaned down and squeezed his hands around her neck. "I would strangle you but I doubt I would survive it. On the other hand, I doubt I will survive the king's punishment either, so why not?"

"You are an earl, no longer the king's guard. It will be all right." And she leaned up and kissed him.

He started cursing again. Merry couldn't help herself—she laughed.

Gilpin called out, "I hear you talking, my

lord. I hear ire in your voice. Who is there with you? Is it an enemy who has sliced upon your gullet and is watching you die?"

"Go to sleep, Gilpin!"

Why not? Merry called out, "I did not gullet him, Gilpin, I am not an enemy."

There was dead silence, then Gilpin stuttered out, "'Tis you, Merry? How can this be?"

31

Everyone always knew everything, no matter the size of the keep, and so it was ridiculous to wait to come down, but she did. When she finally slithered around the final turn of the stairs, the women who saw her stopped talking. Then conversation became louder.

No hope for it. When she stepped into the great hall, Elaine looked her full in the face and gave her a big smile. Then, one by one, the other women did as well.

They didn't mind that she'd bedded the master? Evidently not. Evidently they approved. She grinned hugely at all of them and did a little skip.

Since it was eight o'clock in the morning, all the men and soldiers had already eaten Eric the goat's cheese and Bullic's fresh brown bread and drunk ale, and gone outside to work, as she'd known, except for Sir Lyle. He sat alone at one of the new trestle tables. He didn't smile when he looked at her. And there was Gilpin, sitting in the sunlit doorway, polishing Garron's armor. She looked around the great hall, ignoring Sir Lyle. The air was sweet with lavender and honeysuckle. Lisle lightly touched her old hand to Merry's shoulder. "Come have some fresh bread and cheese. We've waited for you."

They'd waited for her? It was amazing. She felt incredibly blessed.

Women's voices filled the hall. One of the loudest was Miggins, yelling at Gilpin to stop his flirting with the new smithy's daughter, who was only fourteen and too innocent for the likes of him. He started whistling and winked at Miggins.

Merry laughed at his show until she realized—she was no longer innocent. It was a very strange feeling. She supposed she'd expected to look different somehow when she gazed at herself in the polished silver mirror, but she hadn't. She should have looked tired, but she didn't. She looked, quite simply, happy.

When she'd awakened in Garron's bed that morning, he'd been gone, but it hadn't mattered. She felt wonderful except for the soreness. Did he feel wonderful? Was he sore? She didn't know how that worked.

She wondered what he was thinking, what plans he was making. Would he still insist they go to London? Had he made a list? Would he show her his list?

None of the women said a word to her about sleeping in the master's bed the previous night. Gilpin looked at her from the corner of his eyes, and continued whistling. It was a huge relief, but she still felt embarrassed. She had given her virginity to a man who was not her husband. Surely she deserved a bit of damnation, but she didn't care. And still, Sir Lyle watched her. He drank the rest of his ale, then lazily rose from the bench and strode over to her. "I wish to speak to you."

"Short of covering my ears, I cannot stop you."

"You do not wish me to speak in front of all these women."

"Why not?"

He drew himself to his full height, not all that impressive. "I know you are not a priest's bastard. I do not know exactly who you are, but I will know soon, and I will denounce you to Lord Garron. Even though you went to his bed, he will send you away from Wareham."

She gave him a sunny smile. "I do not know exactly who you are either, Sir Lyle, but I will know soon and then Garron will know, and I'll wager he'll kill you dead."

His face darkened with rage and his hands fisted. He looked ready to strike her down. She felt a bolt of fear, but then Miggins was standing at her side. "Here's some sweet bread for ye, mistress, jest out of Bullic's clean oven. I dripped a bit of honey on top." As she spoke, Miggins slid herself between Sir Lyle and Merry.

"Thank you, Miggins." Merry took a bite of the bread. It tasted like fear. She forced herself to swallow, and smile. "It is delicious." All the women were listening now, leaning toward her. What would happen, she wondered, if Sir Lyle struck her? Would the women attack him? She saw them moving even closer.

"Miggins, how is your cough this morning?"

"Nearly gone, mistress, nearly gone. The potion ye gave me was powerful bad, it made my innards creak and groan."

"That means it's working." *I hope*. "You must drink more this morning."

"Oh aye, I'll drink yer potion. Mayhap I'll give some to Sir Lyle, mayhap it will ease his humors. Ye really should step back from the mistress."

"She's naught but the master's harlot. I would not drink anything she has brewed."

Miggins didn't move. "Ye must needs step back from the mistress, Sir Lyle."

"Aye, she's a harlot. Everyone knows he took her to his bed last night."

Miggins smiled with her three remaining teeth. "I begin to question yer brains, sirrah. Step back else ye might find yerself on yer back with all our heels digging into yer chest."

He looked around at the sound of the

women's angry voices. He said over Miggins's head, "This flock of vultures would not dare to touch me."

Merry said, "Do you wish to wager your life on that, Sir Lyle? Look, Talia has a stout broom in her hands and Elaine is holding a chamber pot. Tell me, are you here for Arthur's silver coins? How did you hear of it? Come, tell me, who told you about the silver?"

"'Tis you who are here for no good. 'Tis you who wish Lord Garron ill." He spat on the reeds near her right foot, wheeled about, and walked straight into Garron.

"Sir Lyle, is something wrong?"

"Nay, my lord. I was on my way to meet with my men on the practice field."

"Not this morning. We will leave within the hour for London. Bring two of your men with you."

Sir Lyle merely nodded and strode out of the great hall.

"Merry! Come here!"

He looked windblown, irritated, and she was so glad to see him she skipped up to him, not difficult since Lady Anne's gown was so short, whistling like Gilpin. She gave him a dazzling smile. "Good morning, Garron. I trust you slept well?"

He paused a moment at that smile. It was as beautiful as it was wicked. He automatically searched out the three small braids hidden in her hair. He found only two. Was that the third, nearly hidden beneath that thick plait? He raised his hand to search it out, got hold of himself, and lowered his hand back to his side. "I did not get to sleep all that much," he said.

"Mayhap I should make both of us a sleeping potion of passion flower and woodruff, valerian too, I believe, since, like you, I did not sleep all that much either. But the truth is, my lord, when I did sleep, I nestled with the angels." She tapped her chin. "Hmmm, I must see if such a potion is an infusion or a decoction."

"You nestled with the Devil, more like." He'd held her tightly against his chest until he'd awakened early that morning to the awful realization that his world had changed irrevocably and all because of this girl with her clever braids and beautiful smile. And her lists.

"The Devil, you say?" She arched an eyebrow and grinned shamelessly up at him.

"It seems Gilpin believed me to have an enemy in my chamber."

"Do you think so? You did yell, that is—"

"Be quiet."

"If so, the enemy seems to have laid you low."

He wanted to laugh, but wasn't about to. "Get yourself ready. We go to London to see the king. I would prefer to leave you here but I dare not. You might find Arthur's silver coins and flee to Scotland."

She lowered her voice to a whisper since every ear in the great hall was listening. "I will do just as you say. But surely, do you not think we should wed first? Then everything will be quite clear for the king."

He spoke over her. "You will do as you're told, do you understand me? You will keep your tongue behind your teeth. This is between me and the king. You will not interfere."

"Let us wed first, Garron."

"No. Besides, there is no priest here to

wed us. Your sainted father was killed in the Retribution, do you not remember?"

She ignored his sarcasm because her future was at stake and she couldn't back down. "Where does one find a priest?"

Miggins called out, "Worthward Abbey is not all that far distant, there are many priests there, praying endlessly on their scarred knees, I doubt not, the poor sots."

"Excellent, we can be wed before nightfall."

"No. Be quiet. Get yourself prepared."

She didn't like it. What was he planning to say to the king? How would he talk him around? She saw he was waiting for her to open her mouth, probably to blight her, and so she kept quiet. She was ready to beg the king on her knees to allow her to wed Garron. She was ready to spice up her offer with Arthur's vast cache of silver coins as soon as she found it, if only he would bless their union and leave Garron's head attached to his neck. Everything would be all right.

He cupped her chin in his palm and forced her face up and said low, his mouth not an inch from hers, his breath warm on her cheek, "You got what you wanted, but it wasn't at all pleasant for you. Was it worth such a sacrifice?" He wasn't about to tell her he'd felt like he'd flown off the earth and lazed around in the clouds. Even though this girl was half his size, she was dangerous. And an heiress. "Well, was it?"

She nodded. He tightened his hold on her chin. "I do not trust you. What are you planning now? You will not make a list of arguments to present to the king, do you understand me?"

"Of course I understand you, your whisper is as loud as a yell. You do realize that everyone knows I am no longer a maid. Sir Lyle called me your harlot."

"He would not dare. You made that up because you don't like him."

She shrugged. "Ask Miggins."

"Miggins as well as every other cursed female in Wareham would lie instantly for you."

That was probably true even though she had no idea why. After all, she made them work until they could scarce stand straight at the end of the day.

"I wonder if everyone realizes it was

you who came to me, that I wasn't the rutting stoat to take your valuable virginity?"

"To ensure your continued excellent reputation, I will tell them it was I who took you."

"Damn you, don't make me sound like a puling little lad."

She looked at him thoughtfully for a moment. "Do you know, I have wondered what would have happened had you not believed I was this cow, Blanche. Would you have continued to snore through the night rather than grab me?"

"It is quite possible, since you had no idea what to do. Why do you call her a cow? You did last night as well."

"You said she was bountiful, more than enough for six men's hands."

"I did not say that."

She nodded. "Well, mayhap not precisely that, but all that bounty makes her a cow. I know what to do now. I know everything." And she preened, she actually preened.

He snorted. "You are still as ignorant as Eric the goat."

She said over him, "When I see Blanche the cow, I will thank her for training you."

Garron nearly exploded.

She patted his arm and leaned in close. "Everyone is listening. Garron, I don't want you to worry. I have no need to write out my list, I have already memorized all my excellent points."

"If you do not shut your mouth, I will pull up your gown and smack your white bottom, with everyone looking on, do you hear me, Merry?"

It was on the tip of her tongue to ask him if he liked her white bottom since he'd kept his hands on her bottom a great deal of the previous night, but she saw he looked ready to carry out his threat. "Aye, I hear you. I must fetch us food. How long will our journey be?"

"Three days, no more, unless it rains, then it will still require three days but we will be miserable."

She laughed and skipped away. She did not need three days to perfect her strategy because she already knew she had the most powerful ally in the realm on her side—the Queen of England.

"Miggins!"

The old woman sidled up to him. "Aye, my beautiful boy?"

Garron looked down at that ancient face. "Did Merry's infusion work? How is your cough?"

The old woman cackled. "As dead and gone as the precious maidenhead of my sweet mistress."

32

LONDON
THE WHITE TOWER

The king, Garron was told by Baron Cotswolt, was in Cornwall, visiting his uncle, the Duke of Cornwall. Robert Burnell was with him. No, the queen had not accompanied him.

Merry raised her eyes to the vaulted ceiling and thanked God for granting her fervent prayer. Before Garron could haul her off to Cornwall, Merry asked Baron Cotswolt if Queen Eleanor would see them.

Baron Cotswolt could not think of any reason to deny her, and thus he led the way to the queen's apartments.

When Baron Cotswolt kept Garron back to question him about the Black Demon, Garron sent her a look that threatened death or dismemberment. In return, she gave him a sweet smile that made his belly curdle, and hurried into the queen's solar. She saw the queen was nursing a babe, no surprise since it seemed to her that the queen was always nursing a new babe. She was sitting in a warm splash of sunlight, silk pillows stacked around her, humming a song Merry had written for her.

Alice of Kent met Merry at the door, eyebrows raised over beautiful green eyes. "I cannot believe it is really you. You swore you would never return. At least you are no longer a scruffy child. You have grown up well, Merry. I rather thought you would. I hear you traveled here with Garron of Kersey. It will be lovely to see him again. Tell me, how did this come about?"

How could she possibly know all this so quickly? "How very nice to see you again, Alice." Merry was looking around for Blanche, and there she was, Merry was sure of it, her gown cut low, her mighty breasts on display, smiling at something one of the other ladies said. She was indeed bountiful. Best be sure. "Alice, who is that lady yon? She was not here when I was."

"That is Blanche of Howarth."

The woman looked toward Merry, called to Alice, "And just who is this, Alice? Do not say it is the girl who accompanied Garron here."

Queen Eleanor called out, "Merry? Is it you, child? Welcome. Come here and meet my newest daughter, little Blanche. She is the image of my dear lord. Would you look at all the golden hair and blue eyes, and a nose that will doubtless become long and thin, just like her father's?"

As the queen extended her soft white hand, Merry was afraid that hers were rough. "She is the most beautiful babe I have ever seen, my lady."

Eleanor laughed, released her hand, and patted her cheek. "Of course, she is. All Plantagenet babes are beautiful. She is also hungry, always she is hungry." As she spoke, the queen looked down at her daughter frantically suckling at her breast, dropped a kiss on the babe's forehead, and looked back up at Merry. "You have grown taller. Goodness, you are taller than any of my ladies. Take off your wimple and show me your beautiful hair. Ah, such a lovely red and as glorious as ever. I like the plaits, they suit you. Ladies! Come and greet Merry."

Six ladies dutifully arranged themselves around the queen and greeted Merry courteously. They smiled, noted her too-short, out-of-date gown, the ugly old slippers, and wondered what she was doing here, and with Garron of Kersey.

As suddenly as the queen had called them over and introduced them to Merry, she dismissed them. When the six ladies were out of hearing, the queen cleared her throat, put her babe to her other breast, covered her golden head. "I have heard several of my ladies speak of Garron of Kersey with a great deal of affection. Why are you here with him?"

"I had forgot how quickly news spreads here at court."

"Gossip flows more quickly than my lord's fine wine down our barons' gullets."

"Still, we only just arrived, and Baron Cotswolt brought us directly here."

"One of the pages recognized both you and Lord Garron and immediately came to tell Blanche. The pages tell Blanche everything because she gives them sweetmeats."

So Blanche of the huge breasts passed out bribes. That was smart of her and Merry hated her all the more for it. Merry looked at the queen's lovely face. There was so much to tell her—*My father died, my mother sold me to Jason of Brennan, and I escaped only to be kidnapped and Garron saved me*—

She felt tears sting her eyes. She slipped to her knees and rested her cheek on the queen's knee. "So much has happened, my lady."

Eleanor stroked Merry's hair, fingered the fat plaits, and saw a grown lady, not a girl. "What is it, Merry?"

She whispered, "I wish to wed him, my lady. We seek the king's blessing, but he is not here to give it, and I am afraid Garron will insist on searching him out in Cornwall, and the king will not give his permission and instead he will order Garron to have his head cut off because I am an heiress and no longer a maid and it is Garron who is responsible, only it was I who seduced him, I swear it. He is good and honorable."

Merry looked up when Garron ran into the queen's solar, Baron Cotswolt on his heels, three guards clanking in their wake. He saw the gaggle of beautifully gowned ladies staring at him, but it didn't matter, his eyes were on Merry, who was sitting on a huge silk pillow on the floor beside the queen. He stopped dead in his tracks. "Merry! I did not hear what you said, but shut your mouth!"

He suddenly became aware that the queen's hand was stroking Merry's hair and she was suckling a babe. "Ah, I bid you good health, my lady." He gave her a beautiful formal bow even as he gnashed his teeth. "Forgive me for intruding, but—"

Eleanor interrupted him, her voice soft and pleasant, "Baron Cotswolt, do not be alarmed. As you know, Garron of Kersey was the king's own guard for three years. He is well known to me. You may leave him here without fear for my person," and she dismissed him with a regal nod.

The baron managed not to stare at the queen as she covered her babe's head and her white breast with a pale blue silk shawl. He frowned toward Merry, nodded to Garron, and unwillingly took himself out of the solar.

When the thick door finally closed, Garron realized he didn't know what to do. He saw Blanche and two other ladies he'd bedded, Alice and Mathilda, all three of them staring at him like he was a meaty bone. He would swear in that moment the stones shifted beneath his booted feet, and he knew there was a deep, deep pit beneath those stones, maybe even Hell. Merry was still curled up on the floor next to the queen, not moving, just staring at him. By all the saints' long-suffering mothers, what had she said to the queen? Had he heard the word "seduce"? *He was a dead man*. He remembered Burnell's talk of the executioner and his unfortunate eyesight, and swallowed.

No, he wasn't going to have his head chopped off, not if he did this properly. But he had planned all his arguments for the king—practical reasons, sound reasons, all of those reasons to benefit the king's coffers, and he'd had only minutes to change the nature of his explanations for the queen's delicate ears. He looked at her and saw softness, a lovely gown, and shining hair, and felt like a mongrel caught digging in a bed of roses.

He could but try.

He gave her another bow. "My lady, pray forgive my intrusion." He pointed to Merry. "I hope this one here has told you she is in my care."

"Actually, my lord, she did not tell me that."

"She is in my care, my lady. Ah, what did she say to you?"

The queen laughed. "It seems you are wanted as a husband, Garron of Kersey. What say you?"

He'd only been a moment behind her, well, maybe several moments, and yet she'd managed to get that out so quickly? *What to say?* He cleared his throat and plowed forward. "My lady, I know well it is the king's prerogative to select this one's husband since her father is dead and she has the gall to be a damned heiress and thus men kidnapped her, and I know that I cannot simply wed her." He faltered.

"I pray you be seated, Garron. You are so tall my neck is creaking. Vivien, bring my lord a chair."

The chair weighed more than Vivien did, and so Garron fetched the chair himself. Once he was seated, Blanche of Howarth moved to stand beside him. She placed a proprietary white hand lightly on his shoulder.

Garron was appalled. What was she doing? Didn't she realize Merry was like as not to stick a knife in her ribs? He saw Merry looking from his face to Blanche's hand, her eyes narrowing, and he knew she was wishing for that knife. He wanted to tell Blanche to take three steps away from him, for her own safety. He cleared his throat.

"Wine for our visitor, Mathilda," the queen said.

Mathilda of Matthis poured him a glass of ruby red Aquitaine wine, from Graelam de Moreton. The queen said comfortably as he tasted the wine, "You know Graelam, do you not, my lord?"

"Aye, I know him well. I nearly broke

my neck two years ago when I tried to ride his destrier on a wager. I was doing well until Graelam whistled. The brute threw me into a mess of thorn bushes, the destrier, not Graelam. He was laughing too hard to do anything."

The queen laughed as well. "As Baron Cotswolt told you, my lord, the king is visiting his uncle in Cornwall. A messenger arrived yesterday with a letter from him. He wrote that Graelam and Kassia are in residence, as well as his daughter, Philippa, and her husband, Dienwald de Fortenberry, and their children. The castle is evidently trembling with all the noise. I could tell he wished I was there with our children as well."

Blanche smiled toward Garron. "I remember picking thorns out of you, Garron. There were thorns everywhere."

I'm going to Hell. There is Satan with his arms open ready to receive me.

Merry rose slowly to her feet, her eyes never leaving Blanche's face. "When Garron and I are wed, I will pull all the thorns out of his hide. No one else. You will remove your hand from my betrothed's shoulder or I will prepare a decoction to turn your face blue. I am very nearly a healer."

There wasn't a single breath drawn for a good three seconds.

The queen finally said, "Aye, Blanche, Lord Garron is shortly to belong to another lady. I do not believe your husband would like to have you returned to him with your lovely face blue. Dark blue or light blue, Merry?"

"Well," Merry said, "mayhap she would become a blue cow. The decoction I'm thinking about isn't always predictable."

Blanche's hand bunched into a fist before she finally lifted it from his shoulder.

The queen said, "Do you know, ladies, I have kept thorns out of my own lord's perfect self for years upon years now. It is a wife's duty."

The ladies laughed politely.

The queen said, "I see no reason for you and Merry not to be wed, Lord Garron. You are no longer the king's guard, you are an earl. You now have wealth and rank. You will simply add more wealth and another title. My lord will ensure you will govern both Valcourt and Wareham wisely. Merry, I give you and Lord Garron of Kersey permission to wed. Indeed, I will see to it myself. My lord wrote he would be home within a sennight. It will be done then, unless, naturally, you have committed some foul deed, Lord Garron, then I do not know what will happen to you."

"He is too noble, too kind, to commit any foul deed, my lady."

The queen laughed. "I jest, Merry, please do not faint."

It was too easy, Garron thought, simply too easy. When the king returned, he would look at Garron and denounce him for a worthless upstart. Garron rubbed his neck.

33

LONDON

I will wed him tomorrow. I will make a list of good deeds, and I swear I will do all of them.

She was going to wed him. She wanted to shout it from every rooftop in London, though there probably weren't very many of the incredible number of inhabitants in this mud-soaked filthy city who would know or care.

Merry was wearing one of Vivien's gowns, long in the torso with sleeves that came to a point below her hands and a braided golden belt that fit snugly around her hips. The gown reached the floor, something that made her smile since she'd become used to Lady Anne's too-short skirts. She knew Eleanor had sent a message to Valcourt to have all her belongings sent here to court. Her maid, Ella, would accompany the belongings. She missed the woman who'd raised her from a babe. From her earliest memories, it was Ella's face she saw—

"You are daydreaming, Merry. Just look at your stitches." Vivien of Leicester laughed as she pointed to the four crooked stitches on the soft silk cloth. The queen, seeing that peace reigned, left her ladies to gossip and sew to speak to a courtier, and so Vivien poked Merry lightly in the ribs. "You are seeing your lord naked, are you not? Seeing him come over you and—" Vivien gave a delighted shudder.

The ladies snickered and leaned in close.

Alice of Kent said with great practicality, "She is not a maid, Vivien, so she knows what he will do."

"He must have done it very well since

she dreams away the afternoon," said Mathilda of Matthis. She paused a moment, frowned into the distance. "Although I cannot recall Garron ever doing such things badly." She turned to Merry. "I trust you were a virgin?"

Merry blinked. *Mathilda of Matthis? She and Garron?*

"How many times did he take you, Merry? I know he has great stamina."

Goodness, he would do that more than once? Merry smiled at all of them indiscriminately. She'd forgotten that absolutely nothing was left unsaid even amongst the ladies, and it had embarrassed her horribly before. But not now. "I was indeed a virgin," she said easily. She paused a moment, her head cocked to the side. "I had not expected him to be so very big."

There was silence, then bursts of laughter.

"Ah, that is the truth." Alice patted her knee and gave her a sloe-eyed look that put Merry on the alert. "Lord Garron is well fashioned, several of us already know that well, do we not?" She gave a tinkling laugh. "But never mind that. Tell us, Merry, was he careful with you since you were an innocent? Or was he a bull?"

"He was a bull." *Alice of Kent?* Did the man never sleep?

Blanche said smoothly, "How odd that he did not go easily with you. Mayhap he did not believe you were a virgin, thus his, ah, enthusiasm."

Merry looked at Blanche's white throat, wondering if her hands were large enough to squeeze the life out of the cow.

Alice said, her voice matter-of-fact, "You bring him great wealth. It is a good union." She paused a moment, frowned. "We were told of the Black Demon and how he devastated Wareham and his men raped all the maids. Indeed, we helped the queen make a list of all Lord Garron would need at Wareham."

"Everything the queen sent was used, thank you all."

"But how—"

Merry said, "It isn't important." She shrugged. "I merely tried to fix every-thing."

Blanche laughed. "You, fix everything? How is this possible?"

Before she could answer, Alice added, "Come, tell us how you came to be with Lord Garron. Did he visit Valcourt before your father died? Did you sneak away with him? Tell us why you were with him."

Merry shook her head, but kept a smile firmly in place. "Garron wishes this to remain our secret."

"By all the Devil's cloven hooves, why?"

Merry gazed at Mathilda of Matthis, saw the avid curiosity in her dark eyes, and shook her head again. "Why do we not speak of my new wedding gown?"

Luckily, at that moment, the queen returned, so the ladies were forced to speak of the gown the queen herself was directing made for Merry, her wedding gift to the couple.

When Gilpin fetched Merry an hour later, Blanche insisted upon accompanying her back to her chamber. She walked beside her down the long corridor. Merry heard Gilpin speaking to someone behind her. The corridor was filled with soldiers, guards, ladies, servants, courtiers—all of them talking. Merry shivered. Weren't they cold? The beautiful line of thick wool tapestries covering the walls didn't keep the cold from leaching through the stone, even in deep midsummer. "What do you want, Blanche?"

Blanche looked to see that Gilpin was at least ten paces behind them, flirting with Mathilda's maidservant. "He marries you because he has no choice. You removed all his choice when you whined to the queen."

"Don't be a dolt, Blanche. Think of all the wealth I bring him."

"But he does not like you, that was quite clear to everyone. He thinks you a silly little girl with naught but dreams of daffodils in her head."

"Daffodils? They're very pretty, are they not?"

"Don't you try to distract me. You and your ignorance and your wicked red hair—how could any man admire you if you didn't bring more coffers of silver with you than the King of France?"

"I don't believe there will be any silver. Valcourt's wealth lies in its prosperous land."

"What do you know of anything?"

"I know about Arthur's silver. I plan to find it and give it to Garron as my wedding present to him."

"Silver? What silver? Who is Arthur?" Blanche's voice, once filled with scorn, was now filled with reluctant interest. She pulled Merry to a halt, her fingers tight around Merry's wrist. She shook her. "What silver?"

"Garron's older brother Arthur had a stash of silver coins. The Black Demon attacked Wareham to find it. He failed."

Blanche shook her head. "Doubtless one of your silly tales. You are good at distracting people, but now I wish to speak of Garron. Surely he does not like your wicked hair and those stupid little braids. The braids make you look plain."

Merry remembered a priest who had crossed himself when he'd seen her and muttered about the Devil. How could hair be wicked? Why would the Devil care?

Blanche leaned close. "Indeed, why would Garron want someone as ugly as you are? If you had a single wit in your head, you would know he wants me. That is what he told me last night."

Why don't I have a damned knife? "You

should not tell falsehoods that are so easily disproved, Blanche."

Blanche had the gall to laugh in her face. "I refused to bed with him again, you witless girl. But that is what he told me, his voice all low and hungry. You will never have the man, not the man I have known. You will have only the man who marries the heiress who will doubtless beat you if he has a brain in his head for you surely deserve it. You never shut your mouth."

"I have a question for you, Blanche. Why would you care? You have your own husband."

"Aye, I do, but he is so old, he has no more teeth in his mouth. Can you imagine a man trying to gum you?" She shuddered.

"No, I cannot. So that is why you spend so much time at court?"

"Of course. He is so old all he does is cackle over his porridge. Ah, but Garron, he has a mouth full of white teeth. He smells good, he tastes good. Last night, he was humming a song he said you wrote whilst he was kissing my neck," and she walked away, smoothing her beautiful blue silk gown, her laughter sounding behind her.

Garron nuzzled that cow's neck? She would wager Arthur's silver he hadn't done that. Garron was the kind of man who worked alongside his people until it was too dark to see. He was fair-minded, he would be a fine master for Valcourt. Did he not make lists? Good lists? And what did that say about the man? *He kissed the cow's neck whilst singing one of my songs?*

She did not see Garron that evening because he and the king were continuing discussions on the marriage contract— rather, she suspected, the king was dictating to Garron what he wanted and Garron was trying to salvage what he could without disagreeing overly since he did not want to lose his head for an impertinence the king would decide not to forgive. Merry suspected it weighed in Garron's favor that the king knew him to be an honest man, and when he added a wife, he could expect an heir. Continuity was important to the king.

All the contracts would be completed

by the morrow, before the Bishop of London wedded them. They would bind Valcourt and Wareham together. Both holdings would flourish. She imagined her son would take charge of Valcourt when he was old enough. *Her son.* She touched her hand to her belly. Could it be possible that she already carried a babe?

Since she didn't want any more embarrassing questions from the queen's ladies, she went to her small chamber and snuggled down into the soft feather mattress, pulling the covers to her chin. *Tomorrow*, she thought, tomorrow she would become a wife, Garron's wife.

Maybe, before they left London, she would have a chance to smack Blanche's white face.

Her last thought before she fell asleep was of her mother and what she would do when she discovered her chick had married a man of her own choosing.

Her mother stood over her, her incredible golden hair untouched by gray, just as her face was untouched by lines. "What a little adventuress you are, so resource-

ful. But no more. You will now do as you're told." There was no expression on her face as she spoke, but oddly, her eyes seemed to burn, red and hot, and suddenly her own eyes were burning and it hurt and—

Merry jerked up, coughing and gagging as the bitter smell filled her nostrils. She was shoved back down and a rough cloth was stuffed into her mouth.

She fought like a wild woman, sending her fists into soft flesh, kicking with her feet. She heard a grunt and a cry of pain. A fist struck her jaw. Still she fought, but she couldn't seem to control her hands or her feet. She felt slow and clumsy. She felt a strange numbing sensation sweep through her. Finally, she fell back into silence and blackness.

34

Garron awoke to soft hands stroking down his belly. "Merry, nay, you must stop. You shouldn't be here."

The hands closed around him and he lurched up, grabbing for her hands. "Merry? No, we must wait. We will wed on the morrow. Go back to your chamber."

"One last time." Her hair curtained her face as she leaned down and kissed his belly.

She was kissing him? Where had she learned that? "Merry?" The kisses continued downward. In near pain now, Garron grabbed her hair, and immediately came wide awake. It wasn't Merry's hair. He jerked up and swung his legs over the side of the bed.

"Garron, come back."

The room was dark. He grabbed the honey-scented taper and walked to the fireplace. He went down on his haunches on the hearth to press the wick to the still glowing embers. He raised the lit candle and looked at Blanche's face. She was smiling at him, her eyes bright, her skin flushed, her dark hair spilling about her face and shoulders. He realized he was naked. That wasn't good at all. He set the taper on the chest at the foot of the bed, grabbed the blanket from the bed, and wrapped it around himself.

She laughed. "There is no reason to cover yourself. I have seen you, Garron, all of you, many times, felt you and kissed you. Do you not remember how you always moaned into my mouth?"

"Whatever I remember, it makes no difference now. I am to be wed on the morrow, with the king's blessing and in his presence. Do you really believe I would want to bed another woman?"

"Why not? No one will know." Blanche

shrugged. She was wearing a bedgown that looked like a spiderweb, pale and soft, and he could clearly see her breasts. She said deliberately, "You are not yet hers."

He shook himself. *Hers?* "What do you mean? A man remains a man while a woman becomes the man's possession."

What a ridiculous thing to say. On the other hand, she had baited him. Blanche pulled her bedgown slowly up over her head, let it pool at her feet, let him look his fill. If she wasn't mistaken, she'd frozen him to the spot. He looked to be in pain, yet he didn't move. He quickly turned his back to her. She wanted to clout him. Instead, she managed a laugh, picked up her gown, and pulled it back over her head, letting it settle light as a butterfly's wing against her skin. "Garron, I have no wish to wed you and become a possession, let that arrogant little girl wear your yoke. All I wish to do is enjoy your body one last time."

"No, I cannot. I will not."

"All right. But you know, Garron, when next you visit the king, you will doubtless be bored with her. Then we will see if I still want you. Come, what is wrong with that?"

Wrong. Something was very wrong. Oh God, it was Merry. She was screaming, screaming. He ran from his chamber, holding the blanket around his waist with one hand and the lit taper in the other. He kicked Gilpin in the side with one bare foot, leaped over him. "*À moi*. Now!" The stone floor beneath his feet felt like ice, but he paid no attention, ran faster. Gilpin was soon behind him, running as fast as he could, not knowing what was happening. "My lord, what is the matter? Why are we running?"

"It's Merry," Garron shouted. "Something is wrong with Merry."

Gilpin heard a laugh behind him and turned to see Lady Blanche of Howarth, her gown flowing around her, waving a white hand as she quietly closed Garron's bedchamber door behind her and turned to walk away in the opposite direction.

That wasn't right, Gilpin thought as he tried to catch his master. What had happened? How could his master know something was wrong with Merry?

It seemed an eon passed before Garron

pounded on Merry's door. There was no answer. He didn't hesitate, and slammed the door open. He raised his taper high, saw her narrow bed was empty, a blanket hanging off the side onto the floor.

"No," he said, "no, this isn't possible. Gilpin, get yourself dressed and fetch Whalen, the captain of the guard. Tell him Marianna de Luce de Mornay of Valcourt is gone, kidnapped. Hurry!"

Gilpin, ashen-faced, ran as fast as he could.

Within ten minutes, Whalen was sending out his guards to search the White Tower.

The king didn't want to leave his fine dream. The ground around him was strewn with the bodies of warriors he himself had slain, his tunic soaked with their blood. He was faster than the wind, stronger than his prized destrier, so skilled he needed no soldiers to assist him. He was smiling because he'd won, he'd saved England— he heard a man's voice in the antechamber, it was too loud. He'd take his sword to the lout, he'd—

"Garron! What is wrong?" The queen's voice.

Garron didn't even see she was suckling her baby. "It's Merry, my lady, she is gone, taken. My lord, you must awaken, you must."

"No," the king said, "surely there are more villains for me to dispatch. Will you be quiet?"

"My lord," Eleanor said, lightly touching his shoulder, "these villains are here. Garron needs you. Merry is gone."

The king lurched up in bed. "What did you say, Eleanor? Merry is gone? What nonsense is this? Who would take her? Why did she run away?"

"Nay, sire, she didn't run away. Someone took her." Garron stood in the doorway, fully dressed, his sword in his hand, his eyes wild. "Whalen and his soldiers are searching for her. I don't understand it—who could have taken her?"

The king was known to move very quickly, both his body and his brain, and so he did. "Was it her mother or Jason of Brennan?"

"Either, both, I don't know yet."

"One of the louts fell asleep. Whalen will discover who it was." He paused a moment. "You told me her mother, Abbess Helen of Meizerling, is reputed to be a witch. Do you think she spirited her away, somehow removed the guards' memories?"

"I don't believe witchcraft had anything to do with it. I smelled something sweet in her chamber, a drug of some sort."

Two of the king's servants bolted into the chamber, panting, one of them pulling a short tunic over his head, the other holding clothes for the king. Within moments, Edward was striding into the antechamber. "You were not in her bed with her, were you?"

"I was not." He thought of Blanche, and for an instant, he wondered if she'd known what was happening, if she'd been sent to distract him.

"Then how did you know something happened to her?"

Garron drew up, felt his heart begin to pound. He said slowly, "I don't know how I knew. Really, I do not, it's just that suddenly, from one moment to the next, I knew something was wrong, knew it to my heels. I got to her chamber as quickly as I could but she was already gone. They cannot have gotten far."

Burnell had slipped into the antechamber, wearing a bedrobe as black as a sinner's heart, a black scarf wrapped around his neck. He was frowning, shaking his head. "What you said, my lord, it makes no sense. You must have been dreaming, and it awakened you. You said you simply knew something was wrong? Surely not. Ah, were you dreaming about her?"

"I wasn't asleep, I was wide awake."

Burnell clasped Garron's arm. "Are you ill to be awake in the middle of the night?"

"I was not ill. I was simply awake. I have only six men with me. If her mother has taken her, know, sire, that she has her own private army. I wish to borrow some men, and ride immediately to Meizerling."

"Would her mother take her that far? That is a full day's journey from London." And the king was frowning toward the doorway where the queen stood, holding the babe in her arms, rocking her. She said, "If her mother took her, surely she would expect you would immediately think of Meizerling Abbey. Would she not hide her elsewhere? I would, were I she."

The queen was right. "All right, then I must go to Jason of Brennan's holding. But I do not know where it is."

Burnell said, "I remember some two years ago, Jason of Brennan's father, Lord Ranulf, gave him a small keep called Swaines. It is but a half-day's ride from London."

Garron nodded to Burnell. "If Jason took her there, I know I will find her mother there as well. I have no doubt the two of them decided together to kidnap her."

The king looked amazed. "And they decided to kidnap her out of the White Tower? Out of her bedchamber in the White Tower? That is indeed a great show of audacity."

Burnell said, "Indeed, sire, it demonstrates a great gall. Now, Garron, you know very well that if he has her at Swaines, he will wed her the moment he can drag her in front of a priest. Then he will bed her without delay. I fear it will be done before you can get there."

"No," Garron said. "You do not know Merry like I do. She knows I will come after her. Somehow she will stop him, at least delay him. I would not be surprised if she killed him."

"Your regard for her blinds you, Garron," Burnell said. "She is but a girl, no guile at all, no skills, no ability to hold off a man."

"Do you not remember how she brought down that man who was holding a knife to her neck?"

Burnell, if Garron wasn't mistaken, muttered a very small curse beneath his breath.

The king said, "But surely Jason of Brennan knows I have given her to you, Garron. Is he that great a fool, that mad, to run afoul of me?"

Burnell said, "He doubtless believes once the deed is accomplished you will have no choice but to accept him, sire."

The king grunted. "I doubt not he would agree to give me more than you did, Garron, if I agreed to leave his head attached to his neck." Then the king laughed, punched Garron on the arm. "Go find your maid, my lord. I only hope you find her untouched. Tell Whalen he and ten of his men are to accompany you."

"And I, my lord," Sir Lyle said from the doorway. He was dressed, his sword strapped at his side, his cloak over one arm.

But Garron knew the king would be loath to kill Jason of Brennan if he had already wedded and bedded Merry. He came from an influential family: his father, Lord Ranulf, was long known by the king, one of his most powerful allies.

"It matters not what has happened, sire, I still plan to kill him. Do not forget, he murdered my brother, he sacked Wareham, and killed many innocent people. If he has taken Merry, if he has harmed her, even forced her to wed him, he is still just as dead." In that moment, he pictured Merry studying a scrap of parchment, a thoughtful expression on her face as she detailed another item to her list of what should be done to Wareham. She was smart. "I know her. Somehow, she will stop him."

When Garron was gone, the king turned to Burnell. "I do wonder how he knew Merry was in trouble."

"Men are known for their intuition, sire. Yours, I vow, is the mightiest intuition in the realm."

"Your bedrobe is unbelted, Robbie. I can see your hairy knees."

35

Merry smelled rotten eggs and gagged. She slowly opened her eyes, and wished she hadn't. The room was spinning around her. She quickly shut her eyes again.

The smell of rotten eggs floated by her nose once more, and she heard her mother's voice, brisk, impatient, cold as an ice floe, "Wake up, Marianna. It's past time."

Merry licked her dry lips. "That smell is horrible."

"You will accustom yourself to it soon enough. Open your eyes and sit up. You have been asleep for a very long time.

I was growing worried that my favorite sleeping potion was too strong for you."

Merry sat up, felt a wave of dizziness, and tried to swallow the bile rising in her throat, but she couldn't keep it down. She lurched up and vomited in the basin her mother held in her hands.

She couldn't stop. Her belly convulsed and cramped and she heaved and shuddered until there was naught else to come up, and still she couldn't stop heaving. Her stomach felt like it was grinding itself to pieces.

"Drink this."

Merry could only shake her head and heave again over the chamber pot. She wished for that awful numbing sensation, for her belly was on fire, the cramping so bad she knew she was dying.

Her mother grabbed her braids and pulled her head back. She poured the liquid down her throat, then held her mouth shut with her hands.

She gagged but swallowed. The taste was as horrible as the potion she'd brewed for Miggins's cough. "I'm dying, poisoned by my own mother. Surely, madam, that is very wrong and God will punish you.

Not to mention that my betrothed will gladly stick his sword into your heart." She swallowed and swallowed again. The liquid burned a trail down her throat all the way to her belly. The burning expanded until all of her was suffocating from the inside out. She couldn't breathe, couldn't suck in any air. This was death, she thought. She felt her mother release her and push her back against the pillow. She waited for death, for there was naught else she could do. She didn't want to believe it, but then her belly began to calm. The fire lessened and grew distant from her, but still, she didn't move, even when her mother lightly slapped her face. She waited for the death cramps to return, the awful gagging. But nothing happened. She opened her eyes. Her mother was carrying the chamber pot to the door of the small chamber. "Glenis, come empty this."

Merry thought she saw the outline of a young girl, gowned all in white, from her white slippers to a wimple so large it hid her entire face. Her mother spoke, but she couldn't understand her words. The girl spoke, did she sound upset, even angry?

Why was that? But then the door closed and her mother returned. She looked down at Merry, frowned, and walked to the far side of the room. Merry watched her pull back the fox skin that covered the window. Cool air poured into the room. She sucked in the clean, sweet night air, thinking about nothing else but drawing in the pure air coming into her mouth.

Even though her belly no longer cramped, she continued to rub her palms over herself. *I'm not dying, I'm not dying. She doesn't want to kill me, she wants me alive so she can sell me.* Finally, she could think clearly, and remember. When had they taken her? Not much later than midnight, surely. So, they had brought her directly to Meizerling, to her mother, but how was that possible? Meizerling Abbey was at least a day's ride from London, and it was still night. Had she been unconscious longer than a day? No, she didn't think so. She wasn't at Meizerling, she was somewhere else, and that meant no one would know where to search for her.

Or Jason of Brennan was in the next room. That made more sense.

Wherever they'd brought her, she knew she was on her own.

Merry breathed slowly, lightly, continued to lightly rub her belly, still afraid of the cramps and the horrible heaving to return, but there was nothing but calm, thank St. Cuthbert's tonsured head.

"Thank you," she said, but didn't look at her mother, rather down at her night robe, then at her own bare feet, and she realized she was very cold. She sat up, her back against a soft headboard, and tucked her feet under her and pulled the blanket around herself.

"How long was I unconscious?"

"Nearly six hours."

"Then of course I am not at Meizerling." She hadn't realized she'd spoken aloud until her mother said, "No. You are in a special place of mine, a retreat of sorts where I may study and hone my skills without fear of interruption."

"Where is Jason of Brennan? Is that murdering worm in the next room, waiting with a priest?"

Her mother laughed. "I would imagine at this moment, your future husband is trying his best to find Arthur's silver coins."

"If he finds Arthur's silver, then why would he want to wed with me?"

"Don't be stupid. He gives me the silver and I give him you and Valcourt. He kept muttering about his father, Lord Ranulf, but how could Ranulf know what is happening? Is the silver really his? I don't know, but I suppose so, since where would Jason get that kind of wealth? In any case, once I have the silver, then it will be too late."

Merry said, "Jason will not get himself into Wareham again. Aleric is on the alert, all are on the alert. There is no way for him to sneak in, much less search for the silver coins."

Her mother waved away her words, her smooth white hand graceful as it cut through the air. She actually laughed. "I am certain all the people at Wareham will welcome a tinker with laden mules."

A tinker? By St. Mildred's croaking voice, they would let a tinker in, gladly; she knew she would were she at Wareham. "What a clever idea."

"Thank you."

"Even so, what can one man do? Wareham is a vast keep. It makes no sense, unless Jason has somehow found out where the hiding place is?"

"He told me he did. Who confessed the hiding place to him? I do not know. He only smiled and refused to tell me. Ah, what a blow it was that Arthur died before he could tell Jason where he'd hidden the silver. There would have been no need for the Black Demon, no need for all the butchery at Wareham."

"What do you mean? Lord Arthur was poisoned, at least that is what everyone at Wareham believes."

Her mother only shrugged.

"No one knows where the silver is hidden, no one."

"Evidently you are wrong. Jason is too afraid of me to lie about that. He now knows, but like I said, I do not know who told him."

"Jason is a coward, he would not have the stomach to enter Wareham. It is Sir Halric who will be the tinker, and Aleric will recognize him and hold him for Garron."

"I very much doubt that Halric is any

longer of this earth. He was incompetent. I ordered Jason to kill him."

Merry only wished she could have been the one to kill Sir Halric. She cocked her head at her mother. "Do you really believe this time Jason will find the silver and somehow manage to get it out of Wareham?"

"Since he is following my plan, it is more than possible. I told him how to enter Wareham, told him exactly what to do once he is inside the walls. And since he claims that now he knows where Arthur hid all the coins, I have told him how to get it out of Wareham as well. And when he brings me Arthur's silver, Jason can have you with my blessing."

Her mother walked away from the narrow bed and strode across the room to the fireplace. She realized in that moment that the room was oddly shaped, like a quarter moon, that was it. Where was she?

Her mother turned toward her. "You understand so very little. Do you know, I think it would be amusing if after all his adventures, Jason's father chooses not to plead with the king to let you remain Jason's wife."

"If I were Jason's father, Lord Ranulf, I would travel to Rome to beg absolution for having birthed him in the first place."

"I doubt there is forgiveness for that heinous a transgression. Mayhap the king will remove Jason's head. Then you, Marianna, will be able to wed whomever you wish, or rather whomever the king wishes. I really do not care, for I will have the silver. If Jason claims it was all my plan, that I have the silver coins, why, he is a liar. I am the renowned Abbess of Meizerling."

Helen looked down at the pathetic scrap that came from her womb. Just look at that violent red hair of hers, the loosely braided plaits now unraveling. Wicked, that hair, just like Elevine's hair, that iniquitous witch who was her own mother, who'd misjudged a substance and blown herself apart in an explosion. But not before she'd taught Helen everything she knew. What about Marianna? She had not an ounce of magick in her, Helen had known that since she first held the babe in her arms. She could scent magick, smell the essence of it in the air, and there was nothing coming from the babe. Ella had assured her Marianna was a clever child, and she'd never shown a flicker of natural magick, she'd said, then crossed herself. Clever? Helen wasn't certain if Ella's observation pleased her or not. Hadn't Ella also told her Marianna had learned to read more quickly than Helen had? But she hadn't believed her. She wanted to blight the old bitch, but she held her anger in since she needed her. Ella was her only tie to Valcourt.

Merry watched her mother, wondered what she was thinking. *Reason with her, convince her that this grand scheme of hers cannot work.* "I assume you have spies at court and they told you I am to marry Garron of Kersey today, not only with the king's blessing, but in his presence. Or is Jason of Brennan skulking about and he told you? I wonder if he realized that the queen herself is overseeing my wedding gown? Mayhap he didn't know the Bishop of London will officiate? You must realize, Mother, that the king is going to be very angry when I am discovered missing. Do you really wish to risk the king's anger? He could easily remove you from Meizerling and exile you to France, or behead both you and Jason of Brennan." *Were they to ask me, I would tell them to behead the both of you,* but she didn't say it aloud.

"You have kidnapped me from the White Tower, from under the king's very nose. Garron will know it was you, you have not fooled anyone. If you do not return me, you must realize that your days will be numbered, madam. Garron will kill you, just as I know he will kill Jason of Brennan."

It's working, it's working, she's getting worried, I can see it in her eyes. She's beginning to question herself now.

Merry pressed on, hope filling her now. "Let me tell you about Garron of Kersey, Mother. He is strong and skilled and does not suffer betrayal. He cares for me, madam, truly. Anyone who commits a great wrong against him is wise to fear for his life. He will find me, and you will be in very bad trouble. I do not believe you have given this sufficient thought."

She'd spoken reasonably, fluently, her logic impeccable. Her father would have been proud of her. To her chagrin, her mother actually laughed. "You know so very little, you foolish girl."

"What do you mean?"

"I mean that whatever happened in the White Tower, I have already changed it into what I wished—like that." And she snapped her fingers in Merry's face.

"That makes no sense. I was kidnapped, it happened. All know if something happens, it becomes the past, and no one can change what happened yesterday. Indeed, how can you change anything at all?"

Helen, aware her daughter was following her every move, shook out her beautiful hair, like spun gold, she'd heard both men and women say, smoothed down the soft folds of her white gown, and walked to a long table covered with books. She opened one and read aloud:

"Those who come will turn and leave.
Those who leave will never know
Why they left and where they go.

"Those words are but the beginning to a spell written a very long time ago, even before the Romans came to our rain-soaked island. It sounds clever, don't you think? Does it frighten you, Marianna? And that is only the beginning of the spell. Don't look so witless. You have heard all your life that I am a witch. It is quite true. I could rule England if I so chose. And there is more, so much more."

Merry saw fire building in her mother's beautiful eyes, a deep fire that looked into hearts and brains and cared not if the heart broke or the brain died. *How can you have birthed me? You look like my older sister, not my mother. Did you cast a magick spell on me so I am seeing you the way you wish me to? Or have you swallowed potions to actually make yourself ageless?*

It didn't matter. Merry was so afraid of this woman she felt she might choke on it.

"You look quite stupid, Marianna. Have you nothing sensible to say? Ella told me you never shut your mouth, that you asked endless questions, of everyone, until your father boasted you knew more about shoeing a horse than the smithy. But you never asked about magick."

"Why should I?"

"You heard whispers about me from your earliest years, do not deny it."

"Aye, I did, but it had no meaning to me since you had no meaning to me. You left me. You said that Ella told you these things about me. It appears I did not know her. Did she betray me and Father?"

"Betrayal is nothing compared to loyalty. Loyalty is what counts, what has meaning. Ella came with me to Valcourt when I wed your father. She insisted upon remaining at Valcourt when I left, with you, so I would know you as well as she did. Ella has always owed me her loyalty."

Merry pictured the old woman's face, sure Ella had loved her, hadn't she? Merry wanted to cry, but she didn't.

She looked at the beautiful woman who held an ancient book in her white hands, held it as gently as one would a babe, or a lover. She slowly rose from the cot. "I am leaving now, Mother."

"No, you will not."

Merry walked to the door. She reached

out her hand to grip the bronze knob, then she simply stopped. She couldn't move. No, no, this was not possible. She closed her eyes a moment, then tried to bring her arm back to her side. Her arm didn't move. She tried to take a step back. Nothing. It was as if she were being held by something she could not see. She concentrated on her hand, but her body seemed apart from her, not in her control. Her fingers simply wouldn't obey her.

"Let me go."

36

She knew her mother was smiling, possibly smirking behind her. "Oh no, you will go nowhere unless I decide you will. How does it feel to be my puppet? Shall I pull one of the strings that controls you?"

Merry looked at the bronze knob not six inches from her outstretched fingers. Were those her fingers? Was her mother controlling her, or was it something else? What did it matter?

"I want you to turn around now and walk back to the cot and sit down. Do you understand?"

Merry slowly lowered her arm to her

side. She could move just as she could always move, but it was odd, she felt something vaguely cold lift from her. She wanted to scream, but she didn't. She walked back and sat down on the edge of the cot. She said nothing, she was simply too afraid. She looked over at her mother, still standing at the window. *Do not show fear, do not show fear.* "That was very impressive, madam. What will you do next if I disagree with you? Make my tongue split apart?"

"Who knows? I gave you but a taste of a simple spell. I learned it years ago."

Merry wished in that moment she could do that spell, that she could whisper strange words or flick her fingers and her mother would be held motionless for a hundred years. Maybe longer.

"Why do you hate me?"

A perfect brow arched upward. "Hate you? I do not hate you."

"You left me and Father."

"I had work to do, work more important than any earthly husband or babe. I took over Meizerling within that first year, and it brought me infinite freedom to do exactly as I wished. But now I need more silver, much more, so that I may do truly great things. And I thought of you, the heiress of Valcourt. Sometimes, I will admit it is possible to hate one's tools. But I do not hate you."

She was a tool? "Why do you need more silver? Do you want to buy France?" She managed a sneer at her mother's silence. "You are such a powerful witch, why do you not simply conjure up all the silver you wish?" And she snapped her fingers just as her mother had. "Why must you have that idiot Jason of Brennan try to steal it for you?"

Her mother looked down at the book, and her lips moved. Was she reading a spell? When she looked up, she said easily, "Your ignorance is appalling, but how could it be otherwise? Your father wouldn't have told you about my special abilities, he wouldn't have told you anything at all. So, that means you do not know that magick is an odd science, giving unexpected insights and producing surprising results, some that even I cannot foresee or predict.

"Aye, in the right hands, magick can manipulate the human brain, can stop the human heart, can freeze the body it-self, as you now know, but unfortunately, no matter whose powerful hands mix to-gether what metals, magick will not allow silver to come forth. But I doubt not there will be those alchemists who will continue to search for a magick formula to turn metal into silver, for most of them will be men, and men forever dream."

"Have you tried to make silver?"

"Aye, once. I realized it was impossible almost immediately. You see, there was no feel of *otherness* in it, no scent of the miraculous hidden deep. Let the years pass and let the men dream their foolish dreams."

"With all the silver you say you need, what is it you wish to do that you cannot do now?"

Her mother gently laid the old book down on the table. She ignored Merry and began to pace again, from the win-dow to the door and back again, her stride smooth and long and young. She was treading upon a brilliant blue carpet cov-ered with myriad strange symbols in black. What did those symbols mean, if anything, Merry wondered.

Merry asked her, "That carpet, where did it come from?"

"This carpet? Is it not beautiful? It was given to me by a special friend who came to manhood in that strange black forest that lies east of France. He wanted to command the wild beasts that roamed there, to make them all his minions. He wanted to explore the dark shadowed caves filled with fires that burn ice, or so he told me." She shrugged. "Alas, he is no more. And in all the years that carpet has lain on these stones, it has never gathered dust, and never aged."

Merry didn't want to understand any of this, particularly fire that burned ice, but she couldn't help herself. "What are the symbols on it?"

"They are a secret language from ancient Bulgar, Rostram told me one night when he had drunk too much of my special wine. It is a language that could, if interpreted correctly, grant more power than any mortal has ever known. I will admit I have not managed to unlock its secrets, but I am young, there is time."

"I am not like you, Mother. I do not wish people to fear me because I can blight them with a flick of my finger. I do not wish to spend my life mixing strange herbs together to see if the heavens quake. I want to marry Garron of Kersey. I wish to bear his babes and know life as his wife."

Her mother studied one of her white hands. "Perhaps you will marry this man you find so exciting, eventually. First, however, you will wed Jason of Brennan. You must learn patience, Marianna."

"No, I will not marry him. He is beyond evil."

"Evil? He has not the brains to be evil. He is only a foolish young man who wants more than his father has. He is a braggart who believes himself smart and important, invincible. He is of little account, really, and even his own father, Lord Ranulf, must know by now. Jason will maul you, but it will be over quickly, and he will soon tire of you. If you bear a babe or several babes, it is not important. If Garron of Kersey still wants you when it is done, you will have him."

Merry said, her voice steady, "I will not wed Jason of Brennan, Mother. I mean it."

"So you will poison him then?" Her mother smiled down at her thumbnail.

"No, I will kill him straight and clean, and he will know why I am killing him." She paused, just an instant. "Did you poison my father?"

She saw surprise in her mother's eyes. "Poison your father? Why no, I did not. I much preferred to have him alive. He was a smart man, your father. He knew me well enough not to interfere in what I wished to do. He was also wise enough not to cheat me. He always sent me the exact promised funds over the years to keep me away from Valcourt, away from you, his little angel. But most important, he kept our secret, and made certain that all those at Valcourt who knew as well also kept silent."

"Silent about what? What secret did my father keep for you?"

Her mother ignored her. "Actually, I was saddened when he died. Do you know, the last time I bedded him, I bit his shoulder so deep he bled. Then I licked him, and within minutes, the blood and the bite mark disappeared. He was terrified for weeks." She laughed, still seeing the look of horror on Timothy's face.

"But you were at Valcourt with Jason within a day and a half of his death."

"Ella sent me a message immediately upon his falling ill. And of course you sent a message begging me to come and heal him. Such faith in me. I know Ella believed I could make him well. Did you? Really? But the truth is I knew I could not. What Ella described to me, I believe some organ in his body simply ruptured. And of course there was my golden ball."

"What are you talking about?"

Helen held out her white hand. Upon her third finger was a ring with a small golden ball sitting atop it. "It looks like solid gold, and so it is, most of the time, but when I wish it, it becomes a mirror. I saw it all." She shrugged. "Also, I was busy at Meizerling with a critical experiment and had not the time to spare simply to prove what I already knew. He was a dead man."

Merry was shaking so hard from rage and grief, she didn't think she could stand it. The words spewed out of her mouth. "What you say is madness! You are mad! You cannot be my mother!"

"Mad, am I? Hmmm, how sad that you, my daughter, think in such common terms."

"I also believe you are evil. Unlike Jason, you have the brains."

Another laugh. "You believe evil is loathesome and good is righteous? Those words exist only for churchmen to equate evil to Hell and thus scare the common herd into giving credence to the drivel that comes from their mouths. They want obedience and power, like every other benighted man on this earth, and this is how they gain it—through threats of eternal torture, or, if a man is good, they pour on promises of eternal bliss.

"Good and evil, they having no meaning in the full course of time. Ah, well, nothing much has any meaning, truth be told."

"You cannot mean what you said, you cannot."

Helen turned to the window. "You will never know who I am or what I am, even with my little demonstration. You are really quite common, Marianna. Mayhap I should have kept you with me, made you into something worthwhile, but there was nothing in you to interest me, nothing at all. Could I have given you something to give meaning to your short number of years?"

"Why would you even think to bother, when you say nothing has any meaning at all?"

There was a spark of momentary interest in her mother's eyes. "How odd that you caught me up in my own logic. I suppose that I am distressed at Jason of Brennan's continued failures. But I have seen that Jason will likely succeed in securing the silver coins this time, with my help naturally, if only there is enough time."

"What do you mean, if only there is enough time? Why is time important to you? Won't you live forever? Can't you stop time?"

"No, I can only extend myself so far. A pity, but mayhap there is a way, and mayhap I will be the one to find it. Could it lie in the secret language in the rug beneath my feet?

"Ah, it is dawn. I have always loved to see the sun burst into life yet again each morning. The black clouds thicken. It will rain soon now, enough rain to rut the ground. Soon now." She sighed. "There is so much to study, so much to learn. No matter the number of earthly years, life is still too short." She fell silent as she continued to stare out of the narrow window. She looked back over her shoulder at her daughter. "Mayhap he will come looking for you, Marianna, who knows? But it will not matter."

"What do you mean?"

She paused a moment, then smiled. "In time, you may come to understand, although I doubt it."

37

LONDON

Garron couldn't believe his ears. He stared at the frightened young man Whalen had by the arm.

"This is Thomas, my lord, one of the king's stable guards." Thomas's eyes were as wild as his tangled black hair, panting he was so afraid.

Garron leaned close in. "You say you actually saw two men sneaking past the stables carrying a bundle?"

"Aye, my lord, well, I almost saw them for it was dark with little moon overhead.

I knew there was a body all wrapped up because it was bent in two, not all that big a body, but the men were breathing hard, like they'd walked a long way."

"Why did you not yell for them to stop, Thomas?"

Thomas cast a sideways look at Whalen, lowered his head, and whispered, "I had no weapon, and I was afraid they would kill me."

Garron's fingers were close to wrapping themselves around his neck. "No weapon? You are a guard. Where is your damned sword?"

The young man's Adam's apple looked like it would leap out of his throat. He streaked dirty fingers through his black hair. "My lord," he whispered, "I forgot it when I sat in the jakes with Old Claver."

It was close, but Garron didn't strangle Thomas. "Who in the secret name of the Devil is Old Claver?"

"Old Claver keeps the jakes clean and tells you a story if you must settle in."

Garron wanted to kill Thomas and laugh his head off at the same time.

Thomas hurried on. "I saw my mother's sad face and I knew my duty. I followed them, my lord, waited for my chance, for there are always a dozen guards patrolling near the east wall, so many eyes to see them and call the alarm. How could these two escape? As I neared the wall, I began to see the guards—they were all on the ground and I knew they were asleep and not dead because I heard a lot of snoring. I wanted to yell, but knew if I did and no one came, they would kill me."

Whalen's stone face didn't change expression. "They are all still unconscious," he said to Garron. "We found wine jugs around them. The king's physician will examine them but I believe they were given sleeping draughts. All of them drank." His voice was colder than the ice that had covered the Thames the previous winter. Garron wondered what would happen to the guards once they awoke. Were it his decision, he'd lock them in a dungeon for a week with no food and no light.

Whalen told Thomas to continue.

He looked at Garron, then dropped his eyes again. "I went after them, my lord, I didn't even hesitate, what with my poor

mother's voice speaking to me right in
my ear. Just beyond the outside wall, there
are a score of cooper shops. Beyond the
shops at the end of a dark alley, I could
make out that they tossed the bundle
into the back of a cart and covered it with
a blanket. I managed to climb in without them hearing me. I nearly gagged, it
smelled like offal and sour ale. I felt the
bundle and it was female, but she didn't
move."

Garron did not doubt that Merry's
mother had used a sleeping potion on
the guards. What had she used on Merry?
The same thing? Had Jason of Brennan
been one of the two men who'd taken
her?

"It was a very long time before the cart
horses stopped at the edge of a forest I
didn't recognize. I thought it was their
destination, and I managed to slip out of
the cart without them hearing me. Alas,
they'd only stopped to relieve themselves. I wanted to relieve myself too, but
I knew they might see me in the moonlight, and I saw again my mother's sad
face, and so I suffered.

"When they continued, I had no chance

to climb back into the cart. I ran after them until one of the men must have heard me and turned to look behind him. I was terrified he would see me, and mayhap he did, he called out. I ran.

"I am sorry, my lord, but I do not know how much farther they traveled into the forest. I remember it looked black with only one path leading into it. I knew I had to come back to get help, and so I ran until I could steal a horse and ride back here."

Garron said very quietly, "You saw neither man's face?"

Thomas shook his head.

"You heard their voices. Did they sound old or young?"

"Both sounded like older men, my lord, their voices hard."

So it hadn't been Jason of Brennan or Sir Halric.

"I memorized the way, my lord, I can take you there."

Garron felt a leap of hope. "Get your sword from the jakes. Hurry." He turned to Whalen. "I wonder how they managed to get into the White Tower and down the many corridors to Merry's room. Indeed, how did they know where she even slept?"

Whalen said, "Four of my guards within the tower were struck down, one of them that patrolled near your betrothed's chamber is dead. It shouldn't have happened. By all that's sacred, what if it had been an assassin who had sneaked in to murder the king?" Whalen looked like he would vomit, then he began cursing. Garron thought Whalen knew well enough that he wouldn't be the captain of the king's guard for much longer.

Garron said, "No assassin could get to the king, Whalen, you know that. There are always three guards in the king's antechamber."

"Aye, at night, they patrol for three hours, then sleep. But this—"

"Gather men, Whalen. I need you. I will meet you at the eastern gate. Go." Garron welcomed the anger now pouring into him, it was better than the awful impotence that had rubbed him raw. Now there was a chance. But how much farther had they traveled into the forest after Thomas had run away from them? What if Jason of Brennan had already forced her to wed him, what if he'd already raped her? No, Merry was smart, she would do something to stop him. Besides, even if she was helpless against him, it didn't matter, nothing mattered—Jason of Brennan was a dead man, he just didn't know it yet.

When Garron jerked the saddle cinch tighter around Damocles' belly, his destrier swung his great head around and tried to bite him, but years of experience saved him. He jumped back, smacked his horse's neck. "I'll strangle you if you try to bite me again. We have to fetch your mistress to her wedding."

Garron leaned his face against his destrier's smooth neck for a moment, felt his great strength, and it steadied him. *Merry*, he told her silently, *use that clever brain of yours, tell him you must make a list before you can wed him.* He would swear in that instant that he could hear her saying the words, her voice firm as a nun's. He was smiling when he leapt on his destrier's back, and Gilpin wondered at that smile. He looked over at Sir Lyle, sitting atop his destrier, speaking low to his three men. About what?

Three hours later, Garron was as silent

as the dozen soldiers riding behind him. The sky blackened, the quarter moon disappeared, the air chilled. It began to rain, hard, driving rain that quickly soaked every man to the skin. It was misery. When they reached the forest where Thomas had gotten out of the cart, they saw the narrow road through the trees was well worn, but the rain had washed away any signs of wheel tracks and turned the dirt to mud. Garron motioned them forward. The trees thickened as they rode deeper into the forest, a relief because it provided some shelter from the relentless rain. They came to two rutted paths that struck out from the main track like two stretched-out arms, and disappeared into the trees. The men in the cart could have taken one of the two paths or continued straight. At that moment, it began to rain even harder, rain sheeted down even through the thick trees, and the men huddled in their saddles, heads down, as Garron studied the two paths for any sign of a cart's passage. There was nothing but mud.

He split the men into three groups. He didn't know why, but he simply had a feeling about the path to the right. He, Gilpin, and two soldiers, Arnold and John, left the others and plowed on. He sent Sir Lyle and his men to the left and Whalen took the remainder of the soldiers and continued straight. He'd never prayed so hard in his life that the path he'd chosen was the right one. Some hundred yards farther, the narrow, mud-filled path ended in a small clearing. In the center of the clearing sat a woodcutter's hut, small but stoutly built. Smoke snaked out of a hole in the roof. Just as Garron pulled Damocles to a halt in front of the hut, the rain suddenly stopped. He looked up to see the moon through the black clouds. He dismounted and shook himself like a mongrel dog. "Stay here," he told the men. He pounded on the door, called out, but there was no answer. He pounded again. After a moment, a very old woman, wearing an ancient green gown that was still as green as the impenetrable trees, pulled open the old wooden door. She looked up at Garron, paled, took a fast step back, and crossed herself. She whispered, "Be it ye, the divil? All wet and young and beautiful to gaze upon? At least I think ye're beautiful since there bain't much moon to shine on yer head. Be ye here to strip my soul of its goodness and take my husk to Hell?"

"Nay, I will not harm you." And then, with no thought, the words simply came out of his mouth. "I search for the witch." Why had he said that? Where had those words come from?

The old woman crossed herself again and searched his face in the dim light. "Ye do not want to see her, lad, she'll split yer gullet wide open, and all yer words will spill out of yer throat and fall on yer boots."

"She has taken my betrothed. Tell me where I can find the witch."

She continued to study him, then she nodded slowly, and said so low he could scarce hear her, "Sometimes she comes, not often, and when she does, smoke billows above the trees, black smoke that stinks of Hell itself. Her tower sits not far past the rutted path behind my hut. Aye, she built herself a black tower, or snapped her fingers and it built itself, I know not. It be enclosed behind a high stone wall." She reached out a heavily veined hand

and lightly touched his wet tunic sleeve. "Listen to me, lad, ye don't want to go there. If she's taken yer betrothed, then she is no longer of this earth. Ye don't wish to die, do ye?"

Garron wanted to shake her, but he forced himself to patience. "Have you seen smoke billowing up over the trees?"

Once again she crossed herself. "Aye, I have, several times. I saw her only once, so beautiful she was, all golden and white, and she was laughing, at what I don't know, I saw nothing to make me laugh. She looked glorious, like a princess or an angel, but then she suddenly looked at me, and it was like I was a mirror and she was looking into me and I was looking out at her. I saw meanness deep inside her, aye, and death was behind her eyes."

38

Golden and white? Glorious? What was this about? She was Merry's mother, not some fresh young maid to be admired. Then he supposed any female would seem young to the old woman. *Meanness deep inside her and death behind her eyes?* Aye, he could well believe that. He gave her several coins. She began rubbing them against her palms, stroking them like a lover. "They're lovely, at least I think they are, but I really can't see them. Is the silver bright as the sun?" she said, still caressing them.

"When the sun comes up in a few hours, you will see how bright they are."

"I haven't seen coins like this since my poor deaf Allard finally croaked it after a tree fell right on him. When I laid him out, I found two more silver coins jest like these sewn into his trousers. They were shiny. We'll see. I will bury my coins jest yon, beneath that dripping oak tree. There bain't no one to give them to. Mayhap a druid slept once beneath that tree, mayhap the spirit of the druid will accept my offering and will save ye from the witch. But I doubt it."

Garron said, "Mayhap the spirits will listen, but no matter. I will save myself." Garron swung up onto his destrier's back, nodded to Gilpin, Arnold, and John, and clicked Damocles forward. Why had he asked about the witch? And he'd been right, he was close, he knew it to his soul. And he would find Merry. He would find her in time. They rode past the old hut, out of the clearing and back into the thick forest. Thankfully there was a bit of moonlight coming through the trees, so they could see the path.

It was near dawn and the light was gray. When the trees began to thin, Garron called his men to halt. She was near, he felt it to his bones. "All of you, wait here. I will call if I find something."

"But, my lord—"

He didn't want to argue with Gilpin, didn't want to clout him into obedience, but a sense of urgency was pushing him hard. "All right, Gilpin, you will come with me. Arnold, you and John wait for my signal. Stay alert. A witch lives here. The old woman said she was dangerous. Gilpin, stay in my shadow, or I will kick your belly into your backbone, do you understand?"

Gilpin, not understanding anything at all, nodded.

They came through the thin line of trees into a wide clearing. A stone enclosure sat in the middle of the clearing, forming a rough circle about thirty feet across. The wall was a good eight feet high. A stout wooden gate was built into the wall. Suddenly the gray dawn sky turned black again and thunder boomed loud, once, twice, three times, directly over their heads. Lightning slashed through the trees behind them, splitting an ancient oak in half, not ten feet away. He heard Arnold call out and Garron knew he was afraid. He refused to believe a witch could call up the weather, that was nonsense, but he knew it was a warning, knew it in the deepest part of him, but a warning of what? A warning from whom? *You shouldn't be here, this place will kill you, the witch will curse you, and you will be buried beneath this wall and your bones will molder and no one will ever know where you are—*

There was another boom of thunder, right over his shoulder this time. Gilpin's horse reared on its hind legs. Garron managed to grab the reins and pull the terrified animal close to Damocles, who stood quiet as a nun at vespers. Garron wondered if Damocles was simply too afraid to move.

He looked at Gilpin's white face and said quietly, "It will be all right. Don't be afraid." Gilpin swallowed bile and didn't move. They waited a moment, but there was no more thunder or lightning. Garron dismounted, handed Gilpin Damocles' reins. "Stay here. Keep the horses calm.

Wait for me. No, don't argue, I will be all right."

The rain poured down again, so much hard rain Garron felt the earth beneath his feet begin to slide. It was England, it always rained, there was no magick at work here, no damned witch casting a spell on the clouds.

There was no handle on the gate. He pushed at it, but the gate didn't move. It was barred on the inside, nothing more than that. Garron looked more closely at the stone wall, saw the stones weren't smoothly set one against the other. He found purchase and climbed. When he reached the top of the wall, he turned back and saw only Gilpin's shadow through the thick rain. Thank St. Clement's meaty bones, Gilpin hadn't moved. As for Arnold and John, he couldn't make them out at all through the gray blur.

He lay flat atop the wall and looked down into the enclosure. It was past dawn and he could see there were no trees, no scrubs within the stone walls. The ground was covered with wooden planks leading from the gate to the tower that rose perhaps thirty feet into the air. It looked solid and grim, desolate, not a single sign of life. Three narrow windows marked the three tower levels, all of them facing to the east. There were three small buildings connected to the tower by wooden roofs, and a small stable huddled just inside the gate. He lay still, calmed himself, and listened. He heard nothing save the miserable, endless rain.

His urgency was great now, prodding him, making his heart drum loud in his chest. He had to get inside that godforsaken tower. He knew Merry was in there, and she needed him. He didn't want to turn his back to the tower, but he had to. He didn't want to risk breaking his leg by jumping off the wall. He climbed down several feet, then jumped, lightly landed on his feet. He drew his sword, pulled his knife from his sleeve, and ran to the tower, his boots loud on the wooden planks. In front of him was a tall, narrow black door. There was a symbol painted in white at eye level. Up close it looked like a half moon, no, not quite a half moon, more a sickle, and there were three crooked lines slashed through its middle. He'd never before seen a symbol like that one. What could it possibly mean?

He pushed down the iron handle. He had no hope of it opening, but it did, easily and smoothly, not making a sound.

He took a step inside. The narrow door closed quietly behind him. He whirled about, but there was nothing there. *The wind*, he thought, *a gust of wind blew it closed*, but deep inside him, he knew that wasn't true. He cursed into the silent air.

Before him lay a long narrow corridor, its stone floor bare as the walls, so deeply buried in shadows he couldn't see the other end. On either side of him was a door. He pressed his ear to the right door, listened. He heard nothing. The door opened easily. He stepped into dim light, not as dark as the corridor since there was a single high eastward facing window above his head. It was a workroom of some sort, and he saw it was sickle-shaped, which made sense since he was in a tower. There were baskets of all sizes stacked along a far wall. Something deep inside him didn't want to know what was inside those baskets. Shelves climbed the curving walls, and upon those shelves sat dark bottles and oddly shaped bowls and piles of dried plants. Were the bottles empty? He would swear he saw a flash of movement in one of the larger bottles. No, he didn't want to look. Several benches sat in front of two long bare tables. He stood quietly for a moment, listening, but he didn't hear anything. He was surrounded by stillness and cold, and stale air. Surely no one had been in this room for a very long time.

He walked across the narrow corridor to press his ear to the opposite door. Again, he heard nothing. When he opened the door and stepped inside, he saw this room was deeply shadowed since there were no windows, and it too appeared to be empty. No, wait. The room wasn't empty. He heard a rustling sound. Slowly, he raised his face and looked up.

39

He stared up at a dozen black ceiling beams that stretched the length of the room, some six feet above his head. Atop each beam birds huddled, pressing into each other, seemingly asleep. Crows, he saw, dozens of black crows sitting in a long line. Then he stopped cold. The farthest beam didn't have crows sitting on it, but dozens of bats. The bats weren't asleep. He saw wings stretch out, heard them rustling, then one of them flew directly at him. Garron swung with his arm and hit the bat, knocking it to the stone floor. Another came at him, then a dozen more. Garron jerked open the door and slammed it closed behind him. He heard a bat strike the door, then another. He heard the crows stirring now, heard their harsh caws.

He stood in the dim corridor a moment, trying to calm himself, waiting. Waiting for what? For more of the bats to hurl themselves at the door, to claw through it, and attack him? No, no, the door was stout, he was safe. But how had the birds even gotten into that room? He could make no sense of it.

When silence fell again, he walked toward the back of the tower. The corridor became darker with each step. He saw curving narrow stairs against the back tower wall, winding to the right. He climbed a half-dozen deep, narrow stairs. He paused. It was now pitch black and he simply couldn't see. He placed one hand against the stone wall beside him and kept climbing. He walked upward, ever upward, and the stairs seemed to grow narrower, almost too small for his feet, but it didn't matter. He kept walking, one step after another. At last he reached the second level. And he saw the stairs simply ended. But how could that be, since he'd seen a vertical line of three windows on the outside stone wall? He was sure of it; so that meant there had to be three separate levels in this damnable tower. But how to get to the top level? He shook his head. It didn't matter. It was nothing but tricks, he thought, a witch's tricks meant to confuse him, make him doubt himself.

Garron realized this second level was identical to the floor below him, a room on each side, the long dim corridor separating them.

He walked to the door on the right, listened a moment, then eased the door open and looked inside. Since there was no window, it was all deep shadows. He made out a large bed that sat squarely in the middle of the room, blue velvet hangings enclosing it. A fire burned brightly in a fireplace, but somehow the light given off didn't pierce the black shadows. But it was warm in the room. Unless the witch was presenting him with an illusion, then someone was here and that someone had laid the fire, and kept it built up. But how was that possible? There was no hole for escaping smoke, yet no smoke gushed into the small room.

He saw the thick velvet bed hangings shift, showing a part of the bed. Was there movement in that bed? Was that a woman lying on that bed?

Merry?

He walked as quietly as he could toward the bed. He heard a moan, quiet, then a thin cry. He walked faster now, and it seemed the shadows thickened, somehow formed a barrier, and he was shoving and heaving to get through to the bed. He jerked back the velvet hangings not knowing what he expected to find, and afraid: he couldn't help it. He froze. The bed was empty. His breath whooshed out. His heart wanted to leap out of his chest. How could the bed be empty? He'd seen something move, he'd swear to it, and he'd heard—something. The bed covers were tangled. He touched a blanket. It was warm to the touch. Someone had been here, maybe just minutes before he'd come in. He heard that moan again, this time it was only a sliver of sound and it came from behind him. He whirled around but saw nothing.

No, wait, the moan had come from above his head, that was it. There was another room above this one. There had to be stairs to the third level, they were simply hidden. Slowly, he walked to the door. He turned back to look once again at the bed. He saw nothing at all. It was so still he wanted to drive his fist against the door and pound until something happened, anything to end this deadening silence, to stop the madness. He was more angry now than he was afraid, everything in him was ready to fight, wanted to fight, to do something, anything, to end this absurd game. *It is a game, the witch is playing with me.*

There was nothing to see but deep shadows and darkness. He heard the soft moaning again, and something more—was that a voice? A woman's voice? The moans hadn't come from over his head, they'd come from the room opposite this one. He closed the door behind him and quickly crossed the corridor.

He listened a moment, then opened the door. There was watery light seeping from the window into the chamber, a huge relief. He stepped into a living space.

He saw the room was well used, the rug thick beneath his boots. The rug was brilliant blue and covered with strange black symbols that made his flesh ripple. It was large, covering most of the stone floor. Bound parchments were piled beside a large high-backed chair, a branch of unlit candles sat on a table beside the chair. There was a fireplace on the far wall, a small fire burning on the grate, nearly burned out now. But there was no air hole—no, now wasn't the time to drive himself mad thinking about that. *This is nothing but a witch's game.*

But his hand tightened around his sword handle. Damnation, where had the moans come from? Not this room, no, this room was as empty as the other. Surely he could believe what his eyes saw. Couldn't he? He knew there was something, something just out of sight, something that was hiding, waiting—

He shook off the creeping fear, the questions with no answers. He realized it was cold even though the fire seemed to be burning brighter since he'd stepped into the room. Again, it was a witch's trick, nothing more, and that meant she was close. But where? *Think. Make sense of this.*

He knew there was no one in this room save him, but there was, he knew it to his gut—the witch was here, hiding herself from him. Garron called out, sarcasm thick in his voice, "I know you're here, witch. You've had a fine time playing your games with me, but it's over. Come out from where you are hiding."

"I am not hiding." The soft whispered words seemed to come from all around him.

He nearly leapt into the air, but managed to hold his place. He ignored the rancid fear. "Where are you then?"

"Right behind you, Lord Garron."

Garron turned slowly to stare at one of the most beautiful women he'd ever seen in his life standing directly behind him. She was tall, nearly to the bridge of his nose, slender as a girl, her gown pure white, just as white as her soft flesh, and he thought, *She is golden and white, just as the old woman said.* How had she gotten behind him? He accepted her presence, he had no choice, and now he had to deal with her. Now his questions would be answered. No matter what she did, no matter what she said, he was ready. He felt deadly.

"I have been looking for you. Are you the witch I seek?" No fear leaked into his voice, and rage thrummed in his blood. He slowly raised his knife to her face.

She merely smiled at him. "Marianna said you would come, over and over, she said you would find her. I do not know how you managed it, but come you did. How did you find my sanctuary?"

He held the knife not an inch from her smooth cheek as he studied her face. "You cannot be Merry's mother."

"Do you not see the resemblance between us?"

He slowly shook his head. "Merry's eyes are a dark blue, yours are as gray as old ice. You are nothing alike. You are not her mother. Who are you?"

She continued to smile. "Marianna said you were fine looking, Garron of Kersey, and I see she was right. She also said you were honorable, that there was strength in your center. Did she say you were valiant? I trust not, since 'valiant' is a silly word given to the heroes men invent to make them feel safe. Are you a hero, Garron of Kersey?"

"Aye," he said, his voice strong, calm, "I am a hero. So is Merry."

"What a strange thing for a man to say. How is she a hero?"

"Were I to explain, I still doubt you would understand. Now, where is my betrothed?"

"Do you see her? Come now, you have searched my entire tower."

"Not the third floor. There were no stairs leading up to it."

She laughed.

"Tell me where she is or I will kill you now."

She slowly shook her head, but her smile never faltered. "Mayhap you are a strong warrior and those weaker can trust you to protect them, mayhap you are steady in your beliefs, ignorant and narrow though they be, but in my world, you are only a simple man whose fear of those things he cannot understand turns his heart to ashes. Tell me, Garron of Kersey, how did you find my tower?"

He touched the knife tip to her neck. "I snapped my fingers and found myself facing your ridiculous tower. A black tower, madam? How little imagination you have. And the sickle with the crooked lines slashing through it—what does that mean? Something you hope will frighten people who chance upon this place?" The knife pressed deeper. A drop of deep red blood pooled around the knife tip. "Now you will tell me where Merry is or I will cut your throat."

She lightly raised a soft white hand to touch his cheek. "Aye, you are comely, Garron of Kersey, but there isn't time for me to enjoy you. You are too late."

Her fingers were soft, caressing his cheek now, pressing inward. He jerked his head back. He thought he smelled something sickly sweet but ignored it. He put his face close to hers. "Do not touch me again. What do you mean I am too late? Tell me where you have hidden Merry, or I will kill you right now." And he pressed the knife tip in deeper. Another drop of blood welled up and slid down her white throat to paint a slash of red on her white bodice.

Still she didn't move, still she smiled up at him. She touched his cheek again, then when the knife pressed deeper, she drew her hand back. "Things do not proceed as I had planned, but no matter. What will happen should amuse me. You must leave me now, Garron of Kersey."

"No, I will not leave until I know where you have hidden Merry. You have but an instant, madam, or I will slit your throat."

"Merry? What a silly name," and yet again her fingers touched his cheek, her eyes met his, deep, fathomless. He wanted to slam his knife to the hilt so it would come out the back of her neck, but he felt as if he were moving away from her. Yet this beautiful woman was beside him, both her hands on his face now, drawing him away from himself. He felt his knife fall from his fingers, but they couldn't be his fingers, for he was not really here now, he was above, or mayhap he was beyond this cursed tower. Was that his knife he heard thud softly onto the blue carpet with its strange symbols? He felt his sword slip from his hand, but it wasn't his hand, it was another's. He heard his sword land hard on the stone floor. But he'd been standing on the thick carpet. Was it his sword he heard, or another's? He heard the witch laugh, but he didn't see her now. He was alone, and he was nowhere at all. He felt empty, a shadow. He called out, "Where are you, witch?"

She didn't answer him. He heard nothing now, felt nothing. He was moving away, faster now, into darkness where soft air swirled warm on his face. He thought he saw a flash of fire, but then it was gone, a blur of red and gold, but there was no heat from it, only cold, blistering cold. From a great distance, he heard a soft laugh, the witch's laugh, then he heard nothing at all.

40

A hand slapped his face, once, then yet again, harder this time, then Gilpin's scared voice. "My lord! Please, you must wake up!"

Garron opened his eyes and stared up into his squire's white face hovering above him, seeming somehow detached, floating.

"Thanks be to all God's blessed angels, you are alive! Oh, considerate and generous Lord who occasionally hears his servants' prayers, I will burn a hundred candles to your blessed Holy Mother for saving my sweet master. What happened, my lord?"

He frowned up at Gilpin, whose head was once again sitting on his neck, and tried to make sense of what had happened. He said, "I was gone, where, I do not know. Somehow, she sent me away."

"She, my lord?"

"The witch was within the tower. She said she was Merry's mother, but she couldn't be, Gilpin, she was young and beautiful, all golden and white, but her eyes were this cold ancient gray, like an old tombstone, or dirty ice. She drugged me, the bitch must have rubbed some poison into my skin when she stroked my face." He remembered her fingers pressing into his flesh and shook his head. It all seemed so long ago, yet, strangely, it felt just an instant before. He felt he could reach out his hand and grab her by her long hair. It felt like madness. His fingers flexed. "I wanted to slit her throat, but I couldn't kill her until she told me where she'd taken Merry. But then I was gone from myself. You woke me up." He slowly sat up, Gilpin supporting him. "I failed, Gilpin. I couldn't find Merry. Where are we?"

"We are where we were, my lord, at the edge of the forest. Arnold and John are standing guard over us."

He felt sunlight on his face and looked up. "It's morning."

"Aye, it has been for several hours now."

But how could that be? It was just dawn, wasn't it? "Tell me what happened."

"I saw you climb the wall and drop into the enclosure. Then, a very long time later, you simply walked out of the gate in the stone wall. I called to you, but you simply walked past me toward Arnold. He spoke to you, but you just continued to walk past him back into the forest. It was as if you had something important to do and everything in you was focused on it. You carried your sword in one hand, your knife in the other. You said nothing at all to any of us. Both Arnold and John yelled at you, yet you refused to stop, just kept walking. I grabbed your arm, but you shook me off. All of us grabbed you, but you had great strength, my lord, and you merely knocked us aside. Then you stopped, looked back at the tower, your eyes closed, and you simply fell over. You didn't move, my lord. We thought you were dead. You said the witch drugged you?" Gilpin looked toward the tower and crossed himself.

Garron remembered the witch speaking to him, he could still hear her light laughter close to his face, laughter at him, and her fingers were touching him, and he knew she'd rubbed a drug into his flesh for he remembered the sickly sweet smell. Then he remembered his knife and his sword falling from his hands to the floor, then movement and blackness. Until now.

He saw both his sword and his knife on the ground beside him.

He rolled over and came up on his feet. He did not feel light-headed or dizzy. He didn't feel like anything had happened to him at all. He picked up his sword and his knife. "We must return to the enclosure."

Garron knew they were frightened, but they went with him without hesitation. Arnold and John searched the connecting buildings and the stable. They didn't find the cart, didn't find the horses, they didn't find anything at all, only ruin.

The black narrow door of the tower was locked. They heaved and shoved, but it held. They could cut down a tree and ram it, but Garron didn't want to take the time.

Suddenly, without warning, the door swung open. Arnold and John stumbled back. Garron said, "It is all right. Our last blow pushed it in. Don't be afraid. Come, let's see what is inside."

But just like the connecting buildings and the stable, there was nothing at all inside. It was a hollow tower that reached some thirty feet into the air. The air pulsed with magick, and Garron knew all of them felt the strangeness of it. John crossed himself. Arnold stared at him, but Garron only shook his head.

"It's a ruin," Gilpin whispered, "naught but a ruin, for a hundred years it's been falling in on itself."

"The Devil's work," Arnold whispered so low Garron scarce heard him.

Garron nodded. "It is a ruin," he said, "and isn't that curious?" He stepped back out and looked at the black door. The white painted sickle with three crooked black lines through the middle of it shone bright, as if they'd been painted on only yesterday. At least something hadn't changed. Why did the witch leave the sickle? He didn't look away from it, from the three crooked black lines running through the middle. He lightly touched his fingertip to it, expecting, he supposed, for the paint to be still be wet, but it wasn't. Her face appeared clear in his mind as he touched those crooked lines, and he said to her, *I will find you, witch, and when I do I will kill you.*

He said to his men, "There is nothing for us here. Let us return to London," and without a backward look, Garron strode to Damocles.

Thunder sounded overhead, black clouds formed over them. Not a minute later, cold rain poured down upon them, and the daylight vanished. They endured, there was nothing else to do.

She'd created an interesting illusion for him, then drugged him. He felt his failure to his bones. He'd lost Merry and he didn't know what to do about it.

An hour later they met Whalen and the

other soldiers at the edge of the forest. Whalen shook his head, his face grim. Garron said, "We did not find her either."

Sir Lyle shook his head. "I am very sorry, my lord."

Once they were clear of the forest, it stopped raining.

41

LONDON

It was early evening when they rode through the massive gates into the White Tower's vast inner courtyard. So many people were there, waiting to hear what had happened. But what could he say? That he'd been drugged by a witch who was Merry's mother?

He said only, "We failed to find her."

Garron imagined Arnold and John would have quite a lot to say once they'd poured some ale down their throats, but now they spoke only of finding a strange tower in the forest, abandoned and empty. They said nothing about how he'd acted when he'd come out of the enclosure.

As for Gilpin, he gave Garron a sorrowful look and shook his head. "That empty tower. We all had hopes of finding Merry there, but alas."

"Do you remember when I went in the tower alone, Gilpin?"

"No, my lord, you are not remembering aright. Naturally I would not let you go in that strange place alone, my lord. No, all of us went in and found the tower abandoned." But Gilpin was frowning, and looked bewildered. *He knows there is more*, Garron thought, *but somehow he no longer remembers.*

It didn't matter. Garron knew Gilpin was very worried. Would he ever remember? Or perhaps, he thought, he had himself dreamed all of it. Maybe all there was, was this abandoned ruined tower, built even before William had come to English shores. No, he couldn't accept that. He knew she'd drugged him, she'd planted the illusions in his brain, made them so real he could touch them, taste them, feel them in the air itself.

Garron met with the king and queen. He knew he would be believed mad if he spoke about the witch who was Merry's mother, how she'd drugged him, how she'd made him see things that weren't there, and so he, like Arnold, John, and Gilpin, told them about finding an abandoned tower, but not Merry.

The queen wept. Most of the queen's ladies wept with her. Blanche waved her white fingers at him.

Silence filled the White Tower. There was simply nothing more to be done.

Garron fell into an exhausted sleep. *Merry was standing beside that bed in her nightrobe in the sickle-shaped room. She was holding out her hand to him, speaking to him, begging him, he knew it, but he couldn't hear what she said, nor could he seem to move to her. He heard her calling his name, so clearly, so close.*

Garron jerked awake, his heart pounding. He knew she was in trouble but there was nothing he could do about it.

The next morning, Garron, with Gilpin, Sir Lyle and his two men, and a dozen of the king's soldiers, prepared to leave for Jason of Brennan's keep, Swaines, only a three-hour ride, Burnell told him, in the opposite direction from the forest and the witch's tower.

Merry. He knew to his gut she wouldn't be at Jason of Brennan's keep, but surely Jason had to know where her mother was keeping her. If he didn't find her, he would journey on to Meizerling. Would the witch even be there? If she was, would she admit she'd practiced magick on him? Would she admit she'd drugged him? Would she admit she held her daughter somewhere?

The heavy rains were past. It was a fine morning, warm, the sun was bright overhead. He was preparing to mount Damocles when he heard Gilpin yell, "My lord! My lord, wait! She is no longer gone! She's back!"

"*What?* What did you say, Gilpin?" He turned, impatient, on edge.

"She is here, my lord! Merry, she's here!"

His brain went blank. "What did you say? You said Merry is here?"

"Aye, she said her mother let her leave! Look, she is coming right now!"

Garron looked up to see her running toward him. She was wearing a bedgown, a robe pulled over it, holding the skirts high in her hands. He saw her face, saw her hair wasn't braided, but was loose around her face and down her back, bright red beneath the sun. It was Merry and she was laughing and crying at the same time and running as fast as she could to get to him. For a moment, he simply couldn't believe it, then he was running to her. He caught her up against him and buried his face in her hair. She was real, he could feel her heart pounding against his chest. *She was really here, she'd come back to him*. He raised his head and looked down at her, cupping her beloved face between his two large palms.

"How can this be? Is it really you and not some phantom come to haunt me?"

He felt her warm breath on his face as she leaned up to kiss his chin. "Aye, my lord," she whispered, "I am a phantom come to bedevil you, for all your allotted worldly years," and she kissed his ear, his nose, his mouth.

He said her name even as he kissed her deeply, his hands wild on her back, lifting her hard against him. He didn't want to let her go, ever again. He would help her bathe, he would accompany her to the jakes, he would— Garron became aware of a crowd of men gathering around them. She saw Sir Lyle standing off to one side, looking on, a quizzical look on his face. Slowly, Garron let her slide down his body. He smiled down at her, then looked at those around them. "I thank all of you. She is somehow returned to me. When I learn how my betrothed managed this remarkable feat, I will tell all of you." And he picked her up in his arms.

"My lord!" It was Robert Burnell, his robe flapping around his feet. "I heard the heiress is back. Is this she? Really? I mean, I see all that wicked hair of hers, but how can that be? You could not find her, no one could. How could she suddenly appear?" Robert Burnell, the Chancellor of England, pulled up short and crossed himself.

"She has told me she is a phantom come to bedevil me," Garron shouted with laughter, and carried her away through the crowd.

42

Merry sat on a fat cushion at the queen's feet, Garron stood beside her, not about to let her out of his sight. The queen couldn't seem to stop stroking her hair, long and loose down her back.

The king lounged opposite her in an opulent chair he'd brought back from the Holy Land, a gift from Sultan Baibars himself, his long legs stretched out in front of him, jeweled leather shoes on his big feet.

The queen laid her hand on Merry's shoulder. "It's time for you to tell all of us what happened."

Merry lightly placed her hand over the queen's. It appeared to steady her. "My lady, it is all very simple, really. My mother sent two men to drug me and bring me to her. When I awoke, she told me I would marry Jason of Brennan. I told her he was the Black Demon, that he'd devastated Wareham and killed many innocent people because no one would tell him where Arthur's silver coins were hidden. I told her I wished to marry Garron, that he would make a fine lord for Valcourt as well as Wareham." She paused a moment, then looked up at the king through her lashes. Garron stared at her. He'd never seen her do that before. It was remarkably effective. The king blinked and sat forward in his chair. He never took his eyes off her as he handed her a stuffed fig from a silver platter a servant held beside him.

"And what did your mother say to that?"

Merry smiled as she took a small bite of the fig. Her head tilted just a bit to the side, cascading her hair over her shoulder, to curl around her breast. "Sire, she finally acknowledged she was satisfied with my selection. She gave me her blessing and sent me back here with the two men who'd taken me in the first place. She prays you will not seek to punish her since she was merely concerned that I was being forced into a marriage that didn't please me. All her recklessness, sire, it was only because she felt she had to rescue me, to spare me unhappiness."

Garron stared at her, disbelieving the mad words that had come out of her mouth. *Whose mother are you talking about? Why are you defending her? Your damned witch mother doesn't care about anyone's happiness, you know that. Don't you remember how you had to run away when she first brought Jason of Brennan to Valcourt?*

Had her mother fed her a drug that had somehow rearranged her memory? Was there such a thing?

One of the king's elegant brows went up. "Rescue you? Your mother rescued you only to force you to wed with Jason of Brennan, the man who tried to destroy Wareham for these silver coins I never heard of until recently, a portion of which rightfully belong to me—the Crown." He sat forward, sudden greed lighting his Plantagenet blue eyes.

"Never fear, sire, if the silver coins do exist, if we ever find them, you will receive your fair portion," Garron told him.

Edward nodded for Merry to continue. "You said your mother believed she was rescuing you?"

Merry nodded. "Sire, my mother believed Jason to be the better husband for me until I finally convinced her how very fine Garron was, and at last she believed me."

"Did you make her a list of all my good qualities, Merry?"

She cocked her head to one side. "A list? Why would I make a list, my lord?"

He cocked his head at her in turn. "It is what you do. Always."

"Ah. All your good qualities are imprinted on my brain, each and every one in splendid detail."

"Did you tell her I was valiant?"

"I do not believe so. Don't you believe 'valiant' is a rather foolish word?"

"Not at all," the queen said comfortably. "All know my lord is the most valiant ruler in all of Christendom."

The king turned in his beautiful chair to say to Burnell, "Do you agree, Robbie? Am I valiant?"

Burnell was staring at the fast-disappearing stuffed figs. "If you will allow your miserable servant to avail himself of a single stuffed fig, sire, I will announce to the pope that no one can exceed your majesty in every excellent quality that exists."

"Do you even remember the particular quality we were speaking about, Robbie?"

"I will, sire, very soon now." The king laughed and motioned the servant to offer the silver plate to his chancellor. Garron believed Burnell would swoon. His eyes drifted closed as he slowly chewed. "Aye, sire, I remember. Not only are you the most valiant, you are also the most generous of lords."

The queen laughed and began stroking Merry's hair again.

The king looked complacent.

The queen continued, "Do you know, Garron, that Merry already knew how to make lists when she came to me? I but refined her skills. She left my service a master."

"Aye, I did indeed." Suddenly Merry jumped to her feet. She lightly touched her fingertips to the queen's shoulder. "I thank you, my lady. I believe I wish to have my betrothed stroke my hair now." She turned to the king. Once again, she gave him a look to burn a man's feet. The king, unruffled this time, said easily, "You are tired. Go rest, but do not lie beside your betrothed else you won't be a maid at your wedding."

The queen laughed. "Aye, that is the truth, but a good head rub is a very nice end to the wild adventure you two have enjoyed. Go."

"Your wedding," Burnell said, and took another fig. "What do you wish to do?"

"Why not today?" Garron asked, and thankfully the king agreed.

However, an hour before the wedding, the queen's babe, Blanche, fell ill, and so the wedding was postponed until the morrow.

43

Garron walked beside Merry on the ramparts, London sprawling in front of them all the way to the Thames. They were thankfully too far away for the breeze to waft back foul smells to them.

It was a fine afternoon, Garron observed, even though they weren't to be married, and the air was crisp, a soft breeze blowing. Merry leaned back against the stone rampart wall. Garron said, "You have not worn your hair loose before."

She paused a moment, then smiled. "You do not like it thus?"

"Aye, I like it." He reached out his hand and took a tress, rubbed it against his fingers and palm. "I also like the various little braids you wear hidden in amongst your braids."

"You never rubbed my head, Garron."

"I don't think it such a good idea else I'd doubtless prove the king right, you'd be beneath me in a flash. I'm trying to be strong and honorable, Merry. I will rub your head tomorrow night." He cupped her cheek in his palm. "I have always liked you, Merry, even when I wanted to clout you. I admired you when I realized what you could accomplish. I even told Burnell that you were smart, which, naturally, he didn't believe for a moment. I know you will make me a fine wife, an excellent mistress for both Wareham and Valcourt." He paused a moment, looked out over London. "I was so afraid when you were taken, I believed I would choke on it. I would have faced the Devil himself to get you back safely. But the truth is, when at last I rode from your mother's tower, I didn't believe I would ever see you again. I thought she'd taken you away forever." He paused, watched the breeze lift a stray tress of hair from her forehead. "I have come to realize that I do not wish to be separated from you. I wish you by my side until I die. I wish us to build a dynasty together."

She stared up at him. "Are you saying you love me, my lord?"

He paused, frowned a bit. "I have always believed love is a word the minstrels use to beguile the ladies who listen to their songs. Let caring be enough, Merry, and I care for you a great deal, more than just an hour ago, in fact. Is that enough for you?"

"I have no need of a word that has no meaning to you, my lord. I've always loved my mother, rather I'm sure that I would have loved her had she not left me, yet it isn't at all what I feel for you. I suppose I care a great deal for you also." She began to stroke her fingers over his cheek, lightly rubbing. He felt a bolt of alarm. He grabbed her wrist and drew her hand down. "She did that, she stroked my face."

"Who?"

"Your mother. I believe now she was rubbing a drug into my flesh."

"My lord, you must listen. If she did indeed drug you, it was only because she wished to protect me. She didn't know you. I think she must have feared you. I hadn't yet convinced her that you were my perfect mate, that we should be wedded."

He shook his head. "She did not fear me, Merry. You said when you awoke from the drug one of the men gave you, you were in a room and she was there with you."

"Aye, she was."

"Tell me about the room."

She cocked her head at him, sending her hair tumbling, but she didn't give him the sloe-eyed look she'd given the king, a good thing since he would have laid her out on the ramparts walkway. "It was a workroom. I believe she spent much of her time there, reading, studying, conducting experiments, writing her results. I remember seeing stacks of bound parchments, many of them hers."

"Was there a carpet on the floor?"

She looked down at the distant maze of dark streets and the huddled houses. "I don't remember. I'm sorry, Garron. I suppose the drug was still acting on my brain."

"Did she tell you where you were?"

She shook her head. "I believed I was in Meizerling Abbey, but since it only took three hours to return me to London, I could not have been there. They left me in front of the great gates just below us." Garron looked down to see Whalen surrounded by at least three dozen men, all of them leaning in, listening to him closely. He rather hoped Whalen would remain as captain of the king's guard, a possibility only because Merry had been returned, unharmed.

It sounded to Garron like she had been in her mother's tower in the forest, and that scared him to his boots. He leaned back against the ramparts. "Merry, I do not understand you. Your mother tried to sell you to Jason of Brennan in return for him giving her Arthur's silver coins.

"Why are you defending her, both to the king and to me? Whatever her reason for sending you back here, trust me, it had nothing to do with making you happy. If she said otherwise, she was lying."

"I will admit, at first, I was frightened of

her, and very angry at what she'd done, but then she explained herself to me."

"What did she possibly say to change your mind toward her?"

"I asked her about Wareham and the Black Demon. She denied knowing anything about it. She told me Jason had offered her a lot of silver to marry me. She needed the silver, she told me, and she believed Jason to be a fine man. Why should I not believe her? She is my mother, Garron, my mother."

"What else did she tell you?"

"She said my father had kept me from her, that she missed me every moment of every day, that she'd heard my father was going to give me over to an old man and so she selected Jason of Brennan. She was very distraught when I told her what Jason had done to Wareham."

Garron could only marvel. His bright, very smart girl, and yet she believed these obvious lies? How had the bitch convinced her? He eyed her, then decided to let it go for the moment. He'd believed only a short time before that she was gone forever from him, yet she was here now, standing in front of him. That was enough. He lightly touched his fingertips to her cheek. "When Gilpin shouted to me, I looked up to see you running to me."

She gave him a huge smile that made him forget her mother, Arthur's silver, his own name. Garron leaned forward, cupped her face in his hands, and lightly kissed her. He gave her no time to respond to him, merely pulled her tightly against him and buried his face in her hair. She wrapped her arms around his back and held on. After a moment, he raised his head. "Your hair smells different."

"Different?"

He gathered handfuls of her hair in his hands, and breathed in the scent. "Aye, I do not know the names of different scents, but the smell is different."

"You believe my mother washed my hair?"

"You have no memory of such a thing?"

"No. I was asleep and then I was awake, lying on a narrow bed in this workroom. I remember the room was warm. Did she really bathe me? Wash my hair? I don't know, Garron, but if my hair smells different to you then mayhap she did, or someone did. How did my hair smell before?"

"Like wild sweet smells that lurk deep in the forest. I wanted to bury my face in your hair—in the thick plaits, with the small braids hidden amongst them. I always enjoyed looking for them. You no longer have them either."

She chewed on her lower lip, something he'd never seen her do before. She came up onto her tiptoes, kissed him.

"I never realized how very beautiful my mother is, how she looks like an older sister. Always, I—"

"Always you what?"

She shook her head.

"But you saw her only a month ago, Merry, when she arrived at Valcourt after the death of your father. She came with Jason of Brennan in tow, did she not? For him to wed you? Did you not notice then how beautiful she was, how young she looked?"

She looked confused, rubbed her temples with her fingertips. "Aye, I remember now."

"Do you know, I thought her beautiful

until I saw to the rot beneath, until I was faced with the evil in her."

He saw her face redden, knew she wanted to argue, and quickly raised his hand. "She asked me if I did not see the resemblance between you. I said no. I still do not." He paused a moment. "Somehow, I know to my gut she isn't young and beautiful. I must believe she simply made me see what she wished me to see. You as well, Merry.

"I'm beginning to think so much of what I have always believed to be real, is not. Her tower was lived in, there was even a fire burning in the grate despite there being no air holes. Then, when my men and I came back, the tower was abandoned, the inside as devastated as Wareham. Which is the truth? Is there anything about your mother that is real? Or is all of it a lie? An illusion, a dream she is able to induce?" He frowned into the distance. "I wonder what she is planning now. I wonder if you were ever really there at her tower."

To his surprise, she did not gainsay him. She tipped up her chin, smiled. "Perhaps like my mother, I will not age either, my lord. Mayhap when you are a bent old man, I will still look as I do today."

But he did not smile back at her, his fear, his confusion too fresh, too painfully clear in his mind. "You have blinded yourself to what she truly is. Surely you realize I cannot let her live. She must pay for what she has done."

"I was blind, Garron, but now I see things very clearly. She wants me to be with you. Can you not simply forget her? What has she done?"

"She sent Jason of Brennan to Wareham to find Arthur's silver to give her in exchange for your hand in marriage. He did it with her direction, I am convinced of that. If you wish to forgive her for that unpardonable act, I cannot stop you."

She said, her voice firm, and he heard anger simmering beneath the surface, "Unlike you, my lord, I do not believe she gave Jason such orders. I do not believe she knew anything about it. She knew only he was going to give her a dowry for me, in silver coins. Where is your proof of her guilt? There is none for she did nothing. Kill him, not her."

"Aye, I plan to. I will kill him because he poisoned my brother. I wonder if your mother provided him the poison to murder Arthur. If Arthur were still alive, why then I would still kill Jason of Brennan for what he did to Wareham. She and Jason must have believed the silver would be easy to find, easy to torture one of Arthur's men to tell them where it was hidden, but she was wrong.

"She must pay, Merry. Surely you realize the king will demand it."

"Do you wish to kill her?"

Only the truth, he thought. "Aye, I do. She is very dangerous, Merry." He searched for the right words. "She has blackness in her. I simply do not know as yet how I will destroy her and her blackness, for she has power I do not understand. Your mother will not stop until she has Arthur's silver. I wonder what she is planning now."

"I believe my mother has given up her hopes of acquiring more wealth. I believe she even accepts that there never was any silver at Wareham."

"Why would she accept that? Who would tell her that?"

"I don't know. I know I told her—"

"You spoke to her of Arthur's silver?"

"I must have." She rubbed her temples again, looked confused.

He lightly touched her shoulder. "Do not worry, it will all come back to you."

She shook her head. "But I don't remember why I would speak to her of the silver. Perhaps I didn't, perhaps it's all a dream."

"A dream?" *Had the witch managed to trap them both in dreams?*

"I don't know, I just don't know."

"She drugged you, made you believe her lies. Aye, I believe she has the skills to do that. I do not wish to hear you defend her again, do you understand me?"

She was crying, not making a sound, simply letting tears run slowly down her cheeks. He remembered she could cry at will. It was on the tip of his tongue to tell her to stop it, but she looked suddenly very lost. He brought her against him, rubbed his hands up and down her back, found his fingers threading through her thick hair. "We have our future ahead of us. Your mother has no place in it." He said no more. Never would he believe the witch had given up her plans for acquiring the silver. She wouldn't give up unless he managed to kill her.

But why had she let Merry leave? She hadn't gotten what she'd wanted, yet she'd given Merry her blessing and sent her back to him. It made no sense, but he knew she'd had a reason, the witch would allow nothing to happen without a reason.

Garron raised her face, and kissed her once, lightly, then twice more. He grabbed two fistfuls of her hair in his hands and brought it to his nose. "Aye, different. By Saint Glenda's clacking teeth, I do not wish to wait for you. I want you now, this very moment, but I cannot, I cannot," and he pressed his forehead against hers, held her tight until he felt a chill in the afternoon air.

"It is time," he said, and descended the ramparts ladder, Merry a step above him. When he heard a shout from Aleric, he froze.

"Garron!"

Aleric? No, it isn't possible, Aleric is guarding Wareham. Oh God, what had happened that had brought Aleric to London? He saw Sir Lyle standing behind him, his men flanking him. He leapt down the remaining six steps to the ground and ran full tilt toward him.

44

Garron, we caught him! We caught Jason of Brennan at Wareham! By all that's holy, we found Arthur's silver coins! I came to tell you myself."

Garron came to a panting halt in front of his master-at-arms. He heard the words, but could not accept them. "What did you say, Aleric?"

Aleric was grinning like a madman. "We caught Jason of Brennan. He's locked in Wareham's granary, awaiting your pleasure." And Aleric rubbed his big scarred hands together, his pleasure ferocious to behold.

Garron slammed his fist into Aleric's arm he was so pleased, so very relieved. "Did the fool come again as the Black Demon with many men and somehow find his way again into Wareham? Is everyone all right? Come, spit it out. What happened?"

"Nay, Jason of Brennan did not come as the Black Demon with an army," and Aleric laughed. "Up rides an old tinker with his equally decrepit old wife, leading three mules laden with goods. I spoke to both of them, studied their goods. I saw nothing amiss with them. I knew the mistress needed more goods, and our people were excited, and so I allowed them to enter."

"You are telling me Jason of Brennan disguised himself as an old tinker?"

"Nay, my lord, it is even better than that—he was the old man's wife. She looked as old as the dirt beneath the ancient oak at the edge of the Clandor Forest, ugly as sin, her hair tangled gray knots. I studied the old man's ancient face very carefully indeed, but I will admit I did not study the old woman that closely. I mean I looked at her face, but saw nothing untoward, just ancient seams and wrinkles and black teeth. I saw what I was meant to see. Ah, I am a fool."

"But you said you caught him. How? And how did you find Arthur's silver?"

Men were gathering around them now, listening. Merry pressed close to Garron's side.

"It was Miggins, Garron, she was watching the old crone whilst everyone else gathered around the tinker's mules and looked at all his goods. Since they arrived late, not an hour before sunset, I invited them to pass the night within. I did not question it when Miggins chose to sleep near them in the great hall. Miggins followed the old woman when she went to the jakes in the middle of the night. I was sleeping in the solar when Miggins fetched me. She told me the old woman only stopped at the jakes, then she went to your bedchamber, unaware that Miggins was behind her. Miggins said the old crone was on her knees over the hidey hole where Lisle had hidden Lady Anne's gowns after her death."

"But I myself looked into that hole, there was nothing there. Merry, you and Lisle and Miggins removed all the clothes, the shoes, did you not?"

Merry nodded.

"There was another hole beneath the boards, a larger space than the one above. It was filled with leather pouches filled with silver coins, and the old woman was pulling them out, making a stack next to her. I crept up behind her, clasped my hands together and sent my fists against her ears. She shrieked and fell back. I ripped the wig off and there lay Jason of Brennan."

Amazing, Garron thought, it was not a bad plan.

Aleric bowed his head. "I came to tell you myself so you could punish me immediately for my blindness. I should have stripped those old birds down to their wrinkled hides. You must look to me and at my failure. Aye, I failed in my responsibility, I did not see what was before my own eyes. If it were not for Miggins—"

Garron said over him, "If you had not let the two old people pass the night at Wareham, why then, we would not know where Arthur had hidden the silver coins. I prefer to believe it was your plan all along—to neatly trap Jason of Brennan once you had him within. You set Miggins to watch him. You caught him, Aleric, his arse in the air pulling the pouches from beneath the floor. Did you bring the silver here?"

"Nay, my lord, I did not wish to tempt the king to see all those piles of silver coins. It would strain a saint's morals."

"Aye, it would." Garron sighed. "Still, the king will doubtless remove more than we would wish to give him." He rubbed his hands together. "Was he humiliated to be found in an old woman's gown, with ancient seams painted on his face, his teeth blackened, a grizzled wig on his head?"

"Oh aye, it was a magnificent sight. His rage turned his face red as fresh blood, particularly when I called him by name, and he knew then he could not try to fool me. Do you know, the fool tried to fight me in his gown? I knocked him sideways and sent my boot into his ribs. Then he tried to bribe me, swore he would share the silver with me. I kicked him again. As I told you, he now resides in the granary, his ancient tinker husband with him. I believe I recognized Sir Halric, but I am not completely certain since he did not take off his disguise, and he refused to tell me his name. I left both of them in their ancient old clothes and their hideous faces." A huge grin split Aleric's face. "Oh aye, I see the truth of things now. You are right, Garron. It was my plan all along. I solved the riddle of the missing silver coins and I caught our greatest enemy, the Black Demon. Aye, I was brilliant and I deserve a knighthood. What say you?"

Garron smacked Aleric's arm again. "Why not? Let us see what the king has to say about this." He paused. "Mayhap Miggins should have a knighthood as well."

The king allowed he would consider the knighthood once he'd seen the silver coins with his own eyes. He commanded them to leave at once for Wareham since he feared that villains were lurking behind every tree, and he wanted to take no more chances with the silver. He even suggested Merry and Garron could be wed at Wareham by the king's chancellor.

And so it was that Garron and Merry,

Sir Lyle, and Aleric left London an hour later with all their men and the king's blessing, Robert Burnell accompanying them to ensure, as the king himself put it, "That there be an accurate accounting of the silver and a just amount removed as a tithe to your king."

When Garron saw the king huddled with Burnell, he knew the *just* amount of Arthur's silver was likely to be very great indeed. His last memory of the king was of him rubbing his hands together, his Plantagenet blue eyes alight with excitement.

And Garron wondered, *Where did you get all those silver coins, Arthur? Surely not from Jason of Brennan. And how did Jason of Brennan know where to find the silver this time?*

45

Merry slowly opened her eyes to see blurry bed hangings surrounding her. She blinked several times until her vision slowly began to clear. But the pain in her head still pounded fiercely. She pressed her palms against her temples and forced herself to sit up. She pushed back the bed hangings and swung her legs over the side of the bed. Soft material slid up her legs and she saw she was wearing a gauzy bedgown that covered her from throat to ankle, white, and beautifully stitched. She looked around, saw a low fire burning in the grate. She was in a bedchamber, she was warm, and she was alone.

The only problem was, she had no idea where she was.

She continued to massage her temples until the pain slowly receded. Her mouth felt dry. She picked up the carafe of water on a small table beside the bed and raised it to her mouth.

And she remembered—her kidnapping, her meeting with her mother, then nothing at all. She set the carafe back down. Her mother could very well have drugged the water.

She called out, "Mother?"

There was no answer. Apparently she was indeed alone, unless her mother had either left or made herself invisible, which wouldn't surprise her.

Slowly she got to her feet and took several steps. She was steady. She searched the room, not very large, and in the shape of a near half circle. No, more like a sickle, just like the one in which she'd awakened after those two men had brought her here. Why build rooms in such odd shapes?

Here was where?

She didn't know. She had to get away from this place, she had to get back to Garron. She rifled through a chest sitting at the foot of the bed. She found several gowns, beautiful gowns that the queen's ladies would happily covet. One was green as the richest emerald, another scarlet, the third pure white. And there were matching leather and silk slippers and hose and undergarments. Whose were they? Her mother's?

She quickly pulled off the beautiful bedgown and dressed herself. The gowns fit her perfectly. She didn't understand any of this, but it didn't matter. She had to leave this place, wherever this place was, and get back to Garron.

There was no window in the room. All the shadowy light came from the sluggishly burning fire. What time was it? What day was it? How much time had passed since she'd first been brought here?

She hurried to the door and quietly pulled down the latch. It was locked. Well, what did she expect? A prisoner, that's what she was, her mother's prisoner. Rage filled her and she jerked again on the latch. To her surprise the door opened this time. She looked at the latch for a moment, wondering why it hadn't opened the first time she'd tried it. She looked into a darkened narrow corridor. At the far end of the corridor, she saw a staircase. There was a door directly opposite her, but she wasn't about to go in there. She lightly ran down the stairs. Once at the bottom, she looked through the shadows shrouding the corridor and could make out the main door.

She heard a noise. Was her mother coming?

She heard the latch give on the front door and quickly pressed herself against the wall, deep in the shadows. She watched the thick wooden door open. It wasn't her mother who entered, it was an old woman carrying a basket in her arms, and humming.

She looked neither right nor left, merely walked down the corridor toward the stairs, toward Merry. Evidently she was bringing the prisoner some food. Merry waited until she was nearly in front of her. She grabbed the old woman by the neck and dragged her back against her. She said against that old ear, "Don't you dare drop that basket. I am very thirsty and hungry." She lessened the pressure on the old throat.

"You're bringing me food?"

"Aye. Ye're hurting me, young'un."

"Where are we?"

The old woman was silent a moment, Merry could feel her surprise. "Ye don't know? Why, we are in the witch's tower. I am taking care of ye until she returns."

"When will the witch come back here?"

"I don't know, mayhap another day. I do what she tells me to do, naught more, naught less, else she'll turn me into a lizard. Ye're hungry, are ye, young'un? The witch said she left water fer ye, her special water, and I was to bring ye food today."

How many days had she passed in limbo? Merry knew that if her mother walked into her tower, she'd have killed her in that moment.

"Where do you come from?"

"From the woodcutter's cottage, not far from here. The witch came to me and offered me two ha'pennies to take care of ye. I knew I didn't have a choice since I didn't want to die a lizard. Then a beautiful young knight came to my cottage and asked me where the witch was. I told him, aye, and why not? He gave me two whole silver pennies, so beautiful they were, they shined like God's face in the sunlight when the sun finally showed itself."

Garron. "Did you tell him to come here?"

"Aye, he was searching for ye. Later he and his men rode back past my cottage. I suppose he didn't find ye."

Thank St. Ebert's valiant heart her mother hadn't killed Garron. Had her mother seen him? Spoken to him? She thought she probably had. But she'd wager she'd magicked him, or drugged him just as she'd drugged her daughter. But he was all right, thank the good Lord and all his bearded apostles.

How had he gotten away from her?

"What will I do with my silver?"

Merry eyed the old woman. "Do not worry, I will take all the silver you have and use it well. We're leaving now.

You're taking me back to your cottage, and then you will tell me how to get back to London."

"Think ye the witch will demand back the silver she already gave me? Think ye she will turn me into a lizard?"

"It's likely, so I'll let you keep your coins and you can return them to her when she comes."

"What will it matter? I will be dead by nightfall, she will kill me."

Merry said, "You said she would turn you into a lizard. Well, I believe you would make a fine lizard. Just think how very fast you will climb trees. How long have you been tending me?"

"Two days now. I wake ye up, bathe ye, feed ye, give ye some drink from this bottle of water yer mother left fer ye, and help ye relieve yerself. Then ye drift off again, like a sweet little lamb."

Merry took the basket from the old woman and led her unresisting out the wooden front door.

She looked back at the stark, ugly tower that sat in the middle of an enclosure. Was Garron still in London? Did he believe her dead, and returned to Wareham? She didn't know what to do. But at least she knew how to begin.

"Let us go," she told the old woman. "Quickly."

They walked through the woods, as fast as she could prod the old woman along. Merry wished the old woman *was* a lizard, they'd certainly move faster. When finally they reached the small clearing where the woodcutter's hut sat, Merry stopped and looked carefully around. "How do I get out of this forest?"

The old woman pointed. Merry opened the basket and looked inside. There were slices of partridge, a thick loaf of brown bread, and a flask. She smiled at the old woman. "There is a lot of food here. What would you like to have?"

The old woman immediately picked up the brown bread. When Merry pointed to the meat, she shook her head.

"Would you like what is in the flask?"

"Nay, young'un. Ye're thirsty, ye drink it. And the meat, it'll fill up yer belly."

Merry grabbed the meat, set the basket on the ground, and began running toward the woods. She called out over her shoulder, "Enjoy your dreams."

She'd no sooner reached the trees when she heard a loud whooshing sound. She dove behind a thick, ancient maple tree.

46

WAREHAM CASTLE

It rained only one day on their journey back to Wareham, a light, warm rain that even Robert Burnell didn't mind. He merely wound his long woolen scarf around his head and tied it beneath his chin. All thoughts, all conversation, Robert Burnell's included, was about Arthur's silver coins. Garron actually saw Burnell rubbing his hands together, doubtless contemplating the king's pleasure when he returned to place pouches of silver coins in the king's eager hands. The king had sent twenty of his most trusted soldiers with Burnell to guard his share. *Damn you, Arthur.*

It seemed to Garron that he was the only one who cared where the silver coins had come from.

He looked over at Merry, who was humming a tune he'd heard at court. She wore no covering over her head. Her glorious hair shone beneath the afternoon sun, long and loose, not a single small braid hidden here or there. The queen's ladies must have told her the thick plaits were for a child, not a grown lady who was shortly to marry. He wanted to tell her they were wrong, that he really liked the fat plaits and the small hidden braids, and the smell of her hair. He pulled Damocles close to her mare. "You're thoughtful. Are you making a list of all that you wish to do with Arthur's silver?"

"Lists. Why do you always think I am making lists, my lord?"

He cocked his head at her. "You always are, just as I am."

She cocked her head back at him, then gave him a look that made him want to grab her off her mare's back, set her facing him, and wish them alone, all in the space of a moment. Would she enjoy him this time? Probably not, it was too soon. He needed time and privacy, aye, lots of time, and his wits about him this time. He grinned, looking around at the score of men who rode around them, then back at her.

"Why are you looking at me like that?" Merry asked.

"I am remembering our one night together. I am remembering how your breasts felt in my hands, how you tasted. I am remembering how it felt to tear through your maidenhead." Simply saying that word made him shudder. "And I am remembering how Gilpin thought murder was being done in my chamber."

She said nothing at all, looked straight ahead between her horse's ears.

"I am sorry I hurt you, Merry." Still she said nothing. He arched a black brow. "What is this? You do not wish to berate me? You do not wish to tell me it was all my fault?"

"It was your fault."

"Ha, I was not even there, not really, just the husk of myself. One minute I was dreaming of mighty deeds, the next moment Blanche was astride me, her breasts in my hands. I remember I did not understand why she was still wearing her bedgown."

Again, she cocked her head at him, then in the space of a moment, he would swear she was embarrassed. Well, she should be, since she'd been the one to come to him. She raised her chin. "I have nothing to say about it."

He was charmed. He said, voice low, "You certainly had a lot to say then."

"A lady must speak upon certain occasions or else be ground under."

"Ah, so you're no longer embarrassed about what you did. Now you're all smug and pleased with yourself. I wager if we were walking, you would be swaggering. No, don't look at me like that. It is how you looked at the king and he nearly drooled on you. I will do more than drool, believe me."

"I did nothing to the king. It is merely a look, of little account."

"Did the queen's ladies teach you how to do it? I never saw that look before you poured it full measure on the king."

"My lord, we are nearly home!"

Garron slapped her horse's neck and rode to the front of the column. He looked toward Wareham. His home and it would be his children's home. *A dynasty*, he thought. If life dished out more good than bad, he and Merry would build a dynasty that lasted until time passed into a far-distant future.

He shouted at the top of his lungs, and galloped toward Wareham.

47

There were piles of silver pennies, not a single one was cut, all were whole, glistening in the dull light in the lord's bedchamber, so many of them, piles upon piles, guarded in shifts by a dozen men, and two of his most trusted men, Pali and Hobbs, in charge.

Garron reached down and gathered a handful and watched them slide through his fingers. The silver weighed heavy. The silver also would make him wealthy beyond his wildest dreams, even after the king took his own generous share. There was still so much to be done here at Wareham and now he was wealthy enough to accomplish anything he wished to do.

Burnell said complacently, as he sifted through the piles of silver himself, "Our precious king will be so pleased with you, my lord, I doubt not he will bestow another barony on you. Mayhap even a knighthood for Aleric."

Garron heard Aleric draw in his breath behind him. He looked up at him. "Sir Aleric. Now that has a nice sound to it." And another barony for his dynasty? "Ah, do you believe the king will require more than a *just* share for this barony?"

Robert Burnell did not look up from the pile of silver coins he was counting. "Again you indulge in irony, my lord. We will count the silver, and then we will count it again, and then we will see."

He was distracted when Merry called out, "Miggins tells me Jason of Brennan is now a very smelly old woman. He cursed you and God in the same breath, she says, and he is demanding trousers."

Garron turned to see Miggins standing beside Merry, grinning from ear to ear. He grabbed her up and whirled her about.

"What say you, Miggins, shall we leave the thieving lout in his gown?"

"Aye, lad, he makes a fine old crone. But ye know, he hasn't cursed so much the past two days. Ah, but his rage, Pali told me it still pours off him like rancid oil. I wanted to kick him and so my sweet Pali here stepped aside. I slammed my shoe in his ribs, dug my toes right in. Aye, the little coward yelled proper loud."

Garron said to Hobbs and Pali, "Thank you both for guarding the silver. It is Wareham's future. Pali, that was a fine reward for Miggins." He rose, dusted off his hands, called out to the dozen or so people in the lord's bedchamber, "The silver is well guarded. Let us see what our old crone has to say."

As the procession walked down the narrow stairs to the granary, Hobbs cleared his throat. "A surprise awaits you, Garron."

Garron's eyebrow shot up.

"Nay, you will see," said Hobbs. Each step they took down the stairs, the air became more chill and dank and fetid. There were no windows, just deep shadows even with the rush lights.

Aleric unlocked the cell door and raised the rush light high. "There is Jason of Brennan, in all his glory."

Garron saw that Jason of Brennan had rubbed all the dirt seams off his face and the black from his teeth. He was close to Arthur's age, young and comely, or he would be if he didn't look so very miserable, filthy, and sullen. He hadn't stripped off the old gown because it was too cold and damp to go without. It was a wretched room, and Garron was pleased to think of him spending the past week here.

"At last I meet you, Jason of Brennan. I am Garron of Kersey, Earl of Wareham. And this, I believe, must be your husband?"

He looked down at the old man as he slowly raised his head. He'd also cleaned the lines and seams off his face, rubbed the black off his teeth. Garron looked into Sir Halric's face. *How lucky can a man be?*

Pali said, "Your surprise, Garron. Aleric knew you would be pleased to see the whoreson again."

"I have been hoping Aleric was right.

Let me tell you I find your disguises very clever, but it is over now. I wish the truth now, all of it. Jason of Brennan, you will begin."

Jason gathered as much spit in his mouth as he could and sent it hurtling toward Garron's boot. It fell several inches short. He was heaving, he was so enraged. "I will tell you nothing, you bastard!"

Hobbs said at his elbow, "I knew you wouldn't want them starving and nearly dead, Garron, so I had Bullic feed them well. Now when you break them, it will be all the sweeter."

Hobbs knew him well.

"Sir Halric, the last time I saw you, you were running away from me."

Sir Halric merely stared at him, said nothing at all.

Garron studied Jason of Brennan's face again, then he turned on his heel and walked out of the cell, calling back over his shoulder, "I will see you and Sir Halric again in two days. Perhaps you will feel like talking to me then."

As the cell door clanked shut, Garron heard Sir Halric groan, heard the murmur of low, angry voices.

For two days, Garron said nothing more about the men, merely instructed Bullic to continue to feed them well.

Garron was eating bread and cheese the following morning, when he saw Merry staring at Elaine, her eyes narrowed. "What is this? Has Elaine displeased you?"

She looked quickly over at him, shaking her head. "Nay, I worry about her, that is all. Why is she speaking to that soldier?"

Garron said mildly, "That man is Lussy, one of the king's finest soldiers. As you well know, her husband was killed by Jason of Brennan's men. Lussy is a good man. I'm thinking she might like him. What is amiss with you, Merry? You have always liked Elaine."

Merry was slowly shaking her head, her lips seamed. "I don't believe that is her purpose. I heard her say your name plainly. She is speaking to Lussy about you, Garron. 'Tis you she wants, not Lussy. I know it." At his baffled look, she raised her hand to her forehead and rubbed. "I'm sorry. I don't know what I'm saying. 'Tis a pain in my head that is making me miserable and foolish."

"Have you no recipe to cure yourself?"
She looked utterly blank.

"The pain must be very bad indeed
to make you forget your *Leech Book of
Bald*," he said patiently. "Consult it for a
curative potion. Would you like Miggins
to help you? She does not read, but she
could surely follow your directions."

"Nay, I can do it by myself."

He watched her walk away from him.
He'd been about to ask her if she would
wed with him on the morrow, but he
hadn't. There was indeed still something very wrong with her. He continued
to watch her cross the great hall. She
didn't pause to greet a single woman she
passed. He frowned. She truly believed
Elaine to be interested in him. It made
no sense, and he thought again about
the drug her mother had fed her. It had
changed her utterly.

He heard Aleric yelling something at
Gilpin. Three minutes later, he was laughing so hard he was holding his belly. Gilpin had tied Eric the goat to Aleric's new
bed. Smelling the fresh lumber, the goat
had chewed through one of the bed legs.

———

Without conscious thought, Garron found himself watching Merry throughout the day. He realized she seemed distant from the women, very unusual for Merry, who always had her nose pressed into every single task being performed at Wareham. But what was very strange indeed was that the women didn't come to her as they used to. And the laughter, it had become more and more rare since they'd come back to Wareham. Today, he thought, it was simply gone. He thought again of her mother's drug. What had the witch done to her own daughter? She was simply different, and it had nothing to do with her loose hair, which she wore long and free all the time now, or the smell of her hair.

But there was so much to be done, he had no time to dwell on it. The silver was discussed and counted and discussed more and recounted. He and Burnell agreed to the number of silver coins Burnell would take back to the king. Rather, Burnell announced the amount and Garron, having no choice whatsoever, and thinking about another barony, agreed. After all, it had been his brother's silver in any case, not his. Or Arthur had stolen it, probably from Jason of Brennan's father, Lord Ranulf, but who knew? It was manna from heaven for him, no matter the number of coins remaining to him after the king's large hands delved into the piles.

On the morning of the third day, Garron, Aleric, Pali, Hobbs, and Gilpin went again to the cell in the granary.

48

Garron looked through the bars at the two men who lay silently in their filth. He'd wanted to break their wills, not kill them. He judged them to be ready.

He walked into the stinking cell. Neither man looked up. Neither man spoke. They looked broken enough. "Aleric, bring our two ancients up into the inner bailey, I wish to see them clearly in the sunlight, admire their lovely gowns. Ah, they stink. We'll let them bathe in the well. Merry made some lavender soap, they can use it." And Garron turned on his heel and left the granary, whistling.

He and all his people watched Pali and Hobbs strip the two men down to their skin. There was laughter when the men threw buckets filled with the cold water from the castle well at them, and they yelped and tried to duck and cover themselves at the same time, but with the continuous hooting and shouting of coarse remarks made by both men and women, they soon realized it was pointless. So they set about scrubbing themselves. The lavender soap was sweet smelling indeed.

Merry said to Garron, "This man, Sir Halric, he looks paltry."

"Aye, he does." Garron stood, arms crossed over his chest, and he never took his eyes off the two men. "But then you spent a good deal of time with him."

"Jason of Brennan is young enough and comely, just as my mother told me."

He said lightly, "But you've seen him before, Merry, don't you remember? He came to Valcourt with your mother."

"Aye, I was but giving you her report of him." She turned and lightly ran her fingertips up his arm.

"Mind your virtue, Merry," he said, then

turned back to the two men. He said easily, "I like the smell of the soap. What is
the scent?"

She cocked her head at him. "How
should I know that, my lord?"

Because you made it. He became very
still. Once the two men were dressed,
this time in trousers and tunics from the
goods they themselves had brought to
Wareham, Garron said, "Aleric, bring them
into the great hall. It is time for them to
share their deepest secrets with me."

Garron sat in his new beautifully carved
lord's chair. It was the first time, he realized, that he'd ever in his life sat in judg-
ment. He breathed in the fresh oak and
let the power he knew was his alone settle
into him. Robert Burnell stood off to one
side, not saying a word. *Probably thinking about his silver coins*, Garron thought,
*probably wondering how he could claim
more.*

"Jason of Brennan, I would like you to
meet the person who brought you down."
He nodded to Miggins, who flung her head
back and proudly walked to stand beside
his chair. She gave Jason a big grin and

waved a gnarly fist in his face. "I got ye, ye little bastid, none other, jest me."

Trousers gave a man courage, and so Jason of Brennan yelled, "Old crone, I'll gullet you when I am free."

Robert Burnell called out, "You will never again be free, sirrah. Best not make threats when your miserable life hangs in the balance."

Jason of Brennan knew very well this was Robert Burnell, trusted above all others by the king. A scrawny man, he thought, his head covered with thick, dark hair that curled around his ears, not a single white strand threaded in. His father had once talked of knowing Burnell in their youth, and that meant Burnell was old enough to have white hair, and why didn't he? Jason's father had a mane of white hair. He saw Burnell's bony fingers were covered with ink. His black robe looked musty and old. When all was said and done, Burnell was naught but a miserable scribe, Chancellor of England or not. But he had the king's ear and that meant there would be no mercy, he knew it. He screwed up his courage and said nothing more. Sir Halric stood quietly beside him, the man seemingly as stolid as Jason's father.

"I would like to hear the truth now," Garron said, looking from one man to the other.

Neither even looked at him.

Garron drew his stiletto as he rose from his chair. "You wish me to remove an ear, Jason of Brennan? Will that encourage you to spit out the truth?"

Jason of Brennan said nothing, but his heart began to pound hard and hot.

"I do not know if losing an ear will make you hear less. Do you wish to take the chance?"

Jason of Brennan continued to say nothing. He looked at Garron, and once again, he spit at him. This time his spittle landed on Garron's tunic.

Garron's knife moved so swiftly, it seemed a blur. Garron sliced off his right ear, cleanly and quickly. Jason yelled in shock, grabbed his head, and fell to his knees, keening.

Garron stood over him and calmly wiped off his blade. "You will tell me the truth now, or you will lose your other ear as well."

Jason began to sob, deep in his throat, and rocked back and forth on his heels. "You have made me a monster, a freak!"

Robert Burnell cleared his throat. "Listen to me, you miserable whelp, you will speak the truth now or I will take both you and Sir Halric back to the king. Lord Garron knows naught of torture, thus you lost your ear fast, with no fuss, no real pain, no undue mutilation, so quit your weeping. If you wish to bear unspeakable pain, pain that makes your tongue swell in your mouth so you cannot breathe, I will give you over to the king's men. Stop your howling, do you hear me? By all the saints' wooden crosses, you sicken me. You are a man, act like one!"

Jason of Brennan seemed not to hear.

"Jason," Sir Halric said quietly. "Get hold of yourself. Tell them the truth. It matters not now. Nothing matters any longer."

Slowly, Jason raised his face to Burnell. Blood streamed down his neck, soaking his tunic. It was Merry who silently walked to him, and gave him a folded cloth to press against his head. Garron said nothing, merely watched her from where he sat again on his lord's chair.

Burnell said, "I have known your father for many years, Jason. He was always a hard man, even when we were young, but he was also a man of great bravery and principles, a man who has always supported the king. As you know, your father traveled with the king to the Holy Land. He never left the king's side. The king trusts him.

"I knew there was strife between you and your father, but not the cause for it. You must have shamed him greatly, even as you shamed yourself.

"Speak the truth now, Jason, or I will return you to London and turn you over to the king's men. You would not do well under their tender mercies."

"I was but trying to make amends."

"Amends to whom?" Burnell asked him. "Stand up, you pathetic scoundrel!"

Jason tried to rise. Garron said nothing, remained expressionless, when Merry moved quickly to help him. Once upright, Merry stepped away from him. He squared his shoulders, but his voice was only a whisper when he began to speak, liquid with misery and tears, "I am guilty of naught save trying to find my father's silver coins so that I may return them to him. The silver is not yours, Garron of Kersey, nor was it your damned brother's, who stole it!"

Garron sat forward in his chair, his hands fists on his knees. His knife was back in its sheath at his belt. "You claimed Arthur stole the coins from you. But now you are claiming the hundreds of silver coins do not belong to you, but to your father? And you were trying to steal them back for him?"

"It is the truth. I have no reason to lie, not now."

Burnell said, "How could Arthur possibly have stolen such a vast number of silver coins from your father? How did Arthur even know of the silver?"

"I don't know how he managed it, but he did. He struck my father down in his solar, where he'd hidden the silver. My poor father never even knew who had done it. Ah, but I knew, I knew, for there could be no other."

Garron grabbed Jason by the neck and shook him like a rat. Jason of Brennan struggled, but every shake made the pain of his lost ear send agony through his head. He tried to kick out, but Garron's rage was powerful. "I suppose you believe you can say anything about my brother since he is dead?" He drew his knife. "I think you'll lose your other ear now, you lying whoreson."

"No!"

Garron froze. It was Merry's voice.

He looked over Jason's head at her white face. Sunlight was pouring through the open doors into the great hall, turning her hair to fire. Slowly, he nodded to her to speak.

"My lord, there is no reason to mutilate him further. He will tell you what you wish to know."

Garron said, "You will be silent now, Merry, this has naught to do with you. You, Jason of Brennan, you will speak now or I will slice off your other ear."

He watched her shoot a look at Jason, then she slowly lowered her head.

Jason was holding his palm against

his bandaged head, blood seeping out between his fingers. He shouted, "Your damned brother is not dead! How do you think I knew where to look for the silver? Arthur finally told me where he'd hidden it. You're not an earl, you puffed-up bladder, you're nothing at all!"

Garron roared out of his chair, grabbed Jason around his throat, and lifted him off the stone floor. He stared at Jason's face, white as death, the red blood snaking from beneath the white bandage, turning black against his neck. "You are saying my brother is alive?"

"Aye, he's alive."

Miggins screeched, "Thass a lie! Ye filthy mongrel, I saw Lord Arthur's face fall in his trencher! He was as dead as all the poor souls ye butchered when ye came as the Black Demon to Wareham! Ye poisoned him! We buried him! Ye hear me? We buried Lord Arthur!"

"Nay," Sir Halric said, "Jason does not lie. Lord Arthur was not dead. One of his men in my pay fed him a draught that gave him the look of death. We stole him out of Wareham, and another was wrapped and buried in his place. We took him away so we could question him."

"And just where," Garron asked quietly, "did you obtain this draught that gave my brother the look of death?"

Sir Halric said, "This mangy little liar claimed the credit, but that is absurd. It was all the witch's plan."

Jason yelled, "Aye, it was all from the witch."

"Was it also the witch's idea to plant a traitor in Wareham to open the postern gate so you and your men could enter?"

"Aye."

"But why did you kill everyone? Why did you destroy my home?"

"It wasn't my fault that I had to kill so many. No one would tell me the truth!"

"How could anyone tell you anything at all since only Arthur knew where he'd hidden the silver? How did you even know the silver was here?"

"His men helped him, mayhap women too. Aye, I knew the silver was here. It was Arthur's damned home. Of course he brought the silver here. He deserved nothing, do you hear me? His people deserved nothing! They lied to me just as he did!" Suddenly his rage overcame his desire to survive. He screamed, "By Saint Bartholomew's gilded heart, I hate this place! I delighted in killing all your brother's people, do you hear me, worthless wretches, all of them!"

There was stark silence in the great hall. Then Garron heard murmuring amongst his people, his people who had lost so many to this idiot.

Garron said, "We will speak more of that presently. What did you do to my brother?"

"I did nothing to him, merely took him to a cottage near my home. I waited and waited, but he didn't wake up from the drug. I had no choice but to go again to the witch, and she gave me another plan." Jason whirled on Sir Halric, and his voice was bitter as salt on ice. "You did not argue about the ruse, did you? You said you believed you could convince the starving beggars within these walls to let you in to help them. You did not suggest we should continue to wait to see if Arthur woke up. It was all your fault, damn you, not mine. And you failed yet again, just as you did the first time."

Jason was panting now. "Aye, the witch told you the amount of potion to pour into Arthur's ale, but your man obviously gave him too much. It is all your fault, Halric, all of it!"

Sir Halric grabbed him by the neck. He screamed right in his face, "Just listen to you—you claimed the Black Demon and the Retribution was all your idea. I never believed you, never, but I remember well how you preened and strutted about." And Sir Halric struck his jaw with his fist.

Garron believed Jason of Brennan's heart would burst out of his chest. His face was the color of the blood still slowly seeping through the white bandage. "How dare you strike me? I will kill you for that, Halric! The witch demanded that I kill you, but I did not. Because of you I have lost not only the silver coins, I have lost Valcourt to this bastard!"

"But I am not a bastard," Garron said. "I gather that Arthur finally woke up, didn't he? And since you knew exactly where to find the silver, you tortured him, didn't you, to make him confess the hiding place. Did the witch also give you the plan to get into Wareham this time, disguised as an old tinker and his wife?"

"Aye. It is all her doing, every plan, every ruse. I remembered finally when I was lying in your cell that the witch had magicked me, the wicked creature made me do all of it. None of it was my fault!"

"My mother is not a creature!"

49

The silence in the great hall was absolute. Garron knew he heard Merry's harsh breathing. He raised his hand to hold her silent.

Robert Burnell's rich deep voice broke the silence. "There is something I wish to know. Jason of Brennan, you said the silver coins belonged to your father. How did Lord Ranulf come by all this silver?"

Garron watched Jason of Brennan slowly turn to face the Chancellor of England. It seemed to Garron in that moment that Burnell looked larger, more formidable. He looked like God, a very angry

God, all he needed was a raised staff in his hand.

Jason said, "My father always had the silver. I knew nothing of it until I chanced upon him with the silver when I was but a young boy. He was sitting on the floor of his solar, piles of silver coins surrounded him, and he was counting the coins. He was happy, I could hear it in his voice and see it on his face. It is one of the few times I have ever seen my father happy, before or since. He was counting out loud and he sounded like he was speaking to a friend, or mayhap to a lover, given how he caressed the individual coins. When he saw me standing there, he didn't yell at me or strike me. Nay, he beckoned me to him and said, 'Behold, this is Arlette's gift to our line, Jason. You will never tell a soul about it or I will cut off your tongue and feed it to you. It is our secret. When I am gone, you will take my place, and it will be your turn to guard the silver. You will hold it close, Jason, else you will die a horrible death, and our line will die. Do you understand me?'

"I did not understand then and I do not understand now. Was the silver cursed?

If it were spent, would the one who spent it die this horrible death? How could our line die?

"And I wondered who this Arlette was and how long the silver had been in our family, and so I asked him. He whispered her name again—'Arlette'—and his voice was reverent. 'She drew power from the ancient oak trees, it was told to me. The silver was given to her by countless men who wished her favor. She lived so very long ago.' He said no more, and I didn't either, I was too afraid. I remember I told him I understood, and he told me to leave him and never, never tell another soul what I had seen."

Burnell said, "Then why did you tell Arthur of the silver?"

Jason lowered his head. "I was young, only fifteen. Arthur was eighteen. He and I fought together in a tourney held outside York. We wenched that night, and drank too much ale. He'd beaten me and I suppose I wanted to tell him something that made him feel insignificant, as he was, and so I told him about my family's treasure. The next morning, I remembered I'd told him and I knew such fear I believed

I'd choke on it. When I asked him if he remembered my telling him a tale of silver treasure, he laughed at me, claimed he didn't remember anything, for he'd drunk himself into a stupor. He never said anything to me about it so I believed he had indeed forgotten. We went our own ways after the tourney."

"Did you tell him where your father had hidden the silver?"

He said, "I must have, but I do not remember."

"Did you tell your father what you had done?"

"By all the saints, no! He would have cut out my tongue and fed it to me! My father never makes threats he doesn't mean."

Burnell's voice was so low now, Jason had to lean toward him to hear. "So, because you remained silent in your treachery, your father had no warning at all."

"I tell you, Arthur did not remember! Nothing happened, nothing, do you hear me? Years passed. Years! Then when I was fighting in France with a kinsman, my father sent a message to me, telling me someone had struck him down and stolen the silver from its hiding place. He told me I was the only one who knew of the treasure, even my mother did not know.

"I wasn't about to tell him about Arthur, I dared not else he would have rendered me tongueless, and probably cast me off. I swore to him that I'd never told anyone, but I do not think he believed me. He looked at me sometimes when he did not think I was watching. There was disbelief in his eyes, and I knew to my soul that he knew as well. And I was afraid, but I did not know what to do."

Sir Halric said, contempt in his voice, "Of course Lord Ranulf knew you'd given up the secret, he'd always known, he simply did not know about Arthur. Lord Ranulf told me what you'd done and set me to watch you five years ago. He hoped you would speak to me of it, and you did finally when you realized you had to have my help."

Jason turned on him. He would have clouted him, but when he raised his arm, he felt a shaft of pain in his head so great he nearly fell to his knees. He screamed, "You mangy whoreson! I believed you were my man, but you were naught but a spy for my father! You betrayed me!"

Sir Halric gave him a sneer. "Aye, you should have seen Lord Ranulf roar with laughter when I told him how the witch of Meizerling Abbey had you under her thumb, how you'd told her of the silver coins but you didn't know how to get them. She promised you she would arrange for you to wed with her daughter, the heiress of Valcourt, if you brought her the silver. Lord Ranulf couldn't wait to see what her plan was.

"Your father knew every single move you made, and he was pleased with the witch's plan, though he was furious at your butchery here at Wareham. When I told him Arthur had awakened and confessed, he was content to see what you would do. He laughed when I told him about you making yourself into an ancient old crone. It was your father who ordered me to play the tinker so I would know exactly what happened.

"When he hears of this failure, Jason, he will not only cut out your tongue, he will kill you, for you have lost Arlette's silver.

He knows his line is now cursed. Aye, he told me if he did not die with the silver in his keeping, his line would die out within a generation."

Jason was beside himself. He yelled, "You were the one who failed, Halric! The witch promised me the heiress, and you did capture her for me, but just look what happened. Garron of Kersey got her back. The witch told me to kill you because you failed. But I have a full share of mercy. You had been at my side for many years, and so I didn't kill you, but I will, you bastard, I swear it on my honor, I will slit your bloody throat!"

Sir Halric said, "It was bad luck, naught more than bad luck that this man came upon us, and freed the heiress."

Suddenly, Jason froze. He said slowly, trying to weave his thoughts together over the pain, "Were you really going to bring her to me, Halric?"

Contempt sliced through Halric's voice. "What do you think, you braying little cock?"

Jason actually groaned. "You betrayed me yet again. You were going to take her to my father, weren't you? You were going to give her to him so he could have Valcourt, and I would have nothing."

There was a moment of raging silence, then Sir Halric laughed, a high, full laugh. "Aye, when I found the heiress skulking away from Valcourt and caught her, I did indeed decide to take her to your father. Your father would have rewarded me, as you have never done."

Sir Halric turned to Garron. "Aye, you beat me, sent me running. Your men killed mine, and you brought the heiress here to wed yourself. You are not a fool, are you, Garron of Kersey? When you looked at her, you knew she would bring you great wealth and great power, and you had to do absolutely nothing to earn it. But heed me, my lord, both the heiress and the silver belong to Lord Ranulf, to no one else."

Garron smiled. "Since the heiress did not tell me who she was, believe me, Sir Halric, I had to work very hard indeed to gain her hand in marriage."

Sir Halric turned to Merry. "She's naught but an evil spawn, all that sinful red hair flying around her head."

"I want her," Jason yelled. "She belongs

to me! She wrapped a bandage around my head. I will kill her witch mother and then wed the heiress. It is I who will have Valcourt."

Sir Halric stepped right in Jason's face. He said very quietly, "Are you blind? Are you too witless to understand that you will shortly be dead? You will never have the heiress. You will never have Valcourt. You will never have the silver. You've lost, and you've dragged me down with you. Aye, I deserve to be killed because I obeyed Lord Ranulf when he told me to do what you wished, all the while rubbing his hands together, knowing I would help you recover the silver. I even agreed to make myself into a tinker traveling with his ugly old wife with three mules laden with goods—and just look at what happened when we came here again." He grabbed Jason by the throat and shook him. Jason tried to push him away, but the pain in his head nearly sent him to his knees.

Then Sir Halric released him, stepped back, and shook his head in disgust. "Both of us were caught and humiliated because of that damned witch's mad plan.

Do you know it was your grandmother who passed down Arlette's silver coins to your father? She told him at her last breath he would be the guardian and she explained to him about Arlette's silver, and the cost to him if he lost it."

Burnell said more to himself than to Sir Halric, "Arlette. Was she a Druid priestess, do you think? She gathered silver from men to protect them, to cleanse their sins? Sir Halric, you don't know who she is?"

Sir Halric said, "Lord Ranulf did not tell me anything more, merely that his own mother spoke to him about the silver coins."

Burnell said, "I must study this, determine who this Arlette was. She was of your line, surely. The distant past, I wonder if that is true?"

Garron laughed, he actually laughed until he shook with it. "Sir," he said to Burnell, "you have fallen into this fine old tale—a Druid priestess—but think, sir. The silver coins, you have seen them. They aren't a thousand years old, they are of our time, mayhap amongst the first silver pennies ever issued, probably issued by King Henry. So, Lord Ranulf spun this tale for his son, and for Sir Halric. Jason still spins it. The king must ask Lord Ranulf where the coins really come from."

Burnell, that spiritual man of immense faith, cursed beneath his breath. He looked embarrassed. Then he squared his shoulder. "Aye, a romantic tale it is, and so I forgot what I saw with my own eyes. You are right, Garron, it is Lord Ranulf who has to tell the king the truth."

Garron said to Jason, "I wish to know where you're keeping my brother. Or are you lying? Did you kill him after he confessed the hiding place to you?"

"Arthur is still breathing," Jason said. "I wanted to kill him but I couldn't be sure he had told me the truth. Aye, he lives." He managed a laugh. "So you are nothing, just as I told you, Garron of Kersey, nothing at all, except one of the king's lowly guards."

It was Robert Burnell who calmly walked to Jason and sent his fist hard into his jaw. "No man is lowly, sirrah, when he is in the king's service."

50

Not long after Jason of Brennan and Sir Halric were taken back to the granary, Miggins eased up behind Garron and lightly tugged on his sleeve. "My lord."

"Aye, Miggins? You have more revelations to turn my hair white?"

The old woman quickly looked around, then leaned close. "Ye must listen to me, beautiful lad, ye must."

What now? By all the saints' blistered fingers, there was so much for him to consider, so many decisions to make, and there was his brother, and if he were indeed alive, then Arthur was the earl, not

Garron, and there was Merry, always Merry—he nodded down at the scrappy old woman. "I'm listening."

"Merry has changed. None of us knows what has changed her, but since ye brought her back, she is different. She doesn't know things she should know, like names, though she pretends to. She didn't even remember that Eric the goat was named after little Ivo and Errol's father. She is jealous of Elaine, I've seen her show spite. Something is very wrong. Ye must do something."

Garron said very quietly, "I did not tell you, Miggins, but when her mother kidnapped her, the witch drugged her. I believe the drug must have changed her. We must hope she will recover from it."

But Miggins did not look convinced. She opened her mouth, then shut it because Garron said, "It does not matter now. If Arthur indeed lives, then I am no longer the Earl of Wareham. I will not be allowed to wed her." He thought of the days that had passed, so many days when he could have wed her, but hadn't. But if he had wed her—what would have happened then? Would the king still make him the Earl of Valcourt? He doubted it. Well, it didn't matter now. No matter what her differences, no matter how she had changed, even the scent of her hair, Merry would never be his wife, whether he wanted her to be or not. He gave a low, vicious laugh. Jason of Brennan was right, he would once again become nothing more than the king's lowly guard.

Miggins was frowning. "It is very strange. I knew Lord Arthur was dead, my lord, knew it to my soul. I was wrong, and that's a blow, I tell ye. Do ye believe he really still lives?"

"Jason of Brennan said he could not take the chance of killing Arthur in case he'd lied about where he'd hidden the silver. It is reasonable. Thus, Wareham is his. It is his birthright, not mine." It hurt so much to say those words, hurt all the way to his soul.

"He was a warty master, lad, niver happy with what he had. And now he will lose the silver, ye know the king will not let him claim any of it. Think ye it will go back to Lord Ranulf?"

"Since I don't know where Ranulf got

the silver coins, it is up to the king to judge the matter. It no longer has anything to do with me."

"And those two mangy scoundrels, Jason of Brennan and Sir Halric?"

"Burnell wants to take them and the silver back to London, to the king. I am going with him, to demand my right to kill him. Killing him is little enough payment for what he did to Wareham, much less what he did to Arthur."

"The future is unsettled, lad, too unsettled for my taste."

He could not disagree. "I do wonder who this Arlette was and how she came to get so much silver."

Miggins leaned close. "Mayhap she was a witch, jest like the witch who brought us all the trouble. Will ye kill her too, lad?"

"What are you whining about to my lord, old crone?"

Miggins whirled around so fast, Garron had to grab her bony arm to steady her.

"What is she whispering to you?"

Merry stood, hands on her hips, and death in her eyes as she stared at Miggins.

"She is complaining, isn't she, Garron? She is saying I am not Merry, isn't she? She's claiming I'm an imposter. The old bitch lies! What has she said?"

Imposter?

He looked at the vibrant girl whose hair lay loose down her back, a simple golden band around her forehead. He said calmly, "I am no longer your lord, Merry. We were speaking of my brother, who, if he lives, will once again be the Earl of Wareham. Who knows? Mayhap the king will give you to him to wed. Did you wish to speak to me?"

"You will protect the old crone?"

How can you have changed so utterly? But he merely cocked his head at her.

Merry drew herself up, shook her head so that her glorious hair shifted and danced. "Bullic asks me when we are to wed, my lord. I told him the king's chancellor would not allow it now that you will be stripped of your title." She turned to Miggins. "Why are you listening? This has nothing to do with you. Go away."

Miggins muttered as she walked away, "Aye, 'tis the drug, it has to be the drug that has turned you into a witch like yer mother." She gave Merry a bewildered look, then shuffled out of the great hall.

Merry said, "Since I am not to wed with you, Garron, I would like to return to London with Robert Burnell and ask the king to send my mother a message."

"Do not worry, the king will very much want to bring your mother to London. She has a lot to answer for, Merry."

"What did Miggins say to you?"

"Only that you are different. I told her the drug your mother gave you has somehow changed you. Do you think this is true?"

"Why would you care since I will not be your wife?"

He looked out over the great hall. Wareham Castle would stand forever, but it wouldn't be his progeny to dwell within its walls. He said, "You do not sound at all upset by my changed station in life. Did becoming my wife mean so little to you?"

She met his gaze squarely. "It does not matter what I feel or what I want, for the king will not allow us to wed, you know that. You have no holdings now, no wealth. Even the silver will pass from your hands. When my mother faces the king, she will explain all that has happened. She will prove she has done nothing but try to save me and to save Valcourt."

Who are you? He said more to himself than to her, "When she let you go to return to me, she had to know she would never gain the silver coins. Why then did she let you come back to me? It makes no sense."

Merry only shrugged.

"Do you not remember just a week ago, no more than that, you feared her in equal measure that you hated her? Do you still deny her part in the murder of so many of Wareham's people, and all because she wanted the silver?"

"You make it sound like she wielded a sword. She did not, she merely gave advice and counsel to Jason of Brennan. She had no idea what he would do, the lengths he would go to. I will tell this to the king. Jason of Brennan must confess his lies about her, as will Sir Halric."

He regarded her silently for a moment, then asked her, his voice curious, "Do you really believe them lies, Merry?"

"What do you care what I think? You are nothing, Garron, nothing but a guard."

Oddly, he wanted to laugh. He realized her blow didn't hit deep, and, he supposed, if it had come from the Merry of only days before, it would have crippled him. "A royal guard, Merry, a royal guard. When you came back to me, you kissed me and told me you wished to be my wife. Was that only because you still believed I was an earl with wealth and a valuable holding? Did you ever care for me?"

"Aye, I did, but I must look forward now, not back. You speak of caring, my lord, look to yourself. We could have wedded anytime during this past week, but we did not. I would have wed you, but you made no mention of it. And why is that? Why?"

And there it was, in the open space between them. What could he say to her when he himself only knew in his gut that he simply hadn't wished to? "Tell me, Merry, do you wish to wed with Jason of Brennan if the king lets him walk away whole hide?"

She gave him a cool smile, tossed her beautiful hair. "Jason has only one ear. Who would want to wed with a man with only one ear?"

"Still," Garron said, his voice utterly

emotionless, "if Lord Ranulf convinces the king his claim to the silver is valid, if he offers the king a royal share, then mayhap the king will give Jason over into his father's keeping. If Lord Ranulf allows Jason to live, why then, will he not be his father's heir? Aye, would Jason not be rich and titled upon Lord Ranulf's death?"

He gave her a humorless smile. "What is one missing ear given all that?"

"I will think about it," Merry said, turned on her heel, and walked away.

Garron stared after her, wondering how a man's life, how his very world, could collapse so completely in such a short time. This girl he'd cared for more than he cared for himself but days ago, had become a stranger, a stranger he no longer even liked. *Who are you? What are you? What did your mother do to you?*

Imposter?

He very much hoped the king would destroy Helen of Meizerling. If not, he hoped the king would allow him to kill her; only then would the world be safe from her. He saw again her tower in the forest, saw it whole, then saw it abandoned, as if it had been gutted decades before. Her power was astounding. And because he could not explain it, something deep within him was very afraid. And he thought of how Merry had tried to escape Jason of Brennan because she'd sensed evil in him, as she'd once sensed evil in her mother. But now—

His head hurt.

51

LONDON

It was a fine day in June when Garron stood before the King of England, the queen at his right hand, Burnell at his left. Merry had moved to stand with the queen's ladies along the far wall, which was covered with beautiful tapestries sewn by Queen Eleanor of Aquitaine herself in the last century.

The piles of silver coins were safely locked in the king's coffers. Jason of Brennan and Sir Halric were in the dungeon.

Edward said to Garron, his voice weary,

"There is such strife in the land. The Welsh and the Scots are eagerly slitting any English throats they can catch, and destroying English lands." He sat back in his throne, crossed his long legs, and tented his fingers. "After the Holy Land, I never believed life could become so grim again, but it has. And now you present me with problems that will doubtless fill my royal craw to overflowing." His vivid blue eyes lightened a bit. "At least you bring me enough silver to equip my army so I may crush the Scots, then the infernal Welsh. Very well, let us deal with this. Robbie has told me the substance, but now I require all the needful details. What say you, Garron?"

"I thank you, sire, for convincing Jason of Brennan to tell you where he was holding my brother. I only pray he did not torture Arthur beyond recovery."

Edward did not particularly care, truth be told. "We will see. Lord Ranulf will be here shortly, as will Abbess Helen of Meizerling."

Garron nodded. "You asked me what I have to say, sire. I say that once you have assembled all the players, then our mystery play will begin, and hopefully all will become clear, to both of us."

"Only the final act, Garron, only the final act. I wish to speak to you first for I have never known you to lie or twist the truth for your advantage, unless you have changed. Have you?"

"No sir, I have not changed, even though I was an earl for a short time."

The king gave him a sour smile. "Come with me. Robbie, you wait here."

A servant scurried forward and pulled aside a rich velvet curtain behind the king's throne. The king walked into a small opulent chamber that held a beautifully carved table he'd brought back with him from Sicily, four magnificent gilt chairs, gifts from the Doge of Venice, surrounding it. There were no windows. The walls were covered with vivid Flemish tapestries. It was the king's sanctuary, perfectly silent and private. The king motioned Garron to sit. "Robbie tells me you have willingly given up claim to wed the heiress of Valcourt."

"Aye."

"I believed, as did Eleanor, that you

would make a fine lord for Valcourt. However, given what has happened, Valcourt
will be administered by one of my men
until—well, until there is a new Earl of
Valcourt. But the fact is, Garron, if your
brother lives, you will no longer be the Earl
of Wareham. You will no longer have a
title or holdings, you will no longer have
any wealth at all since you spent it all on
Wareham. All this—if your brother lives."

The king rose and began to pace the
room. His legs were so long it did not
take him long to turn and stride back. "So
what should I do about you, Garron, if
your brother is indeed still alive?"

Garron realized he really didn't much
care. "I suppose there is nothing to be
done. I ask but one favor, sire. I wish to
fight Jason of Brennan. I want to kill him
for what he has done. The witch? I would
also slit her throat if you agree to it."

The king poured two goblets of fine
wine from the Rhineland, and handed one
to Garron. He looked at him closely as
both men drank the sweet red wine.

"I will certainly let you question the
abbess since you have intimate knowl-

edge of her. Then we will see. As for Ranulf, I know him well, as did my father. He will tell me the truth." He added, smiling fiercely, "And then we will see about Jason of Brennan's future."

52

MEIZERLING ABBEY

The king's men, led by Sir Dancy of Arch-
encourt, were conducted to the large
chamber where, they were told by the
Abbess Helen of Meizerling's master-
at-arms that she was within, conducting
her work. He was not happy, but had no
choice but to obey the king's command.
He feared his very fine world was teeter-
ing, given the severity of Sir Dancy's expression, the harshness of his words.

Helen sat at her vast worktable, a quill
poised in her hand above a sheet of

parchment. When she saw the men enter, she slowly rose.

Sir Dancy could but stare. He didn't know what he'd expected, but this incredible creature with her golden hair uncovered by a nun's wimple, and milk-white skin, eyes the color of a foggy sky, was not it.

"L-Lady Helen? Abbess Helen?"

Helen heard his surprise, his admiration, and smiled. She took a graceful step forward. "I am Abbess Helen. How may I assist you, sir?"

Sir Dancy bowed. He remembered Garron's words, remembered how he'd not really believed him: *Be careful, Dancy, do not ever be alone with her, keep your men around you. Do not take any drink from her. She is more dangerous than I can say.*

And Sir Dancy thought, staring at her, feeling lust rise in his blood, *This glorious creature is dangerous? Surely not.*

"I arrive from the king, madam," and he handed her a rolled parchment. It never occurred to him to ask her if she could read. He watched her unroll the parchment, her hands so white and graceful, and read what Robert Burnell had written from the king.

After a moment, she looked up at Dancy. "I require two hours to prepare."

Dancy nodded. "I am instructed to accompany you to your bedchamber, madam." He remembered Garron's words and nodded to all his men to fall in behind him.

So many men, she thought, *too many.* Ah, but she would have the king alone. Surely she could bring that to pass.

Merry listened to Sister Maude and Sister Alice speak outside her cell door. They brought her food twice daily and waited until she had finished, then removed the tray, saying nothing to her, no matter how innocent her questions. They must really fear her mother to obey her exactly. But now, now—the king had sent men to take her mother back to London, and the sisters were whispering about it. Were they pleased? Did they hate her as much as Merry did, or were they more afraid of her than anything else?

She remembered standing at the edge of the forest, near the old woman's cottage, the meat in her hand, when she'd heard that loud whooshing sound. She could see herself whirl about, but there was no enemy, only the dark forest in front of her. And then something had slammed down on her head and she'd collapsed. Had she heard an old woman's cackle? Was it the woodcutter's widow who'd struck her down?

And she'd awakened here in this small cell. Yet again, her mother had bested her, and she'd wanted to weep at her failure.

The king had ordered her mother to come to London, to him, and she thus had no choice. What had he found out? Had Garron uncovered the truth? What had happened?

Now she had another chance.

The witch is leaving. She smiled into the dim light and readied herself.

53

LONDON

Garron looked from Abbess Helen of Meizerling to Merry, who now stood beside her. He watched Merry slip her hand
into her mother's. He watched Helen look
down at her and give her a faint smile.
Beautiful, vibrant Merry, who wasn't his
Merry, and he knew in that instant that
the witch had done something lasting to
her own daughter—or was it something
else? Was she an imposter? But how
could that be?

Lord Ranulf stood straight as a soldier

and watched with no outward emotion as his son and Sir Halric were brought into the king's chamber. Jason saw his father and started forward, but a guard grabbed his arm and held him back. His father nodded toward Sir Halric, which made Jason hiss like a snake.

Garron looked at the man responsible for so much death and misery, the man who'd tortured his brother, and thought, *I shouldn't have cut off your damned ear, I should have stuck my knife through your neck and been done with it.* Would the king allow him to take vengeance? He knew in that moment he would fight him, it didn't matter what the king said.

Robert Burnell, at a nod from the king, said to Lord Ranulf, "You will step forward, my lord, and you will tell us who Arlette is and how she gathered such a huge number of silver coins. You will not speak nonsense about Druid priestesses and curses. You will tell the king the exact truth."

Garron studied Jason of Brennan's father, Lord Ranulf, Earl of Carronwick. He was tall and sturdy, well muscled, very fine of face, just like his son. He wore a black tunic and mail, dusty from his travel to London. He said in a pleasant, deep voice, "Sire, I wove a fantastic tale for my son because he was just a lad when he first saw the silver coins, and would not have understood the truth. I threatened him with curses and punishment to ensure his silence, and he did remain silent until he lost his wits in drunkenness, and told Arthur of Wareham.

"Arlette was no Druid priestess, she was my mother. I was sixteen when she first showed me the silver coins. She told me they came from Philip, King of France. He'd sent her newly issued English round farthings to pay out amongst John's barons to overthrow him, and back Philip's claim to the English throne. Later, however, when I had gained more years, she told me Philip of France had indeed paid her in silver coins, but it was payment for her to poison your grandfather. She told me her father, my grandfather, had sent her to the court in Paris as a young girl. Even at fourteen, she had great maturity, charm, and wit. She became King Philip's mistress. She told me he came to trust her completely.

"As you know, most believe your grand-father, King John, died of dysentery in the fall of 1216, only a year after signing the Great Charter at Runnymede."

Burnell said, "Lord Ranulf, why did the King of France believe your mother could get close enough to King John to poison him? What was she to John?"

"In truth, she was also King John's mistress, sire. Arlette herself told me King John was so ill he could not gain bodily satisfaction from her, but he loved to have her close to him, to look at her, to stroke her. She gave him comfort.

"I remember as a boy I heard people marvel at her beauty, but I paid no particular attention because she was my mother. A few years ago I found a small rendering of her, and saw that her beauty was indeed remarkable."

Edward said, "Some have said John's ale was poisoned, others have said the poison was in some plums he ate. Mayhap your mother did indeed poison him."

"Arlette told me she'd known John's death would come soon enough, with no assistance from anyone. She said when he died, she was surprised when the King of France sent no one to take back his silver. She supposed he believed she had indeed poisoned John.

"Upon John's death, Arlette married the Earl of Carronwick, left London, and took the silver coins with her. She did not spend them, she guarded them for future generations. My father died without ever knowing about the stash of silver coins."

Jason of Brennan took a step forward, only to be pulled back by Whalen. "Father, why did you lie to me?"

Lord Ranulf slowly turned to look at his only son. "You were seven years old, Jason. How could I tell you the truth? You would not have understood."

"I would have understood if only you had told me the truth! I could have drunk a barrel of ale and not said anything had I known this Arlette was my own grandmother. And I have been a man for many years. Why have you not told me the truth?"

Lord Ranulf's expression was austere. "I did not tell you because I knew you were not to be trusted." He turned back to the king. "Sir Halric is my man. When I discovered the coins were gone, when my son swore to me he knew nothing about them, I requested Halric to join my son to keep watch on him. He has been loyal to me, he tried to curb my son's excesses. Unfortunately, this was not always possible, witness the so-called Retribution at Wareham brought by this Black Demon.

"When Sir Halric caught the heiress of Valcourt, he was bringing her to me. He did not realize it was Garron of Kersey who took her from him. I beg that you spare him, sire, for he has been loyal to me for many years."

"What about me, Father?" Jason struggled and heaved against the guard, but it was no use. "The only reason I attacked Wareham was to find the silver coins so I could return them to you! I did nothing wrong!"

Ranulf said nothing, simply stood before the King of England, tall and proud, waiting for the sentence.

Edward desperately wanted to keep all those beautiful silver coins. Were his needs not greater than Ranulf's? Were his needs not greater than any other of his subjects? Was it not his duty to protect

England? And the good Lord knew it required silver. He tapped his long fingers on the arm of his throne and fought with himself. Aye, he would use the silver to help him crush those damned Scots and Welsh—but Lord Ranulf had always been loyal to him, had always met his demands with soldiers and silver. And Ranulf had told him the truth, the entire truth, he knew it to his gut. What to do?

He found himself turning to Garron, a young man who had saved his life twice. "What say you, Garron?"

Jason yelled, "Why would you ask him? He is nothing!"

Garron said, "What I say, sire, is that the silver coins be returned to Lord Ranulf. In gratitude to you, he should pay you the same share I would have, had I been able to keep the silver. Mayhap too, Marianna de Luce de Mornay could wed with Lord Ranulf. Mayhap she can breed him a son with honor." He saw Merry still holding the witch's hand. Honor from a son born of that union?

Lord Ranulf gawked at him.

A lovely melodious voice said, "May I speak, sire?"

Garron, like every other person in the chamber, turned to Abbess Helen of Meizerling.

The king nodded. "Aye, madam, what is it you have to say?"

"I do not believe my daughter should wed Lord Ranulf, rather she should wed his son, Jason of Brennan, and the silver coins should be given to me as her dowry. In return, your majesty will have a just share of the silver, and Valcourt will have an excellent master, one forever loyal and grateful to you, sire. If you will forgive his youthful transgressions."

The king turned to look long at Garron. "What say you?"

Garron didn't want to say anything, even though he knew the witch realized well enough that if her daughter was wed to Ranulf, she would never see a single silver coin. What Garron wanted more than anything was to fight Jason of Brennan and run his sword through his damned belly. And, oddly, he wanted to laugh. In truth, though, nothing mattered except revenge, Garron thought, since he was again what he once was, and that wasn't so bad, was it? "I have changed my mind, sire. I believe the heiress should wed my brother Arthur, the Earl of Wareham. He would keep the silver as reparation for Lord Ranulf's son destroying Wareham and murdering scores of his people."

There was deafening silence in the chamber.

Helen said, "That is not possible. Your brother sleeps deeply. He will never awaken."

Garron said, "Tell us, madam, how do you know this?"

"Jason of Brennan told me your brother never woke up."

Garron continued, his eyes never leaving her face. "Jason has told me that my brother woke up and told him where he'd hidden the silver."

Helen smiled, a beautiful full smile, showing white teeth. "Then I do not know what to believe."

Garron looked from her to Jason. "What is the truth here? Is Arthur alive or not?"

54

Jason said, "He's alive. I already told you that. I had to keep him alive since he might have lied to me about where he'd hidden the silver. I had no reason to kill him."

"Until you'd made sure you got the silver coins," Garron said, and his palms itched to strangle this man who had wreaked so much havoc.

"We will know shortly," Robert Burnell said.

The king said, "I have decided Garron has the right of it. The heiress of Valcourt will wed Lord Ranulf on the morrow. He will have his silver returned, minus the amount justly due to his king and to the Earl of Wareham for reparations, and he will have Valcourt."

There were low mutterings, but the king paid no heed. He smiled faintly toward Lord Ranulf, who still looked utterly stunned.

"No!" Jason yelled. "No! Not my father! He is too old. The heiress should wed with me. The witch promised me. It was all arranged! The witch planned all of it!"

Sir Halric laughed. "This, at least, is the truth, sire. After this puling bastard told the witch of the silver coins, she chose Jason because she knew she could control him." He turned to Jason, who was straining toward him, death in his eyes. "You never were anything but a tool to gain what she wished. And you thought to cheat her, to keep the silver for yourself? She would have cut out your heart, and taken all the silver for herself. Since I have suffered you for five long years, I know that if the king were to make a misjudgment and let you keep Valcourt, it would fall into ruin under your hand, for you are a fool."

Before anyone could speak, the doors

opened and one of the king's soldiers entered. It was obvious he'd ridden hard. He was panting, sweat and dirt covered his clothes. He strode to the king, went down on one knee, his head bowed.

The king asked him, "Did you bring Lord Arthur back with you, Anselm?"

"Lord Arthur of Kersey, the Earl of Wareham, is dead, sire. We were told by a woman who had attended him that he fell back into the dream sleep after Jason of Brennan had tortured him. The next day, she said he simply stopped breathing. She showed us where he was buried."

The king showed no particular surprise. He looked over at Jason of Brennan. "The woman lied for you, didn't she? You were the one to bury him, were you not?"

"No, I tell you, sire, I swear to you, I left him alive. I did not know he died, I did not know. He was merely asleep again. We hardly did anything to him before he told me where to find the silver coins, and then he closed his eyes again. It is true, I told you I could not kill him, not until I knew he had not lied."

Anselm cleared his throat. The king

nodded to him. "The woman told us Jason of Brennan left before Arthur died, sire."

Sir Ranulf could but stare at his son. "It matters not. You doubtless put him to such torture he had no chance to survive."

"It is not my fault he died! We didn't hurt him, only a bit, to give him encouragement. He was nearly well when I left him to fetch the silver from Wareham. It was not my fault! I did it for you, Father, for you!"

His father said, all expression gone from his voice, "All the killing, all the needless slaughter—I pray to God to show me what sins I have committed to deserve you."

The king turned to Garron. "I grant you leave to challenge Jason of Brennan, it is your right." He turned to Helen. "Now I can set things aright, madam. I will give your daughter in marriage to Lord Garron of Kersey, the Earl of Wareham. Half the silver is his, with a share to me and to Lord Ranulf. Ranulf, I believe this is fair since reparations are in order."

Helen called out in her beautiful voice, "No, it is not right, sire. It is not just. A portion of the silver should come to me, the heiress's mother."

The king paused, then nodded to Garron.

Garron said calmly, "Are you a witch, Abbess Helen?"

She laughed. "I, a witch? Naturally not, there is no such thing. I am learned, naught more than that."

"Is it true what Sir Halric said? You would have kept the silver had Jason managed to find it? You truly controlled him that easily?"

"The silver was destined for Valcourt, so that it would remain an important holding."

"Do you spend time in a tower in the middle of a forest?"

She shook her head. "I do not know what you are talking about."

"Did you drug your daughter and kidnap her?"

"Aye, I did. I feared for her. I wished to save her."

"Save her from what, madam?"

"From you, sir, from you. I believed she should have a choice. Ask if she wishes to wed with you."

"Merry, do you wish to wed with me?"

"I will wed whomever the king commands I wed."

"Then tell me why you came to my chamber at night at Wareham."

Her face went utterly blank. Then, "I never went to your chamber! That is an unconscionable lie, sir, unworthy of any man with honor."

"I went to your chamber because I wanted to force you to wed with me."

Everyone turned to the door to see Merry standing there, disheveled, wearing an old, cast-off gown, her hair tangled and coming out of its plaits, hanging down her back. She looked like a madwoman, her face scarlet with rage.

The king raised his hand for quiet. "What is this? You look like another Marianna de Luce de Mornay. How is this possible?" And he looked at them back and forth. "By all the saints' mottled noses, you are twins. Twins. It is amazing."

Merry threw back her head. "I am Marianna de Luce de Mornay, the heiress of Valcourt. I did not even know about this one pretending to be me until your guard outside the door nearly fainted when he saw me and demanded how I'd come out of this room without his seeing me." She turned to her mother. "So this is the secret you told me my father kept, indeed the secret that many people at Valcourt know. You birthed twin girls and you took her and left me with my father."

"No, the bitch lies! My twin? I have no twin, I have no sister. I am Marianna de Luce de Mornay, not this girl! Mother, tell them!"

Merry turned to face the furious girl. It was like looking in a mirror. "I did not even know about you. Did you know about me? Did our mother tell you why she kept you and left me at Valcourt?"

"She took you away, not me! I am the heiress of Valcourt, not you, you dirty little harlot!"

Garron said, "Sire, I believe I can solve this very quickly." He looked from one to the other. "Which one of you can tell me how you escaped from Sir Halric."

Merry stared at her sister, who stood frozen, her eyes darting to their mother.

Garron waited for his Merry to speak, for indeed, he knew to his soul it was her, but then he saw her dirty face change, grow slack, lose all expression. He saw she was looking at her mother, and that her mother was staring at her, her ice gray eyes intense, saw her lips moving. Merry began to sway where she stood.

"Merry, shut your eyes, now!"

But she couldn't close her eyes, she couldn't move, she simply couldn't, and did she really want to? She stared and stared, and felt herself begin to fall, but it didn't feel frightening, this falling.

"Merry! Stop it!"

Why was Garron yelling at her? Wait. This was wrong. Somehow, she had to turn her face away from her mother, she had to—

Garron ran to Helen and struck his fist into the side of her head. The blow lifted her off her feet and sent her flying backward to crash against a wall.

"Merry!"

He caught her up against him, buried his face in her hair.

She slowly felt herself coming together again, but where had she gone? What had her mother done to her? She looked up at Garron, at his beloved face, then down at her mother, who lay on her back, her beautiful white skirts billowing out around her, unconscious.

She said, "You wondered which of us could tell you how she escaped from Sir Halric. I will tell you, my lord. It was you who saved me from Sir Halric, Garron. You."

The king said, "How did you get here?"

"She kept me in her forest tower but I escaped. She caught me again and imprisoned me at Meizerling. I escaped when your soldiers came to get her."

Merry turned to her twin. "Now there is no more pretense. Tell me why you have pretended to be me."

Her twin drew herself up. "Very well, I will tell you. I listened to you and my mother speaking. I listened to you talk about this Garron of Kersey as if he were a god." She shrugged. "I wanted to see what Garron of Kersey was all about." She looked at him holding Merry's hand. "I must say, I was disappointed. I daresay I would have preferred to wed Jason of Brennan with his one ear."

Merry nearly flung herself on her sister, but Garron held her back. "I do not see how you fooled anyone since we look nothing alike." She whirled around and shook her fist under Garron's nose. "How could you believe she was me, Garron, even for an instant? *How could you?*"

He cupped her dirty face between his palms. "Deep down, something in me knew, but the fact was how could she not be you?" He breathed her in. "You smell like horse and sweat." He breathed in the sweet smell of her hair. "Roses, I believe your hair smells of wild roses."

"You whoreson, you've killed my mother!"

Merry's twin leapt at him, fists flailing. Garron set Merry aside, and grabbed her twin's wrists.

"Please let her go, Garron."

He released her. Merry smiled at her twin, raised her own fist, and struck her twin in the jaw.

Both mother and daughter lay unconscious, side by side, on the king's chamber floor.

Garron raised her fist to his mouth and kissed her skinned fingers. "Will you wed with me right now?"

"Right now, Garron?" The king cocked a thick golden Plantagenet eyebrow.

"Aye, sire, if you will. I am afraid that something else will happen to her. I do not wish to let her out of my sight."

Merry threw back her head and laughed. "Aye, please, sire."

The queen rose to her feet. She looked from the unconscious girl on the floor to Merry. "This is all passing strange, but we will do what we must. Merry, you will come with me and I will see that you are readied. Garron, I will keep close guard on her, fear not."

But Garron said, "Please, madam, let us wed now. I want all in this chamber to witness our joining, her mother especially, if she awakens."

The queen smiled. "Very well." She herself took a glass of ale from the marble table beside the king's throne and carried it to where Abbess Helen of Meizerling lay against the wall. She poured the ale on the woman's face.

Helen blinked, opened her eyes to see the Queen of England standing over her. "My lady?"

"Merry wishes you and your daughter to witness her wedding with Lord Garron of Kersey, the Earl of Wareham."

Lord Ranulf asked his son, "Did you know of this twin?"

Jason was looking at both of them, shaking his head. "But I would prefer to wed this one. This other, she is no lady. You saw her use her fist. And she is dirty, she is ungoverned."

His only son, Lord Ranulf thought, what was a father to do? He walked up to his son and clouted him. He caught him before he could sprawl on the floor, whispered close to his one remaining ear, "You will shut your mouth. It is over. When you fight Lord Garron, be a man, not a puling coward."

Robert Burnell took charge. He ordered everyone about, and in the end, all surrounded Merry and Garron, save, of course, the king and queen, who remained seated, the king looking ironic, the queen, pleased.

Merry, wind-blown, dirty, stray hairs tucked into her plaits as best she could, stood beside her betrothed.

Burnell began speaking, his beautiful voice low and melodious, speaking Latin which few understood, but it sounded important and grave, and occasionally the king nodded, as if he understood, and mayhap he did, Garron didn't know.

The moment after Burnell blessed their union, Garron looked over at Jason of Brennan and said, "I challenge you. We will fight until one of us no longer breathes."

55

At your instruction, sire, I, Robert Burnell, Chancellor of England, am recording the happenings of the thirtieth day of June in the year of our Lord 1278 to be sent under your royal seal to His Holiness, Pope Nicholas III, for his deliberation.

I attest that the following account is accurate, without flourishes or embellishment. On this day Lord Garron, the Earl of Wareham, challenged Jason of Brennan, son of Lord Ranulf, the Earl of Carronwick, to mortal combat, this challenge made because of the unwarranted attack by Jason of Brennan upon Wareham and the butchery of most of its people and his murder of the earl's brother.

Both men were well trained, equally matched, both were armed equally, with swords.

When the men stepped into the enclosure, encircled by nearly fifty soldiers, the sky, only a moment before filled with warmth and sunlight, turned black and rain poured down so hard the ground quickly became a quagmire. All witnesses attest that the men fought hard, but footing was difficult, causing many falls. Their swords clashed again and again, but the sounds were muted by the deluge. Lord Garron gained the advantage. He was on the point of delivering the coup de grace when he slipped and landed heavily on his back. Jason of Brennan, although bleeding copiously from a gash in his arm and his side, was still strong through his rage, and ran to stand over him, and all feared he would kill Lord Garron. All attest to how Jason of Brennan lifted his sword to send it into Lord Garron's chest when Lord Garron managed *to jerk his own sword upward to block the blow. The two swordpoints touched and seemed to meld together, to become one. All witnessed that both men were held immobile, their swordpoints locked together. At that instant, a fiery bolt of lightning exploded from the very center of the black clouds overhead and hurled earthward, sharp and clear it was, like a white sword wielded by God. The lightning struck the tip of Jason of Brennan's sword and ripped it from his hand. Jason of Brennan flew back and fell onto the ground, and he was dead. All wondered why the lightning bolt did not strike Lord Garron's sword.*

But it did not. Lord Garron rose to stand over his dead enemy. He was unharmed.

All believe it a miracle.

Robert Burnell studied what he had written. Had it really happened thusly? For perhaps the hundredth time now since this amazing occurrence had come to pass nearly a week before, he saw that wild white bolt of lightning explode Jason of Brennan's sword tip, melded, it had seemed, to Garron's sword, yet Garron had walked away unscathed, save for a single cut delivered by Jason of Brennan to his arm. *Had it truly been a miracle?* he wondered. *Had God truly directed lightning itself, hurled it at Jason of Brennan?*

It was not for him to judge such matters, merely present them to His Holiness, ordained by God himself to rule upon its merits. He rose from his high-backed chair, wiped the excess ink from his fingers, and carried the letter to the king.

His step lagged a bit, for he also had unfortunate news for his majesty. Helen, Abbess of Meizerling, and her daughter, whose name no one knew, had escaped from the tower dungeons early that morning, and no one had wanted to be the messenger to the king. No one could understand how she did it, since no one, absolutely no one, could have escaped the tower dungeons without bribing more than a dozen guards. How had the witch managed to do this? The guards all swore they were loyal, and, Burnell had to admit, their shock and fear of the witch's escape appeared quite genuine. And there was the question—had the witch somehow managed to cast a spell on all the guards? At the same time?

She and her daughter were gone, simply gone, and none had seen them, either within the massive walls or outside. Burnell knew to his soul they wouldn't be found. And who, pray tell, would want to find the witch anyway, and risk being bespelled?

At least, he thought, Sir Lyle of Clive was back at the king's side after his completed task, a special task given to him by the king himself, who had not confided in him, his secretary and his Chancellor of England, and that did indeed rankle. The king had ordered him to guard Garron, to ensure that he did not come to an untimely death as had his brother Arthur. Burnell remembered how the Valcourt heiress, then only a priest's byblow, had disliked and suspected Sir Lyle of treachery. He wondered what she thought when she'd learned the truth.

Burnell thought of the king's share of the silver coins, how that unexpected influx of wealth would undoubtedly buy him at least five hundred soldiers willing to desert their masters and come to him.

And there was another miracle, at least Burnell believed it to be, a miracle no one could have foreseen. Lord Ranulf had told Garron that he did not blame him for the death of his only son, indeed, after what Burnell now thought of as the "divine intervention," Lord Ranulf had embraced him.

Life, Burnell thought, was such an unexpected mixture of the holy and the profane, a man could only wonder.

Epilogue

WAREHAM CASTLE
FOUR MONTHS LATER

Garron and Merry stood side by side on the ramparts of Wareham Castle. It was a fine day in late October, the sun shone bright overhead, the cows grazed in the pasture, now fenced in to the edge of the moat. From the inner bailey, they could hear the muffled sounds of dogs barking mixed with the laughter and shouts of children.

Garron said, "The news the king's messenger brought us surprised me, I'll admit it."

"Come, Garron, you were honestly surprised that my mother wrote to King Edward? After all, she bested him, did she not? She escaped him, made him look like a fool. And now she wanted to put her fist beneath his nose yet again—my sister to wed a French nobleman. Aye, she was smiling when she wrote the letter, knowing we would hear of it sooner or later. Do you think she now owns a wealthy abbey?"

Garron would have given most anything to see the witch dead beneath the heel of his boot for all the misery she had wrought, but it was evidently not to be. He said, "She will probably outlive all of us, our children and their children as well."

Merry said, "It doesn't matter now, Garron. Let my mother parade her magick in France, let her bedevil the French," and she laughed and laid her cheek against his shoulder. "Do you believe my mother might ever come here?"

I pray that she will. "If she does, I will finally be able to kill her." He hadn't realized he'd said it aloud.

Merry said, her voice hard, "Not if I get

to her first. What she did, the evil of it, I cannot bear it that she is my mother. And my nurse, Ella, loyal to my mother, not to me."

His warrior. "You will worry no more about any of them."

"She even managed to take Ella with her when she escaped from England."

"I was wondering if her incredible beauty would last," he said as he picked out one of the small hidden braids tucked in amongst the thick plaits, and raised it to his nose. "It is odd that I knew you by the smell of your hair."

You should have realized within the first five minutes that bitch was an imposter. On the other hand— "At least you knew enough not to wed her."

"Something deep inside me knew the truth, but how could I accept that you were really not you?"

Mayhap he had a point. A very small point.

"I was wondering since my mother loves my twin so very much, why she didn't simply take me away and make her the Valcourt heiress."

He looked out toward the Forest of

Glen. "I think your mother knew there was something in your twin that wasn't right. After several days with her, Merry, I knew I did not want to wed her, there was meanness in her, something unwholesome. Perhaps she feared your twin would turn on her or perhaps she wanted to keep her close." He shrugged. "Who knows why she didn't let her trade places with you?"

"I wonder if she is a witch like our mother." She shuddered. "I will pray that the two of them curse each other and vanish. Aye, I like that notion."

She leaned against the ramparts wall, and grinned up at him. "And just when is Lord Ranulf to arrive for his monthly visit?"

"Possibly tomorrow. He brings Halric with him."

"He dares to bring that villain here?"

He touched his palm to her cheek. "Forgive him, sweeting. I have known many men whose deeds were much blacker than Halric's who still hold the king's trust. Halric wasn't all that great a villain, Merry."

"Ha! I will never trust him. He is still free

to roam the land, free to kidnap another heiress as it pleases him to do so."

His warrior. He laughed, kissed her. "I still cannot believe Lord Ranulf plans to wed a knight's daughter. He hopes to produce an heir to Carronwick. He says he'll be damned if he will allow Arlette's curse to wipe out his name."

"I believe he would like to adopt you, Garron."

He laughed. "If Ranulf has his way, I will doubtless foster any son his new wife manages to produce."

"Or it means that if he doesn't produce an heir, you will eventually have three huge holdings to govern. Can you begin to imagine what the king will expect from you?"

"It does not bear thinking about."

Garron kissed his wife's forehead and thought about life's twists and turns, about fate, and about his brother— *Why, Arthur, why did you steal the silver coins? Surely you knew no good could come of it.*

If, however, Garron thought, Arthur hadn't stolen the silver, why then Garron's life would be very different indeed.

Merry wouldn't be standing beside him, one small braid curving along her jaw. He lightly laid his palm over her belly, wondering whether a son or daughter lay under his hand, and all the intense feelings now burrowed deep inside him, enduring feelings he knew would continue until he died, burst out of him in words simple and abiding. "I love you, Merry," he said.

She laid her hand on top of his. "We love you too, my lord."

The following day Lord Ranulf, the Earl of Carronwick, arrived at Wareham with his new bride of a sennight, Elise, so filled with enthusiasm Garron could only shake his head and laugh.